A

Carol Marinelli ... for her job title. ... answer, she put wr... relaxation and sh... third question asked for her hobbies. Well, not wanting to look obsessed she crossed the fingers on her hand and answered swimming but, given that the chlorine in the pool does terrible things to her highlights – I'm sure you can guess the real answer.

Rebecca Winters lives in Salt Lake City, Utah. With canyons and high alpine meadows full of wildflowers, she never runs out of places to explore. They, plus her favourite holiday spots in Europe, often end up as backgrounds for her romance novels because writing is her passion, along with her family and church. Rebecca loves to hear from readers. If you wish to e-mail her, please visit her website at: cleanromances.net

Cathy Williams is a great believer in the power of perseverance as she had never written anything before her writing career, and from the starting point of zero has now fulfilled her ambition to pursue this most enjoyable of careers. She would encourage any would-be writer to have faith and go for it! She derives inspiration from the tropical island of Trinidad and from the peaceful countryside of middle England. Cathy lives in Warwickshire with her family.

Italian Christmas Nights

CAROL MARINELLI

REBECCA WINTERS

CATHY WILLIAMS

MILLS & BOON

All rights reserved including the right of reproduction in whole or in part in any form. This edition is published by arrangement with Harlequin Enterprises ULC.

This is a work of fiction. Names, characters, places, locations and incidents are purely fictional and bear no relationship to any real life individuals, living or dead, or to any actual places, business establishments, locations, events or incidents. Any resemblance is entirely coincidental.

This book is sold subject to the condition that it shall not, by way of trade or otherwise, be lent, resold, hired out or otherwise circulated without the prior consent of the publisher in any form of binding or cover other than that in which it is published and without a similar condition including this condition being imposed on the subsequent purchaser.

® and TM are trademarks owned and used by the trademark owner and/or its licensee. Trademarks marked with ® are registered with the United Kingdom Patent Office and/or the Office for Harmonisation in the Internal Market and in other countries.

First Published in Great Britain 2022
By Mills & Boon, an imprint of HarperCollins*Publishers*
1 London Bridge Street, London, SE1 9GF

www.harpercollins.co.uk

HarperCollins*Publishers*
1st Floor, Watermarque Building,
Ringsend Road, Dublin 4, Ireland

ITALIAN CHRISTMAS NIGHTS © 2022
Harlequin Enterprises ULC

Secret Prince's Christmas Seduction © 2019 Carol Marinelli
The Count's Christmas Baby © 2012 Rebecca Winters
The Italian's Christmas Proposition © 2019 Cathy Williams

ISBN: 978-0-263-31780-0

MIX
Paper | Supporting
responsible forestry
FSC™ C007454

This book is produced from independently certified FSC™ paper to ensure responsible forest management.

For more information visit: www.harpercollins.co.uk/green

Printed and Bound in Spain using 100% Renewable electricity at CPI Black Print, Barcelona

SECRET PRINCE'S CHRISTMAS SEDUCTION

CAROL MARINELLI

PROLOGUE

'THANKS, BUT I'M really hoping to be spending Christmas with my family.' Realising that she might have come across as ungrateful, Antonietta immediately apologised. 'It's very kind of you to invite me, but...'

'I get it.' Aurora shrugged as she carried on helping Antonietta to unpack. 'You didn't come to Silibri to spend Christmas Day with the Messinas.'

'Ah, but you're a Caruso now!' Antonietta smiled.

The cemetery in the village of Silibri, where Antonietta had loved to wander, held many names, but there were a few constants, and Caruso, Messina and Ricci were the prominent ones.

Especially Ricci.

The Ricci family extended across the south-west region of Sicily and beyond, but Silibri was its epicentre. Antonietta's father, who was the chief fire officer and a prominent landowner, was well connected and held in high regard.

'Do you know...?' Antonietta paused in hanging up the few clothes she owned. 'If I *had* married Sylvester then I wouldn't even have had to change my surname. I would still be Antonietta Ricci.'

'Yes, and you would be married to your second cousin

and living in a property on the grounds of your father's home, with Sylvester working for him.'

'True…' Antonietta started to say, but then faltered.

She had run away on her wedding day, five years ago, in rather spectacular style—climbing out of the bedroom window as her father waited outside to take her to the packed church. Sylvester was popular in the village, and a member of her extended family, so the fallout had been dire—her family had rejected her completely. Letters and emails had gone unanswered and her mother hung up on her whenever she called to try and make her case.

She had spent four years living and working in France, but though she had persisted with the language, and made friends there, it had never felt like home. So she had come back to Silibri, for Aurora and Nico's wedding, but there had been no welcome committee to greet her. Instead she had been shunned by both her immediate and extended family.

Rejecting Sylvester, and so publicly, had been taken as a rejection of them and their closed family values and traditions.

Since Nico and Aurora's wedding she had been working at Nico's grand hotel in Rome, as a chambermaid. But Rome was not home either, and she had often confided to her friend how she missed Silibri.

Antonietta had wanted one final chance to make amends, and Aurora had offered a solution—she could work as a chambermaid in Nico's new hotel in Silibri while training part-time as a massage therapist. The old monastery there had been painstakingly rebuilt, and refurbished to Nico's exacting standards, and it was more a luxurious retreat than a hotel. To train there would be a career boost indeed.

It was an opportunity that Antonietta didn't want to miss—but, given the level of animosity towards her, it was clear she would struggle to live in the village. Aurora had had a solution to that too—there was a small stone cottage, set on the cliff-edge, and Aurora had said she was more than welcome to use it.

'The internet connection is terrible there and it's too close to the helipad and hangar for the guests,' Aurora had explained, 'so it's just sitting empty.'

'Hopefully I shan't need it for too long,' Antonietta had replied. 'Once my family know that I'm back and working…'

She had seen the doubtful look flicker in her dear friend's eyes. The same doubtful look that flickered now, as Antonietta insisted she would be back with her family for the festivities.

'Antonietta…?'

She heard the question in her friend's voice and braced herself. Aurora was as outspoken as Antonietta was quiet, but till now her friend had refrained from stating the obvious.

'It's been five years since your family have spoken to you…'

'I know that,' Antonietta said. 'But it's not as if I've actually given them much opportunity to do so.'

'You came back for my wedding,' Aurora pointed out. 'And you were ignored by them.'

'I think they were just shocked to see me. But once they know I'm properly here, that I'm back for good…'

Aurora sat down on the bed but Antonietta remained standing, not wanting to have the conversation that was to come.

'It's been *years*,' Aurora said again. 'You were only twenty-one when it happened, and now you are close to turning twenty-six! Isn't it time to stop beating yourself up?'

'But I'm not,' Antonietta said. 'It's been an amazing five years. I've travelled and I've learnt a new language. It's not as if I'm walking around in sackcloth and ashes—most of the time life is wonderful. It's just at…'

Just at other times.

Times that should surely be spent with family.

'Christmas is especially hard,' Antonietta admitted. 'It is then that I miss them the most. And I find it hard to believe that they don't think of me and miss me also. Especially my mother. I want to give them one final chance…'

'Fair enough—but what about fun?' Aurora persisted. 'I get that it hasn't been all doom and gloom, but you haven't spoken of any friends. I never hear you saying you're going on a date…'

'*You* never dated anyone until Nico,' Antonietta said rather defensively.

'Only because I have loved Nico my entire life,' Aurora said. 'No one compared. But at least I tried once…'

They both laughed as they recalled Aurora's attempt to get over Nico by getting off with a fireman, but then Antonietta's laughter died away. There was a very good reason she hadn't dated. One that she hadn't even shared with her closest friend. It wasn't just the fact that Sylvester was her second cousin that had caused Antonietta to flee on her wedding day. It had been her dread of their wedding night.

Sylvester's kisses had repulsed Antonietta, and the rough, urgent roaming of his hands had terrified her. And her reluctance to partake had infuriated *him*.

It had all come to a head for Antonietta in the weeks before the planned wedding, when she had come to dread time spent alone with her fiancé. On more than a couple of occasions he had almost overpowered her, and Antonietta had been forced to plead with Sylvester and say that she was saving herself for her wedding night.

'*Frigida,*' he had called her angrily.

And very possibly she was, Antonietta had concluded, because to this day the thought of being intimate with a man left her cold.

At the time she had tried voicing her fears about it to her *mamma*, but her advice had been less than reassuring. Her *mamma* had told her that once she was married it was her wifely duty to perform '*once a week to keep him happy*'.

As the wedding night had loomed closer, so had Antonietta's sense of dread. And that feeling of dread, whenever she thought of kissing a man, let alone being intimate with a man, had stayed with her.

She wished she could speak about it with Aurora. But her friend was so confident with her sexuality, and so deliriously happy in her marriage that instead of confiding in her, Antonietta remained eternally private and kept the darkest part of her soul to herself.

'It's time to live a little,' Aurora pushed now.

'I agree.' Antonietta nodded, even if she didn't quite believe it herself. 'But first I have to give my parents this chance to forgive me.'

'For *what*, Antonietta?' Aurora was blunt. 'Sylvester was your second cousin; the fact is they just wanted to keep their money in the family and keep the Ricci name strong—'

'Even so…' It was Antonietta who interrupted now. 'I shamed my parents in front of their entire family. I left Sylvester standing at the altar! You saw the fallout, Aurora…'

'Yes…'

Apparently a huge fight had broken out in the church. Antonietta hadn't hung around to witness it, though; she had timed it so she had been on the train out of Silibri by then.

'I miss having a family.' It was the simple truth. 'They are not perfect—I know that—but I miss having them in my life. And even if we cannot reconcile I feel there is unfinished business between us. Even if it is a final goodbye then I want it to be said face to face.'

'Well, the offer's there if you change your mind,' Aurora said. 'Nico and I want Gabe to celebrate his first Christmas in Silibri...' Her voice trailed off as she pulled a swathe of scarlet fabric from Antonietta's case. 'This is beautiful—where did you get it?'

'Paris.' Antonietta smiled and ran her hands fondly over the fabric. 'I bought it just after I arrived there.' It had been a late summer's day and, having just written to her parents, she had been buoyed by the prospect of reconciliation. 'I was walking through Place Saint-Pierre and I wandered into a fabric store.'

She had decided to celebrate her happy mood and there amongst the brocades and velvets she had found a bolt of stunning crimson silk and bought a length.

'You have had it all this time and done nothing with it?' Aurora checked as Antonietta wrapped it back in its tissue paper and placed it in the bottom drawer of a heavy wooden chest. 'You *cannot* leave this hiding in a drawer.'

'I might make some cushions with it.'

'Cushions?' Aurora was aghast. 'That fabric deserves to be made into a dress and taken out!'

'Oh? And when will I ever wear it?'

'As a last resort you can wear it in your coffin,' Aurora said with typical Sicilian dark humour. 'You can lie there dead and people can say *Look how beautiful she almost was!* Give it to me and let me make something with it.'

Aurora was a brilliant seamstress, and would certainly make something beautiful, but it was almost reluctantly that Antonietta handed over the fabric.

'Let me get your measurements,' Aurora said.

'I don't have a tape measure.'

But of course Aurora did. And so, instead of unpacking, Antonietta stood, feeling awkward and shy in her underwear, holding her long, straight black hair up as Aurora took her measurements down to the last detail.

'You are *so* slim,' Aurora said as she wrote them all down. 'One of my legs is the size of your waist.'

'Rubbish!'

They were lifelong best friends and complete opposites. Aurora was all rippling curls and curves, and she exuded confidence, whereas Antonietta was as reserved and as slender as her shadow that now fell on the stone wall. The evening was cool, rather than cold, but the year was certainly moving into winter, and she shivered as Aurora took her time, writing down the measurements.

Antonietta tried to hurry her along. 'Nico will be here for you soon,' she warned.

He was checking on the hotel while Aurora helped her settle in, but soon his helicopter would come to return both him and Aurora to their residence in Rome.

'Aren't you going to drop in and visit your parents before you head back?'

'I am avoiding them.' Aurora rolled her eyes. 'Can you believe they want Nico to employ my lazy, good-for-nothing brother as chief groundskeeper for the Old Monastery?'

Antonietta laughed. Aurora's brother was lazy indeed.

'It's no joke,' Aurora said. 'You would need a scythe

to get to work if Nico relented. My brother is as bone idle as yours, but of course now me and Nico are married he seems to think that Nico owes him a job!'

'I hope Nico didn't feel obliged to employ *me*...'

'Don't be ridiculous.' Aurora cut her off. 'You are a hard worker and the Old Monastery is lucky to have you.'

Even so, it was a huge favour for them to give her this cottage as she worked on making amends for the past.

The sound of Nico's chopper starting up made Aurora look out of the window. 'There he is...' She kissed her friend on both cheeks and gave her a hug. 'Good luck starting work and I'll see you on Christmas Eve—if not before. And I mean it, Antonietta. If things don't work out with your family, the offer to join us is there.'

'Thank you,' Antonietta said. 'But Christmas is still a couple of months away; there is plenty of time for things to sort themselves out.'

'You'll be okay?' Aurora checked. 'You really are a bit cut off here.'

'I'll be fine,' Antonietta assured her. 'Thanks so much for this.'

Nico did not come into the cottage; instead he headed straight to the chopper and Antonietta watched as Aurora joined him. They were clearly both happy to be heading back to Rome and little Gabe, who would soon be turning one. She was glad that Nico hadn't dropped in. She was starting work soon, and didn't want her co-workers thinking that she had a direct line to the boss through her friend.

It felt odd, though, after Aurora had gone and she was truly alone.

The cottage was beautifully furnished, with a modern kitchen and a cosy living area, and she wandered through it, taking in not just the furnishings but the stunning view of the ocean from her bedroom. No beach was visible, just choppy waves and crashing foam. Despite the cool evening she opened the window, just to drown out the crippling silence that had descended since Aurora had left.

She was home, Antonietta told herself.

Not that it felt like it.

In truth, Silibri never had.

Antonietta had never quite felt she belonged.

CHAPTER ONE

Six weeks later

ANTONIETTA WAS UP long before the Sicilian winter sun. For a while she lay in the dark bedroom of her little stone cottage, listening to the sound of the waves rolling in and crashing on the rocks below. It might have worked in the meditation of monks of old, and it might be a tranquil backdrop for the guests, but it brought little peace to Antonietta.

It was two weeks until Christmas and since her return there had been little progress with her family. If anything the situation had worsened, with rude stares and muttered insults whenever she ventured into the village, and when she had gone to her parents' home the door had been closed in her face by her father.

Yet she had glimpsed a pained look in her mother's eyes from the hallway—as if her *mamma* had something she wanted to say.

It was for that reason Antonietta persisted.

Sylvester had married and moved away from the village, so there was little chance of bumping into him. And it was good to walk on the beach or in the hillsides she knew. Work was going incredibly well too; her colleagues were friendly and supportive and her training was first class.

Having showered, she went into her wardrobe to select her uniform. It varied—when she was working at the Oratory she wore white, but today she was working on cleaning the suites, so would need her regular uniform.

But as she went to take out her uniform her fingers lingered on the new addition to her wardrobe.

Yes, Aurora was a wonderful seamstress indeed, and the scarlet dress had arrived yesterday! However, just as Antonietta had been reluctant to hand over the fabric, she was even more reluctant to try it on. The dress was bold and sensual and everything she was not.

Still, there was not time for lingering. Her shift started soon, so she pulled out her uniform and got dressed.

The uniforms were actually stunning: the Persian orange linen went well with her olive skin and her slender figure suited the cut of the dress. Antonietta wore no make-up, either in or out of work, so getting ready didn't take long. She pulled her hair into a neat ponytail and then, having slipped on a jacket, made her way across the grounds towards the monastery.

Her little cottage was quite some distance from the main building. Still, it was a pleasant walk, with the sky turning to navy as the sleepy stars readied themselves to fade for the day, and there was a crisp, salt-laden breeze coming in from the Mediterranean.

And there was already activity at the Old Monastery!

A couple of dark-suited gentlemen were walking around the perimeter of the building and Pino, the chief concierge, was looking *very* dapper this morning as he greeted her warmly. '*Buongiorno*, Antonietta.'

'*Buongiorno*, Pino,' she responded.

'We have a new guest!'

The hotel housed many guests, but with the extra se-

curity visible Antonietta had already guessed there was
a VIP in residence.

Pino loved to gossip and was determined to fill her in.
'We are to address him as Signor Louis Dupont. However...' Pino tapped the side of his nose '...the truth is
he is really—'

'Pino...' Antonietta interrupted.

She adored Pino, and always arrived early to allow
herself time to chat with him. Pino had recently lost his
beloved wife of forty years, Rosa, and she knew that
work was the only thing keeping him sane. Still, given
that Antonietta was already a main source of gossip in
the village, she refused to partake in it now.

'If that is how he wants to be addressed, then that is
enough for me.'

'Fair enough,' Pino said, and then he took a proper
look at her. 'How are you doing, Antonietta?'

'I'm getting there,' she said, touched that with all that
was going on in his world he still took the time to ask
about her. 'How about you?'

'I'm not looking forward to Christmas. Rosa always
made it so special. It was her favourite time of the year.'

'What will you do? Are you going to visit your daughter?'

'No, it is her husband's family's turn this year, so I've
told Francesca that I'll work. I decided that would be better than sitting at home alone. What about you—has there
been any progress with your family?'

'None,' Antonietta admitted. 'I have been to the house
several times but they still refuse to speak with me, and
my trips to the village are less than pleasant. Perhaps it's
time I accept that I'm not wanted here.'

'Not true,' Pino said. 'Not everyone is a Ricci—or
related to one.'

'It feels like it.'

'Things will get better.'

'Perhaps—if I live to be a hundred!'

They shared a small wry smile. Both knew only too well that grudges lasted for a very long time in Silibri.

'You're doing well at work,' Pino pointed out.

'Yes!'

And the fact that she had committed to the therapy course was the main reason Antonietta had stayed even when it had become clear that her family did not want her around. With each shift, both as a chambermaid and while training as a therapist, she fell in love with her work a little more. Working at the Old Monastery was so different from the bars and café jobs that had supported her while she lived in France, and she preferred the tranquil nature of Silibri to the hustle and bustle of Rome.

'Work has been my saviour,' she admitted.

'And mine,' Pino agreed.

As she walked into the softly lit foyer the gorgeous scent of pine reached her, and Antonietta took a moment to breathe it in. Apart from the stunning Nebrodi fir tree, adorned with citrus fruits, there were no other Christmas decorations. As Nico had pointed out, many of their guests were retreating to *escape* Christmas, and did not need constant reminders—but Aurora, being Aurora, had insisted on at least a tree.

Still, thought Antonietta, as magnificent and splendid as the tree was, it was just a token, and somehow it just didn't *feel* like Christmas once had in Silibri.

Heading into the staff room, she dropped off her bag and jacket and made her way to the morning briefing from Maria, the head of housekeeping.

Francesca, the regional manager, was also in early, and was looking on as the chambermaids were informed that a new guest had just arrived into the August Suite, which was *the* premier suite of the hotel.

'I don't have his photo yet,' said Maria.

All the staff would be shown his photograph, so he could be recognised and greeted appropriately at all times, and so that all charges could be added to his suite without any formalities.

'Signor Dupont is to be given top priority,' Francesca cut in. 'If there are any issues you are to report them directly to me.'

Ah, so *that* was the reason she was here so early, Antonietta thought. She was always very aware of Francesca. Antonietta liked her, but because Francesca was a close friend of her mother there was a certain guardedness between them.

'Antonietta, that is where you shall be working today,' Maria continued with the handover. 'When you are not busy, you can assist Chi-Chi in the other superior suites, but Signor Dupont is to take priority at all times.'

Antonietta had been surprised at how quickly she had moved through the ranks. She was now regularly allocated the most important guests and Francesca had told her she was perfect for the role.

The August, Starlight and Temple Suites were sumptuous indeed, and the guests they housed could be anything from visiting royalty to rock stars recovering from their excesses, or even movie stars recuperating after a little nip and tuck.

The reason that Antonietta was so perfectly suited to working in the suites was her rather private nature. She had enough problems of her own and didn't care to delve into other people's. Nor did she have stars in her eyes, and she was not dumbstruck by celebrity, fame or title. Generally polite conversation was all that was required, and Antonietta could certainly do that. Silence was merited on occasion, and she was more than happy to oblige. She was polite to the guests, if a little distant, but she did her work quietly and well and let the guests be.

At the end of the handover, Francesca pulled Antonietta aside and gave her the pager for the August Suite. She offered a little more information.

'Signor Dupont has declined the services of a butler. He has stated that he wants privacy and is not to be unnecessarily disturbed. Perhaps you can sort out with him the best time to service his suite—he might want to get it over and done with—but I shall leave that to you.'

A guest in the August Suite could have the rooms serviced a hundred times a day if he so demanded.

'Also, Signor Dupont might need some assistance getting out of bed. If he—'

'I am not a nurse,' Antonietta interrupted. She had firm boundaries.

'I know that,' Francesca said, and gave her rather surly chambermaid a tight smile. 'Signor Dupont already has a nurse—although he seems rather testy and insists that he does not need one. Should he require her assistance, she can be paged. I should warn you that he is very bruised, so don't be shocked.'

'Okay.'

'Antonietta, I probably shouldn't tell you who he is, but—'

'Then please don't,' Antonietta cut in.

For her it really was as simple as that. She did not gossip and she did not listen to gossip either. Oh, the staff here were wonderful, and their gossip was never malicious. Certainly it would not reach the press, which was why there were so many exclusive guests at the hotel.

The same courtesy was extended in the village. The

locals were all thrilled at the vibrancy that had returned to the town with the new hotel, and so the Silibri people looked after its guests as their own. In fact, they looked after the guests *better* than their own—Antonietta had been treated shabbily by many of them.

'I don't want to know his real name, Francesca,' she said now, 'because then I might slip up and use it. Tell me only what I need to know.'

'Very well—he has his own security detail and you will need to show them your ID. He's booked in until Christmas Eve. Although, from what I gather, I believe it is doubtful he will last until then.'

'He's dying?' Antonietta frowned.

'No!' Francesca laughed. 'I meant he will grow bored. Now, he wants coffee to be delivered promptly at seven.'

'Then I had better get on.'

Francesca carried on chatting as they both made their way to the kitchen. 'I have just finalised the roster,' she told her. 'And I have you down for an early start on Christmas Day.'

Antonietta stopped in her tracks, and was about to open her mouth to protest, but then Francesca turned and she saw the resigned, almost sympathetic look on her manager's face. Francesca wasn't just telling her that she was to work on Christmas Day, Antonietta realised. Her mother must have made it clear to her friend that Antonietta would not be invited to partake in the family's festivities.

'Working is better than sitting alone in that cottage,' Francesca said as they resumed walking and headed into the kitchen. 'I shall be here too, and so will Pino and Chi-Chi…'

All the lonely hearts were working over Christmas then, Antonietta thought sadly.

'I'm on over Christmas too,' said Tony, the very portly head chef—which only confirmed Antonietta's thoughts.

Tony was married to his job, and put all his care and love into his food, and there was no exception this morning. There was a huge silver pot of coffee for their new guest, and cream and sugar, but there was also a basket of pastries and bread, a meat and cheese platter, and a fruit platter too. All the chefs, and especially Tony, could not refrain from adding Sicilian flair to every dish.

'Tony,' Antonietta pointed out as she checked the order, 'he only ordered coffee, but you have prepared a feast.'

'He is a *guest*.' Tony shrugged.

'And he's a big man!' Francesca said, holding out her hands high and wide. 'Huge! He needs to eat!'

It was the Silibri way—even in the poorest home there would be *biscotti* and *pizzelles* served alongside coffee. There was no point arguing, so Antonietta wheeled the trolley towards the elevator.

The monastery had been refurbished to perfection, and although it still looked ancient, it had all mod cons. Antonietta often saw the guests blink in surprise when they stepped behind a stone partition to reach the discreet elevator.

She took the elevator up to the top floor and, alone for a moment, slumped against the wall as she dwelt on the message behind Francesca's words. It really was time to accept that her family simply didn't want her. It was time to move on.

Where, though?

Back to France, perhaps? Or to Rome?

But she hadn't felt she had belonged in either place, and there was still her training to complete...

Catching sight of her reflection, she straightened up

and gave herself a mental shake. It wasn't the guest's fault that she was feeling blue, and she put on her game face as she stepped out and wheeled the trolley across the cloister, past the Starlight and Temple Suites, and across to the August Suite.

A suited man stood as she neared. She had known guests to bring their own security detail before, but never to this extent. What with the extra guards outside and within, this guest must be important indeed.

The guard was not exactly friendly, but without a word he looked at the photo on her lanyard and then checked Antonietta's face before stepping aside to let her past.

She knocked gently on the large wooden door. There was no response so, as she'd been trained to do, Antonietta let herself in with a swipe of her key card. Once inside, she turned on a side light and wheeled the trolley through the dimly lit lounge and over to the entrance to the main bedroom. She gave the door a gentle knock.

No response.

Another gentle knock and then, as she carefully opened the door, Antonietta called his name. 'Signor Dupont?'

Again there was no response, and though the room was in darkness it was clear to her that he was asleep. His breathing was deep and even, and judging from his outline Antonietta could see that he lay on his stomach in the large four-poster bed, with a sheet covering him.

'I have coffee for you,' Antonietta said quietly. 'Would you like me to open the drapes? The sun is just about to rise.'

'*Si.*' He stirred in the bed as he gave his groggy reply.

Antonietta headed to the drapes to open them, though it was not a simple matter of pulling them apart. The windows were vast and the dark velvet curtains heavy; pulling with both hands on the cord was truly like parting the curtains at a theatre, as if a play was about to unfold before her eyes.

The August Suite was her favourite. It occupied an entire wing of the Old Monastery, which allowed for panoramic views. The view from the lounge looked across the ocean, and the dining room looked over the valley, but here in the master bedroom there was a view of the ancient temple ruins.

Antonietta drank it in for a moment. There, as fingers of red light spread across the sky, the ocean danced to the rising sun and she felt she could happily gaze on it for ever. The view, though, was not hers to enjoy just now.

Antonietta turned around, and as she did so she started slightly when she first laid eyes on the guest.

He was *nothing* like she had imagined. From Francesca's description she had been expecting a possibly aging, somewhat bedridden and rather large man. But, while he was indeed large, he was certainly not overweight. Instead he was incredibly tall, judging by the amount of space he took up in the large bed. He was also broad and muscular, and thankfully covered by the sheet where it mattered.

And she guessed he might be around thirty.

Francesca had been right, though, to warn her about the bruises, for they really were shocking—purple and black, they covered his arms and chest and one eye, and his top lip was swollen. Signor Dupont, or whatever his real name was, had thick black hair that was rather messy, and also very matted—Antonietta guessed with blood. Of course she made no comment, but for the first time she found herself more than a little curious as to what had happened to a guest.

'Poor decision,' Signor Dupont said, and she guessed

he was referring to the sun, for he was shielding his eyes as he struggled to sit up in the bed.

'I can close them…' Antonietta offered.

'No, leave them.'

He would get used to the bright light soon, Rafe told himself, even as his pulse roared in his ears. But brighter than the sun were the shards of memory painfully surfacing in his brain—the absolute knowledge that this fall had been serious.

Rafe did not fear death for himself, but for a seemingly endless moment he had glimpsed the grief and chaos he would leave behind and had fought to right himself. He could not shake the memory of the looks of horror on his bodyguards' faces, the sense of panic all around, which seemed at odds with the soft voice speaking to him now.

'Would you like me to pour your coffee, Signor Dupont?'

For a moment he wondered who she was referring to. And then he remembered.

Ah, yes, security was extra-tight, for it would be disastrous if news of this near-miss leaked out.

So Rafe nodded and watched as the maid poured his drink, but as she removed one of the linen covers on the tray the sweet scent of bread and pastry reached him, and with it a wave of nausea.

'I only asked for coffee.'

'Ah, but you are in Silibri,' she responded. 'Here there is no such thing as "just coffee."'

'Please tell the chef that he is not to misinterpret my orders,' Rafe snapped.

'I shall pass that on.'

'Leave and take the trolley with you.' He dismissed her with a wave of his hand.

'Of course.'

Antonietta was only too happy to go. 'Testy' didn't come close to describing him. However, there was one thing that needed to be sorted out before she left. 'When would you like me to return and service the suite, Signor Du—?'

'Please!' His interruption was irritated rather than polite, and his dark eyes held hers in reprimand. 'Don't call me that again. Just use my first name.'

'Very well.' Antonietta felt a nervous flutter in her stomach, and it had nothing to do with his surly tone, and more to do with the deep navy of his eyes, which reminded her of the sky that morning. 'So, Louis, when would you—?'

'Rafe!' he snapped, and then softened his tone. It was not her fault there were so many restrictions on publicising his identity. 'You are to call me Rafe. And, no, I do not want my room serviced. If you could make up the bed while I have my coffee, that will suffice.'

He moved to climb out of bed, but then perhaps he got dizzy, because instead of heading to the bedside chair he remained sitting on the edge with his head in his hands, his skin turning from pale to grey.

He should be in hospital, Antonietta thought. 'Would you like me to—?'

'I can manage,' he snapped.

They'd both spoken at the same time, and Antonietta had not finished her sentence. Now she did. 'Would you like me to fetch the nurse to help you get out of bed?'

For some reason what she said caused him to lift his head from his hands and look at her. Antonietta was sure he *almost* smiled, but then his expression changed to austere.

'I *don't* need a nurse and I *don't* need the bed linen changed. Please, just leave.'

His tone was still brusque, but Antonietta took no offence. It was clear to her that Louis—or rather Rafe—loathed being seen in a weakened state. He was holding tightly on to the bedside table with one hand, while the other gripped the mattress, and she was certain he would prefer to be alone than have anyone witness him like this.

'Would you like me to come back later?'

'No.' He gave a shake of his head, which must have hurt, because he halted midway. 'I really don't want to be disturbed today—if you could let everybody know?'

'I shall.'

'And could you block out the sun before you leave?'

It was a slightly oddly worded request, and only then did she realise that Italian wasn't his first language. It took a second to place, but she soon realised that his Italian was tinged with an accent she loved—French.

She wanted to delve. For the first time ever Antonietta wanted to know more about a guest. He had asked that she use his real name—Rafe—and now she wanted to know it in full. She wanted to know where he was from and what had led him to this Silibri retreat to heal in secret.

Antonietta wanted to know *more* about this man.

But instead she wheeled out the trolley while the room was still light, and then returned. 'I'll close the drapes and then get out of your way. But, please, if you need anything then don't hesitate to page me.'

Rafe nodded and glanced at her, and was slightly bemused when he noticed her eyes. It wasn't so much that they were as black as treacle, and thickly lashed, it was more that he had never seen such sadness. Oh, it was not anything tangible—she was not downcast or grim—but there was an abject melancholy in them that tugged him out of deep introspection. And that was no mean feat, for Rafe had a lot on his mind.

An awful lot.

The black-eyed maid took out the trolley, and by the time she returned Rafe was back in bed. Before closing the drapes, she topped up the water by his bed.

'Thank you,' Rafe said, once the room was mercifully back to darkness. He actually meant it, for she had worked unobtrusively and had not, unlike so many others, pushed for conversation, nor dashed to help unasked. He almost smiled again when he remembered her offer to fetch the nurse rather than assist herself.

'What is your name?' he asked.

'Antonietta.'

And that was that.

Well, almost.

She wheeled the trolley back to the elevator and then went down to the kitchen and picked up the tablet to make a note of his requests. The internal computer system for the domestic staff was easy to navigate—she checked the box to say that he had declined having his suite serviced and added a note that he was not to be disturbed.

Yet she lingered a second.

His photo was up now, and she flushed as she looked at his elegant features. He wore black dress trousers and a white fitted shirt and there was a scowl on his lips and his eyes were narrowed, as if warning the photographer off.

She accidentally clicked on his profile, but there was only his pseudonym there.

Signor Louis Dupont.
VVIP

So, he was very, *very* important.

And in the box where normally a guest's requests were noted there was instead a direction.

All queries and requests to be directed to Francesca.
All hours.

'Is everything okay, Antonietta?'

She turned to the sound of Francesca's voice and saw she was chatting with Tony.

'Of course. I was just about to make a note regarding a guest but I'm not able to fill it in.'

'Because all Signor Dupont's requests are to be relayed first to *me*,' said Francesca.

'He didn't even *try* one of my pastries?' Tony was aghast when he saw that the trolley had been returned untouched.

Francesca, of course, thought she should have done better. 'You should have left a selection for him to nibble on.'

'He made himself very clear,' Antonietta said, blushing a bit as she did so, knowing that Rafe's lack of compliments to the chef would not go down well. 'I was just about to make a note—he has asked that the chef…' she hesitated and slightly rephrased Rafe's message '…should please not add anything to his order.'

Even that did not go down well.

Tony flounced off and she later found out from Vincenzo, the head of PR, that he had been discovered in tears.

'You know how temperamental Tony is,' he scolded her. 'And he's especially upset today because the Christmas rosters are out. Could you not at least have diluted such a prominent guest's criticism?'

'But I *did* dilute it,' Antonietta said. 'Anyway, I thought Tony was happy to be working on Christmas Day.'

Vincenzo just huffed off, leaving Antonietta wondering what on earth she'd said wrong this time. Still, there wasn't time to dwell, and for the rest of the day she worked with Chi-Chi. Or rather Antonietta worked while Chi-Chi did the *slowly-slowly*.

The *slowly-slowly* was a way to look busy while getting precisely nothing done, and Chi-Chi had perfected it. She had even tried to share her method with Antonietta.

'You can doze in the cleaning room, but keep some dusters on your lap, so that if Francesca pops her head in you can look as if you're in the middle of folding them,' Chi-Chi had explained when Antonietta had first started working there. 'But never cross your legs while you sleep or it will leave a red mark on your calf, and Francesca will be able to tell you've been in there for ages.'

'I don't want a bar of it,' Antonietta had told her.

She had known Chi-Chi her whole life, but she wasn't a friend, exactly, just someone she knew and, unfortunately, with whom she now worked. Chi-Chi's aim in life was to find a husband and do as little as she could get away with in the meantime. Once, Antonietta had actually seen her dozing on her arm as she supposedly cleaned a mirror, only to suddenly spring into action when Antonietta made her presence known!

'I saw your *papà* yesterday,' Chi-Chi said as she ate one of the turn-down chocolates while Antonietta dusted. 'He couldn't stop and speak for long, though, but he said he was busy getting things ready for the Christmas Eve bonfire. Will you be going?' she enquired, oh, so innocently.

'Of course,' Antonietta said. 'The fire in the village square is a tradition. Why wouldn't I go?'

Chi-Chi shrugged and helped herself to another chocolate. 'What is he like?' she asked.

'My *papà*?' Antonietta said, pretending she had no idea to whom Chi-Chi was referring.

'No, silly! The new man who is staying in the August Suite. I wonder what his real name is? He must be important. I have never seen so much security.'

'*All* our guests are important,' Antonietta said, refusing to be drawn.

Still, at the mention of the August Suite, and not for the first time, Antonietta glanced at her pager. But, no, Rafe had not paged her. Nor, when she checked, had he made any requests for in-suite dining. In fact later that afternoon she found out that his nurse had been given her marching orders for daring to make an unscheduled check on her patient.

Rafe had clearly meant what he'd said about not wanting to be disturbed.

At the end of her shift, as she walked back to her little cottage, Antonietta found she was glancing up in the direction of the August Suite. It was too far away for her to tell if he was on the balcony, but she wondered about him, wondered how he had spent his day and how he was.

For the first time ever Antonietta truly wondered about a man…

CHAPTER TWO

THE CHRISTMAS ROSTER was definitely the main topic of conversation over the next couple of days.

Antonietta was training in the Oratory, which was unusually quiet, but whenever she entered the staffroom it was all that was being discussed.

'It's not fair,' Chi-Chi huffed. 'Even Greta has got Christmas off and she only started three months ago.'

'She has children, though,' Antonietta pointed out.

'How come *you* are off, Vincenzo?'

'Because I live in Florence, and if I am to spend any time with my family then I need adequate time to get there.'

'But it is the Old Monastery's first Christmas,' Chi-Chi said. 'Surely the head of PR should be here and tweeting...or whatever it is you do.'

'I do rather more than play on my phone,' Vincenzo said, and then looked to Antonietta. 'How are things in the Oratory?'

'Quiet...' Antonietta sighed as she peeled the lid off a yoghurt. 'It's fully booked for next week, but the place was dead yesterday and it's almost empty today. I think people must be saving up their treatments for Christmas.'

She looked up as Francesca came to the door.

'Ah, there you are Antonietta. Could I ask you to service Signor Dupont's suite? I know you are meant to be doing your training in the Oratory today—'

'Of course,' Antonietta said, and went to get up.

'Finish your lunch first,' Francesca said. 'He has asked that it be serviced at one o'clock.'

'I'm glad she asked you and not me,' Chi-Chi said, the very second Francesca had gone. 'I've been working there the past couple of days, and he might be important, but he's also mean.'

'Mean?' Antonietta frowned.

'He told me to refrain from speaking while I do my work.'

'Well, I expect he has a headache,' Antonietta said, without adding that *she* certainly did when Chi-Chi was around.

Vincenzo looked at the time and then stood and brushed off his suit, smoothing his already immaculate red hair in the mirror before heading back.

'For someone so vain, you'd think he would have noticed that he's putting on weight,' Chi-Chi said the moment he was gone. 'His jacket doesn't even do up any more.'

'Leave him alone,' Antonietta snapped.

But Chi-Chi would not, and carried on with her grumbling. 'He's only got Christmas off because he's a manager.'

'No.' Antonietta shook her head. 'Francesca is working. I'd better go.'

'But you've barely sat down.'

She was happy to get up. Antonietta was more than a little bit fed up with Chi-Chi's rather grating nature.

'I need to get the linen ready to take up to the August Suite.'

Fetching the linen was one of Antonietta's favourite

tasks. Here at the Old Monastery the linen was tailor-made for each bed and was washed and line dried without a hint of bleach.

Antonietta breathed in the scent of fresh laundry as she walked in. Vera, who worked there, must be on her lunch, so Antonietta selected crisp linen and then walked across the stunning grounds.

A guest who had just arrived that morning had told her that it had been raining and grey in Rome when they'd left. Here, though, the sky was blue, and it was a little brisk and chilly, with cold nights.

The guard checked her ID and actually addressed her. 'He will be back by two, so please make sure you are done and out by then.'

'Certainly.'

Given that it took well over an hour to service the August Suite to standard, guests often went for a stroll, or down to the Oratory for a treatment, or to the restaurant while the maids worked. Usually she was relieved when the guests were out, but today she felt a stab of disappointment that she chose not to dwell on.

Of course she knocked before entering anyway, and when there was no answer she let herself in and stood for a moment, looking around. The place was a little chaotic, and she was wondering where to start when someone came in from the balcony.

Certainly she had not been expecting to see *him*.

'*Buongiorno,*' she said, and then immediately lost her tongue, for Rafe was dressed in black running shorts and nothing else.

'*Buongiorno.*' He returned the greeting, barely looking over. 'I'll be out of your way soon,' he added.

Indeed, Rafe had fully intended to go for a run—his first since the accident. But now he glanced over and recognised the maid from the fog of his first morning here. 'You've had some days off?'

'No,' Antonietta said. 'I haven't had any days off.'

'So why did they send me Chi-Chi?' he drawled, and rolled his eyes.

Antonietta almost smiled, but quickly recovered, because even if Chi-Chi drove her insane she would not discuss her colleague with a guest. Instead she answered as she headed into the bedroom. 'I've been working in the Oratory.'

She paused for a second to let him speak, as she should any guest, but truly she wanted to flee, for her cheeks were on fire and she hoped that he had not noticed. He did not reply.

'I hope you have a pleasant day,' she said.

'Thank you.'

Antonietta put down the list that she always worked from and immediately started stripping the vast walnut bed. She worked quickly, but the exertion was less out of necessity and more to match her heartbeat, which had tripped into a rapid rhythm at the sight of him semi-naked. And when he came into the bedroom to collect his trainers she had to force herself not to look—or rather not to stand there and simply gape.

'You work in the Oratory?' he checked. 'So you are a therapist?'

His voice caught her unawares; for she had not expected the terse gentleman she had met a few days ago to initiate a conversation.

'I'm training to be one,' Antonietta said, and glanced up from the bed.

And then it ceased being a glance, for she met his eyes and the world and its problems seemed for a moment to disappear.

'You look better,' she commented, when usually she would not, but the words had just tumbled out.

'I'm feeling a lot better,' he agreed. 'Although I still look as if I've been paint-bombed.'

She couldn't help but smile, for indeed he did. Those bruises were a riot of colour now, from blue to brown right through to a vivid pink, and they were spread across the left side of his torso and down to his shoulder and arm, and there were savage lines across his shoulder. Rafe's left eye looked as if he was wearing violet eyeshadow.

Yet he wore it well.

In fact, paint-bombed or not, Rafe looked stunning.

And as her eyes briefly travelled over his body, to take in his comment, she found that they wanted to linger on the long, yet muscular arms, and on his broad chest with just a smattering of black hair. More, she found that they lingered on his flat stomach. It was not bruised, so there was no real reason to look there. But Antonietta just found that she did, and a glimpse of that line of black hair had her already hot cheeks reddening as if scalded.

She wanted to ask, *What happened to you?*

Were those bruises from a fight? Or had he been in an accident? For once she wanted to know more, and yet it was not her place to ask.

'I shan't be long,' Rafe said, though usually he did not explain himself to maids, or even particularly notice that they were near.

Crossing the room, he took a seat by the bed she was making and bent over to lace his trainers.

Antonietta did her best to ignore him and not to look at his powerful back and the stretch of his trapezius muscles as he leant forward. Never had her fingers ached to touch so. To reach out with her newly trained therapist's fingers and relax the taut flesh beneath. Only she was self-aware enough to know that that kind of desire had precisely nothing to do with her line of work. He was so very male, and she was so very aware of that fact in a way she had never been until now.

Confused by this new feeling he aroused, Antonietta hurriedly looked away and resumed making the bed. But as she was fitting a sheet he must have caught the scent, and he made a comment.

'The sheets smell of summer.'

Antonietta nodded as she tucked it in. 'They smell of the Silibri sun. All the linen here is line-dried.'

'What about when it rains?'

'The stocks are plentiful—you have to make hay when the sun shines,' Antonietta said. 'Nico, the owner—'

'I know Nico.'

Rafe's interruption said a lot. Nico was prominent, and Rafe had not said I know *of* Nico, or I have *heard* of him. And then he elaborated more. 'It was he who suggested that I come to Silibri to recover.'

That admission made her a little more open to revealing something of herself. 'Aurora, his wife, is my best friend.'

'You are chalk and cheese.'

'Yes…' Antonietta smiled. 'I am drab in comparison.'

'Drab?'

'Sorry,' she said, assuming he didn't know that word. 'I meant…'

'I know what you meant—and, no, you are not.'

Rafe met a lot of people, and had an innate skill that enabled him to sum them up quickly and succinctly.

Yesterday's maid: slovenly.

The concierge, Pino, who had this morning suggested a running route: wise.

His assessments were rapid, and seldom wrong, and as he looked over to the maid he recalled asking her name that first morning. That morning he had not been able to sum *her* up in one word.

Admittedly, he had been concussed, and not at his best, but today he was much better. So he looked at those sad eyes, and, no, he still could not isolate that word.

Their conversation paused, and yet it did not end, for instead of heading out of the balcony and down the private steps to the grounds below he watched as, having made the bed, she headed to an occasional table, where she picked up her notepad and ticked off her list.

'So you are training as a therapist?'

'Yes,' she nodded. 'Although I'm not allowed to be let loose unsupervised on the guests yet. Well, I can give manicures, but that is all.'

'I *loathe* manicures.'

There were two types of men who had manicures, Antonietta had learnt. Those who chose to and those who had been born to. He had been born to, she was quite, quite sure.

She resisted the urge to walk over and examine his hands, but instead looked down at them… Yes, they were exquisite, long-fingered, with very neat, beautifully manicured nails.

'I find sitting there boring.'

'Then why bother?' Antonietta asked, and then pulled back the conversation. 'I'm sorry—that was personal.'

'Not at all,' Rafe said. 'I ask myself the same thing.'

'You could always listen to a podcast while your nails are being done,' Antonietta suggested.

'Ah, but then I wouldn't get to speak with you.'

It was a silly little joke but she smiled.

The girl with the saddest eyes smiled, and when she

did she looked glorious, Rafe thought. Her black eyes sparkled and her full red lips revealed very white teeth. She had a beautiful mouth, Rafe thought, and watched it as she responded to his light jest.

'I would not be allowed to treat a guest in the August Suite.'

He was about to say *What a pity*, but he rather sensed that that would have her scuttling behind the wall she had erected, which was just starting to inch down.

She rather fascinated him, and it was a relief to focus on their gentle conversation rather than deal with the problems he must face. He had intended to go for a run, just to clear his head. Yet instead he carried on chatting as she worked her way through the suite.

'You grew up here?' he asked.

'Yes, I left a few years ago.'

'For how long?'

'Five years,' Antonietta said. 'And though it was wonderful, I came to realise that you cannot drift for ever. Home is home—though it is very different now, and the hotel has changed things. There are more people, more work...'

'Is that why you came back?'

'No,' Antonietta said, and cut that line of conversation stone-cold dead.

It usually took an hour and fifteen minutes to service the suite to standard. Today it took a little longer, although they did not talk non-stop, just made gentle conversation as Antonietta got on with her work, diligently ticking off items in turn to ensure that nothing had been missed.

'Do you have family here?' Rafe asked, curious despite himself.

'Yes.'

Again she closed the topic, and headed into the lounge and dining area. There had been no fire lit last night, and no meal taken, but she dusted the gleaming table, then topped up the cognac decanter and replaced the glasses.

Tick.

He was leaning on the doorframe, watching her. Usually to have a guest watching her so overtly would be unsettling, yet it didn't feel that way with Rafe. She found him relaxing. Oh, her heart was in her throat, and beating way too fast, but that was for other reasons entirely.

She liked it that he did not demand elaboration. So much so that as she put the stopper in the decanter she revealed to him a little of her truth.

'We are not really speaking.'

'That must be hard.'

'Yes.'

The candles in the heavy candelabra were new, and didn't need replacing.

Tick.

She checked that the lighter worked.

Tick.

But she paused for a moment and wondered how used to luxury he must be not to light them each night. Not to need the stunning suite bathed in candle and firelight.

'The August Suite is my favourite,' Antonietta admitted. 'You should use these candles. I am sure it would look beautiful.'

'I'll keep that in mind.'

'I mean...' She was flustered, for she was not used to idle conversation. 'I've always wondered what it must look like.'

'I'll bear that in mind,' Rafe said again, and this time she flushed. 'Which is your favourite view?' he asked.

'The one from the dining room. From there you can see the valley.'

'Show me.'

As easily as that, he joined her at the window.

'When I left,' Antonietta said, 'that whole stretch of valley was black and scorched from wild fires.' She pointed to a large clearing atop a hillside. 'My family's property is up there.'

'Was it razed in the fires?'

'No, the fires stopped short of Silibri, but in the next village, where I also have family, there was a lot of damage. It's hard now to remember that it was so dead and black. I came back in spring, for Nico and Aurora's wedding, and the whole valley was a riot of colour. I have never seen it so alive. I find the view soothing. It reminds me that, as terrible as the fires were, they were good for the land.'

'So you stayed on after the wedding?'

'No,' Antonietta said. 'I went to Rome for a year, but I wanted to be back here for Christmas.' She gave him a tight smile. Certainly, she was not going to reveal that right now a happy family Christmas was looking less and less likely. 'I had better get on.'

'Of course.'

Nothing was left unchecked.

No cushion left unturned or unplumped.

And still Rafe did not go for his run. Instead he made a couple of phone calls, and it turned her insides to liquid to hear his deep voice flow in the language she loved.

'You are French?' she asked, after the second call had ended, although usually she would not pry.

'No,' Rafe said. 'But it is the language of my home.'

'Oh?'

'Tulano,' he added. 'It is between Italy and France…'

'I know where it is,' Antonietta said. 'I visited there once. Only briefly, though.'

His eyes narrowed a touch. In truth, Rafe did not believe she didn't know who he was. The maid yesterday had slipped up and called him by his full first name—Rafael—and the concierge had done the same when recommending a trail to run.

Soon, he was sure, his location would be leaked and the press would be here. The brief respite from the world would be over.

He asked her a question. 'Do you speak French?'

'Some—although not as much as I would like. I was there for four years,' she said, and then switched to French and told him that his Italian was better than her French. *'Votre Italien est meilleur que mon Français.'*

And he responded. *'Ta voix est délicieuse dans les deux langues.'*

She had been away from France for over a year, and it took her a moment to translate it, but as she did a heated blush crept up her neck.

Had he just said that her voice was delightful in both languages?

Were they flirting?

And if they were then why wasn't she halting it?

Why wasn't she running for cover, as she usually did whenever a man, let alone a guest, got a little too close?

Only Rafe wasn't too close for comfort. And Antonietta looked at the eyes that held hers as she responded. *'Ainsi est le tien.'*

So is yours.

It was the tiniest nod to his effect on her, and yet it felt rather huge to Antonietta.

There was another phone call for Rafe, and this time he answered in Italian, taking it out on the balcony.

Though she did not eavesdrop, his low voice reached her and it was clear that he was speaking with Nico. She felt a little flip of disappointment when she heard him state that he would not be staying for much longer.

The call ended and she looked over to where he sat, his long legs stretched out on another chair, his dark eyes scanning the grounds as a prisoner's might, as if looking for a way to escape. She could almost feel his restlessness, Antonietta thought as she headed out onto the balcony to finish her work.

'That was Nico,' he said, though he had absolutely no need to do so. 'Checking that I'm being looked after. He suggests that I take a wander into the village.'

'There are nice cafés there,' Antonietta said, and deliberately kept her voice casual. But there was a flip in her stomach at the thought he might be bored. 'Have you been down to the temple ruins?'

'No—that is where Pino suggested I ran.'

'And the ocean is glorious,' Antonietta said, and then stopped herself. It was not her job to sell the village to a reluctant guest.

'You live in the village?'

'No. Nico and Aurora have been very good to me. They knew coming back would be difficult…' She briefly closed her eyes, instantly regretting revealing so much, and then hurriedly spoke on. 'So they gave me a cottage in the grounds.' She pointed in the vague direction of the helipad, over to the far side of the Old Monastery.

'That must be very…' He hesitated, not wanting to say *isolated*.

Already, for Rafe, no matter how spacious and luxurious the August Suite, no matter how glorious the grounds, cabin fever was seriously hitting. This place really was in the middle of nowhere, and he'd been considering checking out later today.

Yet he was starting to change his mind.

Rafe wanted more of her smile, of her conversation—much, much more of her.

It was not as simple as that, though.

If their relationship were to evolve, then she needed to sign a non-disclosure agreement. She would have to be be vetted by his security staff and her phone would be confiscated before they so much as went out for dinner.

It could be no other way.

Yes, he had had a couple of relationships without such arrangements, but they had been with titled women and potential wives. This Antonietta could never be that. And he must test the waters to find out how she felt.

'That must be very quiet,' Rafe said.

'No,' Antonietta refuted as she watered the jasmine. 'I can hear the waves, and I am by the helipad so there are helicopters coming and going. Believe me, they are *loud* when they're overhead. But most of the time it is nice and peaceful.'

'Still…' Rafe said, and his voice was low as his eyes commanded hers to meet his. 'One can have too much tranquillity.'

Their eyes met and his words travelled through her like a current. Looking hastily away, she saw the slight shake of her hand as she watered the flowers and felt the devilish pull of his smooth voice.

Something told Antonietta that her response mattered, for his statement had felt like a question. More…it had felt like an invitation.

One she rapidly chose to decline.

'I am all for tranquillity,' Antonietta said rather crisply.

And instead of meeting his eyes, or thinking of something witty to add, she went back to her list and added a tick.

The flowers were watered, his suite was done and she gave him a smile—only this time, Rafe noted, it was a guarded one.

'I hope the rest of your day is pleasant,' Antonietta said, and let herself out, exhaling a long-held breath once the door between them was closed. She felt a little giddy.

When she entered the elevator to go down, she walked straight into Francesca.

'There you are! What on earth took you so long?' Francesca scolded the very second she clapped eyes on Antonietta, but then she must have regretted her tone, because she said, 'Oh, Antonietta, I apologise. I forgot that Chi-Chi has been working there for the past couple of days. The place must have been in disarray.'

It was Antonietta who was in disarray, though. Had Rafe been suggesting something?

There was little she could pin on his words, and yet there had been a wicked edge in their delivery—she was almost sure of it.

But she'd had no experience with men.

Not good ones, anyway.

For all Sylvester's attempts, his kisses and gropes had never, not once, made her feel the way that Rafe did with just his voice, just his eyes…

She was not only inexperienced in the kissing department, but in the flirting one too. And they *had* been flirting. Or was she romanticising things? Antonietta pondered as she went about her day. Certainly she was innocent, but she wasn't naïve, and she knew from her work in other hotels that Rafe might have been suggesting *'in-room service'*, so to speak.

She managed a soft laugh at that thought, for if that were the case Rafe was certainly wide of the mark.

And yet he had buoyed her up in a way she could not properly explain…

CHAPTER THREE

RAFE HAD BUOYED her up. The day felt brighter for the time she had spent with him.

And the night felt not so long, nor as dark, and Antonietta awoke the next morning with delicious anticipation.

Yes, even the *prospect* of seeing Rafe buoyed her up.

So much so that she decided to stroll into the village and do her shopping before her shift started.

In so many ways it was wonderful to be back. As Antonietta had explained to Rafe, when she had left Silibri it had been after a summer of fierce wild fires and the mountains and trees had been charred and black.

In fact the village had been slowly dying even before she was born, with shops and cafés closing and the youth moving on. Now, though, with the monastery refurbished, there was new growth all around. The trees were lush and there were winter wild flowers lining the roads. The village itself was thriving. Its produce and wares were now in demand, and the cafés were busy and vibrant.

She had already done some of her Christmas shopping— as well as presents for her parents and brother there was a lipstick for Aurora, which she bought faithfully each year. Just because her friend was newly rich, and could afford a lifetime's supply of the vibrant red cosmetic, some things never changed.

Some things *did* change, though. Aurora was married now, and so Antonietta bought some chocolate for Nico at one of the craft stalls in the village square. And not just any chocolate. Hand-made Modica chocolate, which was so exquisite that even a man who had everything could never have enough.

Bizarrely, she thought of Rafe.

Or perhaps not so bizarrely. Because she had been thinking of him on and off since the previous day. More accurately, he had been popping into her thoughts since the day they had met.

'Could I get the coffee flavour, too, please?' Antonietta said impulsively to the stallholder—and then jumped when she heard her name.

'Antonietta?'

It was Pino.

'Did I catch you buying me a gift?' he teased, when he saw her reddening cheeks.

'No, no…' Antonietta smiled back and then glanced at his shopping bag, which was empty. She knew that Pino was just killing time. 'Are you on a day off?'

'Yes, though I thought you were working?'

'Not till midday. But Francesca wants me to go in a little early. No doubt because of our esteemed guest.' She felt her cheeks go a little more pink.

'That's probably it.' Pino rolled his eyes. 'I heard he has asked not to have Chi-Chi service his suite again.'

'Really?' Antonietta's eyes widened. 'Why?'

'I thought you didn't like to gossip?' Pino teased.

'I don't,' Antonietta said, and hurriedly changed the subject. 'Now, I have to choose *two* presents for Gabe— it is his first birthday next week, and then Christmas too.'

Pino was delighted to help, and soon they had a little

wooden train for him, as well as a cute outfit, and Pino suggested they go for coffee.

'I don't have time,' Antonietta said, which wasn't quite true.

The sweet, spicy scent of *buccellato*—an Italian Christmas cake—wafted through a nearby café, and though she was tempted Antonietta was too nervous about bumping into her family to stop there for coffee and cake.

Instead, having said goodbye to Pino, she decided that she would bake her own, and headed into the village store. There she chose the figs and almonds that she needed to make the cake, and added a few other things to her basket before lining up to pay.

The shopkeeper was awkward with her, and did not make eye contact—and then Antonietta found out why.

'*Stronza!*'

The insult came from behind, and Antonietta did not need to turn her head to know that the word was aimed at her. She had been called worse on previous trips to the shops. Steadfastly, she did not turn around, and though she was tempted to walk out without her groceries, she held her ground.

Another insult was hurled. '*Puttana!*'

They all assumed there must have been another man for her to have run out on Sylvester, or that she had been sleeping with all and sundry in her years away.

Let them think what they choose, Antonietta told herself as she paid.

But as she picked up her bag she saw that it was Sylvester's aunt who was taunting her.

Antonietta said nothing. She just did her best to leave with her head held high—or not quite high, but nor was she head down and fleeing as she had previously. She was determined not to let the incident ruin her day.

But it was about to get worse.

Her parents were walking arm in arm towards her, and both were startled when they saw her.

'Mamma!' Antonietta called.

But together they looked away and crossed to the other side of the street. For Antonietta it was a new version of hell. That they should cross the road to avoid her was not only painful and humiliating, it made her angry too, and hurt words tumbled out.

'I tried to tell you, Mamma!'

Her voice was strangled then, but the words were true, for she *had* tried to reveal her fears about Sylvester to her mother. Antonietta watched as Tulia Ricci's shoulders stiffened. She stopped walking, and slowly turned around.

'You *know* I tried to tell you.'

'Antonietta.' Her father spoke then. 'What are you doing back here?'

And as she saw his cold expression she wondered the very same thing.

It was Antonietta who walked off, refusing to cry.

Even at the hotel she felt an anger building that was unfamiliar to her.

But her shift would start soon, and Antonietta decided she could not think about her family situation *and* do her work, so she fought to set it aside. Tonight she would examine it. Tonight she would sit down and decide whether to stay long enough to complete her training, to give them a chance for a Christmas reunion, but she would not think of it now.

She changed quickly into her uniform and then, with her heart fluttering in her chest and her breath coming too shallow and too fast, she crossed the monastery grounds.

Antonietta was usually a full fifteen minutes early

for work, but so shaken was she by the morning's events that she got there only just in time.

'*There* you are!' Francesca said by way of greeting. 'Signor Dupont has requested that his suite be serviced at midday, when he is out.'

Antonietta nodded and made her way up to the suite. After knocking and getting no answer, she let herself in. There was the scent of him in the air, but not his presence, and she was relieved to be alone and not have to make small talk. She set to work, ticking things off her list, trying to banish all thoughts of this morning.

Except Antonietta could not.

As she smoothed the sheets on the bed all she could see was the sight of her parents, crossing the street to avoid her. She plumped the pillow but found she was crushing it between her hands as the tears started to come thick and fast.

And they were *angry* tears!

She had come here to make amends.

To say sorry to her parents for not marrying a man who had treated her less than gently. A man who had tried to force her to do *that* more than once.

She had held on to her anger for so long, but it was more than seeping out now, and she buried her face in the pillow and let out a muffled scream.

'Agh!'

It felt good.

So good that she did it again.

'Agh!'

And again.

That was how Rafe found her.

He had finally gone for a run—in part to avoid *her*, for such was his cabin fever that he was getting a little too interested in a certain maid.

And that would *never* do.

However, he had not been for a run since his accident, and his endurance was not quite what it had been. He would soon get it back, he told himself, and the next run would be longer.

He made his way up the stone stairs to the private beach entrance of the balcony.

And then he saw her shouting into a pillow.

Rafe did not get involved with the dramas of maids.

Ever.

But when she stopped shouting into the pillow and sobbed into it instead, something twisted inside him even though generally tears did not move him.

She was not crying for an audience; he was aware that he was witnessing something private that she would rather no one saw.

Indeed, Antonietta was mortified when she removed the pillow and saw Rafe.

He was breathing heavily from running, and he looked displeased.

'I apologise,' Antonietta said immediately, for an esteemed guest did not need anything other than quiet efficiency. She wiped her cheeks with her hands and started to peel off the pillowcase as her words tumbled out. 'I thought you were out.'

'It's fine.' Rafe shrugged.

'I ran into my parents…' She attempted to explain. 'They crossed the street to avoid me.'

'I see.' Rafe tried to remain unmoved. No, he did *not* get involved with the dramas of maids.

'I can send someone else up…' Antonietta hiccoughed, frantically trying to regain control. Except her tears would not stop.

'There's no need for that,' Rafe said. 'Carry on.'

'But, as you can see, I can't stop crying...'

'I said,' Rafe snapped, 'carry on.'

And though she did carry on with her work, she found that the tears carried on too, and the anger did not abate.

No pillow was left unthumped!

He ignored her.

Well, not quite. At one point, when anger gave way to sorrow, he gave a slight roll of his eyes and handed his weeping maid a handkerchief.

She carried on with her work.

She just dribbled tears, and she was so grateful for his lack of words, that there was no attempt at comfort, for there was nothing he could say.

She would never have her family back. Of that Antonietta was certain. And it was there in the August Suite that she finally mourned them. Oh, there was no howling. Antonietta just quietly let the tears roll.

Rafe did not involve himself.

He would have liked to have a shower, given he had just been for a run, except he did not want to have a shower while the weeping maid was here.

Of course he could dismiss her.

And yet he did not.

Instead Rafe stood on the balcony and looked out towards the temple ruins, wondering about his teary maid.

He recalled the slight triumph he had felt when she'd smiled, and he found he would like her to smile again.

In turn, she liked the silence he gave her. It did not feel as if she was crying alone, as she had done so many times. And neither did she feel patronised, for there had been no *there, there* or invasive questions.

He let her be, and finally she was done with both her work and her tears.

Every last thing on her list was ticked off and Antonietta felt surprisingly calm as she gathered her things and finally addressed Rafe. 'I am finished.'

'Perhaps before you go down you should go and splash your face with cold water…take a moment.'

She did as she was told, appalled to see her swollen eyes and red nose, but she appreciated the opportunity to calm down, and retied her hair before heading out.

'If you need anything else, please page me.'

'I shan't,' Rafe said, but then he reconsidered, for Antonietta really was proving to be the brightest part of his day… But, no, he would not make up reasons to call her. 'Are you working tomorrow?'

'Just a half-day,' Antonietta said. 'Then I have a day off.'

'Well, I might see you tomorrow, then?'

He hoped so.

So did she.

'Thank you,' Antonietta said as she turned to leave, instead of the other way around.

'No problem.'

Except there clearly was.

'Antonietta.'

He called her name as she headed for the door. And his summons hit her deep and low, and the word felt like a hand coming down on her shoulder. How could the sound of her own name make her tremble and feel almost scared to turn around?

Or rather *nervous* to turn around.

Slowly she did turn, and she knew in that second that she was not scared or even nervous to face him. She was fighting her own desire.

In the room behind him she could see the vast bed, and she wanted to lie with him on white sheets that smelt of summer. To know the bliss not just of *a* man, but of *him*.

Rafe.

Whoever he was.

'Yes?' Her voice sounded all wrong. It was too breathless and low and so she said it again—except it came out no better, was a mere croak. 'Yes?'

Rafe rarely—extremely rarely—did not know how to proceed. Not only did he not get involved with maids' dramas, neither did he take maids to bed.

Added to that, she had been crying for the best part of an hour. He never took advantage.

Yet the air was charged. She looked as if he'd just kissed her, and he could feel the energy between them and her increasing awareness of him.

His sad maid looked exactly as she might if he had her pressed against the wall.

'I could have one of my security detail come and speak with you?'

'Why would they need to speak with me?' She frowned, trying to untangle her thoughts from his words. Trying to remind herself that she was at work. 'Is there a problem with security in the suite?' She was desperately trying to hold a normal conversation as her body screamed for contact with his. 'If that's the case I can let Francesca know.'

She knew nothing about his ways, Rafe realised.

'It's fine,' Rafe said. 'My mistake.'

'Mistake?' Antonietta checked, and he could see that her eyes were perturbed, that she assumed she'd said something wrong.

But she'd said everything right.

For this was far more straightforward and yet way more complicated than a contracted affair.

This was pure, unadulterated lust.

From both of them.

And he actually believed now that she had no idea who he was.

Crown Prince Rafael of Tulano.

CHAPTER FOUR

'RAFAEL, BY ALL accounts you could have been killed.'

Rafe had spoken with his father since the accident, but the King hadn't called to enquire as to his health. 'Had you died as my sole heir,' the King continued in reprimand, 'the country would have been plunged into turmoil and well you know it. Did you think of that as you hurled yourself down the mountain?'

'Actually,' Rafe responded, 'I did.'

As he had fallen—as he had realised the seriousness of the unfolding incident—it had dawned on him that this might well be it and he had thought of his country. He had thought of the royal lineage shifting to his father's brother, of his idle, ignorant, spoiled cousins ruling the land that Rafe loved and their undoubted glee that finally the reckless Crown Prince had succumbed.

'Thank God it has been kept out of the press,' the King went on. 'Our people have thankfully been spared from knowing how close this country came *again* to losing its Crown Prince. But it is not enough, Rafe. You need to temper your ways.'

'Then give me more responsibility. Transition some of your power to me.'

It was the same argument they had had of old. Rafe was a natural-born leader who had been raised to be King and already wanted a more prominent role than merely making staged appearances. He did not want to be a pin-up prince; he wanted active power and to be a voice amongst world leaders, yet his father resisted.

'You know the answer to that,' the King responded tartly.

Yes.

Marriage.

And a suitable bride chosen for him by his father the King.

Rafe did not trust his father with that decision. After all, he had witnessed first-hand the hell of his parents' *suitable* marriage.

There was a reason that Rafe was the only heir to the Tulano throne—after he had been born his father had resumed his rakish ways.

His mother understood her duty to the country, and the impact of a divorce, and so it had never been considered. Emotions and feelings were rarely taken into account at the palace. The King and Queen's marriage was a working relationship only. The Queen met with the King daily, accompanied him on formal occasions and hosted functions with grace, but she had her own wing at the palace and had long ago removed herself from his bed.

And there was no 'family life' as such. Rafe had been raised by palace nannies and had later attended boarding school.

No, there was nothing Rafe had witnessed that endeared him to marriage or to the idea of starting a family of his own.

'I expect you back here on Christmas Eve,' the King said. 'Preferably in one piece and without scandal attached. Do you think you can possibly manage that?'

Rafe wasn't sure.

As luxurious as the Old Monastery was, he was already climbing the walls and ready to check out. In fact, he had been about to call Nico to thank him for his hospitality when the call from the palace had come.

'I shall put your mother on.'

To his mother, he was an afterthought. She would never think to call him herself. Instead, when he spoke to his father, she occasionally deigned to come to the phone.

As he awaited the Queen, Rafe decided that if he was going to hide from the public eye then it might as well be on a yacht. Somewhere warm, with requisite beauties. The Caribbean was calling, Rafe thought as he heard his mother's icy tone.

'Rafe.'

'Mother.'

'What a foolish waste of a great ruler it would have been had you been killed.'

'What a foolish waste it is now,' Rafe responded. 'I am told I'm expected to return for Christmas to inspect an army I can no longer fight alongside because you both deem it too dangerous. Perhaps the balcony I have to stand on and wave from is too high? Too much of a risk.'

'Don't be facetious.'

'I am not,' Rafe responded. 'I am bored with being an idle prince...'

'Then act accordingly and you will be given the responsibility you crave.'

Marriage.

All conversations, all rows, all roads led to that. And the pressure did not come solely from his family but from the people, who longed to see their reckless Prince settled.

'I don't require a wife in order to make decisions.'

'You need to temper your ways. At least in the eyes of the public.'

'So as long as I am discreet I can carry on as before?' Rafe checked, and there was no disguising the disgust in his tone.

But his mother was unmoved. 'You have your father's heart, Rafe,' Queen Marcelle responded matter-of-factly. 'No one expects you to be faithful—we all know that your love is reserved for your country. And that country wants to see its Prince married and with heirs.'

'I decide when.'

'Fine,' said his mother. 'Until then, enjoy waving from the balcony!'

They had had this discussion on many occasions, though the news that he could take mistresses, like his father did, was a new development. But not a welcome one. Rafe admired many things about the King, but abhorred plenty.

He had the last word, Rafe knew. But he could not force him to marry.

And yet he could feel the pressure to conform tightening.

Rafe had not been lying when he'd told the King that his country had been on his mind as he'd fallen. Perhaps it was time to take a break from his partying ways, for Rafe was surprised to find himself growing tired of them.

Back on the balcony, he was thinking of one particular beauty. It was too confined here. That must be the reason why his thoughts had again wandered to Antonietta, for usually he allowed himself to get close to no one.

Her tears had moved him.

He wanted to spoil her. He wanted that smile he had seen so briefly to return to her lips.

One more night in Silibri, Rafe told himself.

And he would not be spending it alone.

CHAPTER FIVE

WHO WAS HE?

For the first time Antonietta truly wanted to know more about a guest—or rather, she corrected herself, about a man.

Her no-gossip rule wasn't serving her well now.

But the Internet service in her tiny cottage really was *terrible*.

To her own slight bemusement, an hour after her shift had ended Antonietta found herself heading out of her cottage and standing on a cliff, typing *Rafe* and *Tulano* into her laptop.

No service.

Agh!

She stomped back to her cottage and told herself she was being ridiculous. Whoever Rafe really was, it was irrelevant, given he'd be gone in a matter of days.

Yet, she wanted to know.

She was too embarrassed to ask Pino, who would generally be her main source of information, having shut down his conversation that first morning. And Chi-Chi, who usually daydreamed aloud about any male she saw as a potential suitor, was unusually quiet. Vincenzo was too discreet.

Oh, how she regretted refusing to let Francesca reveal

his identify to her. She could hardly ask her for more information now—it would only raise suspicion. Nico, and in turn Francesca, were very strict about staff keeping a professional distance from their guests.

It was why she was doing so well.

A knock at the door startled her. No one ever came and visited her at the cottage. Well, except for Aurora, but usually she would text to say that she was on her way. Could it be her parents, feeling guilty about avoiding her earlier in the village? Was she finally going to get the Christmas she had craved?

There was a spark of hope as she pulled open the door. But that tiny ray of hope dimmed when she saw who it was.

Rafe!

Actually, it didn't dim. That little spark shrank and regrouped and then reignited, hot, white and blue, as if the collar of a Bunsen burner had been altered.

'Rafe!'

And it was a Rafe she had never seen before. He looked more like the man in the photo attached to his profile except in that he was scowling. In fact, he was smiling, making no attempt to hide his pleasure at her shock.

He wore a dinner suit, and he wore it so very well.

The first time she had seen him he had been rumpled and his hair matted with blood. Now it was black and glossy and brushed back from his elegant face.

There was still a deep bruise on his eyelid, but the swelling had gone, and he was so elegant and commanding, so unexpected and exquisite, that he was simply too much.

'You shouldn't be here,' Antonietta said immediately.

'I didn't see any signs warning me not to trespass.'

'How did you know where I live?'

'Thankfully there is only one cottage near the helipad.' Rafe shrugged. 'Or I might have ended up at Chi-Chi's—I'd never have got out alive…'

Despite herself, Antonietta found that she was laughing at the vision his words created. The most stunning man stood at her door, and instead of being nervous she was laughing!

But she stopped herself. 'I can't invite you in.'

'I'm not asking to be let in,' Rafe responded smoothly. 'I'm inviting you to come out.'

'Out?'

'After the day you've had, I thought you might like a night of being spoiled.'

'I can't be seen in the restaurant with a guest.' Antonietta shook her head, but as one hand went to close the door her other hand resisted and held it part-way open—a kind of push-pull within her as she offered more reasons to say no. 'And I don't want to be seen in the village…'

'So we go further afield,' he said easily. 'My driver is waiting, if a night out appeals…?'

If a night out appeals?

Her mouth gaped at his choice of words. It more than appealed; pure temptation had come knocking at her door in the delectable shape of Rafe. And yet, as irresistible as his offer was, here came the voice of reason.

He's bored, the voice told her. *You are a mere diversion.*

And the voice became more insistent, rather unkindly pointing out that she was way too inexperienced to handle such prowess and likely it was not just her company he sought.

'I'm not allowed to date guests.'

'Who said anything about a date?'

Those eyes did, Antonietta wanted to respond. They

made her feel warm, and important, and deliciously sought after.

He played it down. 'It is dinner at a restaurant. I could use some company, that is all.' He looked at her. 'And so could you. It is my last night in Sicily. It seems a shame to leave without seeing some of it.'

Her heart sank at the news.

She had been told from the very start, even before they had met, when he had been simply Signor Dupont to her, that he undoubtedly would not last until Christmas Eve and would soon leave. Yet he was *Rafe* now, the man who brightened her day, and soon he would be gone.

Was that why she was considering his offer?

'Where?'

'I shall leave that to my driver. We have to try not to be seen, but it shouldn't be a problem…'

Antonietta frowned. Why would he worry about being seen out? She could think of only one thing.

'You don't have a wife?' she hurriedly checked. 'I know it's not a date, but…' Her voice trailed off.

'Antonietta, I don't have a wife, or a girlfriend. It's my parents who want me to lie low.'

His response gave her some relief, but also confused her. Rafe certainly didn't *look* like a man who worried about what his parents thought.

'Will you join me?' he asked.

A night of reheated pizza, ruminating over her parents' actions that morning and regretting her decision not to join this beautifully dizzying man for dinner? Such a night would be spent loathing her decision and her absolute inability to throw caution to the wind.

In fact, it might even become a lifetime of regret.

'Yes,' Antonietta said. 'I would love to join you.'

* * *

What were you supposed to wear when the sexiest man alive had arrived on your doorstep with a driver, and was waiting to whisk you to dinner?

Antonietta had but one possibility.

And, just as she had reluctantly handed the fabric over to Aurora, she now almost reluctantly slid the dress on.

Because it changed her.

Aurora was a brilliant seamstress. The silk had been cut on the bias, so the dress was as fluid as water and skimmed her body, enhancing the subtle curves The only issue she had was that it was so strappy it showed her bra, and Antonietta did not possess a strapless one.

Thankfully she was small-breasted, and Aurora had lined the top of the dress, but it still felt a little sinful to head out without one.

There was no time to fuss with her hair, so she simply brushed it and settled for wearing it down.

The dress needed no heels, but it certainly required lipstick.

Antonietta had no make-up of her own, and so, promising herself she would replenish it, she opened Aurora's Christmas present and painted her mouth crimson.

No, she would not save the dress for her coffin—and yet she felt like a liar as she stared in the mirror, for truly she was not the woman her reflection portrayed. She was not sexy, nor beautiful, Antonietta told herself, even if the dress said that she was.

Oh, but to Rafe she was.

Antonietta could not know the breath of fresh air that she was to him.

'I lied to you,' Rafe said as she approached.

'You *are* married…'

She knew it! He was simply too good to be true.

'No,' Rafe said, 'but this *is* a date, Antonietta.'

Her breath hitched and that flame spread warmth in her chest and down to her stomach.

'This can go nowhere…' he was very direct in telling her there could be no future for them '…but that doesn't change the fact that tonight I would love to get to know you some more.'

Before she responded, Antonietta knew she had to make something very clear. She did not know his motives, and she would not spend the whole night worrying about them, and so she would be upfront.

'I won't sleep with you, Rafe.'

'You would be a very boring dinner companion if you did.'

'I meant—'

'I know what you meant.' He smiled. 'Don't worry. *I* wouldn't sleep with me either—there's far too much paperwork involved.'

'Paperwork?'

'Come on,' he said, without clarifying what he meant, but she was glad she had told him the night would not end in bed, all the same.

He took her hand and led her to the waiting car, and it made her just a little dizzy that part of her didn't want to know that tomorrow she might wake up and think this had all been just a dream. Perhaps it was.

His driver took them through the village, and Antonietta was grateful for the blacked-out windows because of the number of people who turned and looked at the luxurious vehicle. But as they passed the tiny church—the one she failed to turn up to on her wedding day—Rafe must have felt her ripple of tension.

He turned and looked at her. 'Are you okay?' he checked.

'Of course.'

Except she wasn't. Because a short while later they passed her parents' property and she wondered what they would make of her going out on a date with a guest.

'Don't worry about your parents now.'

'How did you know I was thinking of them?'

'You pointed out where they live,' he reminded her. 'Forget about everything,' he told her. 'Tonight we escape.'

Only not quite.

They drove up the winding hillside and then down into the valley, and there was a certain exhilaration that swept through her at leaving the village she knew so well. But when she glanced behind them, the same car that had followed them out of the Old Monastery was still there.

'Are they following us?' Antonietta asked.

'It's just my security.' Rafe shrugged. 'Don't worry about them.'

But she did.

Not just because Rafe came with a full security detail, but because there was clearly more power to him than she could properly define. She felt as if she had run into the night with a giant—and not just in stature. There was an authoritative air to him that she had never encountered before, even in the most esteemed guests, a commanding edge that both enthralled and unnerved her.

Who *was* he?

Less than an hour ago she had been desperate to find out, but now she was scared to know.

'Do you like to dance?' Rafe asked.

'I don't dance,' Antonietta said. 'Well, I *can't* dance,' she admitted, and then frowned as he pressed the intercom and spoke with his driver.

'The lady likes to dance.'

The restaurant he took her to was stunning. His security team went into the trattoria before them, and she felt a little awkward when they were seated and she saw that the guards had stayed close.

'Do they *have* to be here?' Antonietta checked.

Rafe was so used to them that for a second he was about to ask to whom she referred, but then Antonietta spoke on.

'We're in the middle of nowhere.'

Only it wasn't just for *his* protection that they were close. It was to stop diners taking photos if he was recognised and also, Rafe knew bitterly, to report back to the King.

Rafe lived his life in the presence of staff—maids and aides, advisors and security—and barely noticed them. Yet he could see her discomfort.

'I'll have a word,' Rafe said.

He had several words, and none of them went down very well, for the Crown Prince's behaviour tonight was most irregular.

Still, soon enough they were dining alone.

Wine was poured and Antonietta realised just how hard it was to be in the village day after day after day. Being away from it, she could actually feel the tension leaving, and she let out a sigh as she put down her wine.

'That's better,' Rafe said. 'It's nice to see you looking...'

He didn't really know how to say it—it seemed there was a lightness to her that hadn't been there before. And he felt better being away from the hotel too. It was a relief from the constant weight of planning his next move forward.

'I don't know what to have,' Antonietta admitted, but then her eyes fell on the words 'pistachio pesto' and her mind was made up.

'I've never tried it,' Rafe said.

'Then you don't know what you're missing.' Antonietta smiled.

They ordered their main courses and then, finally alone, they clinked glasses.

'Saluti,' the French-speaking Rafe said.

'Santé!' Antonietta said, and looked him in the eye as they clinked glasses.

He was still looking at her as she took a sip of her drink and then rested back into her seat.

'It is good to be away,' Antonietta admitted. 'It's nice not to be stared at.'

'People were staring when we walked in,' Rafe said. 'Because you look beautiful.'

'Thank you,' Antonietta said. 'It's the dress.'

'Believe me, it's not just the dress,' Rafe said, and he realised he was more relaxed than he had been in a very long while.

It was a gorgeous restaurant, but the atmosphere was peaceful. And Antonietta was right: it was nice not to have his minders so close. Nice to tear bread and dip it in oil and to just...*be*.

Here, she was no longer his chambermaid. Which meant he could ask, 'What happened with your parents?' And she could choose whether or not she answered.

Antonietta looked at this delectable man and, though she would love his take on things, she did not want to bring the mood down. 'I don't want to bore you with it, Rafe.'

'So, give me the short version, then.'

He made her laugh. Oh, there was no *ha-ha-ha*, but his brusque humour teased a single note from her closed throat and stretched her lips to a smile.

He relaxed her. Even while she was nervous and out of her depth, still Rafe's presence somehow eased her soul.

'I was to be married,' Antonietta said. 'I have a very big family, across all the villages, and my father is very well connected...' She stopped herself. 'Sorry, you want the short version.'

'Take as long as you like.'

Her eyes widened, for he sounded as if he meant it. 'I've never really told anyone the whole thing. Then again, I've never had to—everyone already knows...'

'Ah, but do they know *your* version of events?'

'No.' She shook her head and thought for a moment. *'No,'* she said again, for even Aurora had not heard the news from her first-hand.

'It will go no further,' he assured her, 'and I would love to hear it.'

'The day I turned twenty-one I was told that I was to marry my second cousin, Sylvester.'

Antonietta had found that there were generally two reactions to this revelation—a slight grimace of discomfort or a nod of acceptance that said of *course* she should marry into the family, because that was where the money had to stay.

She looked at Rafe to gauge his reaction. There was no grimace and there was no nod. There was just patience.

She looked down. 'At the last minute I decided I couldn't go through with it. I jilted him.'

She dared not look up, but then his hand came across the table and closed around hers.

'Antonietta, can I have the slightly longer version, please?'

She gave a soft laugh, but it was laced with unshed tears—not just because of the subject matter, it was more the bliss of contact, the touch of his skin on hers that somehow cooled her endless scalding shame.

'I should have told him. I know that. Instead I left him standing at the altar. I ran away.'

'In your wedding dress?'

Still he held her hand.

'No. I pulled on some jeans and climbed out of the bedroom window. My father was waiting to take me to the church. By the time he worked out what I had done I was already on the train.'

To Rafe, the waiter coming over with their meals felt like an intrusion, and he wanted to wave him away.

For Antonietta, though, it felt like a reprieve, and her only reluctance at this break in conversation was that their hands had to part.

Then there were flurries of pepper and cheese, and their glasses were topped up, and Rafe could sense her relief not to be talking about herself any more.

He was not used to reticence.

The women he dated—for want of a better word— were only too happy to spend *hours* talking about themselves. Their upcoming photoshoot, their latest role, their clean and green diet, their blah-blah-blah.

And then they would casually ask if he knew so-and-so, which meant could he possibly have a word with them? Not that they wanted favours or anything, they would hastily add.

And then they would sip their thimble of champagne and pretend it had gone to their head, even as they kept all their wits about them, for this was their chance to get ahead, get seen, get a step up on the A-list ladder.

Oh, yes, Rafe knew their game well, because over and over he had allowed them to play it. And even as he told them that this could go nowhere, they countered with how much they liked him. No, no, they insisted, they *really* liked him. For *himself.* It had nothing to do with him being royal—they just liked him *incredibly* much...

He was bored with their fawning, and he knew that he was arrogant and not that nice—he knew there was nothing in him to like aside from his title.

He looked over to Antonietta, who gave an appreciative eye-roll that said her pasta was truly divine.

It was refreshing to sit in silence. To *want* to know more about someone else. And so it was Rafe who spoke. 'What made you change your mind?'

'I never got to make up my mind,' Antonietta said. 'He was the golden boy of the village.'

'Was?'

'He has married and moved away now, but at the time he was the star of Silibri—funny, charming, a hard worker. Everybody loves Sylvester. My father thought he was choosing well...'

'But?'

Antonietta did not know how to answer that. She did not know how to tell Rafe that Sylvester's kisses had left her cold, and that his hands had felt too rough. And that she'd had a sense of fear that had pitched in her stomach whenever she was alone with the man who had been chosen for her.

It wasn't loyalty to Sylvester that halted her, and nor was it Antonietta's propensity never to gossip. Instead it was a new layer of confusion that Rafe had inadvertently added to the mix—for she wanted *his* hand to close again around hers.

They were mid-meal, of course, but his earlier touch had bemused Antonietta, for not only had she liked it, it had felt like the most natural thing in the world. And touch had never come naturally to her.

'Have you seen him since?' Rafe asked when she refused to elaborate on what it was about Sylvester that had caused her to change her mind.

'No. When I got to Paris I wrote and apologised. He never responded and I don't blame him for that.'

'What about your parents?'

'They have had nothing to do with me since. I understand, though. I didn't just shame them. I embarrassed the whole family on both sides…'

'That's surely to be expected when the bride and groom are related?'

'Don't!' She gave a shocked laugh, but then it faded. 'I'm coming to realise that they're never going to forgive me.'

'The question is, can you forgive *them*?'

'Forgive *them*?'

'Antonietta, I'm sure you had your reasons for running away.'

She didn't answer with words. Instead it was Antonietta's skin that spoke, as a blush spread across her chest and cheeks.

'Quite sure,' Rafe said.

'They weren't to know,' she responded, in hot defence of her parents, but Rafe remained unmoved.

'I have known you for only a few days,' he said. 'And I *know* that you had your reasons. I don't know what they were, but I am certain they exist.'

Antonietta swallowed and then reached for her wine, took a gulp and swallowed again.

'You can tell me,' he offered.

'Why would I?' Antonietta retorted. 'You leave tomorrow.'

'That makes me the perfect sounding board,' said

Rafe, refusing to match her sudden anger. 'You never have to see me again.'

It was, she silently conceded, oddly appealing.

'However, if you don't want to speak about yourself any more you can ask about me,' he invited. 'Or perhaps you already know?'

'I don't know anything about you,' Antonietta admitted. 'Some of the staff have tried to tell me, but I close my ears to gossip and I never pry.'

'Pry away,' Rafe said, for although he had done his best to maintain their privacy, there was a chance she would wake up to the tabloids telling her she had dined with a playboy prince.

'You'll answer anything?' Antonietta checked.

'Not necessarily.' He would tell her his title, Rafe had decided. Generally, that more than sufficed.

Yet the question she had for Rafe was not about that. 'Where did you get those bruises?'

His eyebrows rose in surprise at her question. 'Skiing,' he said.

'An accident?'

'Not really. It was more recklessness on my part.'

'Oh. So you're here in Silibri to recover?'

'I'm here to lie low for a while,' Rafe said.

'And you're *not* married?'

'I've already told you, no.'

'Or involved with anyone?'

Rafe's jaw gritted a fraction. Couldn't she just ask the simple question and be done? Once she knew he was the Crown Prince of Tulano this attempt at a get-to-know-you would end.

For no one really knew the Crown Prince.

'I'm not serious about anyone.'

'Have you ever been?'

'Why all these questions?'

'You told me I was free to pry!'

So he had. 'No,' Rafe said. 'I have never been serious about anyone.' He thought back. 'I tried to be once,' he said. He glanced up and saw that she sat still and silent. Patiently waiting. 'Or rather, I tried to make things work. But I was barely in my twenties.' He looked into her sad treacle-black eyes and appreciated her lack of comment. 'I disappointed a lot of people when we broke up. Though I guess you would know all about that?'

'Were you engaged?'

'God, no!' Rafe said. 'If that had been the case there would have been no going back.'

The way he said it made her shiver. That dark note to his tone struck a warning that she had no idea of the power she was dealing with.

As delectable as her pasta was, Antonietta put her silverware down, and as the waiter removed her plate she braced herself to ask the final question.

But when push came to shove she found that she dared not. 'Rafe, on a couple of occasions I have tried to find out who you are. But the truth is I am a little nervous to know.'

'Why?'

'Because...' She flailed around for an explanation. 'Because I don't want to feel any more daunted than I already do.'

'You feel daunted?'

'A bit,' she admitted. 'A lot.'

'I don't want you to feel daunted,' Rafe said, and again he took her hand.

'Which is why I don't want to find out that you're a film star, or a world champion skier...'

She floundered in her poor attempts to label him, for

she was certain he was rather more than that. She knew it from the way he held himself, and the silent command of his presence. She knew that heads had turned as they entered the restaurant, and they had not, despite his kind words, turned for her.

She looked down at their entwined fingers. Oh, it was not just his hands that gave him away, but they had hinted at the truth from the start. Yes, there really were only two reasons that men had manicures: they chose to or they were born to.

She did not want to know.

'So you think I could be a film star or a world champion skier?' Rafe teased. 'Absolutely not, to the former, and I wish, to the latter.'

And then it was Rafe who had a question, and he both frowned and smiled when he asked it.

'Why wouldn't you want me to be a champion skier?'

She blushed instead of answering.

'Why?' Rafe asked again.

'I would like to see the dessert menu,' Antonietta said, and sidestepped the question.

Rafe left it.

For now.

'I can't decide!' Antonietta groaned as she read through the menu, because everything sounded sublime.

'When there is Modica chocolate mousse on the menu,' Rafe said, with barely a glance at the other offerings, 'the choice is already made.'

He gave her a quizzical look as she started.

'What?'

'Nothing,' Antonietta said, thinking of the purchase she had made that morning with Rafe in mind. It would be foolish to tell him, surely? But then she looked into the eyes of the man who had been so very kind to her today and it made it a little easier to reveal. 'I bought some for you.'

'For *me*?'

Antonietta nodded. 'For Christmas. Well, that was when I thought you were staying until Christmas Eve.'

In Silibri, gifts were often exchanged then. Though it wasn't often that a chambermaid bought a gift for a guest, and they both knew it.

She opened her mouth to say that she had bought it because he had been kind when she cried. But of course that would be a lie, for she had bought it before that had happened.

'It's just a small thing,' she settled for instead. 'A tiny little thing.'

Yet it touched Rafe.

'Coffee-flavoured,' Antonietta said.

'With a breakfast banquet at the side?' he checked, taking them both back to the morning they had met.

'No!' Antonietta smiled.

'You were the only good thing that happened that day.'

'I didn't do anything,' she pointed out.

'Antonietta, I find your silence golden.'

Their desserts arrived, and with them a silver platter which, the waiter told them, held real snow from the Nebrodi range. Nestled in it were two tiny glasses of icy Limoncello.

'Is this really snow?' Antonietta asked, pressing into it with her fingers.

'Apparently so,' Rafe said, pushing his own fingers in and finding hers. '*Not* what I need after a skiing accident. It's lucky it's not triggering a flashback.'

He made her laugh.

And to see her laugh felt like a reward.

The mousse was perfect and the Limoncello, though

icy, was warming and a delectable end to their meal. Though the night did not have to end, suggested Rafe. Because they could dance.

'I told you, I don't dance,' she attempted to say. But when he ignored her and stood up, held out his hand, she decided that Aurora was right and this dress did deserve at least one dance.

Or two. For how could he be so tall and so broad and yet so graceful? Antonietta wondered as she melted in his arms.

He carried her through it—not physically, but through her missteps and clumsy efforts. And he only winced once.

'Did I step on your feet?' She gave a worried frown.

'No,' Rafe told her, and he said no more—just held her until she knew how to dance…but only with him.

He felt the tension slide out of her during the second dance, and he knew certain triumph as she relaxed in his arms. Somehow he knew this was rare for her. And he could not remember enjoying a night so much.

A night that could be considered tame by his usual standards, but by royal standards was both reckless and wild. Because she hadn't been palace-approved, as a true date would be, and neither had she signed disclaimers, as his usual companions would.

It was uncharted waters for both of them.

The music slowed further, as if the band had heard his silent request, and now he moved her closer.

Antonietta made no protest, for she wanted more contact and she liked the shield of his arms. The heat from his palm was in the middle of her back and his other hand was on her bare arm. He did not put a finger wrong.

Not one.

Yet her bare arm wished that he would.

She could feel the slight pressure of his fingers and she ached to know their caress. She wished the hand on her back would go lower, so much so that she suddenly found she was holding her breath.

'Antonietta?'

His head had lowered and his mouth was near her ear. His voice, so close, made her shiver.

'Yes?' she said, though she did not lift her face to him. Instead she opened her eyes to the fabric of his suit.

'Why don't you want me to be a world champion skier?'

She didn't answer straight away, and instead swayed to the beat as every exposed piece of flesh—and those hidden away beneath the red silk—burned in his arms.

'Because…' she started.

'I can't hear you.'

Now she lifted her head, and she had to stretch her neck so that her red-painted lips were close to his ear.

'Aren't sportsmen supposed to be insatiable?'

'I don't know,' Rafe said. 'I have never been with one.'

She laughed, but then she was serious. 'I won't sleep with you,' she said again.

It was stated as fact, yet she knew it was a lie, because she was on fire in his arms and she was weak with want.

'Can I ask why?' Rafe said, for he could feel her desire.

She could have told him that she was scared to, or that she did not know how, and both of those answers would have been true, but there was another reason that was holding her back, and Antonietta voiced it now.

'Because I have a feeling that you would pay me.'

'I would pay for your discretion,' Rafe responded calmly. 'Not for the act.'

She pulled back and looked up into his eyes. 'I don't understand…'

'You would have to sign an NDA.' He registered her frown. 'A non-disclosure agreement.'

'That's the most unromantic thing I have ever heard.' She actually laughed.

'Tell me about it,' Rafe said. 'It is very inconvenient at times.'

How was she *laughing* at such a subject?

Why was she imagining them tumbling into bed and Rafe whipping out a contract for her to sign?

'It is just as well,' Rafe continued, 'that I am the least romantic man.'

Except he didn't seem unromantic to her. She had never felt more looked after, or been held with such care and skill, and she had never looked so deeply into a man's eyes while sharing a smile.

'But you can carry on dancing with me,' Rafe said, 'without signing a thing.'

He pulled her in so close that she could feel all she would be missing pressing into the softness of her stomach. His other hand was on her shoulder, toying with the spaghetti strap of her dress and making her breasts ache and crave for the same attention.

'Can you kiss me?' Antonietta asked, and her voice was husky and unfamiliar. 'Without me having to sign a thing?'

'Of course,' he said, in a voice that was completely steady. 'But later.'

Kiss me now, she wanted to plead as his hand moved down to the small of her back and pressed her in a little more.

He smoothed the hair from her hot face and then slid his hand under the dark curtain and stroked her neck and the top of her spine. They hadn't even kissed, yet she was weak and breathless in his arms, and just when she thought she might die from wanting him he released her a touch.

'Why don't I take you home?' Rafe suggested.

He made her wait for her kiss.

Through handshakes with the owner and then out to the delicately lit street.

Now, she kept thinking. *Let it be now.*

But, no.

He took her hand and held it tightly as they walked to the car.

Now, please now, she thought, with the moon high in the sky as they drove through the hillsides.

But of course it would not be now, for she did not want the audience of his driver for their first kiss, even if there was a partition.

Rafe sensed that. He had done far more than kiss in the back of a luxury car, but he wanted this to be right.

He still held her hand, carefully moving it to his thigh, but that was all. And then he loosened his grip and left it there.

She felt the solid muscle beneath her hand and of course she was too shy to move her hand higher. But there was actually no need, for to rest her hand on his thigh was bliss enough.

And then the girl with the saddest eyes spoke and made her first joke to him. 'Champion skiers have very powerful thighs.'

He smiled. 'Perhaps I missed my vocation.'

He made her wait even longer as they arrived at her little stone cottage at the end of a perfect date, and he made one thing very clear.

'Don't ask me to come in, for I might find it impossible to leave.'

'I won't.' Antonietta nodded. She would not lower

herself to deal with 'paperwork', but she did have one request. 'Can you ask your minders to leave, though?'

She was not just quiet, Rafe realised, she was shy, for the cars were all parked well away. He was about to point that out, and even possibly to add that they could not be less interested in a mere kiss, for they had seen far more. In truth, should he be asked in, they were the men who would speak with her first and get her signature on a page.

Except it was not a *mere* kiss.

And he would not be asked in.

'One moment.'

Dismissing Royal Protection Officers was not that easy, for though they were minding *him*, they answered to the King. And this was irregular indeed.

But in the end Rafe was Crown Prince, and when the Crown Prince told you, in no uncertain terms, to back the hell off because you were dismissed for the night, then—albeit reluctantly—you left.

She heard the crunch of gravel as the cars drove away and watched as Rafe walked back towards her—alone. She was nervous, but no longer daunted. He took her little purse from her hands and he took off her shawl. But it wasn't the night air that made her shiver as he placed them on the stone wall, it was the thought of the kiss to come.

He looked right at her as his fingers went to the spaghetti strap of her dress. They made a new language, one without words, for as his fingers toyed with the strap his eyes told her that he had wanted to do this on the dance floor. She swallowed as he pulled the strap down her arm, and she was shaking like a trapped bird as he lowered his head and kissed the bare skin.

Oh, his mouth was warm and soft, and then not so

soft, more thorough and deep, and her lips parted, and her knees did not know how to keep her standing up.

No matter, for his hand slid around her waist and his mouth worked up her neck and then came to her mouth.

'All night,' Rafe said, 'I have wanted to kiss you.'

Antonietta had dreaded Sylvester's kiss, let alone the thought of anything more. She had never envisaged that she might ache for a man's kiss. But now, with her neck damp from his mouth and his hands on her cheeks, she was wound tight with anticipation, and desperate to know the weight of his lips on hers.

It was a soft weight, and at first it satisfied. The graze of his lips had her own mouth pouting to reciprocate and her eyes simultaneously closing. He kissed her slowly until she returned it, and when her lips parted she shivered at her first taste of his tongue.

She had never imagined that a mouth could be so sublime, that his tongue could dance her to pleasure. His hands slipped from her face and moved down her bare arms, and Antonietta remained in his kiss, felt the pleasure building. He kissed her harder, and she felt as if she were nailed to the wooden door by his mouth, by the hands that were on her ribcage and the stroke of his thumb on her breast.

It had her weak and yet faintly desperate. Yes, desperate. For his kiss no longer satisfied. Instead it shot need into her veins. And the way his hand cupped her breast and lightly stroked her felt as if he was stroking her on the inside.

Rafe wanted her.

Badly.

But she had stated her case. So he removed his mouth and looked down at her, flushed and wanting and desirous.

'Go inside,' he told her.

Yet she remained.

For it felt as if the sky had parted and she had glimpsed behind it—as if everything she had been told and all that she had assumed was wrong.

Her body *worked*.

She wanted Rafe's kisses.

She craved Rafe's touch.

Sylvester's taunts had pierced her, embedded themselves so deeply, and yet she felt them lifting now.

Rafe did not daunt her.

If anything, she felt as if he had freed her.

This elusive man, who housed so many secrets, had set her body on fire.

Antonietta glimpsed all that she had avoided and all she had never truly known she was missing.

But would that change if he knew about her lack of experience?

Rafe was used to sophisticated women—something she doubted she could be. Would her innocence douse his desire? For he had made it clear he wanted no strings. And in that moment neither did she.

For the first time in her life Antonietta wanted to be intimate with a man. To taste his kiss again and to know the bliss denied to her until now.

This was so different—so new and so transforming.

And her choice entirely.

Her usual caution lay somewhere between the furthest star and the moon. She knew now how good a kiss should be, and only wanted more of the same.

And so she said what was in her heart.

'Take me to bed.'

CHAPTER SIX

RAFE DID *NOT* recall his minders.

Antonietta removed her high heels and they walked hand in hand across the moon-drenched grounds of the monastery on a clear Silibri night.

Where there had been years of turmoil and angst, now there was clarity and certainty. For there was no thought as to the outcome, or to tomorrow, just the bliss of now and this night.

'We can't go through the foyer,' Antonietta said.

'Of course not,' Rafe agreed. 'I have my own entrance. Though you would…'

His voice trailed off and she felt his grip tighten on her hand. She looked up to see what had stopped him from speaking, though his stride did not falter.

Antonietta looked to where his gaze fell and there at the foot of the steps was a suited man—one of his security detail. She attempted a small joke. 'He can't stop you from entering, surely…?'

And then it was her voice that trailed off as she realised that of course it was not *Rafe* who was the problem.

It was her.

But the security man said nothing. He merely stepped aside. And as Antonietta glanced up at Rafe she saw why—the man would surely not dare to question him, for the look Rafe gave him could freeze molten lava and halt a lion's approach.

'Is there a problem?' Antonietta asked, recalling their conversation about 'paperwork'.

'Of course not,' Rafe said, for he knew he would deal with the issues raised tomorrow. And there would be issues—of that he was certain. For Antonietta had been neither vetted nor approved. And the security guard had unnerved her.

Rafe could not know of her trepidation as he pushed open the French windows and they stepped into the lounge of his suite.

The turn-down service had been in and a fire was lit.

'Would you like a drink?' he offered.

She was about to decline, but then she glanced at the open doors to the bedroom and saw the vast bed. She decided she needed to pause things for a moment, if only to slow her heartbeat down.

'Please.'

She took in a deep breath as he poured, and could not decipher whether it was terror or desire that coursed through her.

Both, she decided as they clinked glasses.

But a drink didn't hold him back for long.

'Come here,' he told her, and put down his glass.

Antonietta did the same, and as she walked towards him it felt less seamless, and his kiss was different too.

It was thorough, it was hungry, and she felt her bravado fading.

She was tumbling with confusion, on an impossible see-saw as she kissed him back. Because he sent her skywards with his hands, with his mouth, with the way he held her against him.

He took her hand and guided it to where he was hard,

and she felt as if the giddy high of the sky and then her nerves had her meeting the ground with a thud.

And she did not know how to reach the sky again.

And she could not fake her way through it.

'Rafe…' She had to tear her mouth from his, had to force her breathless throat to form words. 'I've never…'

Rafe did not care if she had never been into one-night stands.

He did not care if this was not something she often did.

But then he saw her pupils were dilated—and not just with desire. He recognised fear, and though he held her still, he froze absolutely.

'I've never slept with anyone before,' she said.

He dropped her.

Oh, she did not actually tumble to the ground, but she felt the see-saw crash down and she sank further without his touch.

'And you didn't think to tell me?'

'I was hoping you wouldn't notice.'

'Not notice! What the—?'

How the hell could she possibly think he might miss such a detail? But then his eyes narrowed in suspicion.

'Or were you hoping that I'd be too far gone to care?' he accused.

'I don't know what you mean.'

She really didn't.

He watched as she pulled up the straps on her dress, her pert nipples visible beneath the sheer fabric because their arousal remained. It was a fire that would not die, and had her words not halted him they would have been locked together now, with no thought to the consequences.

Rafe knew it.

Absolutely he knew it.

And it was an unfamiliar thing—for he always maintained a semblance of control and never forgot he was royal.

'I don't know what you mean,' Antonietta said again, her voice rising this time, and Rafe felt the anger recede, for she *really* didn't know. She wasn't trying to trap him, he realised. She was clueless, not ruthless.

'You should have told me.'

'Yes,' Antonietta agreed. 'But if I had I would be tucked up in bed alone now.'

'Do you know why?'

'Because you want someone experienced. You want—'

'Antonietta,' he interrupted, 'I leave tomorrow.'

She didn't blink, he noted. At least not until a log on the fire dropped, and it spat sparks and hissed for a moment before it settled.

'I know that,' she said finally.

'If you have waited this long—'

'Oh, please don't!' Antonietta interrupted him now, a little embarrassed and a lot angry. 'Please don't tell me that I must be saving myself for marriage, for Mr Right...'

'Why have you waited, then?'

'*Because.*'

Now she was embarrassed, and she reached for her shawl rather than answer him. She picked up her bag, ready to head out into the night, but he caught her arm.

'Because?' he demanded.

'I've never wanted anyone until now!' She shouted it, and continued to shout. 'My fiancé kept trying and I loathed it. I loathed every touch and every kiss and every attempt—' Her chest shuddered as she took in ragged gulps of air.

'Every *attempt*?' Rafe checked. 'What do you mean?'

'He tried—several times—but I fought him off.'

There—she had said it and the sky had not fallen. She had told someone. In fact she had admitted to this man whom she had known only a few days, something she had never revealed to her family or even her dearest friend.

Perhaps it was because she knew Rafe was leaving, she pondered briefly.

'I told *him* that I was saving myself for marriage; it was the only way I could keep him back. So please don't assume you know my reasons for waiting.'

'Did he hurt you?' Rafe was aware of the anger in his own voice and fought to check it, for his anger was not aimed at her. Then he answered his own question. 'Of course he did.'

'No,' she countered. 'Not really.' For even all these years later there was no neat category for what had taken place on those long-ago nights, and she didn't want to discuss it. 'You are not a counsellor—and I came here to move on, not to look back.'

She looked down to his hand, still closed around her wrist, but looser now.

'I'll say goodnight,' she said.

Yet Rafe could not leave things there. He let go of her wrist, and as he watched Antonietta gather her things there were two people that Rafe loathed right now.

The man who had attempted to force her.

And the man who had tonight denied her.

'Antonietta…' He could see her confusion, could still feel the hum of angry words that hung in the air, and he did not want her leaving like this. 'I would never have brought you back here had I known you were a virgin.'

'We've already established that,' she clipped.

'Listen to me!' he snapped back.

And she liked it that he snapped. She liked his impatience, and the fact that he did not suddenly treat her like fragile glass, that her past did not change them.

'I am trying to explain…'

'You don't want me,' Antonietta said. 'I think you have made that exceptionally clear.'

'Of *course* I want you!'

He sounded cross, and yet his tone did not trouble her. It felt like a row. Yet it did not unnerve her.

For when she looked, when she met his navy eyes, there was desire rather than ire blazing in his eyes.

And it almost floored her.

'Antonietta.'

He took a breath and it seemed to her as if he was preparing her for bad news.

'I *will* be leaving tomorrow.'

Was that it? The bad news? She knew that already.

'Rafe…'

She did not know how best to put it that she was not terrified of his leaving. She was terrified of being sent away!

Tomorrow? She had dreaded so many tomorrows. And she had loathed so many yesterdays.

'I don't care what happens in the morning.'

It sounded reckless, yet right now she felt no caution.

Rafe knew more about her than any other person on this earth. He knew her secrets. And with his kiss he had disproved her own theory, for it turned out that Antonietta *could* want, could be folded over with desire and crave a man's touch.

'I don't care that you're leaving tomorrow,' she told him. 'I care only that you're asking me to leave *now*.'

He weighed her words as he stood there. And they were heavy ones, for she was trusting herself to him.

'I'm not asking you to leave,' Rafe said. 'I'm just asking if you are sure.'

She was.

Absolutely.

As certain as she had been at the door to her cottage.

More certain than she had been as they'd walked on the moon-drenched grass.

Completely certain now.

And nervous.

Yet excited as Rafe took her hand and led her to the master bedroom.

It was warm in there. The turn-down service had been in and the fire was roaring. She wondered if he would open the French windows to let in some cool air, but instead he threw two more logs on the roaring fire and then came over to her.

'What am I to do with you?' Rafe asked, and she did not know how to answer. He smoothed back the hair from her face and his gaze was assessing. 'Are you scared?'

'No,' Antonietta said. 'Well, a bit—but not like I once was.'

The room was too hot, and they stood just a little too close to the fire. But she liked it. For the fire felt like an iceberg and the air seemed cool compared to the heat pooling low in her belly and spreading down her thighs.

Yet Rafe touched her not.

Deliberately so.

This would be no *attempt*.

He loathed it that she had been touched while unwilling, and he would not move even so much as a finger until she approached him, though he'd offer direction.

'Take off your dress,' he told her, and she blinked, because she had thought that Rafe would take care of that. But Rafe did not cajole her, he did not sweet talk or wheedle, he simply made her want.

And it felt delicious.

For the first time ever she rued Aurora's dressmaking skills, for it took her a moment to find the tiny concealed zip at the side. She pulled it down with shaky hands and then stood trembling and a little shy as it fell to the ground.

She stood only in her knickers. As a reflex, she covered her breasts with her arm. But then she pondered her own disappointment if Rafe were to undress and do the same, and she took a breath and peeled her arm away, let it fall to the side.

Rafe cast his gaze the length of her slender frame, to her pert breasts and the dark areolae, the stiffened nipples that he ached to touch—but resistance was a turn-on, he was finding.

She pushed her knickers down without his instruction, and had to put a hand up, resting it on his chest to steady herself. He hissed out a long intake of breath.

He reached out and traced one manicured finger from her collarbone to her breast, until her own breath choked her. The feel of his hand on her breast was sublime and she looked down, somewhat fascinated. For the room felt like a sauna, and yet her dark nipples peaked to his touch as if they were smeared in Nebrodi snow.

He was sure that she was sure.

So sure that he lifted her by the hips and their mouths met as if deprived. She coiled her legs around his torso and his hand roamed her naked body as they kissed.

She did not know how sexy she was, Rafe thought, for he had thought her shy and reticent and yet she came alive in his hands.

He wanted to tear off his clothes, just to feel her naked

against him, but there was a supreme pleasure in her naked warm body wrapped around him.

He placed her down on the bed that she had made that very morning. The sheets that smelt of summer were cool and yet soft on her naked skin, and she made no attempt to cover herself, just lay and watched as he undressed.

She had seen him nearly naked, but on those occasions she had averted her eyes and tried not to look. Now there was no need to be chaste, or embarrassed by her inquisitiveness, and she watched unashamedly as he peeled off his shirt and revealed his chest.

Rafe was impatient to be naked and to join her. Rarely did he have to tell himself to slow down, and yet her hungry eyes beckoned. The rosy blush spread as if she held a fan across her chest and cheeks, and the way she bit down on her lip as he unbuckled his belt made undressing a less than seamless task, for he could not tear his eyes from her.

Nor could she tear hers from him. For she might have seen him *nearly* naked and considered him perfection, but completely exposed Rafe was magnificent.

Far more magnificent than she knew what to do with.

And when she saw him, so strong and erect, there was a stroke of desire so low in her stomach that she pulled up her knees.

'Don't be scared,' he told her.

'I'm not,' Antonietta said, in a voice that sounded too thick and too low.

And then she looked at him again, and wondered how they might possibly fit.

But she was *not* scared. She knew that because before fear had made her fight like a cat and slam her legs closed.

Fear had never made her approach. And it was not

fear that had her rising to her knees and prowling across the bed towards him.

For the first time they were face to face, and yet only for a moment did they look into each other's eyes. There was so much to explore, to touch and to feel, and Antonietta had been resisting doing so almost since they had met, since their first conversation.

But now she could touch those wide shoulders, feel their strength and his warm skin beneath her fingers. Now she could run her hand down his chest and explore the mahogany nipples, pressing the pads of her fingers in. She ached to kiss them, and yet there was even more she ached to feel. She perused the taut planes of his stomach and then turned her hand so the backs of her fingers brushed the snaky line of dark hair.

Daring herself, she touched his thick member, surprised when it twitched as she held him alive and firm in her nervous palm. He slid through her hands and Rafe let her explore him, though his teeth were gritted together, for he longed to wrap his hand tight over hers. But to show her his rhythm would finish him, so he sank into her untutored perusal and explored her instead.

His hands were light on her breasts, yet her nipples hardened further and almost stung, so that she yearned for the wetness of his mouth. He did not give it. Instead his hands slid slowly down, past the curve of her waist, and held her hips, pulling her closer to him and rocking her, so that he nudged against her and left a silver trail on her stomach.

Her breathing hitched and she did not know how to get it back to its rhythm. When his hand slid between her thighs she gave in, and just rested her head on his chest.

Her soft moans spoke of her pleasure as he parted

damp curls. Feeling her warm and ready, Rafe slid his fingers into her warm folds and explored her.

'There...' she breathed.

It was a needless instruction, because he already was there, but she pressed her face into his chest and inhaled his scent. One large hand cupped her buttock as the other burrowed into her tight, warm space.

And she didn't just let him—Antonietta *wanted* him.

She wanted the tiny volts of pleasure he shot through her, and she wanted the salty taste of his skin on her lips and tongue, and the tears that squeezed from her eyes were absolutely ones of pleasure.

And when he was sure she was ready—when he could feel she was on the delicious edge, and when he knew that her pleasure might finish him—Rafe withdrew his hand and opened the bedside drawer.

The tearing of foil felt like a zip tightening low in her stomach, and Antonietta watched, held in a spell of his making, as he sheathed himself.

She bit down on her lip rather than admit that she preferred the velvet skin naked.

But then her lip broke free, and unwittingly she voiced her thoughts. 'I want to feel you in me...'

Rafe pulled a breath in. Those words from anyone else would have served as a warning. Yet tonight those words were a mirror of his own thoughts.

'And you shall,' he told her as he laid her down.

The room was almost stifling, yet it only heightened the pleasure. Her body was flushed and pliant, and when he came over her Antonietta's mouth met his.

He nudged at her entrance and she closed her eyes as he finally took her—took her there and back on a spectrum of pleasure and pain as he filled her.

Her hands gripped his shoulders and he gritted his teeth. 'Your shoulder…' she gasped.

She knew then what his grimace on the dance floor had been about, but as she went to remove her hands his pain was forgotten, and she dug her fingers further in as he filled her so absolutely that it felt there wasn't even enough space to gather in a necessary deep breath.

Instead, she held on to her breath and to a scream.

She had been right. They did not fit.

Yet for Rafe the tight grip of her was so intense that he let out a moan as he fought to stay still while she grew accustomed to the feel of him inside.

She would never accustom herself, Antonietta was sure. Except now his ragged breathing in her ear was coming into focus, and her grip was loosening on his shoulder, and she was so warm she felt she might faint.

'I want a drink of water,' she said, and heard his low laughter in her ear.

He gave her his mouth and he kissed her softly, so that she forgot the agony she was in. More velvet-soft kisses and then he moved deep inside her until she could no longer focus on his kiss.

She slumped back on the bed and he slid an arm under her, and when he moved she did the same.

'Rafe…' She said his name and he tempered himself, fought to slow down, but that was not what she was asking. 'More…'

She had never known anything so delicious—until he put his elbows to the sides of her head and looked right down into her eyes, sweeping damp hair from her face. Then Rafe started to thrust, and she held not his chest, nor his shoulders. She stroked her fingers down his back and felt his taut buttocks, pressed him harder into her.

How did he know? she wondered, because she'd

closed her eyes and told him nothing, but he was thrusting harder now.

'Rafe…' she said again, but there was no instruction she could give when he was playing her like a master.

He felt the shivers of her orgasm even before Antonietta knew what was happening.

He was moving faster, and she could see the concentration on his features. The tension seemed to rip through her, and she clenched tight, but he thrust harder.

Rafe came in blessed relief, and her deep pulses dragging him in were his reward. And then his breathless moan reverberated through her as she convulsed beneath him. He felt her soft collapse as her body relaxed.

'I never knew…' Antonietta was breathless as he lay atop her, dragging in air. 'All I was missing…'

'Because you never knew *me*.'

CHAPTER SEVEN

JUST AS SHE always was, Antonietta was up long before the Sicilian winter sun. And for a moment she languished in bliss. Her head lay on Rafe's chest and she listened to the *thud, thud, thud* of his heart, and in the silence of predawn she focussed only on the sheer pleasure of waking next to him.

The hurt that had become so familiar was held at bay when she was in his arms, and it was incredibly tempting to sink back into the sleep that beckoned. She fought it, though. The consequences of being caught in a guest's bed had started to impinge and Antonietta forced her eyes open.

'Rafe…' She tried to untangle herself from the heavy arm that lay over her. 'I had better head back to the cottage.'

'Not yet,' he said sleepily.

'Yes,' she insisted. 'Your coffee will be delivered soon, and I had better not be here! I ought to leave while it's still dark.'

'I'll walk you back.'

It was an offer without precedent, for while Rafe always ensured that his dates were seen home, it was generally under the care of his driver. Not that Antonietta could know that.

Even so, she immediately shook her head. 'No, the staff will soon be starting to arrive,' she said as she hauled herself from the warm bed and pulled the drapes open enough to allow her to see and scramble for her clothes. 'I cannot be seen leaving your room.'

It really was unthinkable.

Most certainly she would lose her job. And, worse, her reputation in the village—already shaky at best—would flatline completely.

Last night it had felt so simple and straightforward, but the encroaching light of dawn cast shadows of doubt.

Rafe had promised one night, which meant their time was over, but how could this be goodbye? How did she simply walk out of his life as if their parting did not matter to her?

Because it did.

It very much did.

Rafe turned on the bedside light and Antonietta hurried to finish dressing. She turned her back to him, though not because she was suddenly shy—she was trying to hide her eyes. She did not want Rafe to glimpse, even for a second, that last night's bravado had gone.

'Tomorrow' was here.

Which meant he was leaving today.

Antonietta couldn't say that she hadn't been warned. The potential for hurt had been clearly labelled, just as a pharmacist added stickers to a medicine bottle.

May cause heartbreak.
In case of sudden tears do not attempt conversation.

And so Antonietta did up the tiny zip on her dress, pulled on her shoes, and then turned to Rafe and attempted a smile. 'Thank you for a wonderful night.'

He lay with his hands behind his head, watching her dress and wanting to haul her back into bed. Sex had made him hungry, and he would love nothing more than to confuse the chefs and cancel his strict order for coffee only, then tear into pastries and make love to her all over again.

'Stay a little longer. I'll order breakfast.'

'I'm not hiding in the bathroom, Rafe. Anyway, I really do have to go to work.'

She did not want prolonged goodbyes and to be told by him that it had been good while it lasted.

Make that *great*.

Or rather, make that the single best time of her entire life.

And it wasn't just the sex, though her body felt deliciously bruised and awoken. More, it had been the talking and the dancing, and walking across the Old Monastery grounds hand in hand.

And, even more than the sum of all that, it had been the honesty she had found with him. Even if it was impossible to be honest now, and admit that leaving with a smile was the hardest thing she had ever done.

Absolutely the hardest.

She went over and gave him a kiss.

A light one was her intention—except Rafe moved his hand behind her head and pressed her close. Antonietta closed her eyes to the taste and the bliss. She was tempted, so tempted to give in. Was he subtly guiding her to lie atop him, or was she actually drifting that way to the command of his kiss?

Their tongues were more urgent, the kiss deeper as his other hand moved to her breast, toying with it through the fabric of her dress, and Antonietta knew he would have far less trouble with the zip than she.

Rafe's moves were seamless, and Antonietta knew that any moment she would be naked and knotted with him, locked into bliss with no thought as to the ramifications there would surely be.

And she would fall deeper.

Self-preservation had Antonietta removing her mouth, and she looked down for a moment into his deep navy eyes and knew she could very easily drown in them.

Do not take more than the stated dose...

Or she might never recover.

'Be good,' she said.

He gave a slight mirthless laugh. 'I don't want to be good.' But then he was serious. 'You're okay?'

'Of course.'

'You're sure?' Rafe checked, and watched as her eyes narrowed a touch.

Would he prefer that she cried? Antonietta wondered. Well, she refused to allow him back into her thoughts. She had been a willing participant last night and did not regret it for a moment. It was just that she had missed the part in life's guidebook about how to walk from someone who mattered. The lesson that taught you how to be incredibly close one moment and say farewell the next.

'Goodbye, Rafe.'

Yes, walking through the French doors and climbing down the stone steps really was the hardest thing she had ever done.

Leaving a packed church full of people waiting for the bride to arrive had been a very public hurt. Being disowned by her parents had caused anguish and pain. But it was the price she had paid for rejecting Sylvester, and despite the consequences she knew she would do it again.

This was a private hurt that no one knew of.

The guard gave her a bored look as she passed, which told her that a woman leaving Rafe's bed was hardly noteworthy.

The birds were starting to sing and the sky was starting to lighten as she crossed the grounds, and the world carried on as if nothing had changed.

Yet for Antonietta, everything had.

She looked back to the Old Monastery, and more specifically to the August Suite, from which she had just come. The master bedroom was in darkness, and she could almost picture Rafe reaching out and flicking the switch on the lamp before drifting off to sleep.

But Rafe had not gone back to sleep. Instead, he lay in the dark, in a bed perfumed by their union.

He had come to Silibri not just to lie low but to prepare himself for the enormity of what lay ahead, and all that awaited him when he returned to Tulano.

He had come to Silibri to clear his head.

Not to lose it to a maid with sad eyes.

Just this once Antonietta would have liked to do one of Chi-Chi's *slowly-slowly* acts. She was sore, and tender, and she wanted to dwell on last night and wallow a while. But then nothing would get done.

'I think it is mean of Nico to make us work on Christmas Day…' Chi-Chi huffed as she refilled the selection of toiletries in one of the regular suites.

It was stunning, of course, and looked out towards the valley, but it was nowhere near as luxurious as the August Suite.

In truth, Antonietta was happy to have been allocated to the suites well away from there. Her ears were on tenterhooks, waiting for the sound of a helicopter's approach that might signal his leaving.

'Of course some staff have to work,' said Antonietta, dragging her mind to their conversation as she dragged the vacuum cleaner from the doorway. 'Are the guests supposed to make their own beds and get their own food? What would be the point of people taking a Christmas Break?'

'Well, there could be a skeleton staff,' said Chi-Chi, as she needlessly rearranged the herbal teabags. 'That way some of the staff who have been here since the place opened could have the day off.'

'Tell Nico.' Antonietta shrugged.

'I intend to,' Chi-Chi said. 'In fact—'

Whatever Chi-Chi's grand plans were, Antonietta chose not to hear them and switched on the vacuum cleaner. She turned it to full suction and wished that drowning out her thoughts of Rafe was as easy as drowning out Chi-Chi's whining voice.

'Antonietta!'

She heard her name and then heard it again.

'Antonietta!'

'What?' she snapped, wondering what gripe Chi-Chi had this time that couldn't possibly wait—except it was Francesca who was calling her.

'*Scusi,*' Antonietta said and turned off the vacuum. 'I didn't see you there.'

'That's fine. I can see that *you* are busy…' Francesca shot a look at Chi-Chi, who was suddenly polishing a mirror. 'Signor Dupont has asked for his room to be serviced and he has requested you.'

'But I thought he was checking out?'

'Checking out?' Francesca frowned. 'Where did you hear that?'

'I'm not sure...' Antonietta attempted to cover her mistake. 'I thought you said he wouldn't last until Christmas Eve?'

'Well, that might be the case, but for now he is here—and, given that he has been in the August Suite for a week now, it requires a deep service, so I shall come with you.'

Oh, God! Please, no, Antonietta thought as they left Chi-Chi to it and collected linen before taking the elevator and heading along the cloisters.

What on earth was Rafe thinking, requesting *her*? She had visions of him lying naked on the bed as she and Francesca walked in, and was actually sweating as Francesca knocked and then opened the door.

It would seem Rafe had better manners than that, though.

'He's out,' Francesca said, after she'd made herself known but got no response.

Thank you, Antonietta breathed to herself.

'Let's get started,' Francesca said.

It felt odd, being back in the August Suite after last night. There on the table were the glasses that they had drunk from, but Francesca soon whipped them away.

'It looks as if he had company last night. Antonietta, why don't you get started in the master bedroom?'

From riches to rags.

Well, not quite. But she was no longer his lover and she was back to being his maid.

First she swept out the fire before which he had slowly undressed her. It felt as if it had been a dream. And then she rebuilt it, adding kindling under the logs and kneeling back for a moment. But there was no time to daydream, so she went to make up the bed.

As she pulled back the heavy cover she had lain beneath she saw the evidence of her lost virginity.

It had not all been a dream.

Quickly, and with her cheeks burning red, she bunched up the sheet. She was about to toss it to the floor when, glancing up, she saw Francesca standing in the doorway, watching her.

'You're a good worker, Antonietta.'

'Thank you.'

'It doesn't go unnoticed.'

Was it still the bloodied sheet that she held in her hand that made her blush, or was she hearing a warning behind Francesca's words? Had Rafe asking for her to service his suite set off an alarm? Or had they been seen driving off last night?

Surely Francesca didn't know?

'Let me help you,' Francesca said, and together they made the bed with fresh linen, chatting while they worked. 'After this we need to set up the Temple Suite.'

'Is there a guest arriving?' Antonietta frowned, because there had been no mention at handover.

'Nico is flying in to take lunch with Signor Dupont in the restaurant.'

'Oh.'

'Birds of feather.' Francesca gave a tight smile as she wrestled a pillow into its case.

'I'm sorry?'

'Oh, I know Nico is happily married now, but let us not whitewash his past and make him a saint. He was as much a playboy as Signor—'

'Francesca,' Antonietta interrupted, even though Francesca was her boss. 'You know I don't like to gossip. Aurora is my dearest friend and Nico is her husband. Gabe is my godson.'

'Of course.'

The silence between them was a bit strained after that.

With the bed made, Antonietta swept out the fire in the main lounge and then ticked that off the list. Because it was a deep service there was high dusting and ledges to be wiped, but finally it was all finished. And then, because Francesca seemed to be watching everything she did, Antonietta checked each and every candle, despite knowing they hadn't been lit.

It was possibly Antonietta's only regret from last night—not to have seen the August Suite bathed in candlelight.

'I think we are done,' Francesca said. 'Why don't you head off? I shall head down to greet Nico.'

'But we have the Temple Suite to prepare.'

'You're on a half-day,' Francesca pointed out, and then stopped speaking as the door opened and Rafe walked in.

He wore black jeans and a black jumper and his hair was dishevelled. From the sand he'd brought in, Antonietta guessed he had been walking on the beach.

'*Buongiorno*, Signor Dupont,' Francesca said. 'We have just finished.'

'*Buongiorno, signor,*' Antonietta added dutifully, although her voice was barely a croak.

Rafe didn't return their greetings and gave only the vaguest of nods as he walked past them with barely a glance.

She could have kissed him there and then for his arrogant ways, for surely this must put paid to any suspicions Francesca might have.

'Have a nice half-day and a good day off tomorrow,' Francesca said. 'Do you still have Christmas shopping to do?'

'No...' Antonietta said, but then remembered the lipstick. 'Yes—I still have Aurora's present to get, and I would like to get something for Pino.'

And she wanted to get something for Francesca too, Antonietta thought as she left the Old Monastery. Oh, and Vera in the laundry. And then there was Tony and Vincenzo…

She had come back to Silibri to be reunited with her family, and if that didn't work then her plan had been to leave and never look back. Yet, despite making no progress with her family, she was starting to make friends here. Real friends.

But still, it was going to be a very lonely Christmas. And for different reasons than those she had imagined when she had first arrived in Silibri. Christmas meant that Rafe would be gone, and she did not know how she would deal with that.

Nico's chopper was hovering as she crossed the grounds, and she watched as the pilot skilfully landed the beast. To her delight it was not just Nico who stepped out but Aurora too, and she was holding little Gabe!

Aurora looked stunning. She wore a kingfisher-blue dress with killer heels and her hair was a tumble of raven curls as she waved and ran towards her friend. Gabe was all black curls too, and huge black eyes, and Antonietta simply melted when he smiled as she held out her arms to him.

'See,' Aurora said as her son went so readily to Antonietta, 'he knows you.'

'He really does.' Antonietta beamed. 'I didn't think you were coming back until Christmas Eve?' she said.

'I wasn't intending to,' Aurora explained as Antonietta let them into the cottage, 'but Nico has a friend in residence over at the hotel. They are having lunch so I thought Gabe and I could come and see you. I'll join them for coffee afterwards and then we'll head over to my parents'.' She gave a dramatic eye-roll.

'How are they?'

'Still demanding that Nico gives my idle brother work. I have said no, but Nico has backed down. He's going to tell him this afternoon he's got him a role. God help us,' she muttered. 'He didn't even move the logs from Geo's house when there were those wildfires.' Geo was Nico's late father. 'Instead he left it to *me*.'

'That was a long time ago,' Antonietta pointed out.

'And he has grown fatter and lazier since. Honestly, families are—' She stopped herself. 'Sorry. That was insensitive of me.'

'It's fine.'

'Has there been any progress?'

Antonietta gave a non-committal shrug. No, there had been no progress with her family—if anything, they seemed to be going backwards. But there had been progress in her life. She was making friends—real ones—and she was putting down roots too.

And as for Rafe...

That felt like progress too, because even if they could go nowhere he had taught her so much about herself.

'I've brought your Christmas present,' Aurora declared. 'I'll put it under your tree. No peeking...' she said, and then looked at the little lounge, which was pretty much exactly as she had left it some weeks ago. 'No tree!'

'There's only me here.'

'But you love Christmas! Here,' Aurora said, and handed her a parcel—only Antonietta had nothing to give her surprise guest in return.

'I did have yours...' Antonietta blushed. 'Then I borrowed it. I have to get another.'

'Well, hurry up.' Aurora smiled. 'It is only a few days till Christmas.' She looked over at her great friend and gave a quizzical frown. 'Since when do *you* wear red lipstick?'

'Who said I got you red lipstick?' Antonietta attempted, but Aurora knew her too well.

'You always do,' Aurora answered. 'Even when you were in France, and we were barely in touch, you sent the same present each year. So how come you borrowed it?'

'I just decided to give it a try.' Antonietta shrugged. 'You've been nagging me to wear make-up for years.'

'With no luck, though!' Aurora's shrewd eyes narrowed. 'What's going on?'

'Nothing,' Antonietta said, and set about filling the coffee pot, even though Aurora said she didn't want one.

'Just water for me. Antonietta…is everything okay? You seem on edge.'

'Of course.'

Antonietta knew she was holding back, but though she wanted to confide, in this case she felt she could not. Aurora might be her best friend, but her husband was Nico—the owner of the Old Monastery. He wouldn't appreciate a maid fraternising with a guest.

Still, she was saved from explaining her sudden need for lipstick by the sight of little Gabe, tottering around the table on unsteady legs.

'You didn't tell me he was almost walking!'

'Watch this,' Aurora said, and held out her arms to Gabe. 'Show Antonietta what you can do!'

Antonietta held her breath as Gabe turned from the table and took two tottering steps unaided, and then fell into his *mamma*'s arms.

'Oh, look at you!' Antonietta beamed and clapped her hands. 'He's adorable.'

'He is,' Aurora agreed. 'And he knows it. Though he's in for a big shock when his little sister comes along…'

It took a second for the news to sink in. 'You're expecting?'

'Yes! Although only you are allowed to know for now! We're thrilled,' she added. 'I know it means we'll have two under two, but we want them to be close…'

It was wonderful news. This time last year Aurora had been pregnant and practically homeless. Now she was deliriously happy and with *another* new baby on the way!

'I feel sick this time, though,' Aurora admitted.

'Then what are you doing in a helicopter?'

'Flying is fine—it is food that upsets me. That is why I decided not to join Nico for lunch. I don't think me vomiting in front of the Crown Prince of Tulano would go down too well.'

It was the second big piece of news in as many minutes—not that Aurora could know the effect her throwaway comment had had.

'Crown Prince…?'

The smile Antonietta had been wearing slipped from her face, and as her legs turned to water she reached for the couch and sat down. On some level she had always known, but on hearing Aurora confirm it Antonietta crumpled and buried her face in her hands.

'Whatever's wrong?' Aurora said. 'Antonietta, what did I say…?' She came and put her arm around her friend's shoulder. 'Tell me.'

'I can't.'

'Is it Rafe?' Aurora asked—because she had seen her friend pale when she had mentioned his title. When Antonietta neither confirmed nor denied it, Aurora pushed for more. 'Has he been causing problems for you?'

'Problems?' Antonietta frowned. 'No…no.'

'You don't have to put up with it just because you are staff…'

'No, Aurora.' Her friend was on the wrong track. 'The only problem is how much I like him.'

She felt the hand on her shoulder tense and wondered if she had been wise to say anything. But apart from being the boss's wife Aurora was also her best friend, and in truth she desperately needed her trusted advice.

'I *really* like him,' Antonietta admitted.

'You've never said that about anyone before.'

'I've never felt like this before. Rafe took me out for dinner last night and it was absolute bliss. I wore the red silk dress that you made for me and I knew *happiness*, Aurora. He was wonderful to me.'

She saw the doubt in her friend's eyes. The same doubt Antonietta had seen there when she'd insisted her family would forgive her.

'He really was…' she said.

'You're in over your head, Antonietta.'

'I know that,' Antonietta said. 'I already knew that even before I found out he was royal.'

'He has the most terrible reputation with women.' Aurora was both abrupt and upfront. 'Rafe makes Nico look tame, and I don't even know half of what Nico got up to before we were married.' She was genuinely concerned. 'Antonietta, don't let him use you.'

'*Used* was how I felt with Sylvester,' Antonietta admitted. 'I've never felt that way for a moment with Rafe.'

'Listen to me,' Aurora urged. 'Crown Prince Rafael is his father's son—everybody says so. You must have heard all the scandals attached to the King of Tulano?'

Antonietta had. Oh, they weren't sitting there at the forefront of her mind, but there were little memories of her mother tutting over a magazine. And there had been some scandalous articles she'd read laboriously when she'd been trying to improve her vocabulary in France.

'Rafe is exactly the same.'

'Rafe isn't married.'

'That doesn't give him free rein! He is irredeemable, Antonietta, and a complete rake. You must have looked him up?'

'No! I make up my own mind about people,' Antonietta said rather piously, and then stepped down from her high horse and admitted the truth. 'I've tried to look him up, but I can't get on the Internet here and I daren't risk it at work.'

'Well, don't bother—just heed my advice and stay well away from him,' Aurora warned, and then she looked at Antonietta's pale cheeks. 'Or am I right in guessing it's too late for that and he didn't just take you for dinner?'

Antonietta said nothing.

'Oh, Antonietta…'

It wasn't the best catch-up with her friend. Antonietta had wanted advice—only not the advice she had got.

And although Aurora wanted to be delighted for her friend, who had tucked herself away for far too long, she could not bring herself to it.

'I have to go over there now,' she said, picking up Gabe's little jacket. 'I'll try not to kill Rafe when I see him.'

'Please don't say anything,' Antonietta begged.

'Of course I won't.'

'Why don't you leave Gabe with me?' Antonietta offered. 'I can give him his birthday present…'

'You're sure?' Aurora checked. 'He's due for his afternoon sleep and it would be so much easier.'

'Of course I'm sure.'

'I'll leave my phone too,' Aurora said. 'It's got a good signal.'

Antonietta frowned, wondering for a moment why

Aurora would leave her phone here when she was heading out, but then realised she was being given an opportunity to look Rafe up.

'That won't be necessary,' she said, but Aurora was blowing kisses to Gabe as she headed off for coffee with her husband and Rafe...

Rafe had found, during a long and luxurious lunch, that he'd had to keep pulling his focus back to the conversation with Nico. His mind had kept drifting to last night. Or rather it had kept honing in on *tonight*, and seeing Antonietta again.

All thoughts of checking out had gone and, knowing that she was on a half-day, he had decided that he would not wait until evening. If he walked Nico to his helicopter he could make a diversion to the cottage unnoticed...

'Ah, here is Aurora now,' Nico said, and both men stood as she approached the table.

As Rafe greeted her with the familiar kiss to the cheek, it was confirmed that she and Antonietta really were chalk and cheese. A person had to dig deep to get so much as a glimpse of Antonietta's thoughts, whereas Aurora wore her heart on her sleeve.

'Rafe,' she said as they greeted each other.

And, though it wasn't quite the Sicilian kiss of death, he could feel Aurora's wrath and suspicion even as they brushed cheeks, and was certain that she knew what had transpired last night.

'It is lovely to see you again,' Rafe said.

'Likewise.' Aurora gave a tight smile.

'Is Gabe with Antonietta?' Nico checked.

'Naturally,' Aurora said. 'Why wouldn't I leave him with my dearest friend? She *is* his godmother, after all.' She looked over to Rafe. 'I consider Antonietta family.'

'Of course...' Nico frowned, with no idea of what Aurora was alluding to.

Rafe knew, and he could feel Aurora's contempt when she addressed him.

'I was sorry to hear of your accident, though clearly you are feeling much better.'

'Much,' Rafe agreed. 'And I was just telling Nico how much I've enjoyed my stay here.'

'Any time,' Nico said. 'You are always welcome here, and I shall always do my best to ensure that your time in Silibri goes unreported. Consider the August Suite your bolthole.'

'I am sure,' Aurora said, 'that Rafe will soon grow bored with all Silibri has to offer.'

He could feel her animosity, and in truth it was merited. Rafe knew that he had earned his poor reputation with women. And he knew, too, that his time had run out and very soon he would have to settle down.

Nico's suggestion that he use Silibri as a bolthole had rattled Rafe—because it appealed. He sat making polite small talk with his hosts as visions of regular returns to Silibri scrolled in his mind.

And then he shocked himself by imagining how much nicer this gathering would be if Antonietta had joined them.

Rafe had always enjoyed Nico's company, although it had taken a new direction since his friend had settled down, and now took the form of tame lunches rather than parties aboard Rafe's yacht.

But to say there could be no future for himself and Antonietta was the understatement of the century.

Well, no tangible future, anyway.

She could be vetted, of course, and liaisons arranged beyond the reach of a camera lens. But Rafe knew even at this early stage that Antonietta deserved far more than that.

'We should get going,' Nico said now, but as farewells were exchanged, Aurora took another shot.

'So you will be going home for Christmas?' she checked. 'Or, given how well you have recovered, perhaps sooner?'

Rafe heard the veiled threat and was about to make a smart reply—for he did not appreciate being told what to do by anyone, let alone a newly married friend's wife. Except her concern was merited. And in truth he was grateful that Antonietta had Aurora on her side.

'There is a lot to take into consideration before I leave.' Rafe met her gaze, and with solemn eyes told her he had heard her concerns. 'Believe me, I am giving it much thought.'

So much thought that instead of strolling across the grounds to wave them off, and 'dropping in' on Antonietta, Rafe resisted the pull and headed back to his suite.

The thought of being with Antonietta appealed way more than it should. But he was a prince who needed no distractions, and it was time to pull back.

For Antonietta, the conclusion was the same.

She had spent an adorable hour playing with Gabe and the little wooden train. He was an absolutely beautiful baby, with dark curls and big brown eyes, and just the distraction she needed for a confused and troubled heart.

Aurora's phone, resting on the table, had called to her, but Antonietta had resisted.

'Look,' she'd said, waving the train again. But after an hour it had become clear, even though Gabe took it, that all he wanted to do was sleep. Eventually Gabe had thrown the toy down, and Antonietta had only been able to smile, because he'd reminded her then of Aurora.

'You win,' Antonietta had said, pulling cushions from the sofa.

She'd made Gabe a little bed on the floor and in a matter of moments he'd been asleep.

By then Aurora's phone had developed its own magnetic pull, and she hadn't been able to help walking over to it.

You don't want to know, Antonietta had told herself.

Oh, but she did.

It hadn't taken her long to find out that Aurora's dark assessment of Rafe had been correct. Crown Prince Rafael of Tulano did indeed live a life of excess. There were endless photos, taken from a distance, but zoomed in enough, capturing the depravity taking place aboard his yacht. On land he was no better, be it *après ski* or falling out of casinos, and always, *always* with a beauty hanging off his arm.

Yet his lovers remained nameless and they *never* told all.

She'd been able to find no interviews, no bitter tears spilled in the glossies. He paid for their silence, Antonietta guessed, and finally she understood his reference to 'paperwork'.

His life of excess was not just with women. Antonietta had winced at the photos of a sports car wrapped around a tree, from which he had been cut out. And there had been falls from horses and an accident involving jet skis.

Yet through it all his people still adored him, despite seeming to wish for their Prince to slow down.

He showed few signs of doing so.

There were a couple of relationships she'd found, although they went way back. A Lady from England and a minor European royal it seemed he had dated for a while. Although on closer inspection she'd seen that it had been close to a decade ago. The press had gone wild with speculation both times, anticipating marriage, but those relationships had quietly faded and Crown Prince Rafael had reverted to his wild ways.

When Aurora had come to collect Gabe, it had been a shaken but resolute Antonietta who'd opened the door.

'We've got five minutes,' Aurora had said. 'Nico is just meeting with Francesca. How was Gabe?'

'Perfect,' Antonietta had said. 'He's sound asleep. How was your catch-up?'

'You mean how was Rafe?'

'No.' Antonietta had shaken her head firmly. 'I've decided you're right. I won't be seeing him again, even if he asks. And I won't—'

'Antonietta.' Aurora had interrupted her and plonked herself down on the floor beside her sleeping baby, playing with his little black curls. 'What if I'm wrong?'

'You're not wrong, though! I just looked him up and you gave me good advice.'

'Perhaps…' Aurora had sighed.

'Anyway, he's leaving.'

'He gave no indication that he was.' She'd looked up at Antonietta. 'Do you remember that night when the whole village was threatened by fire and you knew Nico was back and staying at my parents'…?'

'Of course.'

'Everyone had told me to get over Nico, yet you told me to go and fix what I could.'

'There was something there to fix, though. You and Nico had been promised to each other for ever…'

'Antonietta, the fact that you like Rafe speaks volumes to me. I don't *want* to like Rafe. I want to tell you to stay the hell away from him and I want to tell him the same, but...'

Then Aurora had taken a breath and told her friend something she never had before.

'When I was in Rome for staff training last year and I ran into Nico he wanted a one-night stand. Another one,' Aurora had added, and given a mirthless laugh. 'I denied him, of course. I refused to be used again. And I walked away. I was so proud of myself for resisting him, but by the next morning it had turned into the biggest regret of my life. I regretted it so much that I threw a coin in the Trevi Fountain and pleaded to have that time over again. And I got it!'

'There's no future for Rafe and me,' Antonietta had pointed out, and then she'd given a wry smile. 'And there's no Trevi Fountain here.'

'What I'm trying to say is that even if Nico and I had never come to anything I would not have regretted the time we spent together in Rome.' She'd looked over to Antonietta. 'You just have to—'

'I know what you're going to say,' Antonietta had interrupted. 'If I see him again I just have to hold on to my heart.'

'No.' Aurora had shaken her head. 'Do you trust him?'

Antonietta had thought for a moment.

Oh, there was a whole lot of evidence not to, but while her head told her to be cautious, her heart said otherwise. She thought of her time with Rafe. The man who had taught her to dance and so much more.

'Yes, I believe that I do.'

'Then you have to do the bravest thing and let go of your heart.'

CHAPTER EIGHT

BUT THERE WAS no opportunity to let go of her heart. No chance to proceed, even with caution, for there was no gentle knock at her door that night.

She slept fitfully and awoke with a jolt, unsure if she had missed the sound of Rafe's chopper leaving. It was her last day off before Christmas, and though Antonietta knew she should head into the village to finish her shopping, she couldn't face it.

This afternoon, perhaps, but right now she had never felt less Christmassy in her life.

She pulled on a denim skirt, a thin jumper and flat shoes and decided a walk might clear her head.

The temple ruins had been her and Aurora's playground. As little girls they would go there to play and lose an entire day, sitting on the steps and watching each other sing, or running through the columns. Aurora had loved the remains of the altar in the cellar area and would dress it with flowers and dream out loud about her wedding to Nico.

Aurora had always known what she wanted—family and home, Nico and babies, and all that she held dear on this very spot on earth…

But Antonietta had always looked beyond. Even as a little girl she had sat hugging her knees and looking out, dreaming of places, some near, some far. Picking up the orange dirt, she would run it through her hands and imagine grains of Saharan sand. There was a whole world she hadn't seen, and as Aurora sang, Antonietta would lie back on the stone and imagine that she lay in a glass igloo, looking up at the Northern Lights, or that she was stretched out on a manicured lawn at the Palace of Versailles...

She had tried that, Antonietta told herself now, and she had been told off for being on the grass.

Her ponderings were interrupted by the sight of Rafe, running in the distance. He was still here, then, and that brought a sense of relief in itself. His form was magnificent, his body a masterpiece, and she admired it for a stolen few moments before he noticed and ran in her direction.

'Hey,' she said as he approached. 'No minders?'

'I'm on the hotel grounds.'

'Not technically.'

She smiled, because the ruins were outside the boundaries of the Old Monastery. Then her smile slipped and she felt suddenly a bit awkward and shy. It had nothing to do with their lovemaking. Now she knew about his royal status, she couldn't pretend. It had been far easier not to know.

'I thought you were leaving yesterday?'

'That was the plan.'

'Why did you tell Francesca that you wanted me to service your suite?'

'I didn't,' Rafe said. 'I told her I did *not* want Chi-Chi.'

'Really?'

'Absolutely,' Rafe said.

He held out his hand and helped her to stand and they

started walking. She offered him her water bottle and he took a long, refreshing drink.

'The ruins are spectacular,' Rafe said.

'I love them,' Antonietta agreed. 'Aurora and I used to play here when we were little. Or rather, Aurora used to play and I used to daydream.'

'About what?'

'The world,' Antonietta said. 'This is where she and Nico were married.' She glanced sideways at him. 'You weren't at their wedding?' She would certainly have remembered if he had been.

'No, I had prior engagements,' Rafe said.

And usually he would have left it at that. Certainly, he rarely explained himself, and yet he found himself telling Antonietta more than he usually would.

'Nico and I are friends, yes, but perhaps not in the way you and Aurora are. It's more that we shared the same social scene for a while.'

'But not now?'

'No, not now. If that were the case I doubt Aurora would be pleased.'

'So, a bit wild?'

'Quite a bit.' He gave a wry laugh. 'You don't want to know.'

'But I do.' And then she was honest. 'I know who you are,' she admitted. 'Aurora told me.'

'And how does that make you feel?'

'Better and worse.'

Rafe frowned.

'Better because I understand now why this can go nowhere,' Antonietta said. 'And worse because I understand now why this can go nowhere.'

Rafe laughed ruefully and they carried on walking. The air was cold on his cooling body and yet the company was invigorating. As they walked he told her something of his life. The endless calls to duty interspersed with a jet-set lifestyle, and the endless stream of heavily vetted company aboard luxurious yachts and invitation-only parties. And he told her how boring it got, for there was no fear of missing out when you were the draw card. And there was no thrill to the chase when all the women in the room had already signed a document to be discreetly yours.

But there were penalties to be paid for living in the fast lane, and he knew his reckless ways upset his people. 'I'm supposed to lie low until the bruises heal,' he said.

'They're still pretty spectacular,' she said, looking at his blackened shoulder and the purple lines there to match the yellow and grey ones she knew were on his ribs. 'And your eye is still black…'

Her voice trailed off because it could easily be covered with make-up, if he chose, since the swelling had all but gone now. Or she could paint him!

Antonietta gave a soft laugh as she recalled a time from her childhood.

'What's funny?' Rafe asked.

'I painted a rash on myself once. I was trying to get out of school.'

'Did it work?'

'I thought it did,' Antonietta said as they walked on in the crisp morning air. 'My *mamma* was worried and told me to stay in bed. I said I thought I might be strong enough to lie in the lounge and watch television.'

Rafe smiled.

'Then she said it was a very serious rash, and she would make me Sopa de Pat…' She glanced over and translated. 'Pig's feet soup. It is the thing I hate most in the world. But my *mamma* said it was the only cure for the rash I had.'

'And was it?' Rafe smiled.

'I did not wait to find out. I washed off the rash and told my *mamma* I felt better…'

And now she would be honest, which would take almost more courage than the other night.

'I would like to paint a rash on you, so you can stay a while.'

'I would like to stay a while too,' Rafe agreed. 'But it won't change the fact that I have to be home in time for Christmas. I am expected to join my family on the palace balcony on Christmas morning.' There was more to it than that, though. 'I've been rather reckless in my ways and those days are over.'

'Have you been told?' she asked.

'I have been told the same for more than a decade,' Rafe admitted, 'but I know that the time is now. I want to work hard for my country, and to do that I have to marry.'

'*Have* to?'

'I have been told that if I want more responsibility then I must tame my ways.'

This was not a conversation he had ever expected to have with a lover, for he always kept his distance, even in bed. Not with Antonietta, though, and Rafe tried, as gently as he could, to explain the future that had been dictated for him before he had even been born.

'I am to marry a bride my father and his advisors deem suitable. One who will further our country's connections and who understands the role of Crown Prince's consort.'

She asked him the same question he had asked her. 'And how does that make you feel?'

His answer was not so direct, though. 'I am the sole

heir to the Tulano throne. The people have been patient long enough.'

'But how do you *feel*?'

'I prefer not to feel,' Rafe said. 'Feelings tend to complicate things.'

'So you choose not to have them?'

'Yes.'

Only that wasn't strictly true, for walking and talking with Antonietta gave him a feeling he would like to capture and store. This morning, walking free, with the winter sun high and Antonietta by his side, his life felt exhilarating rather than complicated.

'And the women you…' she swallowed '…you date? Are you saying that you don't have feelings for them?'

'I am not a machine,' Rafe said. 'Nor am I an utter bastard.' He looked sideways and saw that her head was down. She was frowning slightly as she tried to understand him. 'It is said by many that I have my father's heart…'

Antonietta flushed, because Aurora had said much the same thing. 'And do you?'

'No,' Rafe said. 'I have my mother's heart. I don't get close to people, Antonietta. I am cold like that.'

'Is she cold to you?'

'Especially to me. My parents were young when they married and I think she blames my arrival for my father's philandering ways. She is the epitome of the Ice Queen.'

'Perhaps so—but *I* don't find you cold, Rafe.'

'Because you haven't seen me when I choose to move on. Then I am as detached and indifferent as she. That is why I prefer to pay for company; that is why I choose to have a contract.'

'Yet I haven't signed anything.'

'No.' He gave a tight smile at this.

'So what if I go to the press?' Antonietta asked. 'What if in a couple of years' time I'm on some chat show, revealing all?'

'All?' Rafe checked. 'You mean you would tell the world about the night I took your virginity…?'

He loved it that she blushed, and he loved it that he knew she would never reveal it, and yet he teased her all the same.

'Would you tell them about the morning I took you in the temple ruins…?'

'You didn't, though,' she said, even as he pulled her towards him. 'And you won't—we can be seen from the monastery.'

'If people have binoculars,' Rafe pointed out, but as he moved in to kiss her he could taste her tension and feel her distraction, so he halted their kiss and held her a moment.

Rafe thought of how happy she had been when they'd been away from here. How the tension had lifted from her shoulders, how she had laughed and danced and relaxed in his arms. He thought of his yacht, and the privacy that would be afforded them there.

And he decided.

'Come with me to Capri.'

CHAPTER NINE

HE MADE IT HAPPEN.

Antonietta waited at the cottage while Rafe headed off to change. She would have loved to do the same, but apart from her red silk dress there weren't many options.

She pulled on some tights, and her most comfortable boots for all the sightseeing ahead, and decided she would just have to do.

By the time Rafe returned, dressed in black jeans and a jumper topped with a fine grey woollen coat, his helicopter was out of the hangar.

Antonietta had only ever heard the choppers, or seen them arriving and leaving, but now she sat in Rafe's private one, her stomach lurching as it lifted into the sky.

Capri was well known for the capricious nature of its weather, but it turned on the sun today, and the ocean was azure beneath them. She stared at the white cliffs as they approached the island.

'There it is…' Rafe spoke to her through headphones and pointed down to his yacht in Marina Grande—possibly the most exclusive marina in the world.

But Antonietta was not looking at it. 'I've always wanted to see the Christmas decorations in Capri,' she said, with her hands pressed to the window. 'And to eat *struffoli*. I can't believe you've brought me here!'

They were not in Capri to see the Christmas lights and eat *struffoli*, Rafe thought to himself. He had brought them here for the opulent privacy of his yacht and an awful lot of sex.

Yet his self-proclaimed cold indifference seemed to elude him around Antonietta, and he did not want to disappoint her.

As if his yacht had ever disappointed!

But Antonietta clearly thought they were here on some sort of day trip, so a word was had with his pilot in rapid French, and Rafe had to quickly rethink their day...

'You'll freeze in what you're wearing,' he told her as they sat in a sumptuous café and shared a plate of the famous *struffoli*. 'You need to get something warmer to wear.'

'I'll be fine.'

'We're going out to the Blue Grotto,' Rafe said. He'd go anywhere if it meant getting her out of those appalling tights—and for once he wasn't thinking about sex. 'You'll need to rug up.'

'It's closed in December,' she told him, for she had heard the tourists on the next table grumbling about it.

'It's not closed for me.'

And so they headed to Via Camerelle, with its designer boutiques, and he sipped coffee and insisted that the pale grey woollen dress that hugged her slender frame required a coat, and boots in the softest suede.

'And you'll need a dress and shoes for tonight,' Rafe told her.

'I have to be back at work tomorrow,' she told him.

'And you shall be,' Rafe told her. 'Get a dress.'

He told her he had an appointment to keep, and suggested that while she waited for him she might as well get her hair done.

'Rafe,' Antonietta protested. 'Please don't try to change me.'

'I don't want to change you,' Rafe said. 'But I have never known a woman to turn down a couple of hours in a salon in Via Vittorio Emanuele just to wait in a car.'

The suited men were back. Hovering discreetly, but annoyingly present. And Antonietta could tell they were less than pleased with her.

So, yes, she chose to get her hair done—rather than sit in a car with a driver who looked at her through slightly narrowed eyes.

That was the very reason Rafe needed some time away from her. He headed to the private royal residence for a less than straightforward meeting with his aides and minders, who were all appalled that he had brought a woman onto shore. Not just that, the same woman who had been in the August Suite the other night.

'She has not been vetted,' his advisor warned. 'And you still haven't had her sign the NDA.'

Neither would he. For this was too precious. And he told them none too gently to back off, and that he would deal with the fallout that would inevitably come from a run-in with the King.

It was worth it for this.

Antonietta's long, straight dark hair was still long, straight and dark, but just a vital inch shorter, and so glossy and thick that he put up a hand just to feel it.

And then he looked into dark eyes that were painted smoky and seductive. He took the coat from the doorman, just so he could help her into it himself, and handed her expensive shades.

'Wear these,' he suggested, 'if you don't want people at work to know.'

For Crown Prince Rafael was in Capri, and there was a

stir in all the best restaurants, where they put a 'reserved' sign on their very best table in the hope that he might dine there tonight. And in the cobbled streets the locals soon heard that the Playboy Prince had a woman on his arm.

'Who is she?' they asked—because usually Rafe did not bring his dates in from his yacht, where he tended to party. Perhaps he was finally serious about someone.

His luxurious yacht would not fit into the Blue Grotto cove, of course, so a speedboat took them in. There they transferred to a small wooden row-boat with a single skipper.

'We'll have to lie down,' Rafe told her.

'Really?' she checked, unsure if he was teasing.

'Really.'

He wasn't joking, but she wouldn't have minded if he had been, for it was bliss to lie side by side with him.

And then they entered the grotto. And it was like sliding into heaven as they were bathed in sapphire light.

'It's wonderful…' Antonietta breathed, for the water and its reflection was magical, the cavern illuminated spectacularly. And today, just for them, music was playing, inviting them further in. 'I've never seen anything more beautiful.'

'Nor have I,' Rafe told her.

And she decided that even though he might have used that line many times she would let that thought go. For when he looked at her like that, when he kissed her so slowly, she felt like the only girl in his world. She felt as if she belonged.

Rafe felt Antonietta still in his arms and, concerned, he halted. 'Is everything okay?'

'Yes,' she answered.

And all those years of searching, and yearning, and

never quite fitting in, ended then, and she found her place in the world in his arms.

Oh, it made no logical sense, for it was not about the *place* she was in, it was the connection she had found.

Only then did she understand what Aurora had meant when she had advised her to let go of her heart. For letting go meant no thoughts of tomorrow and a cold, indifferent end. And to let go meant she didn't examine the impossibility of them. She just had to let her heart go and it would fly straight to Rafe.

'Keep kissing me.'

'I can do that,' Rafe said.

He kissed her so deep and so long and with such smouldering passion that she felt as if she were floating, and that if he let go of her she might rise to the ceiling of the cove.

But even Blue Grotto kisses must end.

It was cold and getting dark when he held out his hand and helped her into the speedboat. Instead of going to his yacht, they headed to shore.

The Christmas lights of Capri were truly an amazing sight—not that he'd really paid attention before. They strolled through the square, with its carpets of fairy lights on the buildings and in canopies above them. It was like walking through a nativity scene, with towering musical trees draped in a million lights.

'This is the best day of my life,' Antonietta told him. 'The best Christmas.'

For *this* was her Christmas she decided. Tonight, here with Rafe.

It was cold, though, and their time on the water and the salty ocean breeze meant that not even his arm around her and her new thick coat could keep her from shivering.

'Let's go and eat,' Rafe said.

'I want *ravioli caprese* while I'm here,' Antonietta said, 'and chocolate torte...'

Any restaurant in Capri would serve that. And all the best restaurants, he knew, would have a table reserved for them.

Yet he was sick to the back teeth of restaurants.

There was somewhere else he wanted to take Antonietta.

'Come on, then.'

He called for his driver, and as he saw Antonietta into the vehicle he told the driver where they were headed.

The driver asked him to repeat the location.

'You heard,' Rafe said, although he knew it was *un*-heard of for him to take a date to one of his family's private residences.

They drove slowly up a hill and then turned in at a concealed entrance. She peered out of the darkened windows for a sign that might tell her the name of the restaurant he had chosen, but there wasn't one. Antonietta looked over to Rafe for an explanation as some gates slid open and they drove slowly up a steep path canopied in trees.

'Where are we going?'

'My family has a private residence here.'

'You *family*?' she croaked. 'They won't be here?'

'Of course not,' Rafe said. 'I thought it might be pleasanter than a restaurant.'

Antonietta wasn't so sure... A polite greeting awaited them, but she could sense the caution in the staff when they arrived.

The entrance to the villa was vast, with high vaulted ceilings that seemed to shrink her as they stepped inside. Rafe took off his coat and handed it to the butler, who waited for Antonietta to do the same.

Rafe could feel her discomfort as she handed over her coat and was already ruing his decision to bring her here as he led her through to the lounge.

A huge fire was waiting, and Antonietta stood and warmed her hands as the butler poured drinks.

'They must have been expecting you,' she said, referring to the fire and the fleet of staff. 'But from their surprise I thought you had arrived unannounced.'

The surprise was Antonietta.

Not that he told her.

'They are used to me arriving at all hours,' Rafe said. 'I'm sorry if it feels awkward to be here. I never thought...'

'No,' Antonietta said. 'I'm glad to be here. I'm just...'

She was just overwhelmed—not by her surroundings, but by the fact that he had brought her here. The fact that this man, who had told her he was cold, had lit a flame in her heart. How this man, who was a prince, somehow made her feel not just equal but as if she had found her missing part.

'I'm hungry!' she said, because that felt safe.

'Then let's get dressed for dinner.'

They climbed the stairs, and it felt so different from the monastery—for, no matter how luxurious, that was still a hotel. This was a home, with pictures lining the stairwell, and though it might be one of many homes there were personal touches that no hotel could replicate.

When she stepped into his bedroom it was Rafe's books upon the shelves and his chosen artwork on the walls.

And there was *his* bed.

A high, ornate, dark wooden bed, dressed in jade velvet. She couldn't resist sitting on the edge and bouncing up and down. It felt as delicious as it looked.

He took her leg and removed one of her gorgeous suede boots.

'I would love to sleep here,' she said.

She wanted to know what it was like to sleep in Rafe's own bed, and to know a little more of his life.

'Then do.'

'I have to be back for work,' she reminded him as he removed the other boot. 'I have a shift in the Oratory.'

But she forgot about work after that, liking how deftly he undressed her, lifting her bottom as he removed her stockings, and her panties too, and then pushed her shoulders down so she toppled back onto the mattress.

She lifted up onto her elbows and watched as he parted her legs and exposed her. And then examined her with desirous eyes. She should be shy, Antonietta thought. Yet she was not.

There was no kiss, no preamble. And her legs were pliant, rather than resisting, as Rafe placed them over his wide shoulders.

'I *have* to taste you,' Rafe said.

'Then do.'

He had been right to bring her here. Rafe knew it then. She deserved better than exposed temple grounds, and she did not need the ghosts of his past on the yacht, nor another nameless hotel, Rafe thought as he parted legs that were still cold from their day out.

She was warm *there* though.

He looked at her glistening folds and all he could do was taste…

Antonietta did not know, had not even imagined, that a mouth could deliver such bliss. His unshaven jaw was rough, and though his tongue was soft it made her feel exquisitely tender. There was no desire to pull away. He tasted her slowly and leisurely as her heart seemed to beat in her throat. He explored her more thoroughly, just a little roughly, and her thighs trembled as he tasted her deeply, dizzied her with light suction, then with decadent flicks with his tongue.

And never—not once—did she ask him to stop.

He was probing, and thorough and she found that she was panting, desperate—but for what she didn't quite know. Her hands went up and grasped at the bedcover, but it kept slipping away, like her own control.

'Rafe!' she pleaded—except she didn't know for what she was pleading.

She was back in the Blue Grotto on the crystalline waters. She was floating again, yet held by his mouth. She could hear her own voice calling his name as her fingers knotted in his thick hair.

He moaned into her, and his mouth was more insistent now. He was kneeling up and pulling her deeper into him. There was nowhere to go and nowhere to hide from the bliss he delivered. Every nerve in her body seemed arrowed to her centre, every beat of her heart felt aimed at her sex—until she sobbed and shattered and pulsed to his skilled mouth.

And he tasted her all through it. Even as her orgasm was fading he tenderly caressed those last flickers from her and then knelt back.

His swallow was the most intimate sound she had ever heard.

Antonietta dressed for dinner in the silver-grey dress she had bought earlier that day, then sat at the large dressing table and got ready. Her hair fell into perfect shape as she ran a silver comb through it and Aurora's red lipstick was worn again.

Rafe had never known a woman to take so little time

to get dressed for dinner and to look so breathtaking when she did. But it was not the dress, nor the hair that had transformed her. It was the sparkle in her eyes, Rafe realised, and he felt proud that he had brought joy to her.

'You look amazing,' he told her.

'Thank you.' She smiled and then added, 'You *always* do.'

And never more so than now. Rafe had shaved, his raven hair was brushed back, and he had changed into a deep navy suit.

She understood better the merits of dressing for dinner, for she felt a certain thrill that he had dressed so smartly, so immaculately, even though they were not to be seen, for they were not going out. Rafe had shaved and dressed with care only for *her*.

He took her up to a moonlit terrace, looking out to the Faraglioni rock formations. They sat at a beautifully dressed table, under burners that kept them as warm as a real fire.

'I can't believe I'm here,' Antonietta said.

'I can,' Rafe said.

It felt right.

Dinner was served, and somehow it was an intimate affair, and she gasped when *ravioli caprese* arrived.

'How did the chef know?'

'I told him,' Rafe said. 'Though we might have to wait a little while for the chocolate torte.'

'I don't mind waiting,' Antonietta said. Then asked, 'Do you come here a lot?'

'Not often,' Rafe said. 'My father uses it as a retreat, but I tend to give it a miss and stay out on my yacht.' He saw her slight frown. 'Growing up, I would come here sometimes in summer.'

'With your family?'

'No. My mother felt holidays were pointless. I came here with the nanny, and later I would bring friends.' He gave a wry smile. 'Vetted, of course.'

'But I am not vetted.'

'You have been by me,' Rafe said. 'And I like everything I see.'

'You have my discretion.'

'I know that.' And for the first time in his life he really did.

'This has been the perfect day.'

'An unplanned day,' Rafe admitted. 'I was going to take you to my yacht, but then you said you wanted to see the Christmas lights and eat *struffoli…*'

'You were taking me to your *yacht*?' Antonietta checked. 'For what? Sex?'

'And fine dining.' Rafe smiled. 'Thankfully, I realised just in time that you wanted a day trip.'

And now he had been so honest, she could be honest too. 'I just wanted a day with you, Rafe.'

Well, she'd got it. Rafe had given her a perfect day. And yet the moon moved too fast behind the clouds, and their time together was slipping away.

Dessert was served, and it was delicious—especially when fed to her from his silver spoon.

The second Rafe dismissed the staff she slipped from her side of the table to his knee and they tasted each other again.

She wanted his bed. His velvet bed. She wanted to lie there tonight and to wake with him tomorrow and for their time together to never end.

'We should head back,' Rafe told her. 'If you *have* to be at work.'

She heard the unsubtle emphasis.

'I do,' Antonietta said. 'I can't let them down…'

Rafe would be gone soon, and right now work was the only constant she had.

'I have to get back.'

'I know that.'

'But not yet…'

Not before he took her to his velvet bed.

CHAPTER TEN

ANTONIETTA WASN'T LATE, EXACTLY.

The helicopter pilot made excellent time and they arrived just before the winter sun rose above the horizon—which gave Antonietta just enough time for a quick shower and to change, though she was cutting it fine.

There was no morning chat with Pino.

Antonietta had got away with it.

Rafe hadn't.

Before he had even shrugged out of his coat his father was on the phone. The call was neither unexpected nor pleasant.

'What the hell were you thinking, parading this woman in Capri?' his father demanded.

'Hardly "parading",' Rafe said. 'It hasn't even made the papers.' He knew, because while Antonietta had been dozing beside him on the flight home he'd checked.

'Only because your PR team have been working all night to silence it.' The King was incensed. 'You are supposed to be recovering—'

'I am fully recovered,' Rafe interrupted.

'Then come home.'

'I'm not due back until Christmas Eve.'

'That wasn't a suggestion, Rafe. You have been given an extremely generous length of rope, yet you choose to ignore all the conditions that come with it. Well, no more. You are to return home. And in the New Year there shall be an announcement as to your upcoming marriage. The party is over, Rafe.'

'I am in no position to get engaged,' Rafe answered curtly. 'As you are clearly aware, I am currently seeing someone.'

It was more than he had wanted to reveal—more than he had even acknowledged to himself. But the fact was he was more involved with Antonietta than he had ever been or intended to be with anyone.

'Then *un*see her,' the King said.

Rafe walked out onto the balcony and there, crossing the grounds, was Antonietta. She was dressed in a white uniform and tying her hair back as she walked briskly to begin her shift.

'It's not that straightforward—'

'Are you forgetting who you are conversing with?' his father cut in.

For a moment Rafe had. But he was not under the thumb of his parents—it was the full weight of his title that came crashing down as the King spoke on.

'Your accident caused great concern, Rafe. You have a responsibility to marry and to produce heirs.'

'It is too soon,' Rafe said.

He was not even thinking of himself—more of Antonietta finding out he was engaged a few days after they'd ended.

'As I said, I am seeing someone, and she—'

'*She* has no bearing on this discussion,' the King said. '*She* is a lowly maid, who has been disowned by her own family because of a chequered past...'

'Don't even *go* there!' Rafe shouted.

'I should say the same to you,' his father shot back.

'Rafe, if you are particularly enamoured of this woman, then after your marriage, after an appropriate length of time, you can discreetly—'

'Don't!' Rafe interrupted, and his voice was low and threatening, even if his father was the King. 'Don't even try to give me relationship advice or instruct me on how to conduct my marriage.'

'Again, I remind you of to whom you are speaking,' the King said. 'I shall grant you this day to conclude matters and then I expect your return to the palace this night.'

The King had spoken and he was calling him home.

It was a busy day in the Oratory. As Antonietta had predicted, a lot of the guests had saved their treatments to be taken close to Christmas. And even if Christmas was a somewhat muted affair out in the main building, here in the Oratory it was festive indeed.

She painted many nails red and even performed her first massage on a paying client.

'Busy day?' Pino asked, long after six, when the last client had finally left.

'Very.' She sighed. 'How about you?'

'Lots of activity…' He halted. 'Never mind.' It would seem that Pino had found his discretion button. 'Ready for Christmas?'

'Pretty much.'

'Is that for Aurora?' Pino asked, when she showed him the large bottle of fragrant oil she had purchased with her staff discount.

It was easier to nod—though of course it was for Rafe. Antonietta had decided that chocolate wasn't enough, and had been racking her brains as to what she could get him. What was a person supposed to buy for a prince who had everything?

Including her heart.

She had let go of her heart and lost it to Blue Grotto kisses, and now she had spent half a week's wages on a bottle of neroli oil and had it wrapped in a bow.

Antonietta had never been happier in her life and it had not gone unnoticed—even Pino commented now that she looked brighter.

'I'm just...' But Antonietta could not explain the joy that radiated from her, nor her sudden exuberance, for fraternising with guests was strictly forbidden. So she blamed the season of goodwill for her wide smile. 'Looking forward to Christmas, I guess.'

Which was a lie, because she was actually dreading it, for by Christmas Rafe would be gone.

'Only four more days,' Pino said, and then his phone started to ring. 'Do you mind if I get that? It's my daughter—she's with the in-laws and worried about me.'

'Sure.' Antonietta smiled. 'Say hi from me.'

He gave her a wave and as she stepped into the night she saw that Pino was huddled over his phone, with his back to her, engrossed in his conversation.

There were no guests coming in or out to concern him. No cars arriving or helicopters approaching, nor guests checking in or out.

She could walk the fifteen minutes it would take her to get home, quickly get changed, and then walk the fifteen minutes back to Rafe's suite's private entrance.

Or she could go there now and have an extra thirty-five minutes with him.

And when you only had three days until Christmas Eve, when the man you were falling for was leaving, those minutes counted. And so, instead of walking home, Antonietta walked back inside the monastery.

If Pino saw her she would say she had left her phone, or something.

But there was no need for the excuses she had practised, for so deep in conversation was Pino that she entered unseen, slipped behind the stone partition and took the elevator without being spotted.

Past the Starlight and Temple Suites and through the cloister she walked briskly, wondering which excuse she would give if she was caught.

There was no guard on the door, and Antonietta frowned, because she had never known Rafe's suite to be unattended. And it was not just his suite that was unguarded. As she swiped her card and pushed the door open Antonietta realised that her heart was unguarded too.

For almost the first time since his arrival she *hadn't* spent the day with her ears strained for the sound of his helicopter, signalling that he was leaving. Or for Francesca's voice informing her that Signor Dupont had departed and she should turn over his suite.

And now she stood there, silent and completely unprepared, for she held his gift in her hands and her face still bore the smile she had been wearing when she entered, as if the wind had changed and set it there.

An ill wind.

When she had expected it least, Rafe had gone.

'Antonietta!'

She jumped at the sound of her name, and as Rafe flicked on the light he frowned, for her face was alabaster-white.

'You're early.'

'I didn't go home.' Her voice was strained and she cleared her throat. 'I came straight here. Why are you in darkness?'

'I was taking a shower.'

And that made sense, for he wore nothing more than a towel, but the fire wasn't even lit.

'There's no guard on the door.'

'No,' Rafe said, and he could see the questions in her eyes.

To avoid them, he turned and lit the fire. The guards had not just been there for his protection, they had reported back to the King. And they were not mere 'guards', they were Royal Protection Officers, which meant they were completely within their brief to carry out background checks on her. And when he had told them to leave they had retreated only to the perimeter of the hotel.

But his senior RPO, who had worked with Rafe for years, had stayed back, warning him that he should be back in Tulano by now, by request of the King.

It had been one step down from an order.

'I'm aware of that,' Rafe had told him. 'This is my doing.'

His doing.

'Antonietta…' he started, and loathed the austerity of his tone—but it was surely kinder in the long run, and there was no point prettying up his words.

'I got you a present…' she said.

He glanced down at the bottle she held, dressed in a red velvet bow.

'That was not necessary,' Rafe said.

'Presents shouldn't be *necessary*.' Antonietta smiled, but it wavered. 'It was just something I saw…'

Rafe was more than used to gifts. So *very* used to them. But none had ever shot to his heart in the way this did.

Not only could she not afford it, but it had been chosen with care, and he was loath to cause offence.

'Thank you,' he said.

'Smell it.'

He would rather not, and yet she was already unscrewing the lid.

Rather than offering him the bottle, she poured some into her palm and held out her hand for him to sniff.

'I was worried about your shoulder,' Antonietta said, and attempted to place her oiled hand there, feeling him actually wince at her uninvited fingers, while berating herself for thinking she could possibly spoil a man who could have anything he wanted.

Even her.

'It's too cold in here, though,' Antonietta said, and removed her hand.

She wasn't referring to the temperature of the room. Even though she had tried to ignore it, she could pick up his resistant vibe.

And she refused to beg.

'Enjoy,' she said, and placed the bottle on the table.

Unsure of him for the first time, she turned to go.

'Antonietta.' He caught her oiled hand but it slipped from his grasp, so he caught her more firmly and turned her around to face him. 'Don't leave.'

'I don't feel very welcome all of a sudden.'

'You are *always* welcome.'

He took her hand and placed it back on his shoulder. The contact was her undoing, for she had craved this moment for so much longer than today.

His bruises had all but gone, though there were still two dark lines where the rotator cuff had sheared, and now, when he winced at her touch, it was not in recoil more in targeted relief.

'Did I hurt you that night on the dance floor?' Antonietta asked, and she watched his arrogant mouth edge into a smile.

'A bit,' he said. 'And then you dug your nails into me when we were in bed…'

'I don't have long nails,' Antonietta said, and she pressed her fingers in, exactly where it would hurt.

He sucked in his breath and then exhaled as the muscle was released. 'They felt like long nails,' Rafe said.

He was already hardening, and turned on, and his resolution to avoid break-up sex was fading.

'What pain we both felt that night,' Antonietta said. 'When you took me I thought I might die.'

And as she took him back to that moment Rafe knew that he, the practised seducer, was being seduced by the shy maid with the sad eyes. It was he who had brought this side out in her, Rafe lamented, and he felt a snap of possessiveness at the thought of her out in the world without him. It was a coil in his gut that was unfamiliar as her fingers dug and pressed and kneaded.

She traced a finger around his flat mahogany nipples and then nipped him there with her teeth.

'Antonietta…'

She lifted her head and looked right at him. There was no trace of sadness, and nor was she shy, but he could not bring himself to do what he must and end it.

And so he ripped open the poppers of her white therapist's uniform and scooped her breasts from their flimsy bra. He took some of the oil and warmed it in his palm before playing with them, at first gently, then increasingly roughly.

His towel was gone, and he pushed her dress down over her arms and down past her hips. She stepped out of her knickers along with the rest of her clothes.

Once they were naked, Rafe pulled them both down to

the floor and lifted her hips. It was her hand that guided him as he slipped into her tight space. And they were panting and hot on this cool December night, as he held her hips so he could fill her with his thick length.

Antonietta was up on her knees, holding onto his oiled and slippery shoulders, watching the delicious sight of him sliding in and out of her. Her hair was on his face, and as he brushed it back their mouths met in frenzied, swollen kisses.

They both knew they must stop.

But he could feel her abandon and he craved just a little more.

'We should…' He attempted to speak. He knew he ought to lift her off him, for the protection was in the master bedroom. Except there was no going back now. The condoms might as well be locked in a vault in Switzerland for all the hope he had of getting to them.

He grew careless, as he never had before. It was unthinkable that he should have unprotected sex—not least because Antonietta wasn't on the Pill. But it was *such* a building need… And he *had* to feel her come around him.

'Rafe…'

She delivered her warning that she was close and he hit the snooze button on his thoughts, sinking into the flickering bliss of her grip.

She felt the final swell of him and yelped as he crashed over the edge and lost himself in the hot pulse of her tender flesh.

So careless. Because now he ignored the world outside, and the conversation that needed to be had, and carried her to his bed.

Everything else could wait.

CHAPTER ELEVEN

FOR ONCE, ANTONIETTA was up long *after* the Silibri sun.

Dizzy from lack of sleep, they had crashed at dawn.

Last night Rafe had hit the proverbial snooze button on his mental alarm.

This morning Antonietta had hit the real one.

Outside the warm bed the room was cold, so it had been easy—too easy—to give in to the arm that pulled her into his warmth and drift back to sleep.

'Shall I open the drapes for you, Signor Dupont?'

The sound of Francesca's voice jolted Antonietta awake, although her eyes did not open. Rafe's hand tightened on her bare arm and she lay as if set in stone, with her heart fluttering like a trapped bird in her chest.

'No,' Rafe said. 'That will be all.' And then he added, 'Thank you.'

Antonietta heard the bedroom door close and it felt like for ever until the main door opened and shut. Only then did she sit up and let out a low moan. 'Francesca knew I was here.'

'Of course she didn't. You could have been anyone,' Rafe said. 'The lights are not on...'

'No,' Antonietta said. 'Francesca is the manager. She doesn't bring guests their coffee—not even royal ones. She *knew* I was here...'

'How?'

'She's been checking on me.'

Antonietta climbed out of bed, pulled a throw from the top of it and wrapped it around her. 'That day when she suddenly came to check your suite with me...'

'You're reading too much into things,' Rafe said with stoic calm even as she dashed into the lounge.

'No, Rafe, I'm not.'

Francesca knew—of that Antonietta was certain.

'Did you fold my uniform after you removed it from me?' Antonietta asked as he joined her in the lounge. 'Did you carefully place it over the chair?'

His hand came down on her shoulder and he turned her to face him. Of course he had not.

He wrapped her in a strong embrace. Her head was on his chest and she listened to the steady *thud, thud, thud* of his heart and wished hers could match it.

'I will speak with Nico,' Rafe said.

'No,' Antonietta said. 'I don't need you to do me any favours. I will handle it myself.' She pulled her head from his chest.

'You don't have to.'

'Of course I do.' She removed herself from the haven of his arms. 'How can your intervening possibly help? You weren't the one caught—that was me...'

'Antonietta...' Rafe attempted reason. 'It was both of us.'

'No.' She shook her head. 'You can sleep with whomever you choose, Rafe.' She gave him a tight smile. 'And from everything I've heard you frequently do.'

'Don't do this, Antonietta,' Rafe warned. 'Don't turn this into something cheap.'

But in her head Antonietta already had.

She had struggled to justify sleeping with Rafe even to herself, while all the time knowing that it could go nowhere. In the cold light of day she saw it was impossible to defend it now—especially to others.

She showered quickly and then dressed in her uniform, and came out to find Rafe lying on the bed with his hands behind his head, looking grim.

'I don't blame *you*,' Antonietta said, 'I should have set the alarm…'

'Why does blame have to be apportioned?' Rafe asked.

'Because we are in Silibri,' Antonietta said. 'Finding someone to blame is our national sport.'

'Antonietta,' Rafe said. 'I won't let you lose your job because of me…'

Damn, he hadn't even told her he was leaving today.

'I've lost more than my job to you, Rafe.'

'You speak as if you were an unwilling participant.' His voice came out defensive and derisive, as it tended to when he was feeling caught out.

'I'm talking about my virginity,' Antonietta replied, loathing her own tone, but she felt caught out too.

He didn't know what to do as she flounced off. His immediate thought was to call Nico and put in a word, but he knew she would hate that. Or he could head down and apologise to Francesca…

Rafe felt as if he was back at school.

And then the weight of his own problems arrived at his door.

Antonietta would have barely made it through the cloister when there came a heavy knock.

It was his RPO, looking grim. 'You are to call the palace.'

'I have already spoken with the King,' Rafe responded

tartly. He did not need to be told again that it was time for him to leave.

But he had not understood the message.

'It is the Queen who wishes to speak with you.'

Rafe could not remember a time when his mother had requested to speak with him, and for a moment he felt ice run down his spine. It must be bad news. His mother never called. Not during his schooling, nor when he was injured.

So rare was this request that by the time he had been put through to the palace Rafe had almost convinced himself that his father must be on his deathbed and he was about to become King.

Not now, Rafe thought. *Not like this.*

'Rafael.'

His mother's tone gave him no clue—it was brusque and efficient as always.

'I spoke with your father at length last night.'

'He is well?' Rafe checked.

'Of course he is.' Marcelle sounded irritated. 'Rafe, I understand you are involved with someone?'

'Yes.'

'I have heard your father's poor advice to you.'

For a second he thought he had an ally. That possibly his mother was on his side. But this was not a gentle lead-in. There was no preamble with the Ice Queen.

'End things with her and do it immediately.'

'That's your advice?'

'Of course,' Marcelle said. 'Or would you prefer your father's suggestion to keep her on call? It *is* doable, of course,' Marcelle said. 'I should know.'

Rafe drew in a breath and found that he was holding it. His mother had never discussed his father's ways. At least not with Rafe.

'You took her to Capri?' Marcelle checked.

'I did.'

'You can take her there again…'

Rafe frowned.

'But I will tell you this much, Rafe,' his mother said. 'Your wife must never set foot on that island.'

Rafe had always found his mother cold. In that moment he knew she burnt with humiliation and pain.

'I would never do that to my wife.'

'Good,' Marcelle said. 'Because right now your future wife is being chosen and your engagement is to be announced on New Year's Day. Do as I suggest, and end it with this woman cleanly and quietly. Leave her in no doubt that the two of you are completely through.'

For Antonietta it was quite a walk of shame to Francesca's office.

Yes, she had lost more than her virginity to Rafe. She had lost her pride. For there was little pride to be salvaged when you were found in an eminent guest's bed. But more than that she had lost her heart to Rafe, and that was the part that hurt the most.

It came to her then that this would never have happened had she not been falling in love.

She pressed her eyes closed on that thought as she knocked at Francesca's door.

'Come in.'

Francesca's voice was hostile and so were her eyes as Antonietta stepped in and closed the door.

'Are you here to deliver your resignation?' Francesca asked.

'No,' Antonietta said. 'I am here to apologise. I know it looks terrible, but—'

'Don't make excuses,' Francesca broke in. 'It is forbidden for staff to fraternise or offer favours to guests for reward. Signor Caruso is very clear on that fact.'

'Yes, but I was not offering favours. Aurora knows and—'

'Oh, that's right—you are friends with the boss's wife.' Francesca again cut her off. 'Very well. You can tell your friend that Nico shall have my resignation by lunchtime.'

'No,' Antonietta protested. 'Why would you leave because of me?'

The very thought that Francesca would resign over this appalled Antonietta, who knew the manager loved her work. Francesca worked both day and night, greeting their most esteemed guests, ensuring that every detail of their stay was perfect. She couldn't understand why her actions might force Francesca out.

'If I'd wanted to be a madam then I would have applied for a job at Rubina's.'

Rubina's was the bordello in the next village.

'I am not a whore,' Antonietta said. 'I am not being paid or anything like that...'

'Oh, *please*,' Francesca sneered. 'I don't believe you for a moment.'

'But it's true,' Antonietta insisted, and then admitted a truth she had been trying to resist until now. 'It has nothing to do with money. I love him.'

There was silence from both of them at the enormity of her words, for Francesca knew that Antonietta was not one for passionate declarations.

'Oh, Antonietta...' Francesca sighed. 'You foolish, foolish girl.'

But she said it kindly, and Antonietta knew that Francesca really cared. In truth, she ached for a more mature woman's advice. 'Why foolish?'

'I thought that you at least knew what you were doing and that it was a business arrangement.'

'You'd rather that he was paying me?'

'Yes,' Francesca admitted. 'I'd rather that than you give your heart to a man who is using you.'

'But he *isn't* using me.'

'No—you offered yourself to him on a plate.'

She had.

Antonietta's eyes screwed closed as realisation started to hit and she recalled that first night, outside her cottage, and her reaction to her very first kiss. *Take me to bed.* It had felt at the time as necessary and straightforward as that.

'Sit down, Antonietta,' Francesca said gently.

She offered tissues, and poured water, and then pulled her chair around so she sat next to Antonietta.

The older woman took her hand. 'I won't tell anyone, and neither will I lose my job over this, or you yours, but there is a condition.'

'What?'

'You are to go and tell Signor Dupont—or rather, Crown Prince Rafael—that you have kept your job only on the condition that, after your conversation, you will never speak to him again.'

Antonietta swallowed.

'You are not to be in his suite and he is not to come to your home. There will be no more contact between the two of you.'

'But—'

Francesca spoke over her. 'And after you tell him that I can guarantee that within hours he will leave. Crown Prince Rafael was not expected to stay here for even a few days. I was told that as soon as he was even partway healed he would grow bored and fly out.'

'He didn't leave, though.'

'Of course not. He was getting sex and nightly entertainment. Tell me, Antonietta, why *would* he leave?'

'It wasn't like that—'

'It was *exactly* like that, and I should know,' Francesca said. 'I was taken advantage of by a man a year after my husband left me. I'm guessing that you were lonely?'

Antonietta opened her mouth to argue, but the truth was she *had* been lonely—desperately so. 'Yes,' she admitted. 'But Rafe did not take advantage of that fact. I was complicit.'

'You were out of your depth,' Francesca countered. 'He is a notorious playboy. Have you not seen him in the scandal rags?' Francesca answered her own question. 'Of course not—you wouldn't read them. But, Antonietta, not all gossip is bad. It can serve as a warning.'

'I doubt I would have heeded any warning.'

Antonietta thought back and knew that there might have been a group of protesters on the lawn that first night, as she had walked to his suite, and they could have been holding placards attesting to his reputation, and still she would not have let go of his hand.

'He told me from the start it could go nowhere…'

'Of course not.'

'Even before I knew who he was.'

'And now that you do, be the one to end it.'

Francesca gave her shy and somewhat naive chambermaid a little cuddle, and felt angry on her behalf—and not just with Prince Rafael.

'Antonietta, for what it is worth, I will not tell your mother.'

'I don't care any more.'

She would have dreaded that a short while ago, but

no longer. She had spent these last years frozen at age twenty-one, desperate to reclaim their approval.

'I cannot keep apologising for being me.'

'No,' Francesca said. 'And neither should you. I think your parents' treatment of you has been terrible and I have told your mother the same. We are no longer speaking.'

'I'm sorry.'

'No more saying sorry,' Francesca said.

'One more apology,' Antonietta replied.

In the last hour she had learnt many lessons, and she now felt all of her twenty-six years. She knew that Francesca was being stern out of kindness and to protect her.

'I will always be Aurora's best friend, but I will never use that friendship again. At work, I answer only to you.'

'Thank you,' Francesca said.

It felt right. And for a moment the world felt a lot better than it had in recent years. But now came the hard part. The hardest part.

To let Rafe go with grace and not let him see the agony in her heart.

Antonietta knocked on the door, and instead of being called to come in, or using her swipe card, this time Rafe opened it.

He wore black jeans and a black shirt and was unshaven, yet somehow he seemed so immaculate and regal that Antonietta wondered how she had not known he was royal on sight.

'Come in,' Rafe said. 'How did you get on?'

'Okay, I think,' Antonietta said.

And because she felt as if her knees might give way she chose to take a seat opposite the chair on which Francesca had folded her uniform dress, on the sofa on which they had made love the previous evening.

'I have assured her that it will never happen again.'

'You are hardly going to make a habit of sleeping with the guests.'

'I think she understands that it won't happen again. And I won't be coming to your suite again.'

Rafe actually opened his mouth to dispute that. To wave his royal wand, or rather have things smoothed over, but to what end?

He was leaving, and it was far better to end it now. Cleanly. He did not want to follow his father's example.

Rafe glimpsed it then—a future for them of the kind his father had described. He could return to Silibri at every whim. Take out a permanent lease on the August Suite…

No. Better he followed his mother's example and killed this now.

Or let her think that she had.

'Perhaps that would be for the best.' His voice was steady and he watched her rapid blinking.

'So I'm dismissed?' Antonietta could not keep the hurt at his cold reply from her voice.

'You are the one saying that you won't be returning to my suite,' Rafe pointed out. 'You are the one saying that you cannot see me any more.'

'Yes, but…' She had hoped for some protest, some indication—*any* indication—that this was hurting him even a fraction of how much it was killing her. Yet he seemed unmoved.

'I told you this could go nowhere.'

'You did, but…'

That *but* again. He could hear her attempting to defend them. Worse, he was still glimpsing that future.

And so he killed it, with brutal but necessary words, for he could not drag it out any longer. 'I am to marry,' Rafe said. 'My engagement will be announced in the New Year.'

'Why are you telling me this?'

'At least I have the difficult conversation, Antonietta. At least I don't run from it.'

'That's unfair.'

'Why? Would you prefer it if I just take off and leave and then write you a letter in a few months, explaining my actions? Would you prefer that I return in five years and expect to resume where we left off?'

'Of course not.'

'So what *do* you want, Antonietta?' he asked. 'You tell me that you are no longer coming to my suite and yet you secretly want me to dissuade you?'

'No!' she protested, but that wasn't quite true. 'Perhaps...' she conceded.

Her honesty floored him and made it hard to remain cold, for he could see the confusion in her eyes.

Cleanly, Rafe.

He didn't want it to be over, though. And neither did she.

'One moment.'

He went into the bedroom and from the dresser there removed a slim black velvet box. Then he returned to the lounge and handed it to her.

Antonietta opened it with some difficulty, for she could feel him watching her. She refused to gasp, but held her breath when she saw the gorgeous pendant, with a stone so bold and blue that for a moment she could imagine she was back in the Blue Grotto.

'Thank you,' she said, 'but I cannot accept it.'

'Of course you can.'

'No.' She held out the box to him but he refused to take it, so she placed it on the desk. 'Rafe, I don't know its value, but I am certain that sapphire would buy me a house—not that I would ever sell it.'

He did not tell her that it was a rare blue diamond. Instead he let her speak.

'But how on earth could I keep it?' She looked at him. 'When my life moves on, am I to wear it for special occasions? Perhaps on my wedding day?'

His jaw ground down.

'No,' she answered her own question. 'For that would be crass. So just on dates, or birthdays, or whatever? Or do I buy a safe? And when my lover asks how I came upon it do I tell him that for a few nights I slept with a prince?'

She looked at him, this girl with the saddest eyes, but still there were no tears.

'I don't think that would go down too well.'

She held it out but still he did not take it from her.

'Please, Rafe, don't mark the end of us with this.'

'Take it, Antonietta. Sell it if you have to.'

'I already told you—I refuse to be your whore.'

She stood and placed the box on an occasional table.

'I'm going.' No more kisses, no promises, just one plea. 'Don't get in touch with me. Don't enquire about me from Aurora or Nico. Don't keep me on a thread.'

And so he did what Antonietta wanted and what his mother had suggested—he pushed them to the point of no return.

'That's very conceited of you, Antonietta. I won't even remember your name by the middle of next week. Certainly I won't be looking you up for a replay. You weren't *that* good.'

Ah, yes, Antonietta thought, *he warned me how cold he would be at the end.*

But she had so little to compare this with—so little to go on apart from her heart, which was braver than she. So she walked over to him and looked up to meet his eyes.

And as it turned out she *could* have the difficult conversation.

'Liar.'

She was met with silence.

'I'm going to get on with my life now.'

She walked out of his suite and there, waiting in the cloister, was Francesca.

'I'm proud of you,' Francesca said.

'So am I,' Antonietta admitted.

And so too was Rafe.

'I hope you have had a wonderful stay,' said the concierge.

'Indeed,' Rafe replied, and handed Pino a handwritten note of thanks, as a royal prince was expected to do to someone who had taken such care to ensure his every demand had been met. 'Thank you for your help. The running route you suggested was most excellent.'

'It was a favourite of mine.'

'Was?' Rafe checked.

'I used to walk there with Rosa.'

Ah, yes, Rafe recalled that Pino had lost his wife earlier this year. What *was* it with this place? Usually he did not get involved in staff's lives or dramas.

'It's still beautiful,' Rafe said.

'Not without Rosa,' Pino responded, and held out his hand to the Prince. 'It's been a pleasure having you at the Old Monastery, and I know we are all looking forward to your return.'

But he would not be returning.

Like Pino, the thought of being here without his love meant Silibri had lost its charm.

Love?

Instantly he refuted that. His life would still be beautiful without Antonietta, Rafe told himself. He would return to his country and marry a suitable woman, if it pleased the people, and then he would have the power he required for the changes he craved.

He would no longer be the reckless Playboy Prince.

And Antonietta would move on with her life.

She had been expecting that sound.

Chi-Chi was eating a guest's grapes in one of the standard suites as Antonietta switched off the vacuum. She could hear the whirr of the rotors in the distance and headed to the window.

First she saw Pino and one of the bell boys, carrying luggage, and then she saw Rafe, running across the ground and bounding up into the helicopter.

'He's leaving, then,' Chi-Chi said with a distinct lack of interest.

Antonietta didn't have the energy to respond, and she watched as it lifted into the sky until it was just a tiny black dot on the horizon.

Without his 'amusement' Rafe had not even seen out the day...

CHAPTER TWELVE

RAFE'S HELICOPTER TOOK him to Palermo, and from there it was a private jet to Tulano.

Rafael did not reside at the main palace. He had his own court. As the gates opened it was already dark. But there was no question of sleep. He sat with a pen and tried to work on the most important speech of his life.

It took all night, and, when he finally stood before his father, to his disquiet his mother was there, and her cool gaze was less than encouraging.

At least she was listening. His father didn't even let him past the second line.

'She's a commoner?' the King interjected. *'Non.'*

'Will you at least hear what I have to say?' Rafe bit down on his frustration, for he knew it was imperative that he stay polite.

'There's no point,' the King said. 'So I don't need to hear it. I have been giving your marriage a lot of thought, and we need someone who is well-versed in royal tradition—someone who understands that the crown comes before everything...'

'So a loveless marriage?' Rafe checked.

'Rafe, you have had your freedom, and you have abused that freedom to the nth degree. You are thirty years old and the only heir to the throne—'

'Whose fault is that?' his mother interrupted.

Rafe closed his eyes in frustration. *Here we go*, he thought.

Except his mother truly was the Ice Queen, and Rafe watched as she spoke of the most painful part of her life without a shred of emotion.

'You married me because your father instructed you to. You have stayed married to me purely to avoid a royal scandal, and yet you have created many a royal scandal of your own.'

'And whose fault is *that*?' the King retorted, and he shot a reproving look at the wife who for so long had refused to share his bed.

'Don't speak to her like that,' Rafe warned his father.

'May I remind you to whom you—?'

'I don't need to be reminded,' Rafe retorted. 'I have lived it, and so has your Queen.'

His mother was on his side, Rafe realised. And suddenly he understood her cold nature better and looked back on his childhood with adult eyes. No wonder she had never set foot on Capri, for Rafe could not even fathom taking his future wife there after what he and Antonietta had shared.

He did have his mother's heart after all. She was not cold. She was just bruised by an unfaithful husband, and yet she spoke out for her son now.

'I shall never recommend that you force our son to do the same,' she said.

'I tell you this much,' Rafe said, for though he was grateful to his mother for speaking out he knew his own mind. 'I will never conform to the same.' He faced his father. 'As I have stated, I refuse to take marital advice from you, but I venture to give you some in return: sort out your own marriage before you meddle in mine.'

'How dare you?' the King roared. 'Have you forgotten I am your King?'

'Never,' Rafe responded. 'And for that reason, and that reason only, I stand before you and petition for your permission to propose to the woman I love.'

'She is a commoner,' the King dismissed.

'I have made my choice,' Rafe said.

'A poor one! I will *never* approve this marriage.'

Rafe knew his father well enough to know that he would not back down.

'Will you abide by my decision?' the King demanded.

Would he?

Rafe knew that although his father was King in truth it was Rafe who held the power, for he could simply say no, he would *not* abide by his father's decision. And he would get his own way for his father would loathe the thought of the succession continuing with Rafe's cousins rather than following his own line.

But marrying without the King's permission, even if he remained Crown Prince, would prove a living hell for Antonietta. She would be frozen out by the courtiers and treated with derision by the aides. There would be division in the palace and ramifications that he would not wish on the girl with the saddest eyes, who had only ever wanted to belong.

'Rafe?' the King pushed. 'Will you abide by my decision?'

'Yes,' Rafe said finally. 'I will abide by your decision but I will never forgive you for it.'

'Don't threaten me, Rafe.'

'It is not a threat—it is a fact. And one you should consider. Unlike you, I will do everything in my power to make my marriage work. My wife will never know that I did not wish to marry her. When she asks why I am cold with my father the King I will never tell her the true reason. And when she asks why I don't stand by your side on the balcony I will tell her that it is to do with ancient history and not something she should trouble herself with. And when the heirs you seek are born, and they ask why they only see their grandparents on formal occasions, I will tell them to ask their grandfather to explain why relationships are strained.'

'How dare you threaten me?'

The King stood, but Rafe did not flinch.

'It is a mere glimpse into the future,' Rafe said. 'So think long and hard, Your Majesty, as to how you wish to proceed.'

CHAPTER THIRTEEN

'YOU ARE TENSE,' Antonietta commented as she massaged Vincenzo's shoulders.

As part of her training she was still practising on the staff, but they were actually asking for her now, and a couple of them had told her that they would be her clients if she ever set up on her own.

'Isn't everyone tense at Christmas?' asked Vincenzo, who was lying face-down.

'No!' Antonietta smiled. 'It's supposed to be a happy time.'

'Well, you should be happy!' Vincenzo said. 'It would seem you made the right choice!'

'Sorry?'

'With Sylvester. You know…because his wife left him?'

Her hands stilled on Vincenzo's shoulders.

'You haven't heard?'

'No,' Antonietta said.

As Vincenzo spoke on she discovered that it had been a terrible break-up—and, no, it did not make her happy to hear it.

She poured more oil on her hands and got to work on Vincenzo's knotted neck. Some clients preferred silence, which Antonietta was very good at, and usually Vincenzo was one of them, but today he seemed keen to talk.

'I am so over Christmas, and it isn't even here yet,' Vincenzo said.

'You're off to Florence tonight?' Antonietta checked.

'Yes, but my family are driving me crazy.' He sighed. 'They expect me to come home, yet they don't want me to bring a guest…'

Antonietta's hands paused and, unseen by Vincenzo, she frowned, though she kept her voice light. 'My family don't want me home with or without a guest, so I win.'

He laughed and relaxed a little. 'I don't know how to keep everyone happy,' he admitted.

'I think it's time to make your own traditions, Vincenzo. I know I've been relying on other people to make this Christmas a happy one.'

An idea was forming, though she did not share it with Vincenzo as he was now half asleep. But when he was done, and it was time for her break, Antonietta knocked on Francesca's door.

'Come in, Antonietta,' Francesca said.

'I lied to you.'

Antonietta saw Francesca's curious frown as she took a seat in her office.

'About what?' Francesca asked. 'Are you intending to open a bordello here?'

They shared a small smile before Antonietta answered. 'Of course not. But I do want to take advantage of my friendship with Aurora and Nico. I wanted to speak with you about it beforehand. I don't want to go over your head.'

'I'm curious,' Francesca admitted.

'I came to Silibri hoping for a wonderful Christmas,'

Antonietta said, 'and I've realised I have done little to bring it about.'

Francesca frowned.

'I have left my fate in other people's hands for too long,' Antonietta said. 'I have been waiting for my parents to decide how I spend my days, and what will make me happy, but no more.'

'What do you have in mind?'

'Cake,' Antonietta said. 'And lots of it. And decorations. And a feast shared with the people I care about and who care about me.'

'Who?' Francesca asked.

'You!' Antonietta smiled. 'And anyone else who isn't getting the Christmas they hoped for. Of course it would only take place after all the guests have been taken care of…'

'I have loathed Christmas ever since my divorce,' Francesca admitted—and then perked up. 'We could use the grand dining room,' Francesca said. 'Tony would cook, I'm sure of it, and Pino…' She gave a pained sigh. 'I have been so worried about him spending Christmas alone.'

'And me,' Antonietta admitted.

'I was going to invite him over for dinner,' Francesca admitted, 'but you know how the villagers talk…'

'Believe me, I know,' Antonietta said. 'But of course you are just being…' She was about to say that of course Francesca was just being friendly, but her voice trailed off as her manager went a little bit pink.

Francesca and Pino?

But Pino was grieving Rosa so deeply he would never look at Francesca in that way, Antonietta was sure.

Oh, love was so difficult and cruel—but, given that she couldn't fix her own love-life, she certainly couldn't help anyone else with theirs, so she got back to organising the party.

'We would need Nico's permission.'

'He will never give it.' Francesca shook her head. 'He is like the Grinch. He didn't even want a Christmas tree in the foyer.'

'It's his first Christmas with Aurora and his first as a father...'

'Do you think Aurora could persuade him?'

'Oh, yes.' Antonietta smiled.

'Then on this occasion,' Francesca said, 'I have no problem with you going over my head.'

Antonietta called Aurora. And since Aurora thought it a brilliant idea she said she would be delighted to 'work on Nico'.

'Ha-ha!' Aurora added.

Antonietta would have frowned at that just a few short weeks ago. She had been utterly clueless back then.

'Enjoy!' Antonietta said instead, and then communicated her response back to Francesca.

'We have the go-ahead? Nico approves?' Francesca checked.

'Aurora is working on him.'

'Lucky Aurora!'

Soon they had gathered all the staff who would be working on Christmas Day.

'Do we get paid for staying on?' Chi-Chi asked.

'It's a party,' Francesca said. 'Of course not.'

'Then you can count me out,' Chi-Chi said, and left.

'Well, I think it's a great idea,' Pino said. 'I've been dreading Christmas. I know I said I didn't mind that my daughter is with her husband's family, but really...'

As it turned out, he wasn't the only one who felt lonely at this time of year.

Vera, who worked in the laundry, and could have had the day off but had chosen to work, was another who admitted she struggled. 'I can make a lasagne,' she said.

'No, *I* am making the lasagne,' Tony insisted. 'But, Vera, your cannelloni is the best I have ever tasted...' His voice trailed off as Vincenzo came in.

'What's going on?' Vincenzo asked.

'We're having a meal—a staff party for those who have to...' Antonietta paused '...for those who have *chosen* to work on Christmas Day.'

'Oh!' Vincenzo just stood there.

'Well, it doesn't apply to *you*,' Tony said rather spitefully. '*You're* spending Christmas with family.'

Though it was not quite the perfect remedy for getting over a broken heart, it was fun to organise everything, and in her time off Antonietta baked.

And cried.

But mainly she baked.

Or mainly she cried.

But there was cake involved, which always helped.

What didn't help was finding on Christmas Eve the coffee-flavoured Modica chocolate that she had bought for Rafe.

Well, not really. But she had certainly bought it with Rafe in mind, never knowing that that very night they would make love.

It had been so good.

At least it had been for her.

But then she reminded herself of his cruel departure, and those horrible harsh words, and told herself to get over him.

And she would.

Oh, she would...

But first she had to weep for him.

Yet she knew that once she'd started she wouldn't be able to stop.

She would have to mourn him later, Antonietta decided. For now, the show must go on.

And so, dressing for the Christmas Eve bonfire that night, she put on the gorgeous dress, tights and boots he had bought her.

And though there was no sign of Rafe's black helicopter, still a chariot awaited…

Well, the hotel put on a car to take the people who were working till late into the village for the last hour of the bonfire before everyone headed to church.

Poor Pino, Antonietta thought as she climbed in. He looked pensive as they drove up the winding hill.

But then he gave her a little pep talk. 'If there are any problems tonight, just come and find me.'

'I'll be fine, Pino. My family might not be talking to me, but they're not going to make a scene at the Christmas Eve bonfire.'

'You probably haven't heard the news,' said Francesca.

'I know about Sylvester,' Antonietta said.

'It's nothing to do with you, of course,' Francesca soothed, 'but from what I've heard emotions are a little raw.'

'Emotions are always a little raw with the Riccis.' Antonietta shrugged. 'You're right—Sylvester and his marriage are nothing to do with me.'

She shut down the conversation—and not just because she refused to gossip. She shut down the conversation because it hurt. Though she had no feelings at all for Sylvester, another person's misery still didn't feel like a triumph. There was enough sadness in the world, and right now she was busy dealing with her own.

Antonietta was at the start of her life without Rafe. Oh, they had been together for only a short time, but it had been long enough for her heart to know it was love.

The bonfire would be a nice place to weep unnoticed.

It was huge. The children were all laughing and playing, and there were cheers and celebrations as the orange flames licked up towards the sky—she would blame the smoke for her watery eyes, should anyone see. But she refused to break down completely.

'Antonietta...'

She turned at the sound of her name, and there stood her *mamma*.

'Have you heard about Sylvester?'

'What does that have to do with me?'

'It would seem you were right to have doubts,' her mother said. 'Come to us tomorrow,' she offered. 'Have Christmas Day with your family.'

It was everything she had once wished for. Everything she had come to Silibri for.

And yet Rafe had been right when he'd asked her if she would ever be able to forgive her parents. It had seemed a ridiculous question at the time, but it made perfect sense now.

Antonietta looked at her mother, and though she could stand there now, vindicated and redeemed in her mother's eyes, there was too much hurt.

'I have plans for tomorrow,' Antonietta said.

'Antonietta, don't do this. I have missed you so much...'

'Then why didn't you pick up the phone?' Antonietta retorted, and walked off.

'Hey,' Pino said. 'Is everything all right?'

'I got what I wanted,' Antonietta said. 'Or what I thought I wanted. But it's too little, too late.'

'So carry on the fight, then,' Pino said. 'And we can all be miserable this Christmas.'

He made her smile.

'I know that I don't want to be miserable any longer,' Pino said. 'I was talking to Signor Dupont before he left. He told me to go and look at the ruins. Said that life can still be beautiful even without Rosa.'

'He told you that?' Antonietta said. It angered her rather than soothed her, for she loathed the thought of Rafe just going on with his beautiful life.

'He did. And if he hadn't been a guest—and a royal one at that—I might have hit him,' Pino said.

'But you didn't?'

'No, because I think he might be right. I want to make peace with the past, and I want to embrace the rest of my life. Call me old-fashioned, but I believe life is better with family.'

'Even when they hurt you?'

'Of course,' Pino said. 'Love isn't always easy. My daughter has hurt me...'

'Have you told her?'

'No,' Pino said. 'For there might come a time when I hurt her too. I just have to hope she'll be happy for me...'

Was he talking about Francesca? Antonietta pondered. Surely it was too soon? But then, who was she to judge?

She looked at Pino's tired, kind face and gave him a little squeeze on the arm. 'I'd be happy for you, Pino.'

He'd given her good advice. And so she walked over to her mother, who stood by the fire, when it would have been so much easier, even justified, to walk away.

'I have plans tomorrow, Mamma, but I could come over in the evening, perhaps, for a drink.'

And biscotti and cake and *pizzelles*, no doubt. For there was no such thing as *just a drink* in Silibri.

It would be awkward, and difficult, but it would be a start—and, wrongly or rightly, she could not turn her back on her family.

'I'd love that,' said her *mamma*.

'I'll see you tomorrow.'

'You're not coming to church?'

'No.' Antonietta gave a wry smile. 'That would be too many Riccis under the same roof for me.'

Her *mamma* actually smiled.

And Antonietta smiled too, until she got home. And then she gave in to tears and cried more than she ever had.

She was home.

All was sorted.

Except she had let her heart go to a playboy.

And she didn't know how to even start to get it back.

CHAPTER FOURTEEN

'Buon Natale!' Pino said as she came to the door.

'Buon Natale!' Antonietta smiled.

And then she laughed as she stepped into the foyer. Nico had let them pull out all the stops, and there was now a small nativity scene on the reception desk.

'We have bon-bons.' Francesca beamed as she came over. 'And Signor Caruso is throwing in champagne. Aurora must have been working overtime on him.'

And, despite her blue heart, Antonietta laughed. *'Buon Natale*, Francesca.'

She was so grateful for her wonderful friends and colleagues who had supported her. And she was grateful too for Francesca. Yes, her words had hurt at the time, but Antonietta knew she had got off very lightly.

Well, not that lightly, because she still had to work with Chi-Chi, and they had been given a full list of suites to service in an impossibly short amount of time while the guests were at breakfast or the Oratory or church.

'My back is killing me,' Chi-Chi grumbled.

'One more suite,' Antonietta said, and knocked on the door.

'Good,' Chi-Chi said. 'They're out.'

The suite looked like a tornado had hit it. There were champagne bottles and glasses in the lounge, half-drunk mimosas on the bedside tables, and wrapping paper all over the bed.

'Don't just throw it away,' Antonietta barked, as Chi-Chi scooped up the paper. 'There might still be gifts in there...'

Foolish words.

'My back is killing me,' Chi-Chi grumbled. She sat on the sofa and commenced her *slowly-slowly*, folding the wrapping paper piece by piece as Antonietta made the bed. 'I just need five minutes.'

Antonietta rolled her eyes as Chi-Chi turned the television on. Really! She wanted a few moments alone and so, having made the bed, she went and serviced the bathroom. For a tiny second she allowed herself the dream of her and Rafe sitting in bed on Christmas morning, sipping mimosas as they unwrapped their presents.

Did she regret her time with Rafe?

No, not for a single second.

Oh, she regretted that they had been doomed from the start...and perhaps she regretted how hard she had tumbled into loving him.

But no, she refuted, she did not regret that.

As she came out of the bathroom she glanced at the television and saw the Vatican, and the Pope giving his Christmas address.

Antonietta stood watching for a moment, and saw an image of the Christmas celebrations in France, and then Germany, and then the British royal family heading to church...

And then her difficult Christmas became an impossible one—for there were the King and Queen of Tulano on the palace balcony, and beside them stood Crown Prince Rafael.

It was a mere glimpse, but it burned in her brain: the

sight of Rafe in all his military splendour, looking so impossibly handsome and so utterly beyond her, and worst of all so happy, for he had been smiling. Smiling a natural, relaxed smile that told Antonietta he was truly happy.

Of course she wanted him to be happy—but not quite yet. Not when her own heart was so raw and bleeding.

But even as Antonietta cried out in recognition the footage moved on to Austria, and how Christmas was being celebrated there.

'He's mean,' Chi-Chi huffed. 'Do you know, he left letters for all the staff who had dealings with him, and a tip, yet he left nothing for me?'

'Nor me,' Antonietta said.

Well, he had tried to give her a necklace. But that was one thing that didn't make sense.

It could not be a coincidence that the sapphire he'd tried to give her had been the exact shade of the water in the Blue Grotto. Surely?

Get over yourself, Antonietta, she warned herself.

He probably had a collection of sapphires. And all the women he took to the Blue Grotto and made love to were probably gifted one.

There was probably a Blue Grotto Sapphire club, Antonietta decided bitterly.

'Time for me to go,' Chi-Chi declared at five minutes to three. '*Buon Natale*, Antonietta.'

'*Buon Natale*, Chi-Chi.'

But *was* it a happy Christmas?

Antonietta brushed her hair and applied Aurora's red lipstick, which clashed a little with her Persian orange dress.

She had managed to get a replacement lipstick for her friend, and had baked gifts for everyone else. Well, everyone except Pino.

Antonietta collected her gifts from her locker and arrived only a little late to the party she had herself organised. And suddenly it really was a *Buon Natale*.

There was a canopy of lights that stretched across the ballroom, and in the corner stood a huge tree dressed in ropes of lights. It reminded her so much of her magical time in Capri that for a moment tears filled her eyes.

'Who did this?' she asked.

Francesca didn't even have to answer her, for a moment later there were footsteps, and Antonietta turned to the sight of Nico carrying little Gabe, with Aurora by his side.

'You're here!' Antonietta beamed. 'And you've been so busy!' she exclaimed. 'The ballroom looks beautiful.'

'Doesn't it?' Aurora said as she hugged her. 'And of course I'm here. To tell the truth, my family were driving me crazy. It is wonderful to escape!'

'There is no escape...' Nico sighed. 'And we have to head back by five for an announcement.'

'Announcement?' Antonietta frowned.

'Don't pretend you don't know,' Aurora said, and then blinked. 'My brother is getting engaged.'

'Oh!'

'To Chi-Chi!' Aurora groaned.

'No!'

'Yes,' Nico groaned. 'How the hell do I fire her now! Antonietta, you cannot leave Silibri. I swear the two of them will move into the cottage and we'll never get them out.'

For the first time since Rafe had left, Antonietta found that she was properly laughing. 'Every pot has its lid!' she said.

'And that lid is going to be my sister-in-law!' Aurora sighed, but then brightened when she saw Vincenzo arriving, weighed down with presents. 'I thought you were off!'

'I am,' Vincenzo said. 'But since when did I ever miss a party?'

Antonietta frowned, a little surprised that Vincenzo wasn't in Florence. But then Tony walked in, carrying silver trays laden with seafood and all kinds of delicacies, smiling proudly. He almost overbalanced when he saw that Vincenzo had arrived.

She turned and looked as a flush crept up Vincenzo's cheeks when Tony smiled at him. *Oh, my!* No wonder Vincenzo was putting on weight. Imagine if Tony was trying to constantly feed you!

'Is Tony the reason you aren't home for Christmas?' Antonietta asked with a smile.

'I *am* home for Christmas,' Vincenzo said. 'Here is home. It just took me a little while to work that out. My family have refused to accept Tony and me. So it is time to start our own traditions...'

'Good for you,' Antonietta said.

The table was groaning with the most delicious food. Christmas Eve was the Feast of the Seven Fishes, and there was lobster, *scungilli*... And as they sat and laughed it was impossible not be happy.

As the feasting ended the speeches started, and she looked around the table and saw that these people were the ones she loved.

Nico started by thanking his staff, and Antonietta for her marvellous idea. And there was clearly too much champagne flowing, because they all toasted Aurora for persuading him.

Then Francesca spoke. 'My staff have never let me down...'

Antonietta flushed a little at that.

'Never,' Francesca said. 'There is nowhere I would rather be than here this Christmas.'

And then Antonietta stood, and though her speech was short and sweet it came from her heart. 'I am so lucky to have you all.'

She truly was, Aurora knew. She finally had her magical Christmas.

'I might go for a walk in the temple ruins,' said Pino. 'And burn this dinner off.'

'A good idea!' Francesca smiled.

For a second Antonietta thought Francesca was going to suggest joining Pino, but there was something in his stance that suggested he wanted to be alone.

'Enjoy your walk,' Francesca said.

'Thank you.' Pino smiled.

But one day Francesca would join him. Antonietta just knew it.

It really was a two-by-two world, Antonietta thought as she bounced little Gabe on her knee and looked over to Vincenzo and Tony, who were happily holding hands.

'Antonietta,' Francesca whispered in her ear. 'Sorry to pull you away, but I need someone to take a trolley up to the August Suite.'

And it seemed that 'someone' would be her.

'Here,' Antonietta said, and handed little Gabe back to Aurora. 'I have to take a trolley up. I shouldn't be long.'

'We ought to get going,' Aurora said.

'Yes.' Antonietta forced a smile. 'You have an announcement to get to.'

Antonietta could hear the laughter wafting up from the ballroom as she pushed the trolley along the cloister. She hadn't been back to the August Suite since her cruel parting from Rafe, and it didn't help that it was Christmas Day.

And that everyone was happy except her.

She pressed her fingers into her eyes and rued the champagne she had drunk, because guests did not need a chambermaid with tears in her eyes.

'Service,' she called after knocking.

When she got no reply, she swiped her card and let herself in.

'Service,' she said again.

And then stepped into a room that was not in complete darkness, for though the drapes were drawn, every candle in the suite had been lit. The August Suite was softly illuminated with twinkling lights that stretched and danced to a gentle breeze she hadn't even been aware existed.

It felt like a church, or a ballroom, as if the stars had been brought down from the sky.

'*Buon Natale*, Antonietta.'

She jolted at the sound of his voice.

'Rafe!'

She must be dreaming. Hallucinating, even. For he was dressed in military finery, and now that her eyes were adjusting she saw that the August Suite had a Christmas tree, with presents beneath it. And a dining table set for two.

Yes, she was dreaming, Antonietta decided. She would wake up in a moment and her pillow would be wet with tears and she would be late for duty...

'I forgot my present,' Rafe said when she could not speak.

'I gave you your present, Rafe. The neroli oil, remember?'

'Of course. It is on my dresser at home. I meant the chocolate.'

'I gave it to Pino,' Antonietta said, utterly unsure as

to what was going on, and expecting him at any moment to disappear.

Except he did not disappear. In fact, when she walked over he wrapped her in his arms, but that only served to confuse her further.

'I saw you on the balcony…on the television,' she said.

'That was a couple of hours ago. It would be a break with tradition if I did not appear…'

'Rafe.' She pulled back. 'I cannot do this. Does Francesca—?'

'Stop,' he said. 'There is no conflict—this is no clandestine meeting. She knows that I am here, and so do Nico and Aurora.'

'They know?'

'Of course. And they agree that Christmas Day should be spent with the people you love. *Oui?*'

Yes. Did that mean birthdays too? And all the other special days? Would he return to Silibri on a whim?

'I have *ravioli caprese* for us,' said Rafe, 'and chocolate torte too…'

'I've eaten, Rafe.'

Perhaps it was not the kindest reply, when he had gone to so much trouble, but Antonietta didn't know what his being here meant.

When she didn't lift the cloche, Rafe did.

But it was not a romantic dinner for two that lay beneath.

It was her Blue Grotto stone. She would recognise it anywhere, even set in a ring.

'It's beautiful, but…'

Rather than pick it up, she cast anxious eyes up to him.

'Please don't play with my heart, Rafe. Please don't tell me that this sapphire means you will one day return…

that we will kiss and be together again in the light of the Blue Grotto...'

'I would never do that,' Rafe said. 'And it is not a sapphire, Antonietta. It is a diamond. Forgive me for ever thinking it should be a pendant. We *shall* kiss and be together again in the light of the Blue Grotto—but as husband and wife...'

'How...?'

'How not?' Rafe said. 'How could I ever marry anyone else? It would not just be unfair to us both, but it would be cruel to my wife also. I have my mother to thank for that insight.'

He told her the truth.

'My father used to take his lovers to Capri, and I confess, for a while I considered doing the same with you. And Nico said that Silibri could be my bolthole...'

'Never!' Antonietta shook her head.

'Silibri can be *our* bolthole,' Rafe said. 'I know it will be a huge change for you, and I know you might need time to think, and it's a lot to take in...'

'No,' Antonietta said. 'I don't need to think—you are my lid.'

'*Scusi?*'

'Every pot has its lid. And you, Rafe, are mine.' She picked up her Blue Grotto ring and placed it on her own finger. 'I would love more than anything in the world to be your wife.'

And then, when her bravery ran out, when she was daunted by all that lay ahead, Rafe carried her to the candlelit bedroom where he made her his lover for life.

EPILOGUE

'I HAVE TO go to my parents' house later…'

They lay in bed as she stared at her ring, which sparkled in the fading candlelight.

'I said I would go there for a drink.'

'You are speaking to each other now?' Rafe checked.

'It would seem so.'

'That is good,' Rafe said. 'Tell them that I have married you.'

'Not yet!' Antonietta laughed. 'You must ask my father's permission!'

'Oh, no,' Rafe said. 'We will be married by then.'

'Don't be ridiculous.'

'There will be a huge formal wedding in a few weeks,' Rafe told her. 'And there will be duty and cameras and parades…' He looked over at his bride-to-be. 'But I want you to know how committed I am before I take you home. Life is going to change for you, Antonietta…'

'I know.'

'But my love for you never will.'

'I know that too,' Antonietta said. 'But, Rafe, I have nothing—and I mean *nothing*—to wear.'

Enter Aurora. The best friend, the best seamstress and the best keeper and sharer of secrets that a girl could ever have.

Antonietta's dress was a sheath of Italian white lace, so slender that for a second Antonietta was sure that Aurora had got her measurements wrong.

'Hold still,' Aurora warned. She wore gloves just to do the zipper up. 'Oh, Antonietta, look!'

Aurora was crying—she actually was—as she admired not only her handiwork, and the pretty shoes she had selected, but her best friend's happiness.

And then Francesca arrived and dotted her hair with flowers, handed her a little posy.

'I am so happy for you,' Francesca said. 'And I take back every word I said about him.'

It was the most intimate and unofficial wedding in Tulano history. But what it lacked in paperwork, it made up for with love.

Rafe slid a heavy ring on her finger and said, 'I loved you the morning I met you, though I told myself I had a head injury.' Everyone smiled. 'And I hope every day to see your eyes smiling.'

And Antonietta smiled up at her impossibly handsome groom and said, 'I love you, and that is never going to change.'

'I know,' Rafe told her, and he kissed his shy bride who melted solely for him.

He held her hand as Pino read her favourite verse from Corinthians and choked up a little, for it was the one that had been read at his and Rosa's wedding. One that was still relevant now…

'"And now these three remain: faith, hope and love. But the greatest of these is love."'

And Nico did a speech, during which both Aurora and Antonietta sat, just a little tense, hoping he would not share too much of the groom's chequered past.

He did not.

'Aurora considers Antonietta family. So I guess,' Nico said, looking over to Rafe, 'that my old friend is now almost my brother-in-law. Welcome to our family.'

Christmas had delivered its magic.

With Rafe by her side she belonged in this world.

And with friends like these surrounding her as she danced with the love of her life, Antonietta had got her for ever family...

* * * * *

THE COUNT'S
CHRISTMAS BABY

REBECCA WINTERS

To my darling son John, a wonderful husband and father, who started skiing at four years of age and can ski like a champion. His experience and expertise both in the Utah and Colorado Rockies have helped me to add authenticity to the many mountain scenes in my books.

CHAPTER ONE

"PAT? It's me."

"Where are you?"

"At the Grand Savoia eating lunch in my room. You were right. It's a lovely place with every amenity. Thanks for arranging everything for me."

"You're welcome. How my gorgeous baby nephew holding up?"

"He's taking another nap right now, thank heaven. That's giving me time to pick up where I left off last evening."

"Couldn't you have phoned me before you went to bed to tell me how things were going? Your text saying you'd arrived in Genoa was hardly informative. I waited all day yesterday expecting to hear more from you."

"I'm sorry. After I reached the hotel, I began my search. But the telephone directory didn't have the listing I was looking for. When I realized I wouldn't find the answer there, I talked to the clerk at the front desk. He hooked me up with one of the chief phone operators who speaks English who was more than happy to help me."

"Why?"

In spite of the seriousness of the situation, her suspicious sister made her laugh. "It's a *she,* so you don't need to worry I'm being hit on. When I told her my dilemma, she couldn't have been nicer and tried to assist me any way she could. But by the time we got off the phone, I was too exhausted to call you."

"That's okay. So what's your plan now?"

"That operator suggested I should call the police station. She gave me the number for the traveler's assistance department. She said there'll be someone on duty who speaks English. They're used to getting calls from foreigners either stranded or in trouble and will help me. I'm going to do that as soon as I hang up from you."

"And what if you still don't have success?"

"Then I'll fly home in the morning as planned and never think about it again."

"I'm going to hold you to that. To be frank, I hope you've come to a dead end. Sometimes it's better not to know what you don't know. It could come back to bite you."

"What do you mean?"

"Just what I said. You might be walking into something you wish you could have avoided. Not all people are as nice and good as you are, Sami. I don't want to see you hurt."

"You're not by any chance having one of your premonitions, are you?"

"No, but I can't help my misgivings." Pat sounded convinced Sami had come to Italy on a fool's errand. Maybe she had.

"Tell you what. If he's not in Genoa, then I'll be on the next plane home."

"I'm going to hold you to that. Forgive me if I don't wish you luck. Before you go to bed tonight, call me. I don't care what time it is. Okay?"

"Okay. Love you."

"Love you, too."

Sami hung up, wondering if her sister was right. Maybe she shouldn't be searching for the grandfather of her baby. If she did find him, he might be so shocked to find out he was a grandfather, it could upset his world and make him ill. Possibly their meeting could turn so ugly, she'd wish she'd never left home.

That's what worried Pat.

If Sami were being honest, it worried her, too. But as long as she'd come this far, she might as well go all the way. Then maybe she could end this chapter of her life and move on.

She looked at the number she'd written down on her pad and made the phone call. The man who answered switched to English after she said hello. "Yes?"

His peremptory response took her back. "Is this the traveler's assistance department?"

"Yes—"

"I wonder if you could help me."

"What is it you want?"

Whoa. "I'm trying to find a man named Alberto Degenoli who's supposed to be living in Genoa, but he's not listed in the city phone directory. I've come from the United States looking for him. I was hoping y—"

But she stopped talking because the man, whom she'd thought was listening, was suddenly talking to another man in rapid Italian. Soon there was a third voice. Their conversation went on for at least a minute before the first man said, "Please spell the name for me."

When she did his bidding, more unintelligible Italian followed in the background. Finally, "You come to the station and ask for Chief Coretti."

Chief?

"You mean now?"

"Of course." The line went dead.

She blinked at his bizarre phone manners, but at least he hadn't turned her away. That had to account for something.

Next she phoned the front desk and asked them to send up the hotel's childminder. Sami had interviewed the qualified nurse yesterday and felt good about her. While she waited for her to come, she refreshed her makeup and slipped on her suit jacket.

Only four people knew the private cell phone number of Count Alberto Enrico Degenoli. When the phone rang, Ric assumed it was his fiancée, Eliana, calling again to dissuade him from leaving on a business trip in a few minutes. She was her father's puppet after all.

Now that Ric was about to become the son-in-law of one of the wealthiest industrialists in Italy, her father expected to control every portion of Ric's life, too. But Ric had crucial private business on Cyprus no one knew about, and it had to be transacted before the wedding.

Love had no part of this marriage and Eliana knew it. The coming nuptials were all about money. However, once they exchanged vows, he planned to do his part to make the marriage work. But until Christmas Eve, his time and business were his own concern and his future father-in-law couldn't do anything to stop him.

When he glanced away from his office computer screen long enough to check the caller ID, he discovered it was his private secretary phoning from the palazzo.

He clicked on. "Mario?"

"Forgive the interruption, Excellency." The older man had been in the service of the Degenoli family as private secretary for thirty-five years. But he was old-fashioned and insisted on being more formal with Ric now that Ric held the title. "Chief of Police Coretti just called the palace requesting to speak to you. He says it's extremely urgent, but refused to tell me the details. You're to call him back on his private line."

That would have irked Mario, who'd been privy to virtually everything in Ric's life. In all honesty, the chief's secrecy alarmed even Ric, whose concern over the reason for the call could touch on more tragedy and sorrow for their family. They'd had enough for several lifetimes.

"Give me the number."

After writing it down, he thanked Mario, then clicked off and made the call. "Signor Coretti? It's Enrico Degenoli. What can I do for you?"

He hadn't talked to the chief since the funeral for his father, who'd died in an avalanche in January. The chief had been among the dignitaries in Genoa who'd met the plane carrying his father's body. The memories of what had happened that weekend in Austria would always haunt Ric and had changed the course of his life.

"Forgive me for interrupting you, but there's a very attractive American woman in my office just in from the States who's looking for an Alberto Degenoli from Genoa."

At first his heart leaped at the news, then as quickly fizzled. If this American woman had been looking for him, she would have told the police chief she was looking for a man named Ric Degenoli.

Ric and his father bore the same names, but his father had gone by Alberto, and Ric went by Enrico. Only his siblings ever called him Ric. *And the woman who'd been caught with him in the avalanche.*

"Does she know my father died?"

"If she does, she has said nothing. To be frank, it's my opinion she's here on a fishing expedition, *if* you know what I mean." He cleared his throat. "She's hoping I can find him for her because she says it's a matter of life and death," he added in a quiet voice.

What?

"Since she's being suspiciously secretive, I thought I should let you know before I told her anything."

The intimation that this could be something of a delicate nature alarmed Ric in a brand-new way. He shot out of his leather chair in reaction. Up to now he'd done everything possible to protect his family from scandal.

Unfortunately he hadn't been able to control his father's past actions. No matter that Ric was a Degenoli, he and his father had differed in such fundamental ways, including the looks he'd inherited from his mother, that the average person wouldn't have known they were father and son.

One of Ric's greatest fears was that his father's weakness for women would catch up with him in ways he didn't want to think about. With his own marriage coming up on New Year's Day, it was imperative nothing go wrong at this late date. Too much was riding on it.

His father had been dead less than a year. It wasn't a secret he'd been with several women since Ric's mother's sudden and unexpected death from pneumonia sixteen months ago. He recalled his mother once confiding to him that even if his father were penniless, he would always be attractive to women and she had overlooked his wandering eye.

Ric couldn't be that generous. If the woman in Coretti's office thought she could blackmail their family or insist she had some claim on his deceased father's legacy, then she hadn't met Ric and was deluding herself. "What's her name?"

"Christine Argyle."

The name meant nothing to him. "Is she married? Single?"

"I don't know. Her passport didn't indicate one way or the other, but she wasn't wearing a ring. She called the traveler's aid department and they turned it over to me. At first I thought this must be some sort of outlandish prank, but she's not backing down. Since this is about your father, I thought I'd better phone you and learn your wishes before I tell her I can't help her and order her off the premises."

"Thank you for handling this with diplomacy," Ric said in a level voice, but his anger boiled beneath the surface. To go straight to Genoa's chief of police to get his attention was a clever tactic on her part. She wouldn't have taken that kind of a risk unless she thought she had something on Ric's father that the family wouldn't like made public. *How convenient and predictable.*

She'd probably met Alberto at a business party last fall when he'd decided he didn't want to be in mourning any longer. More often than not those dinners involved private gambling parties. Many of them were hosted for foreign VIPs on board one of the yachts anchored in the harbor where the police had no jurisdiction.

There'd be plenty of available women, including American starlets, to please every appetite. But it would be catastrophic if this last fling of his father's was the one that couldn't be hushed up and resulted in embarrassing the family morally and financially.

Not if Ric could help it!

Anything leaked to the press now could affect Ric's future plans in ways he didn't even want to think about. He saw red. Before the wedding, the negotiations in Cyprus *had* to go through as planned to safeguard his deceased mother's assets so Eliana's father couldn't get his hands on them. Ric refused to let anything get in the way.

"*Per favore*—keep her in your office until I get there. Don't use my title in front of her. Simply introduce me as Signor Alberto Degenoli and I'll go from there." This woman wouldn't have gotten involved with his father if he hadn't had a title, but Ric intended to play along with her ruse until he'd exposed her for a grasping opportunist.

"Understood. She went out for a while, but she'll be calling me in a few minutes. If you're coming now, I'll let her know you're on your way."

His thoughts were reeling. "Say nothing about this to anyone."

"Surely you don't question my loyalty to the House of Degenoli?"

"No," Ric muttered, furrowing his hair absently with his fingers. He stared blindly out the window of the Degenoli Shipping Lines office. For well on 150 years it had overlooked the port of Genoa, Italy's most important port city. "Forgive me, but when it comes to my family…"

"I understand. You know you can rely on my discretion."

"Grazie." Ric's voice grated before he hung up.

Whatever was going on, Ric didn't want wind of this to reach his siblings. Claudia and Vito lived with enough pain and didn't need to take on more, especially with Christmas only a week away. It was absolutely essential this be kept secret.

After he told his driver to meet him in the side alley, he rang security to follow them and left the office with his bodyguards. He needed to take care of this matter now, before he left for the airport.

For the second time today, Sami paid the taxi driver and got out in front of the main police station in Genoa with trepidation. The police chief had told her one of his staff had found the number of the man she was looking for and had contacted him.

It was a miracle! She couldn't have done it without the phone operator's help. After searching for Alberto Degenoli without success, she'd almost given up hope.

No telling what would happen at this meeting, but she had to go through with it for her baby's sake. His existence would come as a total surprise to Mr. Degenoli, but her son deserved to know about his father's side of the family.

Of course, the baby was too little to know anything yet. It was up to Sami to introduce them and lay a foundation for the future, *if* Mr. Degenoli wanted a relationship. If not, then she'd go back to Reno and raise him without feeling any attendant guilt that she hadn't done all she could do to unite them.

Once through the doors, she realized it was just as busy at four o'clock as it had been earlier. Besides people and staff, it was filled with cigarette smoke, irritating her eyes and nose. The nativity scene set up on a table in the foyer reminded her how close it was to Christmas and she'd done nothing to get ready for it yet. But she'd had something much more important on her mind before leaving Reno than the upcoming holidays.

Having been in the building earlier, she knew where to go. She'd just started to make her way down the hall when a man strode swiftly past her and rounded a corner at the end. He was a tall male, elegantly dressed in a tan suit and tie. Maybe he was in his mid-thirties. For want of a better word, he left an impression of power and importance that appeared unconscious and seemed to come as naturally to him as breathing.

Sami passed several men and policemen who eyed her in masculine appreciation before she turned the corner and entered the reception area of the police chief's office. With the exception of the uniformed male receptionist she'd met before, the room was empty. Where had the other man gone?

After she sat down, the receptionist picked up the phone, presumably to let the chief know she'd arrived. Once he'd hung up, he told her she could go in. After removing a few blond hairs from the sleeve of her navy blazer, Sami thanked him and opened the door to the inner office.

To her shock, the stranger who'd passed her in the hall moments ago was standing near the chief's desk talking to him. Obviously the chief of police was busy, so she didn't understand why his secretary had told her she could go in.

At a glance she took in the other man's lean, powerful physique. Her gaze quickly traveled to the lines of experience etched around his eyes and mouth. Maybe she was mistaken, but beneath his black brows, those dark eyes pierced hers with hostility after he'd turned in her direction. That wasn't a reaction she was used to receiving from the opposite sex.

Of medium height, she had to look up to him. His unique male beauty fascinated her, especially his widow's peak formed by hair black as midnight. Swept back like that, it brought his Mediterranean features and gorgeous olive skin into prominence.

The chief spoke in heavily accented English, drawing her attention away from the stranger. "Signorina, may I present Signor Alberto Degenoli."

Sami's spirits plunged. *This isn't the man I'm looking for.* But perhaps he is a relative? "How do you do?" she murmured, shaking the hand of the striking Italian male who'd extended his. He had a strong, firm grip, like the man himself.

"How do *you* do, Signorina?" His polished English was impeccable with barely a whisper of accent. But it was the depth of his voice that sent a curious shiver through her body, recalling an echo from the past. Maybe she was mistaken, but she thought she'd heard that voice before.

But that was crazy. They'd never met.

"You've gone pale, Signorina. Are you all right?"

"Yes—" Sami gripped the back of the nearest chair. "I-it's just that you're not the person I'm looking for and I'm disappointed," she stammered before gazing at him again. "You have his name, but you're...too young. Obviously there's more than one Alberto Degenoli living in Genoa."

He shook his head. "No. There's only one."

"You mean *you?*"

"That's right."

"Perhaps instead of Genova, you meant Geneva in Switzerland, Signorina," the chief inserted. "Many

Americans become confused by the two similar spellings."

She frowned. "Possibly I misunderstood. Mr. Degenoli's in shipping."

"So are others on Lake Geneva."

"But he's Italian."

"Thousands of Italians live in Switzerland."

"Yes. I know." Maybe because of the differences in pronunciation, she'd gotten the name of the city wrong. How odd. All this time... "Thank you for the suggestion." She looked at Mr. Degenoli. "I'm so sorry you've made this trip to the police station for nothing. I've put both of you out. Please forgive me."

"Perhaps if you gave me a clearer description of him?"

"Well, he'd probably be in his sixties. I'm not sure. I feel terrible about this. Thank you for coming here on such short notice." She glanced at Chief Coretti. "Please excuse me for taking up your time. You've been very kind. I'll leave now so you can get on with your work."

At her comment, he squinted at her. "You sounded desperate when you came to me, Signorina. Therefore I will leave you to get better acquainted with this gentleman you've inconvenienced, and the two of you can discuss...business."

Business? "What on earth do you mean?"

"Surely you're not that naive?" the chief replied.

Upset by the distasteful insinuation, she felt heat rush to her cheeks. "You've evidently questioned my motives, but whatever you're thinking, you'd be wrong—" she blurted.

At this point she felt oddly reluctant to be left alone with the intimidating stranger studying her with relentless scrutiny. "I haven't found the person I'm looking for, so there's no point in this going any further. I truly am sorry to have caused either of you any inconvenience."

Chief Coretti gave her a nasty smile. "What is going on, Signorina? You said it was a matter of life and death."

"It is." She hated the tremor in her voice.

He threw up his hands. "So explain!"

"I know I've been secretive, but I'm trying to make this inquiry as discreetly as possible to protect all concerned. When my other searches failed yesterday, I came to you for answers and hoped nobody would get hurt in the process. But the fact remains I'm looking for an older gentleman. I suppose he could even be in his early seventies."

Time seemed suspended as Mr. Degenoli swallowed her up with those jet-black eyes of his. "Signor Coretti— if you'd be so kind as to leave us alone for a moment."

"Of course."

After he left, the room grew silent as a tomb except for the thudding of her heart. It wouldn't surprise her if the stranger could hear it.

His lips twisted unpleasantly before he moved closer. "You've been secretive long enough. I'd like to see your passport." Sami had the strongest conviction he was curious about her, too. At this point she knew she'd heard his voice before. But where? When she'd come to Europe a year ago, she hadn't visited Italy.

While she rummaged in her purse, her mind was

searching to remember. He stood there waiting, larger than life with an air of authority much more commanding than any police chief's. She handed the passport to him. After he read the information, he gave it back.

"I've never heard of you." His eyes glittered with barely suppressed anger. "The Alberto Degenoli I believe you're looking for is no longer alive, but I think you already knew that. How well did you know him?" he demanded.

Ah. Now she understood the police chief's earlier remark about "business." Both men assumed she'd been involved with the man she was looking for. Sami lifted her head. "I didn't know him at all. In fact I never met him, but I'd h-hoped to," she stammered. Sadness overwhelmed her to realize she'd come to Italy for nothing.

"What did this man mean to you?"

Wouldn't he just love to know, but he'd be so wrong! She took a fortifying breath. "Since he's dead…nothing."

"How did you hear of him?"

Sami had heard of him through his son, but he was dead, too. If this man was the only living Degenoli in Genoa, then what the chief of police had said was probably true. She should fly to Geneva to start her search there before flying home.

"It no longer matters." She tried to swallow, but the sudden swelling in her throat made it difficult. "Forgive me for bothering you." She spun around and made a quick exit.

As she flew down the hall to the entrance of the police station, she suddenly realized what had been bothering

her. The man she'd just left had the same kind of voice as
her baby's deceased father. That's why it had sounded so
familiar and disturbing…except for one thing.

This man didn't have that tender, caring quality in
his voice. His tone and manner had been borderline ac-
cusatory. Her body gave a shudder before she stepped
into the first taxi in the line-up in front of the building.

Ric had caught only a glimpse of tear-filled green eyes
before she dashed from Coretti's office. Could there be
two American women in existence who sounded that
identical? He supposed the coincidence was possible,
since he'd never seen this woman in his life.

For months he'd looked for the woman he'd been
trapped in the snow with, hoping she would come looking for him, but by summer he'd decided she must have
died in that avalanche.

He closed his eyes for a moment, remembering the
way this woman's husky voice had trembled. Much as he
hated to admit it, a part of him had felt her emotion was
genuine. The classic features of her pale blond beauty,
so different from his own countrywomen, already bothered him in ways he was reluctant to admit.

But great as her acting had been, Ric was convinced
Signorina Argyle had lied to him, or at least hadn't told
him the whole truth. Whatever her secret, he was determined to find it out.

Running on pure adrenaline at this point, he buzzed
Carlo, his head of security, and told him to follow the
twenty-six-year-old blonde American woman leaving

the police station. When she reached her destination, he wanted to know exactly where she went from there, so he could arrange a private meeting.

Now hadn't been the time to stop her. The conversation he intended to have with her needed to be someplace where they could be strictly alone with no chance of anyone else walking in on them.

With his visit to the chief's office accomplished, he went out to the limo. Within a few minutes he learned she was booked in at the Grand Savoia—one of the best, if not *the* best hotel in Genoa. It was expensive any time, but especially over the holidays. He told the driver to take him there. Carlo indicated Ric would find her on the third floor, to the right of the elevator, four doors down on the left.

Before long he alighted from the limo and entered the hotel. Deciding to take her by surprise, he dispensed with the idea of phoning her and took the stairs two at a time to her floor. When he reached her door, he knocked loudly enough for her to hear.

"Signorina Argyle? It's Signor Degenoli. We need to talk." He got no response, so he decided to try a different tactic. "Why were you trying to find Alberto? I would like to help you if you'd let me."

Carlo had told him she'd gone into her room and hadn't come out again, but she might be showering. He gave her another minute, then knocked again. "Signorina?"

A few seconds later the door opened as wide as the little chain would allow. He saw those green eyes lifted to him in consternation, but they were red-rimmed. By the look of it, she'd been crying. That much was genuine.

The champagne-gold of her collar-length hair gleamed in the hall light. She'd discarded her jacket. From the little he could see, a curvaceous figure was revealed beneath the silky white blouse she'd tucked in at the waist of her navy skirt. Every inch of her face and body appealed strongly to him.

"I didn't realize the police chief had had me followed." The natural shape of her mouth had a voluptuous flare he'd noticed back at the station. But right now it was drawn tight. She hugged the door, as if she didn't trust him not to break in on her.

Ric lounged against the wall. "Don't blame him. I asked one of my men to keep an eye on you until I could catch up with you."

"*Your* men?"

"My bodyguards. If you'll invite me inside, I'll be happy to explain."

A delicate frown marred her features. "I'm sorry, Mr. Degenoli, but as I said at the station, there's nothing more to discuss and I have other plans."

"As do I." He was already late leaving for Cyprus. "But we have unfinished business," he rapped out. To his disgust, he wondered what her exact plans were. Deep inside, his gut twisted to think that he could be this intensely attracted to a stranger. His interest in her made no sense, but the sound of her voice and the way she talked still played with his senses.

A sound of exasperation escaped her lips. "Please believe me when I tell you how badly I feel that you were called into the police station for nothing. If you'd like me to pay you for the inconvenience, I could give you fifty dollars to cover the gas money. It's all I can spare."

If that were true, then she'd chosen too expensive a hotel to stay in. "I don't want your money. To be frank, I knew you were upset when you left the station." He cocked his head. "I can tell you've been crying. Now that we don't have Chief Coretti for an audience, you can speak freely with me."

"I probably could, but there'd be no point." She wiped her eyes with the back of her hands. "I've come to the end of my search. I have to say goodbye now."

There was no question in his mind she was holding back something vital. He put his foot in the door so she couldn't close it. "Not until I get more answers. For one thing—" He only got that far because he heard a baby fussing. The sounds came from the other side of the door. *I knew it!*

"Not so fast." Ric put his weight against the door so she couldn't shut it on him. "Whose baby is it?"

"Mine."

"And Alberto's?" With his mind firing, all Ric could think was that his father had made love to this woman and she'd come to present him with the fruit of that union, but it was too late.

"No—" she cried.

"Then prove it to me."

CHAPTER TWO

IN HER mind Sami could hear Pat's dire warning, but she hadn't heeded it.

This situation had hit rock bottom and was exactly what she'd hoped to avoid, but this man wouldn't let it go and had followed her to the hotel. Since she'd started this, she decided that if she didn't want to deal with Chief Coretti again, she'd better let him in.

After undoing the chain, she hurried across the room to the crib. Once she'd picked up the baby, she cuddled him against her shoulder in a protective gesture. Kissing him, she said, "You heard noises and they frightened you, didn't they, sweetheart? Don't worry. It's okay." She flicked Mr. Degenoli a curious glance. "Our visitor will be leaving soon."

The arresting-looking Italian had already come inside the room and locked the door behind him. She shivered a little as he drew closer to look at her baby.

Sami decided *this* Mr. Degenoli *had* to be a relative of her baby's father. That's why his voice sounded so familiar to her. Back at the station he'd been as cagey as she'd tried to be in her effort to protect people and reputations, even to the extent of possibly lying about his name, but with both father and son dead, there was no worry now. The only thing to do was answer his questions, then go home to Reno in the morning.

"Excuse me while I change him." Reaching for a towel, she spread it on top of the bed and put the baby down.

"Where did you leave him while you were at the police station?"

Sami undid the baby's stretchy blue suit. "Here, of course. Don't you know the last place for a baby was that smoke-filled building? This hotel happens to have an outstanding child-minding service." Sami's sister had made the reservation for her. "That's the reason I booked in here. They sent a qualified nurse to watch over him while I went to the police station."

He didn't look as if he believed her. "I didn't kidnap him. If you're so skeptical, call the front desk and ask them yourself. They'll verify who I am."

At this point his eyes were riveted on the baby. "How old is he?"

Sami used the baby wipes and discarded everything in a plastic bag. After powdering him, she slipped him into a fresh diaper. "Two months, but that information wouldn't have any relevance for you. I couldn't bring him to Genoa to meet his grandfather before now."

"Grandfather—"

"Yes. Why do you seem so shocked? Most children have them. I'm heartbroken that my son is never going to know him or…his father." Her voice faltered.

She kissed the soft baby hair that was dark and too

beautiful for a boy. His handsome face was all flushed, but he stopped crying long enough to notice the intruder who was thoroughly inspecting him.

After fastening the snaps on the stretchy suit, she wrapped him in his quilt and picked him up to snuggle him. "I think you're ready for your dinner, young man." She walked over to the dresser for a fresh bottle of ready-mixed formula and sat down on a chair to feed him.

"Your voice sounds familiar to me, Signorina."

So she wasn't the only one imagining their connection. "Yours does to me, too. Strange, isn't it, when I know we've never met?"

His dark brows furrowed. "More than strange. Were you in Europe on holiday recently?"

"Not for close to a year, but I've traveled to Europe before."

"I'd like to see your passport again."

"Let me feed my son first, then I'll get it for you."

He was a good little eater, but he'd been awakened before his nap had been over and was ready to go back to sleep. She burped him, then put him back in the crib and covered him with the quilt.

Aware of Mr. Degenoli's eyes watching her every move, she walked over to the dresser and pulled the passport from her purse. "In case you were wondering, I applied for this passport several years before my baby was born."

Her visitor took it from her and studied the pages with the various entry stamps. "This last one dated in January says you visited Austria—"

"Yes."

"*Where* in Austria?" The inflexible male sounded in deadly earnest.

"Innsbruck."

At the mention of it, his complexion took on a definite pallor. "Why that town?"

"Because my sister and her husband own a travel agency, and I was checking out some hotels for them there and in the surrounding areas. They're always looking for new places to book their clients into."

Mr. Degenoli appeared so shaken, she decided to end their inane question-and-answer session. Without hesitation she reached for her purse and pulled out a brown envelope. "Here—" Sami handed it to him. "I brought this to show my baby's grandfather. It will explain everything."

He eyed her suspiciously before he opened it and pulled out the birth certificate.

"As you can see there, I named my baby Ric, after his daddy. Ric Argyle Degenoli. You see, b-both Ric and his father, Alberto, were caught up in the same avalanche I was buried in last January." Her voice faltered. "I assume Alberto was a relative of yours. Maybe your uncle?"

Her uninvited guest didn't make a sound. It led her to believe he was finally listening to her. "I'd just stopped in one of the hotels for a minute to check it out and get a hot drink in the dining room. As I was about to go outside again to do a little sightseeing, the avalanche swept through the three-story hotel like a supersonic freight train.

"Ric and I were entombed for several hours. I knew he'd died before I lost total consciousness, but until you told me at the police station, I didn't realize Alberto had been killed, too.

"After I woke up in a clinic, I assumed Ric's father had survived, because only one male victim named Degenoli was listed among the fatalities. That was Ric, of course. His father must have died later from his injuries, after the list was put out."

Sami couldn't stop the tears from spurting. "It was a nightmarish time. My sister came to Innsbruck to get me and fly home with me. I didn't realize until six weeks later that I was pregnant. At that point I determined that one day I'd look up Alberto and let him know he had a grandchild. But as you've let me know, this trip was in vain."

The man listening to her story had gone eerily quiet.

"My sister calls my son Ricky, but I love the Italian version. I named him after his heroic father to honor him."

"Heroic?" he questioned in a gravelly voice.

"Yes. One day when Ric is old enough, I'll tell him how courageous his father was."

"In what way?"

"You would have to have been there to understand. Ric was an amazing man. After the snow buried us, he kept me from losing my mind. You see, I suffer from claustrophobia. You can't imagine what being trapped did to me. I wouldn't be alive if it hadn't been for him.

"We were total strangers sealed in a black tomb together. We heard each other moan, but had no idea what the other one looked like. I know I was on the verge of a heart attack when he started talking to me and urged me to relax, because he believed we'd get out of there if we didn't panic. He pointed out that by some miracle, we were trapped by beams that kept the whole weight from falling on us, providing us a pocket of air and room to wiggle.

"At first I thought I was dead and that he was an angel the way he took care of me and never let me panic. But when he reached for me and held me in his arms, promising me we'd be all right, I knew he was mortal.

"His only thought was to protect me. At first his kisses on my cheek held back my terror. I returned them, needing his comfort while we lay there slowly suffocating. We talked a little. He told me he'd just come from a wedding with his father, Alberto. I explained I was on a trip, but we didn't go into details.

"As time went on and no help came, we realized we were going to die. At that point we drew warmth and comfort from each other's bodies." She took a fortifying breath. "We made love. It happened so naturally, it was like a dream. Then I heard a shifting sound. The next thing I knew a piece of wood had pierced his forehead."

A sob caught in her throat. "It knocked him unconscious and his warm blood spilled over both of us. I couldn't get a pulse and knew he was gone. When I woke up in a clinic, the last thing I remembered was that he'd died in my arms.

"We'd been literally tossed together with the broken

walls and furniture in the darkness of a catastrophic avalanche that hit the hotel. But for the time we were together, hanging on to life because we knew they were
our last moments on this earth, I felt closer to him than
to anyone I've ever known.

"When I look at my adorable Ric, I know I'm seeing
his father. My only hope now is to raise him to measure up to the great man who gave him life. I know he
was a great man because he was so selfless in the face
of terror. He never once thought of himself, only of me.
So now I hope that explanation answers your questions,
Mr. Degenoli."

She stared at the tall figure still standing there. His
face had gone ashen. The birth certificate had fallen to
the floor. How odd he'd left it there...

"If you still don't believe me, then I don't know what
more I can say to convince you. Maybe now you'd answer
a question for me. Was Alberto your uncle?"

"No," he answered in a voice as deep as a cavern. "He
was my father."

"Chief Coretti introduced you as Alberto, but that
really isn't your name, is it? He did it to protect you. I
can understand that."

He moved closer to her. "Let me explain this another
way. My father was christened Alberto Enrico Degenoli,
and was called Alberto. I was also christened Alberto
Enrico Degenoli, but I go by Enrico. However my immediate family calls me...Ric."

As Sami stared at him, the world tilted.

"But you *couldn't* be that Ric. I wasn't able to waken him. He died in my arms—"

"No, Sami," he countered in a husky voice. "I'm right here."

She was so staggered to hear him use her nickname, she clutched the crib railing with both hands. A small cry escaped her lips. "*You're* Ric?" She shook her head, causing her hair to swish against her pale cheeks. "I—I can't believe this is happening. I—"

The room started to swim. The next thing Sami knew, she found herself on the bed with the man who'd made her pregnant leaning over her. He sat next to her with his hands on either side of her head. "Stay quiet for a minute. You've had another shock."

He spoke to her in the compassionate voice she remembered—exactly the way he'd done in the avalanche. With her eyes closed, she could recall everything and was back there with him in spirit.

But the minute her eyelids fluttered open, she saw a stranger staring down at her. In her psyche Sami knew he was Ric. But she couldn't credit that the striking, almost forbidding male who'd swept past her at the police station was the same Ric who'd once given her his passion and the will to live.

Sami's hair spilled onto Ric's fingers. If he closed his eyes, he could recall the same silky mane he'd played with in the darkness. The strands had been as fragrant as every part of her face and body. It was the same now, but at the time he'd had no idea its coloring resembled spun gossamer.

Still noticing her pallor, he got up from the bed to get her a cup of water. When he returned from the bathroom, she sat up. He handed it to her and she drank thirstily. "Thank you," she whispered in a tremulous voice before lying back again like a spent flower.

Ric put the empty cup on the side table, then sank down next to her once more. "Our survival was a miracle," he began.

"Yes. I'm still trying to deal with the fact that you didn't die and are here where I can see you."

She wasn't the only one. "When we were trapped together, I would have sold my soul to know what you looked like," he confessed emotionally. "Feeling you told me that you were a lovely woman, but I must admit that no dreams I've had of you could measure up to your living reality."

Like someone shell-shocked, she lifted one of her hands to his face in wonder. She traced his features, bringing back memories he would never forget. "Ric—" Her fingers traveled over his lips. "Maybe I'm hallucinating again."

He kissed the palm of her hand. "It was never an hallucination. We were mortal then and now."

Tears trickled out of the corners of her eyes, eyes that were alive like the green of a tropical rain forest. "When I thought you were dead, I wanted to die. While you were still breathing, I could hold on. But after that beam hit you and I couldn't get a response, it was the end of my world."

Ric heard the same pain in her voice he'd carried around for months afterward. He studied her facial features, overlaying his memories of her through eyes that could see the throb at the base of her slender throat. Tears trembled on the ends of long dark lashes so unusual on a blonde.

She kept looking at him with incredulity. "I feel just like I did after the avalanche struck. Maybe I'm hallucinating and none of this is real, but it *has* to be real because I'm touching you and it's your voice. You're actual flesh and blood instead of the stuff of my dreams."

"You were the flesh and blood I clung to while we were entombed," he confessed. "You saved my sanity, too, Sami. Like you, I felt I was in this amazing dream. When we made love, I remember thinking that if it was a dream, I never wanted to wake up from that part of it. Everything about our experience had a surreal quality."

Sami wiped the tears off her face. "I know. Until I found out I was pregnant, there were times when I thought I'd made it all up." She stared at him. "What happened to you after you were rescued?"

He grasped her hand. "I was told that another few minutes and the medics wouldn't have been able to revive me. I knew nothing until I woke up in a hospital in Genoa. I was in a coma for two days. When I came out of it, I was surrounded by my family. My first request of the doctor was to find out if you were one of the victims.

"He came back with the message that you must still

be alive because there was no name of Sami or anything close to it on the list of fatalities. After hearing that news, I determined to go after you once I got better. After our family held funeral services for my father, then I started looking for you."

"I can't believe it."

"Why are you so surprised? What we'd shared together was something so unique, I'll never forget. But when your name didn't show up on any established tour-group lists in the area, I had to look further afield. I remembered you'd told me you were from Oakland, California. That's all I had to go on. I put my people on it while we searched for you for several months."

"Oh, Ric—" she cried softly before sliding off the other side of the bed to come around.

He got to his feet. "You were my first priority, but you weren't listed in the Oakland phone directory. No flights leaving Austria for the States with your name. No planes arriving in Oakland or San Francisco had a name that could be traced to you. It was as if you'd disappeared off the face of the earth."

"That's because you didn't know my real name," she cried out in dismay. "I was nicknamed Sami because my father's name was Samuel. After my parents died, my grandparents took over raising me and my sister, and my grandfather said I reminded him so much of his son he started calling me Sami, and it stuck."

"I thought it had to be short for Samantha, but your passport says otherwise."

"That's what everyone assumes who doesn't know

me. To think you searched all that time for the wrong name. I can't bear it."

He couldn't either, considering the promise he'd made to his father when they'd gone to Austria for an important family wedding. Ric had done everything humanly possible to find her. When he'd exhausted every avenue to no avail, he'd got on with his life and eventually fulfilled that promise.

"It's true I was born and raised in Oakland," she went on to explain, "but after I went back to college, I started to feel ill and went to a doctor. When he told me I was pregnant, I couldn't believe it. My sister, Pat, insisted I move to Reno, Nevada, to be with her and her husband. Their travel agency is growing all the time. They're the ones who gave me a working vacation during my break from college."

Nevada... The avalanche had changed both their lives in ways Ric was only beginning to understand. "Were you ill the whole pregnancy?"

"No. After the morning sickness passed, I didn't have other problems. Since Pat's my only family and I wanted to be close to her and their children, I moved to Reno and started classes there. Without my legal name, no wonder you couldn't trace me."

He rubbed his chest absently while he was digesting everything.

Her anxious gaze fastened on him. 'Do you have any ill effects from your head wound?"

"Only the occasional headache," he answered, touched by her concern.

"I'm so glad it isn't worse. That was the most terrifying moment." Her voice shook.

"Thankfully, I don't remember."

"I don't like to think about it. Throughout my pregnancy I decided that after Ric was born and I'd had my six-weeks checkup, I'd take him to Genoa and look up his grandfather. My own parents had already died, and I thought it would be wonderful if Ric grew up knowing he had at least one grandparent who was still alive." She hugged her arms to her waist. "How tragic you lost your father."

"Yes," he whispered, but right now everything else seemed very far removed.

"I thought about him all the time," she said. "Naturally I feared how he would take the news. It might have been the worst thing he could hear, but I hoped it might comfort him a little to know you weren't alone when you died."

Ric's breath caught. "*Ringrazio il cielo* you looked for him! Otherwise I would know nothing! Be assured my father would have wanted to be a grandfather to our son." *Once he'd gotten over the shock of learning the circumstances of his grandson's conception.* Ric was still having trouble taking it all in.

She bit her lip. "I didn't know the right thing to do. That's the reason why I was so secretive with the police chief." Ric warmed to her for her desire to be discreet. "I didn't want to embarrass your father or cause him pain in front of anyone else. I really thought if I could find him, he'd refuse to believe me and that would be the end of it. But for the baby's sake, I felt I had to try.

"When the police chief suggested maybe I had the wrong city, I didn't know what to believe. I thought you'd told me you were from Genoa. The thought of flying to Geneva and starting another search sounded overwhelming, but I was prepared to do it for your son's sake. Oh, Ric—"

The woman he'd been trapped with had to be one in a billion.

His eyes strayed to the crib. The baby sleeping so peacefully was his son. It was unbelievable! Throwing off his own shock, he walked over to the crib and looked down at the baby—*his baby*—lying on his back with his arms outstretched, his hands formed into fists.

"In spite of all that death and destruction coming for us, we managed to produce a son!"

"Yes." She'd joined him. "Incredibly, he's perfect."

Ric had thought the same thing the second he'd laid eyes on him. In that moment he'd suffered pain thinking his parent had fathered such a beautiful child with *her*. Ric had been so convinced of it that he was still having trouble getting a handle on his emotions.

But it wasn't his father's— It was his own!

His elation was so overpowering, he reached for the baby and held him against his shoulder, uncaring that he'd wake him up again. Ric *wanted* him to wake up so he could get a good look at him. Warmth from the little bundle seeped into his body's core, bonding them as father and son.

The baby must have sensed someone different was holding him. He started wiggling and moved his dark silky head from side to side. He smelled sweet like his mother. He was such a strong little thing that Ric was forced to support his head and neck with more strength. He lowered him in the crook of his arm so he could pick out the unique features that proclaimed him a Degenoli and an Argyle. Both sets of genes were unmistakable.

"*Ciao, bambino mio.* Welcome to my world." He kissed his cheeks and forehead. His olive-skinned baby grew more animated. Ric laughed when those arms and legs moved and kicked with excitement. The *first* Degenoli in this generation to live.

His sister, Claudia, had barely learned she was pregnant before she'd suffered a miscarriage. It had happened soon after she'd heard their father had been killed in the avalanche. His sorrow for her and her husband, Marco's, loss would always hurt, but as he looked down at his son, there wasn't room in his soul for anything but joy.

When Ric looked up, he caught Sami's tear-filled eyes fastened on the two of them. After wondering what she'd looked like, he couldn't get his fill of staring at her.

"I can't fathom it that you're alive, that you're holding him," she cried. "When I left the police station, I was heartbroken. If I didn't find Alberto in Geneva, it meant going home knowing my baby would never know the Italian side of his family. What if you hadn't followed me here?" she cried.

"Nothing could have stopped me. I had to find out who

you really were because I couldn't believe there was an-other woman alive who sounded like you."

"I know what you mean. The second you spoke to me, I should have stopped trying to be cautious and just called you Ric to see what you'd do. It would have saved us both so much trouble."

Ric would have responded, but his cell phone rang. It jerked him back to reality. He had a strong idea who it was.

"I'll take the baby while you answer it." Sami plucked the baby out of his arms and walked the floor with him.

He watched his little boy burrow his head in her neck. The action brought a lump to his throat before he wheeled away from her and checked the caller ID. Though he'd finally come to the end of his search for the woman named Sami, time had passed during that search and other dynamics had been set in motion.

Ric groaned when he thought of how this news was going to affect negotiations with Eliana's father, let alone with Eliana herself. Theirs was no love match, but news of an unknown baby would be difficult for any bride-to-be to handle. He'd need to deal with her carefully. As for his own family, they would be in shock.

"Eliana?" he said after clicking on.

"I thought you would call me before you left the office, but your secretary said you weren't there."

He rubbed the back of his neck absently. "I'm on my way to the airport and planned to phone you before my jet took off." It would have been the truth if something else hadn't come up. Something that had changed the very fabric of his life. The Sami he'd been entombed with was alive and had just presented him with his *son!*

There was a distinct pause. "Are you all right? You sound...different."

Different didn't begin to cover what was going on inside him.

"It's...business. I'm afraid I'm preoccupied with it. Forgive me." It was the kind of business Chief Coretti had referred to at the station. But it had everything to do with Ric, not with his father. When he thought of the way his suspicious mind had worked trying to get answers...

"Of course I forgive you, Enrico."

Ric took a steadying breath. Before they were married, those words were going to be put to the test in the cruelest of ways.

Sami had called him a great man. How honorable did it make him if he kept this revelation from Eliana? But he couldn't tell her yet. It wasn't possible when he could hardly comprehend it himself. With this news there would be so many ramifications, he needed time to think how he was going to handle everything.

"I'll phone you from Cyprus tomorrow."

"That had better be a promise."

He gripped the phone tighter. "Have I ever broken one to you?"

"No, but I'm still angry you've let business interfere so much. After we're married I intend to keep you occupied for a long time. For one thing, I want to give you a baby. Hopefully a male heir."

Ric closed his eyes tightly. *Someone got ahead of you in that department, Eliana.*

His fiancée was a beautiful, polished product of her aristocratic upbringing. He couldn't fault his future wife for voicing her womanly expectations. But neither could he do anything about the new state of affairs. Fate had blown in with the avalanche, altering his world forever.

"Forgive me, Eliana, but I have to go. We'll talk tomorrow."

"A domani, Caro."

He ended the call and turned to Sami.

The baby had fallen asleep against her shoulder. She eyed Ric steadily. "While you were on the phone, I've had time to gather my thoughts. Maybe I'm wrong, but I sensed a woman was on the other end of that phone call. Judging by the tone of your voice, she's either your wife or your girlfriend."

During those hours they'd been trapped, they'd crossed all the boundaries waiting for the end. It didn't surprise Ric she wasn't only intuitive, but forthright. "My fiancée, Eliana."

Not one dark eyelash flickered. "Were you—"

"No." He knew what was on her mind. "I didn't get engaged to her until long after I'd lost all hope of ever finding you. I kept the thought alive that since I'd told you my last name, you might come back to Genoa to look for me. Now that I understand you were carrying our son all that time, I know why you didn't come until now."

"Did you ever tell your fiancée about us?"

"Not her, not anyone," he whispered before moving closer. "Are you involved with someone? Married?"

"No." Her single-word answer shouldn't have filled him with relief, but it did. "I'd just broken up with a man I'd been dating before I left for Europe on my trip in January. As you can imagine, I wasn't the same person when I returned.

"When Matt found out I was back, he called me and told me he hadn't given up on us." Ric could understand why. "I told him it was over for me, but he said he was going to keep trying to get through to me. When I discovered I was pregnant, I told him the truth of what happened to me in Italy so he'd give up."

Ric bit down hard. "And did he?"

"No. He said he'd marry me and help me raise the baby as if it were his own."

The idea of another man parenting Ric's son didn't sit well with him. "He must love you very much."

"Yes, I believe he does. I love him, too. He's really wonderful, but I'm not in love with him. There's a huge difference. That why I broke up with him in the first place, because I didn't want to hurt him.

"He's been very good to me, but I know it hurt him horribly that I would make love with a stranger, especially when he and I hadn't gotten to that point." Her voice faltered. "No matter how I tried to explain the circumstances, I realized it sounded incredible."

"It still does," Ric confessed. "Even to me, and I was there."

Color crept back into her cheeks. "It would be asking

too much of him to forget it. I know he's still hoping I'll change my mind, but I can't see that happening." She kissed the baby. "How soon is your wedding?"

The wedding to Eliana...

"January first."

"New Year's—that's coming soon."

With Sami standing there cuddling his son, Ric found it impossible to think about his upcoming nuptials. The shock still hadn't worn off.

Her eyes searched his. "I realize it isn't every day a man is confronted with a situation like ours—" she said anxiously. "If I'd known you were alive, I would have handled everything differently. But now that you know you have a son, I'm aware you need time for the information to settle in before you can tell how you really feel about everything."

"How I feel?" he questioned, not understanding the remark. "You've just presented me with my child. I didn't know that being a father would bring me this kind of happiness."

Neither Ric nor his siblings had ever been close to their father. He was gone so much, they rarely saw him. Though he'd ruled over their family, he left the child-rearing to their mother and the house staff.

Not until college did his father take an interest in Ric. Even then it was all about duty and money. When Ric thought about how his father had always ignored Vito and Claudia, his insides twisted into knots. Early on he'd decided that if he were ever to become a father, he'd get totally involved in his children's lives from day one.

For Ric, today *was* day one. He eyed the mother of his child. "I didn't know learning I was a father would make me feel reborn in a whole new way."

"Nevertheless, you're getting married before long and have all this to talk over with Eliana," she said in a pragmatic tone. "It's a good thing my flight for the States leaves in the morning. Ric and I will go back to Reno while you let this sink in. Now that we know of each other's existence and can exchange phone numbers, there's no hurry."

He frowned. "No hurry? I've missed the first two months of my son's life and don't intend to miss any more."

"But with Christmas and your wedding almost here, this isn't the time to—"

"To what?" He cut her off. "Decide how to fit our baby into my life? He wasn't conceived on your schedule or mine, but he's a living breathing miracle. Unlike my father, who hardly acknowledged the existence of his children until they were grown, I want to be with my son all the time that you and I can work out."

Her face closed up. "There's nothing to work out the way you mean. We live on separate continents. He's my reason for living. After you and Eliana are married, I'll bring him for visits the way I would have done if your father had been the one who was alive. My sister will help me so the flights won't be expensive. When it's possible, you and your wife can fly to the States to see him."

Ric was listening, but the woman who'd given birth to his child was still a stranger to him in ways he had yet to understand. However, that was about to change, because he had no intention of letting her fly out of his life with their son.

CHAPTER THREE

"WE'LL talk about that later. For now we need to get better acquainted." Already he sensed she would require careful handling first. "I'm on my way to my second home on Cyprus to do vital business, so I'm taking you there with me tonight."

Her eyes widened in surprise.

"You said you wanted Ric to know about the Italian side of his family. My mother came from Cyprus. I spent most of my childhood there. As Ric grows older, it will be his second home, too. I want you to be with me for the next week and see my world in relaxed surroundings. It has the warmest climate in the Mediterranean during the winter months. Tomorrow it's supposed to hit seventy degrees, warm enough to go swimming."

She let out a small cry. "I couldn't do that, Ric. I only intended to be here a few days."

His body stiffened. "But you didn't know you'd find *me*. Now that you have, everything's changed for both of us. Our baby needs to be with his family. If your sister can't rearrange your flight for a different day, *I* can."

"I've no doubt of it," she conceded, "*if* you didn't have a fiancée who won't understand."

"She isn't expecting me back until Christmas Eve day. Until then, what I do with my time while I'm not in Genoa is my business. You and I have to talk things through. For you to go home tomorrow is out of the question."

"But—"

"Sami—" he broke in. "You wouldn't refuse me this time with you and the son I didn't know I had. We need time together to process the fact that the three of us are alive." He sucked in his breath. "We were given a second chance, not only to live life but to rejoice together in our beautiful son."

"Still—"

"There's no *still* about it. After what happened to us at that resort in Imst, I'm not taking any chances of another unexpected disaster. Anything could go wrong on your way back to Reno. Don't say it wouldn't happen, because we know better. I need this time with you and Ric. Be honest and admit you need it, too, now that you know I'm alive."

Sami looked away. "Even so, your fiancée will be devastated when she finds out the truth. How long do you plan to keep her in the dark?"

His eyes narrowed on her features. "For as long as it takes. I don't have a better answer."

"I'm afraid for her, Ric. I saw how the news affected Matt and we weren't even dating anymore. The revelation about the baby will be so terrible for her, she might never recover from it, especially if you don't tell her right away. I know if I were in her shoes and—"

"Let's not anticipate what might or might not happen," he interrupted her. "Your boyfriend heard the truth and told you he still wants to marry you."

"Maybe, maybe not," she answered honestly. "I told him I needed time and haven't seen him in months. But if we did get together for the sake of the baby, I'm afraid that over time he would learn to resent me for what I did. He wants children one day.

"If we married, it would be normal for him to love a son or daughter of his own body more than he loved Ric. I couldn't bear for that to happen. That's been one of the things holding me back from getting involved again. I won't let anything hurt Ric if I can help it."

"I hear what you're saying, Sami." He loved it that she guarded their son's happiness so fiercely. "I have those same protective feelings. That's why I have to be careful before I tell Eliana anything. She'll be hurt in ways I can promise not even *you* have thought of yet."

She shook her head. "This is such an incredible situation."

"But not insoluble. Ric's been your first priority or you wouldn't have flown to Genoa to find his grandfather. Now that I know of his existence, he's *my* first priority. I want to get up in the night and feed him. Over the next week I want to bathe him and do all those things a new father does. In that amount of time I'll know better how to approach my fiancée."

"I—I'd feel better if Eliana knew I was with you," she stammered. "What if someone tells her?"

"Who? My staff and pilot are all loyal to me. Chief Coretti knows better than to discuss my business with anyone."

"Even so, I—"

"Even so nothing— Unlike you, I haven't had the advantage of nine months to think things through while waiting for the arrival of our baby. Once I've spent time with you and Ric, I'll be better equipped to know how to deal with Eliana and anticipate her questions. For you to turn around and fly back to Reno in the morning would be a knee-jerk reaction that will only complicate our situation."

She still wouldn't look at him. He admired her for wanting to protect Eliana, but the baby was a fact of life. While they'd clung together in the claustrophobic darkness, he'd made her pregnant. Little Ric was their creation. Despite the fallout when the news surfaced, the knowledge filled him with a wonder and excitement he'd never known before.

He darted her a glance. "The remarkable woman I was buried with wouldn't begrudge me those privileges. Has she changed so much in eleven months?"

That brought her head up. "But you're not prepared for a baby."

"Is anyone? If you're talking about his physical needs, you've brought everything he requires with you for the moment. Whatever is missing, I'll take care of it. With one phone call, a crib and bedding can be delivered."

"I don't know, Ric." She still wasn't convinced.

"Don't tell me you're uncomfortable with me, not after everything we've been through?"

A faint flush filled her cheeks. "No. Of course not."

"Then there's nothing to stop you from agreeing to come with me. I'll have one of my men check you out of the hotel."

She eyed him in confusion. "Who are they exactly?"

"My bodyguards."

"I remember you telling me you were in shipping. What I don't understand is why you would need that kind of protection."

"I'll explain later."

"But you're not ready for guests," she argued, "especially not an infant."

"Guests?" he exploded. "Ric's my son, and you're his mother. That puts you in an entirely different category from anyone else in the world. Would you rather I stayed here with you for the next week?"

"You mean at the hotel?"

He heard panic in her voice and realized with satisfaction that she wasn't any more indifferent to him than he was to her. "I mean in this room. After all you've gone through to find my father, do you honestly think I'd budge from here without you?"

"I thought you had vital business on Cyprus," she said quietly.

"My son is the only business more vital. I thought I'd made myself clear. But keep in mind that on the island you'll have your own bedroom with the Mediterranean only steps outside your suite. We'll set up a crib next to you where you and Ric can live in total comfort. But we can stay right here if that's your wish. The decision is up to you."

She pressed her lips together, further evidence she didn't like either option. "When were you going to leave?"

"Two hours ago. A limo is parked for me in front of the hotel."

He waited while she mulled everything over in her mind. "I'm frightened," she finally whispered.

"The woman who sought help from Genoa's chief of police to find Ric's grandfather was a warrior. It pleases me more than you know to realize my son has inherited that trait from you."

"You don't know that," she answered shakily.

Ric shifted his weight. "What do you think are the chances of a fetus to survive what you lived through both emotionally and physically?"

Her haunted gaze collided with his, giving him his answer. "If you'll get your things together, I'll take them down. It's a few hours' flight to Paphos. Once we're in the air, we'll have dinner. I don't know about you, but I'm famished."

She looked at the baby, then glanced back at him. "If you're sure about this," she murmured.

"I've never been more sure of anything in my life."

After another long hesitation, she walked over to a closet for her suitcase. With that action, the tautness left his body. He pulled out his cell phone to call his housekeeper in Paphos and give her some instructions. While

he waited for Sami to finish her small amount of packing, he spoke to Carlo and the driver, alerting them to
his plans.

Earlier, on the drive to the hotel from the police station, he'd entertained the thought that his father had in-
dulged in an affair with this woman. No way on earth
could he have known that Christine Argyle would turn
out to be *Sami.* Even more astounding was the knowledge
that the baby he'd heard crying from behind the door was
none other than his own son.

Sami's legs felt shaky. The mixture of shock and hunger
had reduced her to this state. For Ric to be alive didn't
seem possible, yet here he was, this tall, hard-muscled
Italian male who held the baby to his shoulder with one
arm, and carried her suitcase in his other hand.

But he had a fiancée! The news of it flickered off and
on like a giant neon sign. How could she just go along
with him like this knowing he belonged to someone else?
She'd tried to reason with him, but he'd refused to listen to her fears.

"This is heavy," he said in an aside, oblivious to her
state of mind. "What's in here?"

"Baby formula. I had to bring a lot in case of an emergency."

He broke out in laughter, causing people to stare. She
walked alongside him holding the car seat and diaper bag.
For all the world the three of them looked like a married
couple staying at the hotel for the Christmas holiday,

yet the woman he intended to marry was somewhere in Genoa, not knowing what had happened.

Sami's guilt was so overwhelming, she barely noticed that the hotel had been festively decorated for Christmas. All she sensed was Ric's pride as hotel guests and staff alike smiled to see him carrying his baby.

She also saw the envy in the eyes of women young and old who found Ric drop-dead gorgeous. That's what he was. A thrill darted through her to realize their son would grow up to look like him. It was followed by another stab of guilt to be thinking about him like this when he had a fiancée.

When he ushered her through the main doors to the outside, he'd said his car was waiting. But there were no cars parked in front, only three black luxury limousines. The center one had special smoked glass and a hood ornament with a unique gold figure of what looked like an ancient seaman.

Two of Ric's bodyguards opened the doors to help her inside and deal with the luggage, including securing the car seat into place, with little Ric firmly settled into it. Their deference to him caused her to stare into his inky-black eyes once they were seated across from each other. The limo started moving. "Ric? What's going on?"

"We're heading to the airport." His deep voice oozed through her body, kindling her senses without her volition.

"But in *this*?"

"You're not comfortable?" Behind his hooded gaze she thought he might be smiling in amusement.

"That question doesn't deserve an answer. Why did the driver address you as Excellency? I may not understand Italian, but I heard him distinctly, so don't tell me I mis-understood. Are you an important government official?"

He kissed the top of the baby's head. Ric was still sound asleep. "My business is shipping, remember?"

She expelled the breath she'd been holding. "You do a great deal more than that! Who are you? Please tell me the truth." He could be a terrible tease, something she hadn't expected. Though they'd shared the most intimate experience between two people, she knew next to noth-ing about him…except the most important thing.

He was a man of character who'd welcomed his son without hesitation, even though he was engaged to be married. How many men would do that?

"I'm Alberto Enrico Degenoli the thirteenth."

"All of your predecessors had the same name?"

"Yes."

She made a sound that came out more like a squeal. "That's very interesting, but I know you haven't told me everything. When we were buried, you never said a word about any of this."

One black brow lifted. "You never mentioned you were a student or where you were enrolled. If you'd told me, I could have found you months ago."

If by those words he meant that their lives might be different, it was too late now! Her body trembled. "If you recall, we decided we shouldn't talk much."

"True. Instead we communicated in a more funda-mental way under the most death-defying circumstances.

I believe making love in total blackness added a thrilling element that increased our pleasure, thus producing our son."

With those words, the memory of what had transpired caused her body to break out in feverish heat.

"One day," Ric continued, "he'll be indebted to us for giving him life against those odds, don't you agree? I know I'll be undyingly grateful to you for taking such meticulous care of him in my absence, Sami."

Though she was warmed by his compliment, the implication that his absence was now over rocked her to the core. She'd heard the steel behind it. Chief Coretti had jumped the moment Ric had suggested he leave the room. His own office! Come to think of it, the police chief had been able to locate Ric immediately. On the verge of asking him one more time who he really was, Sami was distracted by the limo coming to a stop.

"We've arrived," he murmured. On cue the doors opened for them.

She climbed out to see a gleaming green-and-white private jet with the word "Degenoli" printed in gold on the side with a logo of a mariner beneath it. Before she knew it, one of his staff escorted her to the jet with her luggage. She started up the steps with Ric right behind her holding the baby.

The steward showed her to one of the posh white leather seats in the club compartment. Ric strapped the car seat into the seat between them, then settled the baby, who'd fallen asleep again. As soon as she sat down, the

Fasten Seatbelts sign flashed on. Soon the engines started up and the jet began to taxi out to the runway.

Though she knew she wasn't living in a dream, the revelations of this day were still unreal to her. When she really thought about her and Ric being alone together again for a whole week, her body shivered with a barrage of new sensations.

She should have phoned Pat in Reno to tell her everything, but Ric was like a force of nature. Everything had happened too fast. Now wasn't the time to get into a conversation with her sister while Ric sat nearby, able to listen. But when they landed in Paphos and got settled, she'd make the call.

Pat was in for the biggest surprise of her life. She would have fits when she heard Ric had a fiancée who still didn't know about the baby.

When the jet reached cruising speed and the seatbelt light went off, the steward served them a delicious pasta and chicken dinner accompanied by a sweet white wine. After Sami took a sip, Ric eyed her intently. "I take it you aren't nursing."

Sami put the glass down. "I tried it, but my milk jaundiced him, so the pediatrician told me to put him on formula. He loves it at room temperature and has been a good eater from the beginning."

His gaze wandered back to the baby. "I noticed he drank every drop of his bottle back at the hotel. I'm eager to feed him when he wakes up again."

Little Ric must have heard his father's voice because it wasn't a minute before he opened his eyes and started making sounds. That was all Ric needed to release the baby from the seat and nestle him in his arms.

Having finished her dinner, Sami got up and searched in the diaper bag for a new bottle of formula and a clean burping cloth. "It sounds like you're hungry again, sweetheart." She leaned over to kiss his cheeks before handing Ric the bottle. "Just put it in his mouth and he'll do the rest." On that note she placed the toweling cloth over his right shoulder, then sat down again.

Ric laughed as he played with the baby before feeding him. When the steward came in, Ric lifted his son for the other man to look at. They both smiled and spoke in Italian before he took away their dishes.

Sami could see Ric was a natural at being a father. She was the slightest bit jealous their baby seemed content for his daddy to do the honors, but it also touched her heart. Little Ric was wrapped up in his silky blue baby quilt with the white lace around the edge. He made a beautiful picture against his father's tan jacket.

No doubt he wore a custom-made suit produced for him by a famous Italian designer. When they'd clung to each other in the darkness, he'd been wearing a shirt. But whoever said that clothes made the man hadn't met Ric.

Whether in the light or the dark, *he* made the man.

Stop thinking about him like this, Sami. He was about to be someone else's husband.

She felt his eyes flick to hers. "Our son is perfect."

Sami had been thinking the same thing about Ric. Out of all the men in the entire world, how had she happened to be caught in the same avalanche with *him?* "He reminds me of a baby prince in one of my old books of fairy tales."

"Not a prince," Ric corrected her before kissing his son on the cheek. "A count."

She blinked.

"The first Alberto Enrico Degenoli went to sea and amassed a fortune he brought back to Genoa. For that, the ruling power made him a count. Through various ventures in shipping, that fortune grew over the years. Our family history dates back to the thirteenth century."

Sami hadn't thought she could be shocked a second time in one day. Now, when she thought about it, the gold seaman ornament on the hood of the limousine made sense, but too many revelations in just a few hours had her reeling.

Her hands gripped the sides of the chair. Ric was literally Count Degenoli. In a few more weeks his fiancée would be *Countess* Degenoli. Good heavens!

"When you had the baby, you didn't realize you'd given birth to Alberto Enrico Degenoli the Fourteenth. He's my firstborn son. By rights he should be the next count after me."

Sami understood what he meant. That honor would go to the son he and Eliana would produce. Little Ric could never be the next count because he was the *illegitimate* son.

"After my father died, the title passed to me," Ric continued in a conversational tone, "but the title means nothing in this day and age, so forget it, Sami. To his friends, our son will be Ric Argyle Degenoli."

The ramifications of what all this meant made it hard for her to swallow. "Ric—I'm not naive. Knowing you're a count means your engagement is of public importance. Any move on your part will produce a ripple effect with serious consequences."

"You're right, but you agreed to come with me, so no one else knows yet. Later on we'll talk everything over. For the present I intend to enjoy this time with you and our son. Can you let your reservations go that long?"

Some nuance in his tone got to her. Sami bowed her head, attempting to come to grips with this latest revelation. She didn't know if she could do what he asked. But when she tried to put herself in his shoes, she could understand why he needed emotional time away from responsibilities and duties to deal with being a brand-new father.

"There's no precedent for what has happened to us," she admitted at last. "I'm sorry to keep fighting you on it. You're right for reminding me I had the whole pregnancy to realize I was going to be a mother. You only found out this afternoon that you're a father. I'll try to control my anxiety for a few days."

In the silence that followed, he leaned forward and put his hand over hers. She felt heat travel up her arm and through her body. "That sounded like the woman who helped me get through those first horrifying moments when we figured our time was up."

Tears filled her eyes. "I'm so glad it wasn't— Ric's the sweetest, most wonderful thing that ever happened to me."

"We did good work, didn't we?" he said in a husky voice before lifting his hand from hers.

She half laughed. "Yes. My family and friends go crazy over him." Pat had said more than once that the baby's father had to be some kind of Italian god to have produced a child as handsome as Ricky. As Sami eyed Ric covertly, she thought she could tell her sister that Ric was more sensational than any statue. She had to remember that soon he'd be another woman's husband.

"Tell me something. Are you rich?" she teased with a smile.

He kissed the top of Ric's head. "That depends on one's definition."

With a gloomy answer like that, he'd sidestepped the issue. Their son had a father like none other. "Is Eliana's family rich?"

A shadow crossed over his attractive face. "Yes."

Suddenly Ric did a loud burp and they both laughed hard. She was glad to see his father's frown had disappeared. There was nothing like a baby to reduce everything else to the unimportant.

"Forgive me for being curious. I've never known a count before."

"I don't like to be reminded of it, Sami. It's meaningless."

She rolled her eyes. "Not to the men who called you Excellency."

He grimaced. "Old habits die hard."

"I'm glad you told me how you feel. I'll never make

the mistake of calling you count. It will be up to you to tell Ric one day."

Sami heard his sharp intake of breath. "Since you're his mother, I'm going to let you in on a secret no one knows about yet. After my father died, I took the steps to have the title officially abolished. I made it legally binding so that it can never be bestowed on anyone else again, which means Ric's life is going to be free and his children after him."

She studied him anxiously. "Has it been such a burden?"

He flashed her a bleak glance. "You'll never know."

"Tell me about it." *Help me get my mind off the woman you love.*

"The title is always bestowed on the first male heir. It was all I heard about from the moment I can first remember. All the attention was focused on me—my education, my social life, my duties, my future wife. But my siblings were ignored.

"Vito and Claudia were fixtures in the background of our lives. My brother became a shell of himself with no confidence or sense of accomplishment. Claudia was a girl and virtually forgotten in the scheme of things.

"Every time I received an honor from my father, I flinched inside, knowing my brother and sister were left behind and in some cases forgotten."

"How awful," Sami whispered.

"You have no idea. It sickened me and I swore that the day I became count, I'd have the whole reign of terror obliterated. That day came after we buried our father."

Sami thought long and hard about what he'd just told her. Titles were still de rigeur in certain societies, but apparently Ric abhorred the whole idea of them so much, he'd taken steps to rid himself of his title. That took an unusual man with the strength of his own convictions. She admired him more than he would ever know.

His siblings wouldn't have believed at first that he could do such an extraordinary thing, but since he was still the count, he had the right to do as he pleased.

Sami had to admit the title had a certain ring. She secretly treasured the knowledge that when they'd made love, another Count Degenoli had been conceived. A very little one. For the short time left, she could fantasize about how romantic it all sounded.

But that was shameful of her when she knew how diabolical the system clearly was in Ric's eyes. Since the drive to the airport, Sami had felt as though she was living in a fairy tale; she was the young maid—being spirited away by the handsome prince to live in his castle. But there were two important caveats to this tale.

By Christmas Eve the spell would be broken and Sami and her baby would return to Nevada to get on with the rest of their lives. By New Year's Day, Ric would be married.

She sat up straighter in the chair. "What do you think Eliana will say when she finds out your title is gone?"

His answer wasn't a long time in coming. "She'll have to handle it. That's what she's been raised to do."

"Not if it wasn't her dream." For no good reason, her

heart rate accelerated. "When are you planning to let her know?"

"As soon as I receive word. I expected to hear a week ago, but the courts are slower here than in the States."

"I didn't know that was possible."

Another chuckle escaped his throat. "It's my Christmas present to myself, but your gift trumps anything I could have conceived of in this world or the next."

"You can think of Ric as your Christmas baby."

"*Our* baby," he corrected in a thick-toned voice before switching him to his other shoulder. She could see he was totally enamored by his son. Sami could relate. "I believe our little *bimbo* is sleepy."

"Bimbo?"

"It's another Italian endearment."

"That's sweet," she murmured. "He's easy right now because all he basically does is eat and sleep. In another month everything will change."

Ric nuzzled the baby's neck. "Did you hear that, *figlio mio?* How about we change your diaper before you sign out again?"

Sami chuckled as she laid everything out for him. "I know the diaper looks tiny, but it does the job." They smiled at each other before he got down to business. After a little too much powder, and a couple of tries to attach the tapes right, he'd managed to change their son's diaper. "Bravo," she exclaimed.

He picked up the baby and eyed her over his head. "I'll do better next time."

"I can't tell you the number of times I put the diaper on the wrong way. Ric was so patient."

By tacit agreement they both sat down with Ric hugging the baby to his chest. "Tell me about the delivery. Were you in labor long?"

"About eighteen hours."

His eyes grew serious. "Were you alone?"

"No. My sister and her husband took turns staying with me. I owe them everything."

His jaw hardened. "I should have been there. Did you know you were going to have a son ahead of time?"

Her lips curved. "Oh, yes. I called him Ric the second the technician handed me the ultrasound pictures. She told me I had a boy in there and everything looked great. I'll admit I wished you'd been in the room to hear the news with me. While I lay there, I had this fanciful notion that maybe you were watching from above or somehow knew, and I hoped it would make you happy."

"I think you know exactly how I felt when you handed me his birth certificate. It was the supreme moment of my life." The throb in his voice gave evidence how deeply his emotions were involved.

"Ric? Tell me the truth. Was the reason you looked for me because you wanted to know if you'd made me pregnant?"

His gaze wandered over her. "No. To be honest, I was afraid you might have died in the hospital you were taken to. You could have lost consciousness the way I did and never come to. I had to be sure."

"Why?"

"Because if you were alive, I wanted to meet you face-to-face. I wanted to understand why two strangers could connect the way we did. I thought if we talked, maybe I'd get answers to questions that have plagued me ever since."

She made an assenting sound. "I have the same questions, but am no nearer to an explanation. For us, it wasn't a physical attraction in the literal sense of the word. Maybe you'll think I'm crazy, but the only way I can describe it is that our spirits spoke to each other."

"Or recognized each other on some other level?" he inserted.

"Yes, as if we were bidding each other a final farewell which we did with…our bodies."

"I've had the same thoughts, Sami. They're not crazy."

"I'm glad you feel that way because I've gone over and over it in my mind and it's the only conclusion that makes sense." She stirred restlessly. "When I first got back to Oakland, I felt so empty inside. I knew you'd died and I felt this great loss. It alarmed me. It wasn't just the fact that we'd made love. What we did wasn't for the normal reasons. I mean—"

"I know what you mean." He read her mind with ease.

"While we were trapped, I'd assumed we would die. The thought of getting pregnant never entered my consciousness."

"Nor mine," he murmured. "The thought of using protection was the furthest thing from my mind."

"All we knew was that we were facing the end."

"But during those hours, I felt I'd lived a lifetime."

He'd taken the words right out of her mouth. "When I was released from the hospital, at first I thought what I was feeling had to be sadness over the way my father had died. But after a time, I still had that same heaviness. No matter how deeply I searched for the source of it, *you* were always at the bottom of it."

"That's how it was for me, too," she volunteered. "Matt thought I was having some symptoms of post-traumatic stress disorder because of the avalanche. He knew I'd been trapped with you, but I didn't tell him everything at first. I was hoping I'd pull out of whatever was going on inside me. Then I found out I was pregnant."

She glanced at their baby sleeping so trustingly on Ric's chest. "Maybe I shouldn't have been overjoyed by the news, but I was. Of course I had to tell Matt everything. But he never truly understood." After a pause she said, "I can promise you now—Eliana won't understand either."

"No. And once she learns the truth and meets you, she'll assume you're the reason why the physical side of our relationship has been unsatisfactory."

Sami squirmed in her seat. "I shouldn't have come to Genoa."

"You know you don't mean that."

No. She didn't… "For you to be engaged, I'm sure your love can weather anything."

"Sami—I'm not in love with Eliana."

What?

"We're marrying to secure the financial welfare of our two families. Don't get me wrong, Eliana has many admirable qualities and I care for her, but I don't love her. Unfortunately, when I asked her to marry me, I didn't know the 'for worse' part of the ceremony would precede taking our vows."

Sami stirred restlessly. Maybe he didn't love Eliana, but she couldn't imagine Eliana not being head over heels in love with him. What woman wouldn't love him? The knowledge of a baby would tear his fiancée to pieces. Sami was about to question him further when the Fasten Seatbelts sign flashed on. "We're in Cyprus already?"

Ric was on his feet in an instant to secure the baby for the descent. "I told you it's not a long flight. When we step off the plane, you'll notice a difference in the temperature. Whenever I breathe that air, it reminds me of my youth and carefree days. Do you know I haven't taken a real vacation here in a long time?"

"Not even with your fiancée?"

"She's never been here. Eliana's not fond of the water. But now that you're with me, I'm ready for one."

"But you've come on business."

"I'm capable of doing both."

CHAPTER FOUR

SAMI had barely paused for breath since meeting Ric again. Who would have thought a few short hours could have changed so much in her life? Now she and little Ric had flown on Count Degenoli's private jet to an exotic island in the Mediterranean. Whether right or wrong, she was too physically and emotionally exhausted to think about the wisdom of her decision to come with him. Tomorrow would be soon enough to face the consequences of her actions.

The drive from Paphos airport hadn't taken long before the car entered a flower-lined private estate isolated on a point overlooking the water. Within ten minutes Ric was showing Sami through a fabulous, white, two-story Grecian villa. The colorful Mediterranean furnishings against white walls caught her eye everywhere she looked.

A cushion of blue here, an urn of yellow with an exotic plant there, an unexpected Greek icon in predominantly red and gold colors around the corner. So many choice armoires and tables placed around on tiled floors with a definite flair revealed a luxurious treasure trove.

Beyond the villa was the sight of the water through the window and doorways. Ric's second home was paradise. Sami could only imagine the elegance of his first home.

She marveled that his staff had managed to buy a crib so fast and have it set up in one of the guest rooms on the second floor. Besides fresh flowers, they'd provided everything needed to make her and the baby comfortable. To her delight each room of the villa contained a charming Christmas crèche surrounded by lighted candles. Ric explained that Christmas trees weren't amongst their local traditions.

He introduced her to Mara and Daimon, an older couple, probably in their sixties. He told her they'd been living here taking care of the villa and grounds for years. They'd worked for Ric's mother's family and spoke good English.

When Ric showed them the baby, the dark-haired couple cried out in delight and took turns holding him. Whatever they thought about Ric bringing home a foreign woman and a child, they didn't let it show and honored him like the favorite son he evidently was.

Mara smiled at Sami. "Anything you want, you ask me."

"I will. Thank you."

"The little one is beautiful, like you. He has your mouth."

"You're very kind. I think he looks like his father."

Daimon nodded. "I knew he was a Degenoli the minute I saw him."

"I see Vito in him," Ric inserted.

"A little," Mara said. "He also has Claudia's shell-like ears, but his shape and size and those brilliant black eyes are all yours, Enrico."

Daimon nodded. "He's well named."

Sami glanced at him. "What does it mean?"

"Ruler of the household."

Ric's black orbs kindled with warmth as he studied their son. "For now he's our *piccolo.*"

"There's another word I don't understand."

"It means little one."

"That's a darling endearment for him," she exclaimed, "especially the way you say it in such beautiful soft Italian. Your language has lots of words I love to say, like *ciao* and *cappuccino.*" She'd emphasized the *chee* sound, causing him to chuckle.

Sami noticed an aura had come over him since they'd entered the house, as if he'd dropped his worries outside the door. She couldn't deny he looked happier. In truth he no longer resembled the intimidating male at the police station in the tan silk suit who'd glared at her with barely suppressed hostility the moment she'd walked in.

All of a sudden his gaze swerved to hers with concern. "It's almost midnight. You must be dead on your feet. If there's anything you'd like to eat or drink, Mara will bring it to you before we say goodnight."

She shook her head. "After that meal on the plane, I couldn't, but thank you anyway."

"What you and the baby need is a good sleep after your flight from Genoa." Mara kissed little Ric on the cheek before she and Daimon disappeared to their room at the back of the villa on the main floor.

Sami turned to Ric. "They're wonderful."

"They're like family to me. I trust them with my life. Our baby will be pampered and spoiled while we're here."

"What a lucky little boy. I'll just bathe him and put him down, then get ready for bed."

"I'd like to do the honors if you'll show me how." He led them upstairs to her guest room.

"You're not too exhausted?"

He gave her a speculative look. "I'm so wired, as you Americans say, I don't know when I'll be able to sleep."

She let out a gentle laugh. "Then bring the diaper bag into the bathroom and we'll get started. He loves the water."

"That's because he's a true Degenoli. The first one went to sea and now seawater runs through all our veins." His comment made her chuckle. As for the pride in his voice, it was something to witness.

"We'll have to be careful not to keep him in too long or his fingers will start to look like dried grapes." Ric's burst of laughter rang throughout the villa. "Go ahead and undress him while I fill the sink."

They worked in harmony. When the temperature felt right she said, "Lower him in the water and let him enjoy it."

It tugged at her heart to see the care he took with the baby, who got terribly excited. He wiggled and moved his arms and legs with sheer enjoyment as the water lapped around him. In the middle of so much pleasure, the baby urinated, creating a fountain that had Ric's shoulders shaking with silent laughter.

She couldn't hold back her own giggles. "As you can see, his plumbing works just fine. We'll have to start this again." While Ric held the baby in a towel, she let out the water and put some more in. His little chin quivered from leaving the warmth. He was so adorable. Soon he was lowered back in.

"This is glycerin soap to wash his hair and body. It's gentle. He needs his hair washed. Be sure and get into the creases around his neck and behind his ears where the milk runs."

While he did a pretty masterful job for a beginner, she set out a fresh towel ready to dry the baby.

"He's strong, Sami."

"Of course. He's what we Americans call a 'chip off the old block.' Not that you're an old block, but you know what I mean."

His eyes glinted as they shared a silent look of mutual understanding. This time he powdered his son just the right amount and diapered him without any problem. Sami got out a yellow stretchy suit. Ric fitted him into it and fastened the snaps.

"He's almost finished." She handed Ric the little hairbrush. He took it from her and played with the baby's soft hair for a minute.

When he was through, he lifted Ric and turned him to her. "What do you think, *mamma?*"

The use of the Italian version of *mommy* caught her by the throat. Everything felt so natural, she'd forgotten she was a guest in his house. She'd almost forgotten he had a fiancée who had no idea what was going on.

"No one would know you'd only learned you were a father today. He loved his bath with you. I have a feeling he's going to want you to do it all the time. Our baby likes the masculine touch, don't you, sweetheart?"

Sami had already gotten past her jealousy into an area where she was enjoying this way too much. Judging from the emotion streaming from Ric's eyes, he had the same problem. However it was one thing to bathe the baby with Sami looking on, and quite another to imagine Eliana helping him after they were married. Pain filled her chest at the thought of it.

Little Ric was so loveable, but it would take a super-human woman to love him when she hadn't given birth to him. Eliana's resentment toward Sami would always be there because she wasn't the mother of Ric's firstborn child, count or no count. It would boil beneath the surface and the baby would pick up on the tension.

Over the years Sami had met women who were making successes of their second marriages. But it was a struggle combining two families to form a new one. Sami's situation couldn't be compared to theirs. For one thing, she and Ric had been strangers, not husband and wife.

For another, Eliana hadn't had children yet. Her whole life had been lived in preparation for marriage to an aristocrat, a marriage in which the bearing of children was bound to be of the greatest importance, especially the first one. Ric might not want to be Count Degenoli, but

Sami knew in her heart it was part of who he was. Eliana was in for a double shock when she heard the title had been abolished. Sami felt horribly sorry for her.

Deep in thought, she handed Ric a fresh bottle of formula. "While you feed him, I'll clean up the bathroom and take a shower before bed."

Ric stood where he was, snuggling the baby, who was looking for his bottle. "Where did you go just now?" His voice may have been quiet, but she heard the demand in it.

Maybe it was a case of both of them having an extra dose of ESP in their makeup. He was keyed in to her thoughts far too easily.

"I'm pretty sure you know," she answered in a dull tone. "But as you said earlier, let's not get into it right now. This is a time to enjoy the baby. Do what you want with him. Since your room is across the hall from this one, you'll probably hear him cry in the night. If you want to feed him, feel free to come in my bedroom and get a new bottle out of the diaper bag. I'll leave the door open."

His veiled eyes played over her features until her legs shook. "Sleep well, Sami," he murmured before leaving the bathroom with the baby. She shut the door after him and leaned against it, waiting for the weakness to pass. To her alarm, it never did.

Ric had only seen Sami in her suit and blouse. When she walked into the breakfast room at ten the next morning dressed in jeans and a chocolate-colored top, he caught himself staring. Slowly his gaze dropped from her green-eyed blond beauty to the gorgeous mold of her body. His intimate knowledge of her eleven months ago would always be fresh in his mind, and made the visual reaction to her now a hundred times stronger, forcing him to look away.

"Well, look at you two!" She made a nosedive for the baby, who was lying in the carrycot Ric had set on the breakfast table so he could play with him.

"I just fed him his morning bottle, but he hasn't fallen asleep yet. It's giving us time to get better acquainted."

She came around to kiss the baby's face. "Are you having fun with your daddy? Is he already reading the newspaper to you while he enjoys his coffee? If he could talk, he'd probably be calling you *Daddy*. How do you say it in Italian?"

"Papa."

"That's what Pat and I called our grandfather!"

Her enthusiasm caused the baby to grow more animated and made Ric smile. While he watched her poke his son's tummy gently, he inhaled her peach fragrance. She'd just come from the shower. It took all the willpower he possessed not to grab hold of her womanly hips and pull her down on his lap.

"He loves mornings and usually stays awake for a while," she chatted. "No doubt being with you has stimulated him so much, he might not close his eyes till much later." She glanced at Ric. "Has he been good?"

"I think you already know the answer to that question."

She looked away first and sat down on one of the

chairs opposite him. He got the impression she was nervous about getting too close to him. How ironic after what they'd experienced in Austria. "I didn't hear him cry in the night."

"You were exhausted. When I saw you lying there, I realized you'd had the whole care of our son these last two months and no one to wait on you or give you relief."

"I could never complain. Having a baby has been the joy of my life."

"Not all women feel that way," he muttered. Sami was so hands-on with little Ric, he couldn't help but wonder what kind of a mother Eliana would be.

"Do you and your fiancée plan to have children?"

"Definitely. It's what I've been looking forward to most."

"Some men don't want to be fathers."

Ric knew a few like that, but his own father fitted into a different category. He'd wanted an heir, but didn't want to do the fathering that should have gone on. As Ric played with his baby's toes, he realized his father had been the loser on every count.

His mind wandered to Sami. What if this ex-boyfriend Matt stayed so persistent, she ended up marrying him? What kind of a stepfather would he be to little Ric? More and more he didn't like the idea of it.

"Did you get up with him?" she asked.

Her question jerked him out of his dark thoughts. "I did. Around four I thought I heard him fussing. He needed a complete diaper change."

Sami grinned. "Uh-oh. How did your first solo experience go?"

"We made it through, didn't we, *piccolo?*" The baby's tiny fingers still clung to his little finger. They were the same shape as his. He realized no force on earth was as strong as the pull of that miniature hand on his heart. Ric found he didn't want his son to hold on to any other man's finger but his. Until now he hadn't understood how possessive he'd already become over what was his by fatherly right.

Mara walked into the room to refresh Ric's coffee. "Good morning, Sami. Now that you're up, I'll serve breakfast. Coffee for you, too?"

"Just juice if you have some. Please don't go to any trouble."

"How could you be trouble?" she cried. "You won't let me do anything for you, and the *bambino* never cries. I've been waiting for the excuse to hold him!"

"Don't worry," Sami said. "Before long you'll hear him loud and clear. You have my permission to grab him. Just remember his cries can be quite terrifying."

The housekeeper laughed before going out of the room.

"She likes you, Sami."

"That's because she loves you, and therefore loves your son, who I must admit is irresistible."

So is Sami. The unexpected things she said and did had the alarming ability to charm him. Maybe that's why he'd found himself making love to her in the blackness of the avalanche.

At the time he hadn't thought of what she might look like. She was young and afraid, and all he knew was gratitude that he didn't have to die alone. They'd needed each other and taken comfort from each other before they'd both lost consciousness.

It wasn't until he awoke in the hospital and remembered everything that he wanted to find her, talk to her. He was naturally curious to see what the woman looked like who'd helped save his sanity. But it never occurred to him she would be so physically appealing.

When she'd walked into Chief Coretti's office yesterday, he'd found himself attracted to the blond stranger beyond a normal interest in a good-looking woman. Ric had known and been with a number of beautiful women in his life, his fiancée being one of them. But this attraction was different.

The fact that she'd instigated the meeting with the police chief while being so secretive about his father should have been a total turnoff for Ric, but the opposite had held true. She had that spark not given to many people.

As they sat there at the breakfast table, Ric realized the chemistry he felt for her was growing stronger, something that wasn't supposed to happen. Bringing her to Cyprus might have been a mistake after all.

He still needed to phone Eliana, but had been putting it off. Once he heard his fiancée's voice, the magic of this time with Sami and his infant son would evaporate. He wasn't ready for that yet.

Already the baby was his whole life. It had happened the instant he'd walked over to the crib in the hotel room and had seen him lying there so small and helpless. The Degenoli likeness had only increased his wonder.

While he was immersed in thought, Mara had served them. By the time they'd eaten, he'd come up with a plan to stay busy. It would prevent him from thinking too much. Ric refused to think right now and wanted simply to relish this fleeting time.

"Sami? How would you like to take a boat ride in the cabin cruiser?"

"That sounds wonderful!"

"Good. You'll be able to see Paphos from the water. The sea is calm and the air is getting warmer by the minute. Ric will love it. We have swimming costumes and wetsuits on board for your enjoyment. We'll take Daimon and Mara with us."

She lowered her glass. "Did you hear that, sweetheart? We're going on an adventure. We'll have to dress you in your little green sweater and overalls."

Just like that, she'd gone along with Ric without voicing a reservation. Her eagerness to fall in with his plan could mean several things. If she'd wanted a distraction to push her fears away, then he'd just provided an outlet. But if she was nervous being around him for any length of time because she found herself attracted to him, too, he was curious to find out, even though it was the last thing he should be thinking about.

He phoned Daimon and asked him and Mara to join them, then he carried Ric upstairs into her bedroom to get him dressed. Afterward he went to his room and slipped on his bathing trunks and a T-shirt.

Between them, they gathered everything they'd need and headed out of the house for the boat dock. While she held Ric, he found life preservers for all of them. After putting them on, they climbed in. Daimon helped push off before joining Mara at the back of the boat.

Ric's cruiser had a galley and a roof. Both provided shelter for the baby. To his satisfaction Sami sat next to him on the padded bench while he took the wheel. Once he undid the ropes, he idled out to the buoy, then opened up the throttle and they whizzed through the peaceful blue water. Ric kept looking at his son who was wide-awake.

"Do you think he likes it?" he asked her.

Sami smiled at him. "You're asking me when he already has seawater running through his veins?" Ric's white smile turned her heart over. "I'm sure the sound and the vibration have him enthralled."

"How about you?"

"I adore the water, but it's been a long time. This is pure luxury. I've been to Europe several times with Pat and her husband, but never this far south. Cyprus is beautiful."

"It's full of history." He pointed to the city in the distance. "This is the new Paphos. My mother's family home is there."

"Who lives there now?"

"My uncle and his family. It may interest you to know there's an old city there, too. It dates back three thousand years to the Mycenaean period. One of the big attractions is the Temple of Aphrodite."

"The Greek myths! We had to study them in my high-school English class. I loved them. But *you* grew up with them. What a playground you've had here and in Genoa. As I told you before, my grandparents raised Pat and me. Growing up in Oakland we had a view of San Francisco Bay, but here the sea is at your doorstep."

"I confess I love being able to walk out of my house to the water."

"Who wouldn't?" Her voice trailed.

"Tell me what happened to your parents?"

"They were on the freeway driving home when an earthquake hit. We were little girls and don't remember them, but our grandparents kept them alive for us."

"I'm sorry for your loss. Tell me about them." He cut the engine before turning to her.

"Dad was a chemical engineer and Mom stayed home to raise us. I grew up thinking I'd like to follow in his footsteps, but discovered I like computers, too. A year ago last fall I started graduate school to become a computer engineer. If there's been any one thing lacking in my life, it's been the loss of parents I never knew.

"Growing up I envied my friends who had moms and dads. Don't get me wrong. I adored my grandparents, but in a just world, nothing takes the place of a loving, caring parent."

"*Loving* and *caring* being the operative words," Ric mused aloud. More than ever he was determined to be there for his son no matter the obstacles.

He rubbed the side of his jaw. "When you first mentioned your studies, I assumed you were talking about your undergraduate studies. I'm impressed you're pursuing your career while being an exceptional mother at the same time. You have fire in you, Sami, a very rare thing."

She broke into an unguarded smile. "Flattery will get you everywhere."

"It's the truth," he came back. "What brought you to Europe that last time?"

"During the winter break in January, Pat gave me a free pass for a short trip to Innsbruck. I knew if I didn't go, I wouldn't get another vacation for a long time and I'd just broken up with Matt. She wanted me to check out several hotels in the area and give them feedback. They send a lot of ski-tour groups to Austria.

"On the day of the avalanche, I'd taken the train on a side trip to see some of the villages. While I was in Imst, I stopped at the hotel to check it out and wait for the storm to pass." She paused for a minute. "You know the rest."

He watched her through veiled eyes. "While you were waiting, I'd just left my father's room. He felt like a nap, so I decided I'd walk around the village to stretch my legs. After grabbing my jacket from my room, I headed for the stairs to go down to the lobby.

"Before I had a chance to put the jacket on, it felt like a bomb had gone off in the hotel. The next thing I knew, I was trapped in the darkness. I heard someone moaning and was grateful I wasn't alone. That person turned out to be *you*. The chances of our coming together on that day, at the moment, are astronomical, Sami."

"I know."

"It seems I have your sister to thank for our baby's existence. Have you told her you found Alberto Degenoli?"

She broke eye contact. "Yes. I was on the phone with her before I came in to breakfast."

"What was her reaction?"

Sami's head reared. "What you'd expect. Shock and shock."

"Did you tell her everything?"

"Yes."

"And of course she doesn't approve of you being here with me."

"No, but she's a mother, too, and knows Bruce loves their children desperately. In that regard she understands you and I are in a very precarious situation with no precedent."

"So she didn't give you advice?"

"No."

"I like her already."

"You'd love her. She's selfless…like you."

"Before you give me credit, remember I have yet to tell Eliana anything. My own siblings would call me a selfish swine for putting off the inevitable while I enjoy my son in private."

"They aren't in your shoes. I understand that now." After fighting him about coming here, her defense of him came as a gratifying surprise to him. She looked around them. "Why are all those boats out there?"

"People are scuba diving. Below them is the wreck of *Dhimitrios*. This is a popular area of the island."

She eyed him curiously. "Do you dive?"

"I did a lot in my youth. What about you?"

"No scuba. I've done some snorkeling and surfing in the summer in Carmel, but Matt's the expert."

Matt again. "Why don't we take a dip? Mara and Daimon will watch Ric. You'll find a locker below with all the swim gear including my sister, Claudia's, wetsuit if you need one. There should be flippers in there, too."

"Does your fiancée dive?"

"No. She's a horsewoman at heart. When I can get away, we go riding on their estate, but I must admit I prefer water sports. What about you?"

"I'm a jack of all trades, but excel at none."

"None?"

"Maybe table tennis."

He squinted at her. "Let's find out what kind of a swimmer you are."

"You're on. I'll be up as soon as I change."

After she kissed the baby and went below, he walked back to talk to his staff, who were clearly delighted to have charge of Ric for a while. Sami resurfaced faster than he would have supposed, wearing a wetsuit that hugged her body, revealing the lines and curves he'd memorized long ago. Desire for her overwhelmed him.

She sat on the end of the bench to put on the flippers. Trying to look at anything but her shapely legs was an impossibility. "I'm ready whenever you are."

Excited, Ric discarded his T-shirt. "Let's go." He helped her over to the side of the boat so she could jump in. He went in behind her. When her wet head appeared, he thought he'd never seen anyone so naturally alluring.

"We'll swim to that big rock. It's not far, but if you get tired, let me know and Daimon will bring the boat along. The sea gets rougher there."

Sami was glad they'd started swimming. In the boat she'd noticed his long powerful legs stretched out in front of him while they'd talked. The gorgeous sight of him almost made her lose her train of thought.

He paced his strokes so they stayed abreast of each other. The flippers gave her the momentum she needed to keep up. The closer they got to the rock, the bigger the swells became. When they were quite near, she could appreciate the beauty of the setting sun against the stunning blue of the sea.

Ric reached the rock first and caught her hand to pull her in so she could cling to it. "What is this place?" She was a little out of breath, but that had a lot to do with him being shirtless. His well-developed body made her mouth go dry. She'd had the same reaction when they'd been trapped. Without seeing him, she'd felt him and knew he was exceptional in many ways.

"The Goddess Aphrodite's birthplace. She was born out of the foam breaking on this rock. If you wore your blond hair long and flowing, you'd personify my own image of her."

Even though her heart was thudding, she laughed and threw her head back. "Oh—you Italian men are priceless."

"I'm half Cypriot," he declared, "raised on the stories of Zeus. Afraid her beauty would create jealousy among the other gods and cause war, he married her to Hephaestus."

Her smile deepened. "I know that story, too. But to his chagrin she was unfaithful to her husband and had many lovers."

One of them was the young god Adonis. With his wavy black hair and olive skin warmed by the sun, Ric could be a more adult version of him. However, she'd never seen Adonis depicted with hair on his chest. She decided she didn't dare tell Ric her thoughts to his face. He was engaged to be married. *Remember?*

"She had many children as a result," Ric teased.

A chuckle broke from her. "I've just had one. I'm afraid he's all I can handle."

Ric's black eyes grew shuttered. "Our baby's so perfect, he would make the gods jealous." The tone of his voice gave her gooseflesh.

"Then let's be thankful Zeus doesn't exist." It was frightening enough that Eliana didn't know about the baby. Sami feared her reaction when confronted with Ric's child.

Sami shouldn't be out here alone with him like this. Much too aware of him, she looked around her, noticing the pebbled beach in the distance. "It's all so natural here. Nothing's spoiled it."

"Perhaps not right now, but later you'll see tourists come here to the café above the beach. They believe these waters have mystical powers to soothe the troubled soul. You'll notice them clustering in the evenings to watch the sunset. That's the beauty of arriving by boat. When we want, we can slip back out to sea away from everyone else to witness the sun falling into the sea."

She believed that growing up in these waters had cultivated a poetic side to him. "Are you telling me you're a loner?"

"Sometimes. With the right person, you don't need anyone else," he said in a remote tone.

He'd said he wasn't in love with his fiancée. Maybe he was missing some woman from his past who'd been important to him. Sami had no idea. "Thank you for bringing me to this famous spot. How lucky am I? When I came to Italy, I couldn't have conceived of being at Aphrodite's birthplace two days later."

"Then you can imagine my incredulity that the woman I was trapped with is holding on to this rock with me."

She averted her eyes. "I think we ought to get back to the boat. Even if Ric is fine, I don't want Mara and Daimon worrying about us being gone so long."

"Never fear. My bodyguards are keeping watch."

"From where?" she asked in surprise.

"The shore and that sailboat out there."

Sami hadn't really noticed. Ric's masculine presence dominated everything. "They're very unobtrusive. It must be hard to watch you when you're having fun. I hope you pay them a good salary."

His laughter filled the sea air, mesmerizing her. Their gazes met in shared amusement. "I can't wait to tell them what you said."

She felt her cheeks grow warm. "Are they the same ones you told to follow me from the police station?"

"I'm not sure. They trade off shifts."

"Do you think they're scandalized to see you with someone other than Eliana?"

"Maybe. The only thing important is that they've been told that Ric is our son. They're too busy guarding us with their lives to do much else."

Though the sun was shining, she felt a dark shadow pass over her. "Have you had many threats on your life, Ric?"

"Enough to warrant protection, but I don't want you worrying about it."

"I'm not. I felt perfectly safe with you in the avalanche and feel the same way now."

"I'm relieved to hear it. Shall we go?"

"I'm ready."

"I'll race you back to the boat."

Her brows lifted. "Since you fly through the water like that striped dolphin you pointed out on the way here, what chance do I have?"

His lips twitched. "Those flippers give you an edge."

"Hmm. We'll see." Filled with adrenaline from being this close to him, she shoved off, determined to give him a run for his money even if the water was more difficult to handle. She thought she was doing fine until three-quarters of the way, when she lost power. Weakness had taken over.

Ric took one look and told her to get on his back. "Hold tight to my shoulders."

She obeyed him and let him do all the work. The sensation of swishing through the water on top of him gave her another kind of adrenaline rush. When they reached the ladder to the boat, she let go of him, afraid for him to know how much she'd enjoyed the ride. She'd never thought to be that close to him again.

He turned around. The motion tangled their legs. She let out a tiny gasp.

"Are you all right, Sami?"

"I—I'm fine." What a great liar she'd become.

"I'll remove your flippers so you can climb in."

No... She didn't want him touching her, but it was too late. He worked too fast. Like lightning he eased them off and tossed them in the boat. With no more impediments, Sami was able to heave herself up the rungs. Ric was right behind her. Their limbs brushed as they both got in.

Daimon was there to hand her a towel. "Welcome back. Did you enjoy it?"

"Yes, thank you. It was a wonderful trip, but before I do it again, I need to get in some conditioning. Poor Ric had to save me at the end." It was nothing new. He'd saved her eleven months ago.

"Surely you realize that was no penance?" he whispered near her ear before he headed for the front of the boat to check on their son. She felt the warmth of his breath against her skin in every atom of her body before following him.

Mara sat beneath the roof feeding the baby. She smiled at both of them. "He's been an angel. I hoped you would stay out longer."

"Please keep doing what you're doing. I'm going to run downstairs to shower and change."

"Take all the time you want."

What heaven to have a babysitter like Mara, but Sami didn't dare get used to such luxury.

Once she was out of her wet things, the warm shower felt good. She washed her hair. Afterward she put her jeans and top back on and walked out of the bathroom with a towel. As she started to dry her hair, a pair of strong hands took over.

She'd thought Ric would have stayed upstairs by the baby.

No man had ever dried her hair before. With Ric, she'd experienced all the wondrous aspects of being a woman. She was loving this too much. When she couldn't bear his touch any longer because she wanted more, she took a step back and pulled the towel from his hands. Unable to look him in the eye she said, "Thank you. I can manage now."

He was blocking the way. She suspected it was on purpose. "You were fantastic out swimming," he said in his deep voice. "After having little chance to swim since giving birth to our son, you're in amazing shape. That's no swimming pool out there. I'm impressed."

Sami needed to lighten the moment before she threw herself into his arms. She smoothed the hair out of her eyes. Being by the water had made it curlier. "I think I'm impressed, too." Or at least she had been until her energy had run out.

"I've enjoyed today, Signorina Argyle."

"The feeling's mutual."

"When you're ready, join me in the galley and we'll fix dinner for all of us."

She flicked him a glance. "You like to cook?"

"It's in my blood."

"I thought it was filled with seawater," she quipped.

"It's all part of the same thing." He kissed the end of her nose. "When we've dined to our heart's content, we'll pull up anchor and head back."

CHAPTER FIVE

AFTER eating a Greek smorgasbord of his favorite foods, Ric felt replete and glanced at the baby in his carrycot. He'd finally fallen asleep. Just he and Sami were on deck to watch the sunset. The other two had gone below. The evening was idyllic.

"Sami? I'm curious about something. If you hadn't traveled to Innsbruck, do you think you would have changed your mind about Matt?" The possibility that those two could still get together had been troubling him to the point he had to ask her about it.

"No."

"Yet since the avalanche you've left a door open for him."

She sighed. "Learning of my pregnancy, I realized another little person was going to be totally dependent on me. When I was young, my parents were taken from me. I was sad my baby would also be deprived of a father, so I determined I would be there for my son or daughter every minute.

"But Matt's a great guy and I have no doubts he'd be a great father. Maybe in time I could learn to love him as I should. I'm sure you know what that's like. But if we married, I'm worried he would feel he comes in second best with me because of the baby. That wouldn't be fair to him. He deserves to start out marriage with a woman who doesn't have a history like mine. *No one* has a history like ours, Ric," she half moaned. Her face closed up.

"Maybe I'll change my mind later and get in touch with him. But by then he might have found someone else. I just don't know. For a while longer at least, I've got to find my own way."

Hearing those words, Ric felt as if someone had just walked over his grave. His dream of a week alone with her and the baby had just gone up in smoke. What they were dealing with was too heavy, too serious, for him to live in denial any longer.

"So do I," he ground out. "The air's getting cooler. It's time to go home."

He hoped she would beg him to stay out longer, but she said nothing. With his gut churning, he pressed the button that pulled up the anchor and they headed back to the villa without further conversation.

Eventually they reached the point. By this time Daimon and Mara had come up on deck. As Ric pulled up to the dock, Daimon jumped out to secure the boat with the ropes. Ric helped him. Still hunkered on the pier, he looked down at Sami. She was busy removing the baby's life preserver.

"I've made a decision, Sami." She glanced up at him nervously. "Eliana's waiting for me to call her, but I need your input first before I make that call, because whatever happens from here on out, we're in this together."

Her expression sobered. "In what way?"

"Shall we fly back to Genoa in the morning? Once we're settled in the palazzo, I'll bring her over to meet you and Ric. Or, I can tell her to board her family's jet and fly down here tomorrow afternoon. Which option do you prefer?"

She handed him the baby before climbing onto the pier with the diaper bag. "I'm thankful you've decided to tell her. It's the right thing to do. I think we should face her here where there's no possibility of anyone else being around. As your future wife, she deserves every consideration we can give her. This is going to be very painful for her."

"I agree." Sami's courage and decency made her a remarkable woman.

"She'll be Ric's stepmother," she added. He heard the quiver in her voice. It reached deep inside him. "If it's possible, I want to be friends with her. But I realize that will take time considering the shock she's going to receive."

With those comments he'd just discovered Sami had a goodness in her not found in most people. For their baby to have a mother like her thrilled and humbled him.

"So be it. I'll call her when we go inside and tell her I want her to join me tomorrow evening. I won't indicate the reason until I pick her up at the airport. Until then, I'd like us to enjoy our vacation as long as possible. You'd like to spend time out by the swimming pool tomorrow, wouldn't you, *piccolo?*"

Ric clutched the baby to him, recognizing he only had another twenty-four hours before everything changed.

Sami headed for the villa and went up the stairs to the bedroom where she put the baby down. Ric followed. The baby had fallen fast asleep. After she covered him with a light blanket, she started to rise up and found herself too close to Ric. Instead of moving out of her way, he lifted his hands to her shoulders and kneaded them with increasing restlessness.

His eyes, so black and alive, devoured her features. "If you and I had been taken to the same hospital after the avalanche, we would have been able to get to know each other in the light and hold each other while we thanked providence our lives had been spared. Instead, it's taken all this time for us to finally meet. This is long overdue. After spending today with you, I need to hold you for a minute, Sami, so don't fight me."

He pulled her in to him, not giving her time to answer. The second he buried his face in her hair, she felt his hands rove over her back. Sami moaned and instinctively moved closer to his hard-muscled body. The feel of him, the enticing male scent of him, all were too familiar. The way he touched her and kissed the side of her neck brought déjà vu, sending a river of molten heat through her body. His touch had the power to turn her insides to liquid.

This was like before. She'd could hardly get enough

air then, and she had the same problem now, but not because of being enclosed by tons of snow. This time there was room to stand, and the fragrant air from the flowers growing outside moved through the windows and alcoves of the villa. Once again he'd intoxicated her, filling her with rapture that made her senses spiral and silenced her conscience.

"You're the most naturally beautiful woman I've ever known, Sami. I want you even more than before," he cried urgently before his mouth sought hers in a frenzy of need neither of them could control.

She didn't remember being carried to the bed. Somehow she was there with him, responding to her growing desire for this man who was thrilling her senseless. Every kiss created pure ecstasy. She felt herself going under, deeper and deeper.

"Since the avalanche, I've dreamed about us so many times. To think you're alive… *Sami*—"

"I know." She half sobbed the words. "I can't believe it either." She kissed the scar where the beam had hit his forehead. But in the act of doing it, she was suddenly seized by a cognizance of what was happening here.

When Ric would have found her mouth again, she rolled away from him and got to her feet, just far enough away that he couldn't reach her. She lost her balance and grabbed on to the end of the dresser.

"Don't do this to us. Come back here," he begged. His eyes were smoldering black fires.

She was one trembling mass of desire. "You think I don't want to? But we can't just do what we want, Ric.

It's clear you and I feel an attraction because of what happened during the avalanche and the miracle of meeting up again. But that's all this is. So far we've done nothing to be ashamed of. That's why this has to stop here and now, and never happen again."

He got up from the bed. She thought him even more gorgeous with his black hair disheveled. "So what are you saying?" he said in a voice of ice.

She backed away from him. "I'm saying that in Austria you and I were like two colliding heavenly bodies out in space. But those bodies have long since orbited away from each other despite the pull we've felt today. I suppose it's understandable since we both thought the other was dead."

He folded his arms. "So now that we've discovered we're amazingly alive, what about the next time we see each other and feel the pull?"

Sami took a shaky breath. "We'll deal with it. We *have* to. Yes, we shared one amazing connection together in the avalanche, but it wasn't real life. You have a whole new married life about to unfold. I have my studies."

When he didn't respond, she added, "In January I'm going to get on with my school work. I need a good career to be able to provide for me and Ric."

A tiny pulse throbbed at his temple where he'd been injured. "Where exactly?"

"At the University of Reno. I transferred my credits there when I left California. The nice thing is, the computer engineering department has a program that lets you go to school at night, so I'll be with Ric during the day. I've already arranged for several babysitters who've agreed to trade off helping me nights. It will all work out.

"As for you, you'll be married in a few weeks. After you and Eliana talk things over tomorrow evening, the three of us will sit down and work out a mutually beneficial visitation arrangement for our son. I'm praying that if she's a part of it, then she'll be more accepting of the situation."

Ric moved closer. "You think it's all going to be that simple?" he asked in a dangerously silky voice.

"No," she said, still looking at him. "Do you have a better solution? If so, I'm willing to hear it. But not tonight. I'm really tired after my swim. We all need a good night's sleep."

Stillness surrounded him. "If you should want me for any reason, I'll be in my study downstairs making a phone call."

Please leave now and get it over with. Sami's willpower was nonexistent.

Ric must have heard her plea. In the next instant he was gone.

Sami slept in late. When she came downstairs the next morning, she discovered Mara had served breakfast out on the patio surrounding the pool. There was no sign of Ric or the baby, but his carrycot was there. As she sat down to eat, Ric came through the alcove holding her little darling. Their eyes met.

"Good morning. I'm sorry I got up so late."

He walked over so she could kiss the baby. "That's the

idea when you're on vacation. It gave Ric and me a chance to go for a walk and have a talk together, man to man."

She smiled. "Did you two set the world straight?"

"Of course." He reciprocated with a heart-melting smile of his own.

On the surface, you wouldn't think they had a care, but Sami couldn't take the invisible tension she was feeling any longer. She needed an answer to one burning question. "Were you able to reach Eliana last night?"

He nodded without noticeable emotion. "She'll be arriving at six-thirty this evening."

"I realize she doesn't suspect anything. That makes me nervous."

"If it will ease your anxiety, I did tell her I had something of great importance I needed to talk to her about. It put her on the alert, which was good." He expelled a deep breath. "If there were someone to blame in this... but there isn't." His voice trailed. "You and I clung to life until the last breath. If that was a sin, then so be it, but I won't allow our son to suffer because of it."

"I believe you."

Sami didn't know how she was going to stand meeting Eliana, but she had to go through with it. No doubt Ric's fiancée was an outstanding woman, otherwise he wouldn't be marrying her. But tonight when he would introduce them and they would look at each other, Eliana's eyes would be staring at the woman Ric had made love to in the dark with the result of pregnancy.

Could Sami expect to see any understanding, or would bitter resentment always cloud the other woman's vision?

She looked up at the powder-blue sky. The weather had warmed up to seventy degrees at the pool and was almost balmy. With such brilliant blue water beyond the point, it was hard to believe it was December.

Sami cast a covert glance at Ric, who'd gone over to lie down on one of the sun loungers to play with the baby. He'd dressed in a wine-colored polo and white cargo pants. His well-honed body made it difficult to look anywhere else.

Another sigh escaped. She could only imagine what was going through his mind right now. Once he told Eliana the truth, the word would be out. It wasn't just his fiancée he would have to placate. His family and hers, their friends, everyone who knew and loved him would have questions he would have to answer.

What made this so hard was to realize that a very private act between the two of them—an act even *they* had trouble explaining—would become public knowledge. Because of Ric's prominence, both he and Sami would be the targets of gossip, in some cases malicious. She would hate the notoriety, but she and the baby would be back in Reno where she wouldn't have to be around the paparazzi on a twenty-four-hour basis. Ric would bear the brunt of it.

Of course he'd handle it, but his marriage would suffer. And though she knew he'd go to the greatest lengths to protect their son from being hurt when he was on visitation, it was inevitable the baby would feel it and have to live with it growing up.

Her desire to lift Ric's spirits until Eliana arrived

prompted Sami to get up from the table. "Excuse me for a minute. I'll be right back."

"Hurry. We like your company."

His little personal asides made mincemeat of her emotions. She dashed through the villa and up the stairs for his gift. She'd started making it for his father after finding out she was pregnant. Little did she dream she would be giving it to Ric himself.

Formula wasn't the only thing at the bottom of her suitcase. She opened the lid and pulled out the scrapbook which she'd wrapped in Christmas paper ahead of time. Hugging it to her chest, she hurried back downstairs to the pool.

He was so preoccupied with the baby, he didn't see her coming. "Merry Christmas again, Ric," she called to him, announcing her presence.

He looked up in time for her to hand it to him. "I brought this to give your father for Christmas. I've decided now would be the best time for you to have it."

While he sat up to open it, she picked up the baby and stood there to watch him leaf through the pages.

Sami had put everything in there: pictures of her, her grandparents, more pictures of her sister's family and their parents, the apartment in Reno, the picture the hospital had taken of Ric right after he was born, cards from friends, comments from the pediatrician, more pictures of him turning one week, then two, then three, his room, his crib and baby toys. Everything she could think of to preserve memories for his grandfather.

"Those three photos are the ultrasound pictures. Can

you believe that's our little Ric there? The technician said he had a strong heartbeat and everything looked normal. You'll never know my relief."

Ric went so quiet, she wondered if something was wrong. Then he looked up with those jet-black eyes suspiciously bright. "I'll cherish this forever, Sami." She hardly recognized his voice it was so husky.

Thrilled with his response she said, "When you told me you'd missed the first two months of his life and didn't want to miss any more, I was doubly glad I made this. While you enjoy it, I'm going to put this little guy to bed for a nap."

"Wait— Stay right where you are." He got up from the lounger and dashed into the villa. Not a minute later and he came back outside with Daimon.

"He's going to take a picture of us with my cell phone," Ric explained. In the next breath he came to stand next to Sami and put his arm around her shoulders, pulling her close enough to set off a burst of adrenaline.

"This one's for posterity and will go in the last page of the book. Take a dozen pictures, Daimon. Then we want to take pictures of you and Mara holding him. Before long I intend to fill up a whole new scrapbook with memories."

But when, Ric? Here on the island isn't real life.

After all the picture-taking was done, they went upstairs to put the baby down, then tiptoed out of the room. Sami assumed Ric would use this free time to do the business he'd come to Paphos to accomplish. Nothing could have surprised her more than when he told her he wanted her to drive to town with him.

"I've arranged for Mara to watch the baby while we're gone. I want to show you around the ancient part of the city."

"What about your work?"

"It's getting done."

When? In the middle of the night? How did he do it and still get up with the baby?

"If you feel you have time, I'd love to do some sight-seeing." As long as she could be with him, she honestly didn't care what they did. She was storing up memories before she had to go back home.

"The weather's warm enough to go without a coat, but if you want one, I'll wait for you downstairs."

"I'm fine the way I am."

When his eyes smiled like that, she felt complete. "Then let's make the most of the time."

Within minutes they were driving on the A-6 toward the city they'd passed on the cruiser yesterday. He gave her a running commentary about the origins of the sprawling modern coastal town of 47,000 people.

Once in the busy part of the new Paphos, Ric stopped to buy a stroller for the baby. "We'll need one. It'll be nice to push him around whether we're out walking around or at the villa."

Sami saw a clothing shop and popped in to buy an extra couple of outfits for herself. Everything was decked out for Christmas. Nearby Ric found a sweets shop that sold drinks and *loukoumades*. He bought a sack of the delicious donut balls with syrup for them to eat along the way. "My friends and I used to stuff ourselves with these."

"I can see why. I can't stop with just one."

They drove on. No one was more fun than Ric when he was lighthearted. She became the pushover who went along with all his ideas because she couldn't help herself.

"Ahead of us is Palaepaphos, the old city. It was the island's capital in Greco-Roman times and the main focal point of Aphrodite-worship for the entire Aegean. I'm taking you to see some outstanding mosaics that still remain in the Roman governor's palace."

For the next two hours they explored the remains of everything from villas, palaces and theaters to fortresses and tombs. "Oh, Ric, this is all so incredible."

"Isn't it? I spent all my holidays here, pretending it was my secret world. Come on. I want to show you one more thing before we go back."

Sami dreaded the fact that this time with Ric was almost over. Nothing would be the same after Eliana arrived. If it were in her power, she'd make this time with him last forever.

They soon came to a jewel of an ancient church. "This is the Agia Kyriaki Chrysopolitissa parish church, one of my favorite places. My mother loved it and always brought us here."

"Is it still operational?"

"Yes. They even hold English mass."

She loved its architecture. "There's a very spiritual aspect about the whole place."

His dark eyes fastened on hers. "This city was blessed when Paul of Tarsus visited here in the first century A.D."

Sami reflected on Ric's upbringing. "You were blessed to have a mom you loved so much raise you."

He moved closer to her. "Now you understand why I'm full of gratitude for the way you love our son. Your grandparents did a wonderful job with you."

"Pat and I weren't the easiest children. They'll get a crown in heaven, that's for sure."

While she was caught up with so many feelings she didn't dare express, she was conscious of a clock ticking away. "I think Mara will wonder if we're ever coming back."

Ric's mouth turned up in a half smile. "She hopes we won't."

They started for the car. "Do she and Daimon have children?"

"Yes. Both their married daughters live in Nicosia. They visit back and forth with the grandchildren on a regular basis."

"That makes me happy to hear it." She glanced at her watch and couldn't believe how long they'd been gone. "It's almost time for Eliana's plane to arrive. We need to hurry home."

"Relax. We'll make it."

Ric seemed in no rush. Sami tried to heed his advice, but she was too restless. When they reached the villa, she hurried inside to find the baby. Holding him always calmed her down.

Mara had put him in the carrycot while she was in

the kitchen cooking. Sami entered with Ric to find their son lying there open-eyed and perfectly content until Ric hunkered down to talk to him. The second he saw his daddy, he started crying, wanting to be held. On cue, Ric was right there to pick him up and nestle him against his chest.

Sami burst into laughter. "What a little faker he is. I swear that happens every time with you."

A smile lit up Mara's face. "He knows his *papa*."

"Unfortunately his *papa* needs to get ready to leave for the airport," Sami said. Her gaze shot to Ric. "I'll take him so you won't be late."

She felt his hesitation before he handed the baby over.

"At least Ric still acts happy to come to me. I'd begun to fear he might have forgotten me because of his new infatuation with you."

"Sami..."

Afraid to look in Ric's eyes she said, "I'm taking this young man upstairs. Thanks for everything, Mara."

"My pleasure. He won't need a bottle for a while. I think he's getting sleepy."

"All right then. Let's go change you."

Ten minutes later he'd fallen to sleep. As Sami turned to go take her shower, Ric made an appearance. He looked too gorgeous in a silky charcoal dress shirt and black trousers she hadn't seen before. Her heart pounded outrageously.

"I wanted you to know I'm leaving now."

"I—I'll see you later then." She stumbled over the

words. Fear for what was going to happen had chilled her blood. "I'll pray things go well."

Without saying anything, he went over to the crib and rubbed their little boy's head. "I'll be back, *tesoro mio,*" he whispered.

"What did you just call him?"

"My treasure." His gaze swerved to hers. "When you came to find my father, you brought me the world, Sami."

His words liquefied her insides. "He's my whole world, too." She struggled to keep her voice steady. "Do you have any advice for me for when I meet Eliana?"

A brooding look stole over his handsome face. "Simply be yourself."

That didn't help her. "How old is she?"

"Twenty-five."

A year younger than Sami. "Have you—" She stopped herself, needing to bite her tongue out.

"Have we been intimate?"

"It's none of my business."

"The answer is yes."

Sami had no right to feel wounded by the admission, but she did. Horribly. But she was glad she knew. It put things into perspective. He was a man with a man's appetite and Eliana was his fiancée, after all. Women always dramatized everything.

Well, Sami refused to be like that. Everyone knew that the majority of couples, engaged or not, didn't wait for marriage to sleep together. The fact that Sami hadn't been intimate with a man except Ric put her in that tiny minority.

He darted her a quick glance. "I'll answer the next question you haven't asked yet. I've enjoyed my share of women over the years."

"If Eliana knows that, then perhaps she won't be as hurt when you tell her about us."

His lids drooped over his eyes. "That's a nice thought. Let's hang on to it, shall we?"

"Ric—"

"I should be back with her within forty-five minutes."

Her body trembled. "I'll be ready. What shall I wear?"

He scrutinized her from her hair to her sandaled feet. "You're breathtaking with or without clothes. Put on whatever feels the most comfortable."

After Ric had left the bedroom, Sami stood in the shower paralyzed by what he'd said. How could he reduce everything to its most intimate and personal when he was preparing to pick up his soon-to-be wife at the airport?

Yet, on the heels of that thought, she had to remember he'd been intimate with both Sami and Eliana. The situation didn't fit any scenario she knew of.

Coming to the island had been a mistake. They'd gotten into a false sense of vacation mode. Last night things had almost spiraled out of control. Because of the baby, she assumed that was the reason they'd both subconsciously let down their guard. But one thing was certain. She refused to put herself into such a vulnerable position again.

The only thing to do was get through the next few hours while they all talked, then she'd fly home in the morning. She'd done her part so Ric could enjoy the baby, but now it was over. It didn't matter if he wanted their son with him all the time. That wouldn't be possible. Reno and Genoa were thousands of miles apart. After his marriage and honeymoon, they could talk on the phone and plan how to arrange visitation.

While her mind pored over how she would tell him she was leaving, she did her hair and makeup. After that she opened the closet door and put on her navy blue suit, matching it with a lighter blue silk blouse. The rest of the clothes she'd brought with her comprised a few casual jeans and tops. Sami wanted to look her best. Nothing but the suit was dressy enough for this first meeting with a princess, no matter how casual the surroundings.

When she was ready, she went downstairs and asked Mara to listen for the baby while she walked out to the private marina to take in the view. She hoped Ric and Eliana would arrive while she was away from the villa. Ric could show her the baby before she had to face Sami.

Mara acted delighted and offered to feed him if he awakened. Sami thanked her and stepped outside.

The sun had set an hour ago. Sami presumed Ric would be back fairly soon. Twilight had come on fast and the air was cooler, yet she glimpsed sailboats and cruisers out enjoying the evening. From the corner of her eye she saw a jet climbing in the sky from Paphos airport. Under the right circumstances this time of night could be magical, but all Sami experienced was a heavy heart.

She walked along the path bordering the sand. Everyone knew weddings were for the bride. A bride had the right to expect that the days leading up to her wedding would be filled with excitement. It killed Sami to imagine that because she'd come to Genoa looking for Ric's grandfather, Eliana's excitement would now vanish as if it had never been.

Again Pat's predictions came floating back at her.

Neither Sami nor Ric could change things, but she would go out of her way to appease Eliana in any way she could in order not to do more damage. Lost in thought, she didn't realize she'd been out longer than she'd planned. It had grown dark. She retraced her steps back to the villa and met Daimon coming toward her.

"Enrico sent me to find you."

"I purposely stayed out to give him time to be with Eliana and the baby."

"They've been here awhile. He was worried about you."

"I'm sorry. Where are they?"

"In the living room by the fireplace."

Sami walked inside and made her way through to the front of the house. She peered around the corner to see the couple over on the couch. In the open-necked charcoal shirt and dark trousers, Ric had never looked more appealing. He'd nestled the baby against his shoulder. His little head bobbed, signaling he was awake. Both were heartbreakingly attractive.

Eliana was seated near him wearing a stunning watermelon-colored suit. She had class written all over her and could have been a model for the latest princess doll with her dark blond hair falling in curls over her shoulders.

CHAPTER SIX

"HELLO?" Sami called softly to announce her entrance.

At the sound of her voice, Ric's black eyes shot to hers and he sprang to his feet. The way he was looking at her underlined what Daimon had said about him being worried. She hadn't meant to alarm him.

Her gaze strayed to Eliana whose head had turned in her direction. Large amber eyes gave Sami a wintry stare of condemnation. Otherwise her classically Italian features were devoid of animation.

Little did Eliana know she didn't have anything to fear from Sami. But the baby was another matter, because Ric had claimed him. He loved their baby to the depth of his being and intended to be a hands-on father whenever possible.

At the moment his remote countenance was more pronounced than it had been when he'd told her the reason he'd gotten rid of his title. She groaned inwardly for him.

"Christine Argyle, please meet my fiancée, Princess Eliana Fortulezza."

Sami had known he was marrying nobility, but hearing his fiancée's title and seeing her in person at last still took some getting used to. "How do you do, Princess Fortulezza?"

Eliana rose to her feet. "Signorina Argyle," she said and they shook hands.

Ric's fiancée studied Sami without revealing any visible emotion. Though Ric had been honest about his reasons for marrying Eliana, no one could know what was in his fiancée's heart. She'd been trained to maintain her dignity, but now that this ghastly moment was upon them, Sami thought the other woman was awesome.

"Come on," Ric said. "We'll go into the dining room where we can sit around the table to talk." Sami followed them, noting Eliana's tall, slender figure and the three dazzling diamonds of her engagement ring.

The carrycot was still perched on the table. Ric put the baby down in it, then pulled out chairs for her and Eliana. Since her little boy seemed content, Sami sat down without kissing him. She didn't want to get him all worked up and create a fuss.

Mara came in to serve coffee and biscotti. Ric thanked her before she left them alone. His dark, solemn eyes slid to Sami. "I've told Eliana everything that happened last January."

Having said that much, the onus was now on Sami. She cleared her throat and eyed Eliana. "Then you realize that when I went to the police station two days ago, I was expecting, or at least hoping, to meet Ric's father."

"Yes."

This was so painful for Sami, she could only imagine how shocked and hurt Eliana had to be. "I can't tell you how sorry I am to have caused you this kind of grief. I had no idea the elder Mr. Degenoli had died, or that Ric had survived the avalanche." Her voice faltered. "When he lost consciousness, I thought he was dead. Neither of us dreamed we would ever leave our tomb alive."

"So Enrico explained. Did he tell you to call him Ric?" she asked in heavily accented English.

Out of all the questions she might have asked, that was the last one Sami would have expected. "When I realized I wasn't alone in the dark, I asked who was there. He said he was Ric Degenoli. I was thankful he spoke English and told him my name was Sami."

"Sami?"

"My father's name was Samuel. That's how I got the nickname." She leaned forward. "Eliana—please believe me. I have absolutely no intention of ruining your life. I know you're going to be married on New Year's Day. Tomorrow morning I'm taking the baby back to Reno with me."

She purposely didn't look at Ric while she spoke to Eliana. "Once the wedding and honeymoon are over and you've settled into married life, then visitation can be discussed. But be assured my life is in America."

The other woman studied her for a minute. "Enrico tells me there's a man who wishes to marry you."

Sami couldn't fault Ric for telling his fiancée everything. The whole truth and nothing but. No doubt it would make things more bearable for Eliana if Sami were to say that she and Matt would be getting married shortly. But she couldn't, because it would never happen. Sami didn't love Matt with all her heart and soul. In the past twenty-four hours, she'd had that confirmed beyond any lingering doubt.

"There is, but I've decided against marrying him." Her announcement caused something to flare in the recesses of Ric's eyes, whether surprise because she'd been so frank about it, Sami couldn't tell. Eliana didn't flinch. "Perhaps if I give you a little background, you'll understand.

"I was young when my parents died. Though I adored my grandparents, I ached for a mother and father. When Ric was born I made a vow. Since he would never know his father in this life, I would devote my life to raising my precious son to the very best of my ability.

"For the last two months I've thought of nothing else and don't see another man giving my baby the love he'll need." Watching Ric in action with their child had settled the question for her once and for all. Anyone other than his own father wouldn't do.

"How will you live?"

Sami had half expected Eliana's practical question. Ric's fiancée could be forgiven for thinking Sami was out for everything she could get from him. It was time to reassure her on that point.

"Did Ric mention to you that I was in graduate school before I flew to Austria?"

"He said something about it."

"I intend to go back to it. Being a computer engineer will provide me with a good living to help me take care of the two of us and pay back my loans."

"How in debt are you?"

Again Sami understood why she was curious. "By the time I've received my master's degree, I'll probably owe at least $40,000, but I'll pay it back slowly after I'm employed. I'm fortunate to go to a university where I can be with the baby all day and attend classes at night.

"Once I'm back there, I'll email you my schedule. We'll work things out so Ric gets to see his son when it's convenient for you. Do you have any other questions you want to ask me?"

After a few seconds she said, "No."

Then there was nothing more to talk about. Good. Sami couldn't sit here any longer. If Eliana was struggling to hold it all together, she didn't give anything away.

Sami stood up without having tasted her coffee. "If you'll excuse me, I need to put the baby down and go to bed." She went around to lift him from his carrycot. On her way out of the room, she paused for a moment. "I'm glad Ric brought you here tonight so we could meet, Eliana. I wish you two every happiness on your forthcoming marriage."

Even though Eliana and Ric hadn't been engaged last January, Sami had the conviction that the strange circumstances surrounding the baby's conception had driven a wedge that could never be closed. "Since I know you have a lot to discuss, I'll say good-night."

Eliana looked relieved. So was Sami, who hurried to the bedroom, thankful the dreaded meeting was over. Once inside, she hurried upstairs and put the baby down long enough to change and slip into her robe. After that she bathed him and gave him his bottle, needing to feel him close to her.

She still shivered from the look on Ric's face before she'd rushed out of the dining room. It said she hadn't had the last word when it came to her going back to the States. But despite how crazy he was about their baby, he had to face reality. The only way to relieve the tension was for Sami to go home.

As soon as her little cherub had fallen asleep, she put him down in the crib. Afraid she'd toss and turn in agony all night, she took a sleeping pill and turned off her lamp before climbing into bed.

If the drug worked and she fell into a deep enough sleep, she knew Ric would get up in the night with the baby. The experience would give Eliana a taste of what it would be like when it was their turn to take care of him.

While she lay there waiting for needed oblivion, her mind went over the scene in the living room. Sami had given out enough information for Eliana to put her own spin on it. No doubt she believed Sami had come to Italy hoping Ric's father would fund her graduate-school costs. When she'd found Ric alive, that was even better. The count was worth a fortune and would do anything for his son. He'd already proved it.

Surely by now it had entered Eliana's mind that a lesser man with his kind of money could have paid Sami off and been done with the problem without any knowledge of it coming to light. *Not Ric.* He not only loved the idea of being a father, he genuinely loved playing with the baby and seeing to all his needs. You couldn't fake that kind of caring.

Eliana had to be seeing a whole new side to her fiancé. It ought to reassure her he'd be a marvelous father to any children they would have one day. But Eliana would have to get past this obstacle before she could begin to appreciate how exceptional Ric really was.

Still in turmoil, Sami turned on her other side. For the three of them to meet and talk had been the only thing to do, but none of them had come out of it unscathed. Her gaze lit on the baby, who had no idea what was going on. Her sweet little baby... Hot tears trickled out the corners of her eyes.

When next Sami knew anything, she discovered it was after 10:00 a.m. That pill had eventually knocked her out. With her timing off, it meant she would have to hurry to arrange for an evening flight out of Paphos.

There was no sign of the baby. Ric and Eliana must have come in to take care of him. If not them, Mara. With her pulse racing, Sami quickly dressed in jeans and a blouse before hurrying downstairs. She expected to find him with Ric and Eliana in the breakfast room of the villa. Instead the housekeeper was the one to greet her.

"Good morning, Sami. Enrico is at the pool with the baby. I'll serve your breakfast out there."

"Thank you, Mara."

She rushed through the alcoves to reach the pool at the side of the villa. As he'd been yesterday, Ric was seated at the umbrella table, but this morning he was dressed in a pale blue suit and tie. Rather than reading the newspaper, he was playing with the baby, whose animated responses touched her heart. An empty baby bottle lay next to his coffee. Apparently Eliana wasn't up yet.

Ric saw her and got to his feet, the quintessential Genoan aristocrat. *Her baby's father.* Not in a hundred lifetimes could Sami have dreamed up this picture.

"I'm glad you're awake," he said as she approached. "We have to talk. Ric has been looking for you."

Sami leaned over their son. "I think your *papa* is just teasing me to make me feel better. You've been having a wonderful time, haven't you?" She caught his little hands and pressed kisses all over them and his face and neck. After she lifted her head, she turned to his father. "Is Eliana still in bed?"

His eyes roved over her features for a moment. "No. I just got back from driving her to the airport. She flew home in her father's company jet."

Sami's composure slipped. "I'm sick for her, Ric," she cried. "The news had to ruin her dreams. With your wedding so imminent, I don't know how she's handling it."

Lines marred his striking face. "She's not" came the grim admission. Sami's heart plummeted. Ric rubbed the back of his neck as she'd seen him do before. "There's much more to Eliana's reaction than even I had imagined."

"You're talking about the inevitable scandal," she whispered. "I know it will be awful, but compared to a little baby who needs a father and mother, surely she'll come to terms with this in time?"

The lines marring his features made him look older. "The baby plays a negligible part in what's happened."

Sami frowned. "What do you mean?"

"Early this morning I heard from my attorney. The title is now officially gone." His eyes narrowed to slits. "What you said in passing was prophetic. Knowing she'll no longer be addressed as Countess is what has destroyed Eliana's dream. She's demanding that I have it reinstated."

"Did you tell her that's impossible?"

"She doesn't understand the word. As for little Ric, she has no intention of being a stepmother to my child."

"She's saying that now because she wants her own children with you, Ric."

"Not if there isn't a title to bestow on our firstborn son. Her solution to the problem is unthinkable," his voice rasped, igniting her panic.

"What do you mean by that?"

"She won't consider visitation. Either I give up all rights to Ric and never see him again, or the wedding is off. She's giving me until Christmas Eve day to make a final decision. In the meantime she won't discuss this with anyone."

Sami swallowed hard. "She's not a parent yet, or she wouldn't have laid down those rules. Eliana doesn't mean what she said. It was her pain lashing out. You have to give her time. Though the pain's excruciating, in a few days she'll have recovered enough to think more clearly."

"No. She's thinking clearly now. Until last summer Eliana and I only knew each other socially and were never in any kind of relationship. What happened between you and me had no bearing on her, but now she's in a rage because I never told her about you. I explained that I'd gone looking for you and couldn't find you. For all I knew, you had died. Even if I'd found you, I wouldn't have dreamed I'd made you pregnant."

"I had to explain the same thing to Matt. When the doctor told me the reason why I hadn't been feeling well, I almost fainted and had to stay lying down for an hour before I could leave his office. He talked to me about diet and prenatal vitamins, but I hardly heard him for the shock I was in.

"If I hadn't become pregnant, none of it would have come out." Sami shook her head. "Eliana could have no idea how this situation has affected you and me, but it's so hard to explain."

"She doesn't want an explanation. All she cares about is the title."

"Ric—I have to believe that when the worst of her agony subsides, she'll realize she wants to be your wife under any circumstances."

"That's where you're wrong. You weren't raised a princess with specific expectations to be met."

Sami hugged her arms to her waist. "Do you think she's capable of understanding what it would mean for you to give up your parental rights to Ric?"

"She doesn't want to understand, because the baby isn't a factor."

"But he's your son!"

"Eliana grew up in her father's world of black and

white. His daughter is a product of that environment. When he hears about this, he'll demand I get the title back, because he puts his desires above everything else. He'll tell me to pay you off for the child I fathered by some freak accident."

She shuddered. "I've known all along no one would believe what happened to us."

"Certainly not Eliana. When I told her you were in Austria on a working vacation for your sister's travel agency, she's convinced you targeted me when you found out Count Degenoli was registered there. Employing your wiles, you ended up sleeping with me in the hotel before the avalanche struck, and decided to use the tragedy as an alibi to cover our flirtation."

Sami sank into the chair. "Actually I can't blame her for thinking that."

"Nor I. She assumes you came to Italy as soon as the baby could travel in order to extort money from me. Moreover she thinks I decided to rescind the title because you phoned me from Reno and told me about the pregnancy a long time ago.

"Because I was already engaged to her, she assumed I immediately made the necessary arrangements so I'd be able to legally claim Ric as my firstborn, thus cheating her."

"You can't fault her logic, Ric. I'm afraid everyone who learns about us will think the same thing. Do you think Eliana always hoped to marry you?"

"I have no idea." He came to a standstill, gripping the back of one of the dining-room chairs until his knuckles showed white. "Our fathers have brushed shoulders in the same business circles for years, but I didn't consider getting to know her until June of this year. In November I asked her to marry me and we set a date for the wedding."

"She's very lovely. Not very many women in her kind of pain would have handled our meeting with so much poise."

"Interestingly enough, she said the same thing about you."

Sami couldn't look at him. "Unfortunately if Eliana thinks you've lied to her about our first meeting, then she *does* see me as a menace. It wouldn't matter how many times I tell her I won't stand in the way of her happiness, she won't listen."

He cocked his dark head. "Perhaps deep down she does believe it. That's what bothers her more."

"Why do you say that?"

"Do I need to spell it out?" he fired. "Not every woman and man trapped in a situation like ours would have sought comfort as we did."

Again her body grew warm. "I know," she admitted reluctantly.

"I'm still haunted by those feelings and why we acted on them. I can assure you my life hasn't been the same since that experience."

"Neither has mine," she confessed in a tremulous voice. "Maybe it was because we believed our time had run out and we were both single and free at the time to act without hurting anyone else. But the same can't be said of us now."

"No," he murmured. "Since then, we have a marvelous child who needs his mother and father." Without warning he scooped up the baby, laughing triumphantly. The happy sound was a revelation. He alternated kissing and cuddling him close. Ric treated their son as if he'd always been in his life.

Her heart ran away with her. "But everything has changed—"

"I agree. We've all changed. Last night Eliana could feel a certain tension between you and me she couldn't cut through. Don't forget you kissed me back yesterday and the day before, Sami."

"I've forgotten nothing!" When he'd laid her down on the hotel bed in Genoa to talk, her body had come alive again without her volition. Yesterday they'd reached blindly for each other in the bedroom after putting Ric down. She'd only come to her senses at the last second.

He eyed her with a penetrating glance. "I'm glad to hear you say it, because you're not going back to Reno yet. Since you've flown this long way, the three of us are going to stay here and enjoy this time together while Eliana works this out in her mind.

"Maybe the impossible will happen and she'll decide she wants this marriage badly enough to compromise. It'll mean going up against her father, but she knows my terms. Without visitation, I won't marry her."

Sami couldn't stop shivering. "This is all so mean. She's been looking forward to her wedding day since you announced the engagement in November. To defy her father's wishes in order to keep you will be a hard thing, Ric. If she isn't able to go against him, then she'll be forced to call off the wedding and suffer the humiliation of having to undo all the arrangements of a huge public marriage like yours."

"That's where you're wrong, Sami. With my family still in mourning, we'd already planned our wedding to take place in the privacy of the palazzo chapel with only our families in attendance. No reporters will be allowed inside. The news will leak out, it always does, but there'll be no photo ops or press releases, no official reception."

"The poor thing." Tears filled her eyes. "Why didn't you fly back with her?"

"After you left us last night, I told her I'd take her back to Genoa in my own plane this morning and we'd talk to her parents together while you and the baby remained here. She agreed. But when we reached the airport this morning, she suddenly changed her mind and told me she needed to talk to her parents alone first."

That's why he was dressed in a suit. "Why do you think she didn't want you to be with her when she faced them? With you there explaining everything, how could they possibly doubt your honesty?"

"You want the truth?" he rapped out.

"Ric—if we don't have that, we don't have anything!"

"She assumes you and I have slept together since your arrival in Genoa. Last night she asked me not to touch her."

Sami moaned. "Does that mean—"

"It means she slept in the other guest bedroom," he answered.

She bit her lip. "Did she help you with the baby when you got up in the night to feed him?"

"If she heard me and Ric, she didn't make an appearance."

"Obviously she was in too much pain."

He exhaled sharply. "It's commendable how much credit you give her."

"I'm not the woman who has been looking forward to her marriage to you. She's crushed. In the face of what she's dealing with, I admire her more for her honesty, no matter hard it is on both of you."

Ric raked a hand through his black hair. "You're an extraordinary woman, Sami."

"No, I'm not—" she cried. "This is so awful for both of you. I have my own life to go back to, but you two have to wade through so much to make this work!" She buried her face in her hands. "Did you disabuse her about us?"

"In what regard?" he drawled.

"That nothing has happened between us since I came to Italy."

"I wouldn't say that," he countered in a tone that sent little darts of awareness through her body.

Exasperated she said, "You know what I mean."

"Just because you and I haven't ended up in bed yet doesn't rule out what goes on whenever we're near each other." Her trembling started up again. After a pause he added, "Even if I'd assured her we didn't pick up where we'd left off in January, do you imagine it would have done any good?"

Her shoulders slumped. "I should never have come."

"We've been over this ground before," he said in an iron-clad voice. "Don't ever say that again."

She took a deep breath to pull herself together. By acknowledging his son from the start, Ric hadn't given his fiancée a choice. Surely Eliana was aware of his strong will. He wouldn't capitulate. It was up to her to decide what she could handle. No doubt she wanted to scratch Sami's eyes out or worse.

"You need to fly back to Genoa where you'll be close if she wants to see you. I'll leave for Reno on the next plane out of Paphos."

"No. That you *won't* do. For the sake of propriety, she's already set down the condition that you and I stay away from the city until the twenty-fourth."

"Ric—tell me the truth. If she doesn't come around and there's no marriage, then what will it cost you besides the woman you asked to marry you? Don't insult me by pretending this won't shake your world."

He wore an implacable expression. "That's for me to worry about."

"But I *do* worry!" she declared. "My reappearance in your world has done irreparable damage. If anyone should go to her parents, *I* should. I'll ask my sister and her husband to come with me. They'll verify what we've told Eliana.

"If we can convince her parents that I wasn't out to extort anyone or try to break you up, then it's possible they'll forgive you for having a human weakness. Good heavens, they're parents and will have to understand you want to be able to see your son on a regular basis. If

Eliana is willing to accept the baby, then the marriage can still take place."

His smile wasn't reflected in his eyes. "Your reasoning is without fault, Sami. You'd make a very convincing courtroom lawyer. But the crux of the real problem lies in the loss of the title. Eliana has been imagining herself as Countess Degenoli."

"You honestly think she can't get over that?"

"Not her or her father," his voice grated. "She's conflicted at her foundation. It wouldn't matter if you and your family were there to plead my case and win over her parents. She has her own war to fight inside. As I told you earlier, I'm going to find out what's really important to her."

Ric was a wonderful man. A prize. All this time Sami had assumed Eliana had learned to love him more than life. But what if that wasn't perfectly true? What if she loved him with strings?

Since this was virtually an arranged marriage, it was obvious there was a voice inside Ric that had always entertained his doubts about her. He'd gotten rid of his title as soon as he could. Maybe it had been a test. When Sami had asked him if it was such a terrible burden, his answer had left her in no doubt.

While she stood there trying to analyze his psyche, he peeled off his suit jacket and loosened his tie, as if he couldn't wait to remove the shackles of society. "After I've changed, we'll take another boat ride, this time in the other direction."

"What if someone who knows you and Eliana sees us together with Ric?"

"If they do, it won't matter because the person who needed to know the truth was Eliana. By now she's talked to her parents on the phone. If I'm not mistaken, they've already laid out a strategy to deal with the gossip in case Eliana says she wants to end the engagement. Until then, that leaves you and me free to play. When the time comes for us to leave Cyprus, you'll have seen many of my favorite haunts."

Warning bells were going off. "You said you were here to work. If I go home, it will give you the time you need."

His body stiffened. "If you can give me one good reason why..." His voice snaked through to her insides.

"Even if Eliana has set up the rules for this intolerable situation, it's not right for us to be together like this while you're still engaged."

He moved closer to her. "I think the real reason goes deeper than that. You're afraid to be alone with me."

She clutched the baby tighter. "My greatest fear is that your fiancée will always consider me an immoral woman. I felt it without her having to say it. If she's willing to work out visitation so your marriage can go through, I don't want her to hate me forever. Otherwise it could reflect on little Ric.

"To be honest, it hurts me that she doesn't know the real me. For that matter, neither do you. These last few days haven't been an example of real life, Ric. We're still strangers with our own individual lives to lead once I'm gone."

The silence between them was tangible. Finally he spoke. "Then let me get to know my son and his mother better while we have this rare free time together. Since we'll be sharing him for the rest of our lives, why not start this minute?

"You felt strongly enough about Ric's Italian ties to come to Genoa in search of them. Let's not waste your efforts this trip. It's a fact you're here with our son. Until you have to go back, we'll enjoy him. I swear I won't do anything you don't want me to."

If there was one thing she knew about Ric, it was that he'd stand by his word.

"We'll fill our days with fun and laughter. It's been ages for me, and I daresay for you since that's happened."

There was a nuance in his voice. A longing for something he wanted, needed to trust. Her heart ached for him. Between that and his promise to be circumspect around her, his logic had once more defeated her.

She kissed the baby's soft cheek to hide her emotions. "I'll need to let my sister know I won't be coming home quite yet."

A glint of satisfaction lit his eyes for a moment. "There's a seaside restaurant further along the coast with the most luscious purple grapes hanging from the ceiling. You won't be able to resist them. The food just keeps coming. Taramasalata, tahini, kebabs, dolmades, eggs, feta cheese and homemade bread and beer. You'll love it. So will our *piccolo*."

Again the years seemed to have fallen off him. Despite her effort not to feel anything, his excitement was contagious, infecting her. He was right about one thing. For the rest of their lives they'd be parenting Ric. A few more days together while they got to know each other better would pave the way for harmony in the future.

Sami had to be honest and admit she wanted this, too. Knowing what made Ric tick would give her more insight into him when their son was older and wanted to talk about him during times of separation.

She'd had hundreds of talks with her grandparents about the mother and father she never knew. Without their input, her life wouldn't have been as rich. For her baby's sake, she would stop worrying about Eliana for the time being and amass as many memories as possible with his father for the time they had left.

CHAPTER SEVEN

SAMI had done some snorkeling in Southern California, but nothing as exciting as this trip to the sea caves near Cape Gata. Taking advantage of the warm weather, they'd gone snorkeling to different spots over the last two days. In that time she'd become addicted. With Mara and Daimon along, they could all take turns spelling each other off to swim and watch the baby.

Today, after climbing some cliffs, Sami followed Ric around in the crystal-clear waters while he identified new varieties of fish for her. He'd spent a lot of years in these waters and had obtained his SCUBA certification in his teens. This afternoon had been their coolest day; the temperature had only climbed to sixty-seven degrees. It was warm enough to enjoy being in the boat, but her wetsuit felt good once she'd entered the water with her goggles and fins.

Every time they returned to the cruiser for a snack and a drink, Ric asked her if she'd had enough, but she shook her head and rolled over the side to hunt for new species. He stayed right with her. This round he pointed out mullet and a school of colorful perch. What a delight!

But the next time she lifted her head out of the water, she was surprised to see the sun much lower in the sky. Feeling herself getting tired, she made a signal to Ric that she was ready to get back.

Sami hadn't gone far when an ugly-looking brown fish she hadn't seen before swam directly for her. Before she could think, Ric grabbed her hips and pulled her out of its path. When they reached the ladder on the back of the boat, she pulled off her head gear. "What happened out there?"

Ric removed his gear and tossed both apparatuses in the boat. "You barely escaped the sting from the front fin of a weever fish. Are you all right?"

"I'm fine."

For the last while they'd had such a wonderful time swimming in different waters, she'd forgotten he could look that forbidding. Their bodies brushed against each other from the wake of some other boats passing in the distance.

"I've been stung by one before, so it's obviously not fatal, but its poison is stronger than a wasp sting. They sink in the sand to hide. He came in front of you so fast, I almost didn't get you out of the way in time."

Because of his protective instinct, his dark eyes continued to peruse her features, as if he were still doubting her. By now she was feeling fragile, but it was his nearness that had brought on a need for more oxygen.

"Thank you for saving me," she whispered. With their mouths so close, she ached to her bones to taste him. From sunup to sundown she'd had the time of her life playing with him. There was no one more intelligent or exciting.

But so much togetherness had resulted in her desire for him growing out of control. If she gave in to the temptation to press her lips to his right now, then she was worse than a fool. Calling on the little self-control she had left, she turned back to the ladder.

As she hoisted herself into the boat, she wasn't able to escape the touch of his hands on her hips. He might be trying to help her, but they clung to her as if he were having difficulty letting her go. Weakness attacked her body, making it almost impossible to function.

Thankfully Mara and Daimon were there to greet them and provide towels. Otherwise she would have proven Ric right and thrown herself in his arms because she could no longer resist him.

Without looking at him, she dashed down to the galley to remove her wetsuit. After a shower, she changed into the sweats and T-shirt she'd bought in Paphos the other day. Once dressed, she hurried back up to lavish her emotions on the baby, but Ric was holding him.

As she came forward, he gave his son's dear little head a loving kiss before handing him over. The baby immediately snuggled into her neck. "Our son has missed you," Ric observed. "There's nothing like a mother's love."

"I noticed him clinging to you before I came along. He knows his *papa* now."

Her comment produced a light in his eyes. "I think you're right." On that note he helped them into their life jackets and took his time buckling her up. His gaze rested on her. The look of longing in his eyes sent warmth spiraling through her bloodstream. Her desire for him was so palpable, he couldn't help but notice. Yet he still kept his promise not to do anything she didn't want him to do. *That was the problem.*

The other two stayed in the rear of the boat, leaving Ric to take the wheel. He finally started the engine for the trip back. En route he surprised her by pulling into a marina where there was a wonderful seafood taverna. The place featured dancing and bouzouki music. When he asked her to dance, she declined. No more touching.

Ric didn't seem to mind she'd turned him down. He ate up the attention their little boy drew from waiters and patrons alike. Everyone raved over the beautiful baby. Daimon and Ric took pictures. At the rate he'd been snapping photos on their outings, he'd fill that second scrapbook in no time.

After experiencing another halcyon day, they cruised home through the calm blue water. Except for certain breathless moments she was never prepared for, Sami discovered she was comfortable with Ric. Whether they built sand castles on an isolated beach with their son, or walked along in companionable silence, she relished every second with him.

On the ride home, she stayed up in front of the boat with him to shield the baby from the wind, glad for the obvious excuse because she didn't like to be apart from him. Last night had been the worst. After they'd bathed the baby together and put him down after his bottle, Ric got out some maps and talked about their plans for today before he'd disappeared from her room. She hadn't wanted him to go. She'd almost begged him to stay. That was forbidden.

Sami decided he'd left the villa to conduct the vital business he'd mentioned. It had to be then, or early in the morning. She didn't know and didn't dare ask. One thing she was certain of: he continued to see to the baby around four every morning. Mara told her he was always up before she could take a turn. That brought a secret smile to Sami's lips.

Tonight as they neared the point, she verged on panic because it dawned on her they only had two more days left until he had to return to Genoa. So far Ric had honored his promise to keep things under control by including Mara and Daimon in their activities.

Perversely she hoped he would ask her to stay up with him for a little while tonight after everyone else had gone to bed, if only to talk. Even though she knew it wouldn't be a good idea, the realization that there'd never be nights like this again once she went back to Reno tore her apart.

Within minutes he drove the boat to the dock. Before long they entered the villa. Ric carried the baby while Sami followed him with the carrycot and diaper bag. As they walked down the hall past the living room to the stairs, an unfamiliar female voice called to him.

Out of the corner of her eye, Sami watched a stunning visitor with stylish black hair hurry toward him dressed in elegant eggshell pleated pants and a peacock-blue sweater. She resembled Ric. If it weren't for the baby, Sami was convinced his sister would have thrown her arms around his neck. A stream of Italian escaped her lips. She sounded distressed.

"Claudia?" Ric said in a low voice. "Speak English, *per favore.* If I'd known you were coming, I would have met your plane. Is Marco with you?"

"No."

Ric's eyes glittered with emotion, enough to convince Sami something was wrong. "Meet my house guest Christine Argyle from Reno, Nevada."

The introduction proved to Sami he hadn't told anyone about her. Otherwise he would have added something like "You know—the woman I was entombed with in that avalanche."

"How do you do," Claudia responded. Though polite, she was clearly impatient to talk to him alone.

"Sami? This is my only sister, Claudia Rossi. She and her husband, Marco, live near the family palazzo in Genoa."

"It's very nice to meet you, Claudia. We've just returned from snorkeling and are a mess and exhausted. Since you and your brother will want to talk alone, I'll get the baby's bath started."

"I'd rather you stayed." Ric spoke before she could take the baby from him. He turned to his sister. "What emergency has brought you down here?"

"That's what I came to find out."

Ric's brows formed a black line. "Are Vito and Donata having problems again? I'd hoped they were doing better since he's taken over the operations of the company."

Claudia shook her head. "That's not what this is about. Yesterday Eliana called and asked me to go Christmas shopping with her."

His lips formed a thin line. "So this has to do with my fiancée."

"Yes. We had dinner afterward and I asked her how the wedding plans were coming. She told me you would know the answer better than she did. Then she got up from the table and said she had to go home. She walked off without her packages."

"Eliana should never have involved you."

Claudia's gaze flicked to Sami, then back to him. "I didn't know what to do. I've tried to reach you, but you've turned off your phone. I told Marco this was serious and he agreed I should fly down here and find out what's going on."

Ric wasn't at all surprised Eliana had engineered Claudia's visit. She knew how far to go to create an emergency without giving away her secret.

Eliana had been waiting for him to break the silence and tell her he was giving up his son for her and he'd had the title reinstated. But the wait had gone on too long, so she'd resorted to other tactics. By involving his sister when Eliana had promised to keep quiet until Christmas Eve, she'd made a fatal mistake.

Trust was everything to Ric. Without it a marriage could survive, but for all the wrong reasons.

"Let's sit down, shall we?"

When they were seated around the fireplace he said, "Sami and I have a story to tell you. It's a true story."

As the revelations about the avalanche and Sami's pregnancy unfolded, Claudia's worried expression underwent a drastic transformation. "He's really your baby?" she blurted in complete shock.

It *was* so shocking, no one would ever understand what had happened to two desperate people trying to hold on to life eleven months ago.

"*Si.* Already he's the joy of my life. Why don't you hold him, then you'll know beyond a doubt he has the Degenoli genes."

Ric walked over to his baby-hungry sister and put his son in her arms. He undid the quilt so she could see his limbs, too. The movement brought the baby awake. His eyelids with their black lashes fluttered open.

She looked down at him. "*Oh*—you little angel—"

Her cry of emotion was so heartfelt, he and Sami exchanged glances.

Claudia lifted a wet face. "I see the whole family in him. I see his mother in him, too." She smiled at Sami. "He's the most adorable baby I ever laid eyes on."

The second she spoke, little Ric burst into tears, not liking the strange face and voice. He turned, looking for his father. It caused Ric's heart to leap that his son wanted him. He had never heard him cry like that before, and he picked him back up to hold him. Once in his arms, the baby calmed right down.

"Oh, Ric." Claudia laughed through her tears and stood up so she could get another look at him. Already his sister was smitten with her new nephew. She deserved a baby of her own. If it hadn't been for the avalanche, she might not have lost hers.

But if it hadn't been for the avalanche…

"Eliana won't consider visitation."

"What?" With that one exclamation, he knew which side his sister stood on.

"Eliana asked me to give him up by signing away my parental rights. She's given me until the twenty-fourth to tell her my answer. Otherwise the marriage is off."

Claudia's eyes closed tightly for a minute. "If she said that, then she doesn't know the most important thing about you."

Ric was gratified to hear that. "There's something else, Claudia." He told her he'd had the title abolished. "You've always known I find it an archaic custom that should never have existed in the first place. Once the word is out, I'll have made a lot of enemies, but it doesn't matter."

Her eyelids flew open. "How long ago did you petition the court?"

"After Papa's funeral. Two days ago my attorney called and told me it's official. I'm no longer Count Degenoli. The title's gone forever so no one in our family's future will ever have to be hurt by it."

"Does Eliana know what you've done?" she cried.

"Yes. I told her when she came down here earlier in the week. But I've told Mario I don't want this story leaked to the press until Eliana and I have resolved things. I'm not about to embarrass her or her family."

"Of course not. You wouldn't do that." She suddenly threw her arms around him, baby and all. "I'm so glad,

Ric! When Vito hears this, I honestly believe it could make him a new man. He never felt good enough for Papa, and has always felt inferior to you.

"I think it's the real reason he's always had problems, especially since he got back from military service. He hasn't felt as though he fitted in. This will force him to reevaluate his thinking."

"It would be nice if we could be brothers again in the real sense. That's what I'm hoping for."

She hung on to his arm. "Ever since the avalanche, you've been different. What's happened to you and Sami defies description."

"Discovering I have a son has changed my entire world. I've been committed to Eliana, but without being able to have Ric in our lives, I can't marry her if she won't agree to visitation."

"Of course you can't." His sister eyed the baby. "I've learned to care for her very much and am so sorry for this terrible hurt, but if she thought I would come to her defense on this, then she doesn't know me either. I'd give anything to have a son like baby Ric, even if he weren't mine."

Bless you, Claudia.

"By forcing you to choose between her and your child when it doesn't have to be that way, she'll be making the greatest mistake of her life." Her voice shook. "I need to talk to Eliana in person and convince her of that. Maybe I can get her to put back the date of the wedding for a little while longer until she gets over the worst of the shock and can think clearly."

Ric shook his head. "It won't do any good. It's the title she wants back, but that can't happen now." If anyone could succeed, it would be Claudia. But in his gut, Ric had the premonition neither Eliana or her father would give an inch.

"Thank heaven!" She kissed his cheek. "If you and Sami will excuse me, I've got to phone Marco and tell him I'll be flying back in the morning."

"While you do that, Sami and I are going to get our son ready for bed. Tomorrow we'll all have breakfast and see you off at the airport."

His gaze fell on Sami who said goodnight to his sister, then walked out of the living room with him. After they reached the bedroom at the top of the stairs to start Ric's bath, she glanced at him. "She sounded so emotional when she held the baby. Aren't they able to have children?"

"Yes, but in the aftermath of the avalanche that killed our father, Claudia suffered a miscarriage. She'd been two months along at the time."

"Oh, no— That would have been so devastating for her."

"Our babies would only have been two months apart."

Sami made a soulful sound. "The poor darling. To see you with a baby you had no idea was alive has to be bittersweet for her. She needs to get pregnant again."

"I agree. The doctor says it would be the best thing for her, but Marco says she's been fighting it for fear of losing another one."

"Pat had a miscarriage between children. She went

through the same fear before she got pregnant again. It's a very frightening time."

Ric dripped water on the part of the baby's tummy that wasn't submerged. His little legs kicked so hard, he splashed water. He was a miracle. The idea of a permanent separation from him and the mother who had born him was anathema to Ric.

"I saw that fear with Claudia," he murmured, "but tonight that all seems far away. I'm still celebrating the birth of our son and there's no room for sadness right now." He kissed his cheeks. "You know, I think he's hungry."

"I'm sure he is since it's an hour past his usual time. I'll get a new bottle for him and you can feed him."

"After he's asleep I need to talk to you privately, away from the villa. I'll ask Claudia to listen for him. Between her and Mara, he'll be well taken care of while we take a drive to the harbor. It's one of the major attractions I think is best seen at night."

Sami felt all fluttery inside as Ric drove them along the coast road to the city's harbor.

She'd been waiting to be alone with him. Tonight he looked marvelous in a dark green crew-neck sweater and jeans. The estate car smelled of the soap he'd used in the shower. Combined with his own male scent, her seduction was complete, but he had no idea what his nearness was doing to her. Except that wasn't true. She was sure he did, but he wouldn't act on it.

She forced herself to concentrate on the sights out the

window. Tourists from all over the world—lovers, old couples, teenagers—meandered in and out of the colorful shops beautifully decorated for Christmas. The holiday excitement was contagious. Cooking aromas drifted from the restaurants lining the curving seawall. The area was made all the more romantic by the sight of Paphos Castle lit up for Christmas against a dark blue sky.

Ric pulled to a stop on a rise away from the other cars so she could get a good view. "This used to be a Byzantine fort that was rebuilt by the Lusignians, then redone by the Venetians and finally restored by the Ottomans. What you're looking at is one of two towers built in 1222. Sadly, the other was destroyed by an earthquake."

"Being on Cyprus is like living in an ancient open-air archaeological museum. I'm in awe. Thank you for bringing me here, Ric." She clasped her hands in her lap. "I'd be remiss if I didn't thank you for everything you've done for me the last few days, the excursions in the boat—I appreciate how much you've gone out of your way to make this an enchanting time."

"I've enjoyed it, too. More than you know. It's given me time to think about the future. That's what I want to talk to you about. Our lives are going to be connected from here on out. We might as well start laying the groundwork."

Suddenly her pulse sped up. She swung her blond head toward him. "How can you plan anything when you don't know if you're getting married or not?"

"The one doesn't have anything to do with the other.

No matter what happens between Eliana and me, Ric is a part of my life now. I want to talk about how you and I can share our son with the least amount of difficulty."

"There's no such animal, Ric, not when we live on separate continents."

"Then maybe we can change that."

Her heart pounded outrageously. "How?"

He stared at her over his strong arm stretched across the top of the steering wheel. "If you moved to Cyprus."

Sami's eyelids squeezed shut. "You can't be serious."

"Just hear me out. You and Ric would live at the villa. There's a department of computer engineering at the university in Limassol. It's a ten-minute helicopter ride from my house to the campus. With Mara and Daimon here to help, you could get your master's degree and be with our son the same as you would in Reno."

"I don't know Greek!"

"With your brain, you'll pick it up fast and I'll help you."

"Ric—you don't really mean what you're saying."

"Why not? If I'm married, I'll fly down from Genoa every Friday evening after work and fly back Monday morning. You'd have that time to get away, study, travel. Anything. It's a workable solution to our problem so our son sees both of us on a regular basis. We'd bring your sister and family over to visit often. Neither Claudia nor Vito's wife, Donata, would be able to stay away. Donata wants a baby. When Vito sees himself in Ric, he'll want one, too."

"And of course Eliana would be all right with that—"

She was so shaken, her voice was virtually unrecognizable.

"If we're married, then she could either come with me or stay in Genoa. The choice is hers."

"She'd never stand for it."

"Eliana would have to. It would be part of our marriage agreement."

"The idea is ludicrous."

Something flickered in the dark recesses of his eyes. "Can you think of a better one?"

Her thoughts were reeling. "I couldn't just move here—"

"Not even for Ric's sake? How much are you willing to sacrifice to give him a stable home with his own mother and father?"

"That's not fair."

He moved his arm and rested it on the back of the seat. His fingers were within inches of her hair. "I can make it fairer by providing for you and Ric so you don't have to worry about money and paying back student loans."

"You're not my husband!"

"I'm Ric's father," he shot back calmly. "My son means everything to me."

She trembled. "He's my raison d'être!"

"Precisely. That's why we need each other to make this work so everyone's happy. I want to give you and Ric everything. You went through the whole pregnancy alone and have been raising him without help. Now that you've found I'm alive, I'm prepared to do whatever it takes. It's my turn and my right as Ric's father."

"I'm overwhelmed by your generosity, but what you're asking is impossible."

"Not impossible—practical. Flying down here once a week to see Ric makes more sense than for me to fly to Reno on a weekly basis to see him. But I'll arrange it if I have to."

"You couldn't do that—" she exclaimed, alarmed for him. "Your life wouldn't be worth living. You wouldn't have a company to go back to, and your wife wouldn't be able to handle it!"

"Nevertheless it's what I'll do if you can't see yourself moving here. I'll give Vito more responsibility. Claudia's observations about him have given me food for thought."

"But Ric—"

"No buts, Sami. After being trapped together and given a second chance at life, how can we not give our son as much joy as possible? If you can't bring yourself to move, I'll buy a home on Lake Tahoe to be near you. The high elevation makes a perfect setting."

"When were you there?"

"Right before I started college, I traveled to the States with some friends. It's one of the most beautiful lakes I've ever seen. I'll buy a boat for Ric and me to enjoy. But as I said, you have a ready-made home right here on the Mediterranean. Ric will grow up being trilingual, which will be a great advantage to him."

As usual, he had a way of getting to her. She couldn't argue with his logic. He had the financial means to make anything he wanted happen, but he refused to consider the elephant in the room. "Until you know what Eliana has decided, then there's no more point to this discussion."

"I agree. I've told you what I intend to do one way or the other. You have until Christmas Eve to decide what plan sounds best to you," he said on a satisfied note.

He started the car and they headed back to the villa. In the process, he had to remove his arm which brushed her shoulder. The slightest touch sent little fingers of delight through her body. She grasped at any topic to cover her reaction. "Maybe Claudia will be able to make Eliana see reason."

In the darkness of the interior, his expression looked almost savage, sending a different shiver down her spine. "If by that time my fiancée hasn't come to terms with everything on her own, then she's not the person I thought she was."

He sounded so distant, she couldn't pick up on anything else.

"Maybe she doesn't have the capacity to love without qualification. Some people don't. But if growing up as a princess with money and power means so much to her that she can't accept your situation, then that's something else."

Sami had to give Matt credit. Even though the news about her pregnancy had been brutally painful for him, he'd still insisted he wanted to marry her and would love the baby. But that was before she'd discovered Ric was alive and wanted his son.

If she decided to marry Matt now and live in Oakland with him, Ric would buy himself a home there in order to be with the baby. There was no way out. By coming to Genoa, she'd changed destiny.

"In a few days I'll have my answer, Sami."

She bowed her head. "I'm beginning to understand why you did away with your title. More than ever I'm thankful you abolished it. I want our son to grow up having a normal life, never thinking he's better than anyone else."

He exhaled a heavy sigh. "That's the whole idea."

If Eliana didn't love Ric enough to let go of her pride and accept his child, then she didn't deserve him. Having said that to herself, Sami had to admit she'd fallen in love with him. Crazily in love so she could scarcely breathe whenever she heard his voice or saw him enter a room.

"Ric? Tell me something honestly."

"I'll do my best," he said in a slight drawl.

"Was there another woman in your past before Eliana? Someone you wanted to marry?"

His bark of laughter wounded her. "You think my heart's desire spurned me years ago, putting me off women for the rest of my life?"

Her cheeks grew warm. She shouldn't have said anything.

"Don't try to figure me out. You won't succeed. The truth is, I thought I was in love with every woman I got close to. But to my parents' regret, I could never see myself married to any of them." He shifted in the seat. "What about you? Why weren't you married long before now?"

His question brought her up short. "I never met the right one."

"The right one… I wonder if there is such a thing."

"Did your father press you to marry Eliana?"

"He had his hopes, but no." His answer was unequivocal. "I decided to marry her of my own free will, for my own reasons and no one else's."

She hadn't been expecting that revelation. It hit her with the force of the avalanche. His comment put a different slant on everything. After finally deciding to spend the rest of his life with Eliana, she had disappointed him by wanting the title and not being willing to accept his baby. The hurt had gone straight to his heart and meant he was suffering, but he'd never let it show. Sami wished she could shield him from that pain.

"Did your parents have a good marriage?" she asked quietly.

"For an arranged one, it worked remarkably well. Father had his affairs and Mother overlooked them."

That would explain his cynicism.

"I don't know about my siblings' marriages at this stage," he went on speaking. "They were both in love, but these are early days with more difficult times to come. What else would you like to know?" They'd arrived at the villa. He parked the car in the drive and shut off the engine.

"I'm sorry if I've offended you with my questions."

"Offended—" He turned to her. The moonlight pouring through the windshield reflected in his black eyes. "I find it totally refreshing. Nothing's changed since we were caught in the avalanche. I found *you* totally refreshing then, too. For the first time in my life, I was with a woman who knew nothing about me, who couldn't have identified me.

"We took each other as we found each other, Sami. No preconceptions. Whatever came out of you was genuine and honest. I believe that foundation put into motion what happened between us. After spending time with you, it's not a mystery to me any longer."

It wasn't for her either. But she feared that if she stayed in the car another minute, she'd blurt out her love for him. "We'd better go in and check on Ric, just in case he awakened and found us both gone."

"Don't leave yet," he suggested. "Mara would have called me if there was a problem. I thought with this full moon we'd take a walk on the beach. The light brings the dollar fish to the surface. You'd enjoy the sight. I brought a jacket for you."

Heaven help her but she didn't want to go in yet. At least walking would keep her body in motion. Sitting out here in the dark with him amounted to an open invitation to forget rules and beg him to kiss her. But if he did what she wanted, it would be her fault. She wished he *weren't* so honorable, but of course she didn't really mean it.

"As long we're only gone a short while."

"We'll come back whenever you say."

If there were no Eliana, he'd have a long wait.

He reached in back for the black leather bomber jacket and handed it to her. After thanking him, she got out of the car and put it on before he could come around. It was too big, the sleeves too long, but it smelled of him and she loved the feeling of being wrapped in it.

They made their way past the marina, their bodies close together, but not touching. No one else was out walking along the shore. The moonlight made a pale gold path across the water, following their progress. Lights from a cruiser far out from the coast twinkled in the darkness. Sometimes perfection was too perfect. This was one of those times, deepening her ache for Ric.

Keep moving.

"Come look over here, Sami."

She'd been so deep in her thoughts about him, she hadn't realized he'd stopped. When she turned, she saw he was hunkered down close to the water. She walked over.

"Oh—they look exactly like silver dollars!"

"These fish like to come up to the surface at night and moon-bathe."

"How adorable. They look like they don't have a worry in the world. I'd like to do that myself. Where are their babies?"

He chuckled. "I've never thought about it. In summer we'll swim here at night and find out."

He was sounding as though her move to Cyprus was already a fait accompli. "They don't sting?"

"No. Like our son, they're harmless, but not helpless. If they sense danger, they disappear like those heavenly bodies you once compared us to. Amazing how our separate orbits collided again." He stared up at her. "Only this time I can see your hair. Its glow rivals the moonlight. I'm surprised it didn't illuminate our heavenly prison. Once we'd reconciled ourselves to our fate, that time with you *was* heavenly, Sami. Wondrous."

Tears stung her eyelids. "I'll never forget it. Every time I look at Ric, I remember."

"That's why he's perfect, because it was so perfect for us. You thrilled me, Sami."

She was dying inside. "Please don't say things like that and make this harder than it already is," she begged him. "Let's go back and promise not to talk about it again."

He rose to his full height. Ric possessed a virility she had no immunity against. "I promised not to do anything you didn't want me to, but you can't make me promise *that*. You became a part of me. We became parts of each other and it produced our baby. From now on we'll be wrestling with that reality. It's pointless to pretend otherwise."

Sami bit her lip. "So you think talking about it is going to help?"

A grimace marred his hardened features. "No."

Not waiting for anything else he might have said, she started running and didn't stop until she entered the villa. No one was around as she dashed up the stairs to her bedroom and walked over to the crib. Their baby slept soundly. While she looked down at him, examining every precious part, Sami felt Ric's hands slide to her shoulders from behind. She hadn't heard him enter the room. The contact made her feel light-headed.

"I've made a decision." When he spoke, his lips brushed her temple. "We're going to fly back to Genoa with Claudia in the morning. I need to talk to Eliana in person. She should have made up her mind by now. The fact that she hasn't phoned yet seems to prove she doesn't want the marriage. I refuse to play games and wait until the twenty-fourth. Be ready by six to drive to the airport."

CHAPTER EIGHT

AFTER squeezing her shoulders gently, Ric let her go and vanished from the room. Sami stood there for a long time afterward before she started packing. Even when she'd finally put on her cotton pajamas and climbed under the covers to go to bed, she could still feel the imprint of his hands. Talking about the past reminded her how much pleasure he'd given her. If she was going to be haunted by those memories for the rest of her life, she'd go mad.

Sami didn't know when she fell asleep, but it was only ten to three when the baby's crying brought her wide-awake. She turned on the lamp and flew out of bed to pick him up. Since coming to Cyprus, this was the first time she'd gotten up with him in the night. Ric had claimed that job from the beginning.

Though she tried to settle him down, he cried harder. Afraid he was sick, she put him on her bed to change him, but saw nothing wrong. She felt his face and forehead, but he wasn't running a temperature. While she put a clean diaper on him, a disheveled Ric, wearing a brown robe, swept into the room barefooted.

"What do you think's wrong?" He sounded anxious. "Our *piccolo* has never awakened this early in the night."

"He probably had a gas pain."

The second the baby looked at his father, he cried harder than ever. On a burst of inspiration, Sami snapped up his stretchy suit and handed him to Ric. The moment he cuddled him against his shoulder and spoke Italian to him in an incredibly tender tone, the baby quieted down. Every so often a little half sob escaped, shaking his body.

She smiled. "It's obvious there's nothing wrong that his *papa* can't fix."

"Sami..."

"It's true. He's feels safe with you. Every son wants a father like you, but not all sons are that lucky." She walked over to the dresser for another bottle of formula. "Here. While you feed him, I'll go to sleep for what's left of the night."

She turned off the light and went back to bed, assuming he'd sit in the chair as he always did. Instead, he walked around the other side of the bed and lay down on top of the covers, putting the baby between them. "I think he'll be happier if he's here with both of us."

No, Ric—

"He's hungry!"

Sami could tell. The baby made noises while he was wolfing down his formula, provoking laughter from Ric that shook the bed. "After watching you eat, I've decided he must take after you."

"So you've noticed."

Heat spread through her body. She noticed every single detail about him. "It was hard not to when you ordered a third helping of those *mezes* at the seaside restaurant."

"I confess I'm a fish lover."

"They were delicious."

"If Ric grows up here, he'll become addicted. Do you have anything like them in Reno?"

"Not even remotely and you know it! It'll be hamburgers and pizza." The idea of living on Cyprus hadn't left her mind, but she could never do it. It wouldn't be fair to Eliana or their marriage.

And if he didn't marry her?

It still wouldn't be right. In everyone's eyes Sami would be a kept woman. But in Reno, she'd be the head of her own home. He'd be a father who came on visitation, like other divorced fathers. They wouldn't be sleeping together. She'd made her mind up about that, too. Sami hadn't lived her life this long to end up being a man's lover and nothing else, even if that man was the most wonderful man on earth.

She had no illusions where he was concerned. He'd told her he thought he'd loved every woman with whom he'd ever had an intimate relationship, but he'd never wanted to marry any of them. Whatever reason had caused him to propose to Eliana had its underpinnings based on other things he hadn't chosen to reveal.

Sami believed Eliana would break down and agree to anything to be married to Ric. She just needed more convincing, and was waiting for Ric to come to her. Well, her plan had succeeded because he was cutting this vacation short to be with her again. Six o'clock would be here before they knew it.

A loud burp resonated in the room. She grinned. "I heard that. Why don't you put him back down in the crib so you can get some sleep before we leave?"

"Did you hear that, *figlio mio?* Your *mamma* wants to get rid of us."

"I do," she lied.

She felt the side of the bed dip. "Then we'll let you get your beauty sleep. In case you were wondering, you don't need it."

Keep that up and I'm yours forever.

At nine the next morning, Ric's jet landed in Genoa. During the flight Sami had got better acquainted with Claudia, who was a lovely person in her own right. They talked about her miscarriage and Ric's birth. Sami felt that in other circumstances they could be close friends.

A limousine was waiting at the airport to transport them. As Sami glanced around before getting in, she noticed the hood. The special ornament was missing!

Like Pharoah, who'd had the name of Moses erased from every pillar and historical record, Ric had wiped his life clean of its former title. His bodyguards no longer called him Excellency. If all of this pleased him, he didn't mention it. Naturally his thoughts were on the meeting he was about to have with Eliana which accounted for his deep preoccupation.

"We'll take you home first, Claudia."

They passed many of the city's architectural wonders

and eventually reached Claudia's stately villa, one of the Degenoli properties. Sami could tell it was by the gold crest of the ancient seaman on the grillwork of the gate.

Claudia embraced her brother with the promise to get together later. Then she gave Sami a hug. "I can't wait for Marco to meet you and the baby."

Sami grasped her hand. "I'll call you," she whispered out of Ric's hearing. His sister pressed Sami's fingers, as if to say message received. She was a quick study and understood it wasn't an idle remark. After another kiss to little Ric's cheeks, Claudia got out of the limo and ran inside the villa.

Ric told the driver to head to the palazzo. He must have asked him to take the scenic route. They drove slowly through an area Ric pointed out the market of Saint Porphyrius. Local craftsmen displayed their Christmas products along the streets, and squares of the old town were dotted with huge nativity scenes.

Sami loved him desperately for always putting her pleasure and comfort first. She was no longer the same person who'd arrived in Italy fearing a bad reaction from Ric's father, even if she were able to find him. Since discovering Ric was alive, *she'd* come alive. Ric had become her life.

The limousine rounded a corner and climbed toward a beautiful medium-sized palace on the hill. "How beautiful!" she exclaimed to him. "What's its history?"

"Genovans call it the Palazzo Vermiglio. It was built in the seventeenth century. In English it means *vermillion,* so named because of its orangish-red exterior."

"I noticed the unique color right off. The interior must be incredible, too."

"Would you like to see it?"

"Not today, Ric. Remembering your reason for returning to Genoa, don't you know the last thing on my mind is sightseeing?"

"I'll make this the one exception." His playful tone threw her. He could be a tease. She'd seen evidence of it before, but this time she wasn't amused.

"Ric—I'm serious."

"So am I."

The limousine passed through a gate and wound around to the side. When it stopped, several of Ric's bodyguards opened the doors. He got out to help her with the baby.

"We'll go to your room first," he said in an aside before he spoke Italian with the others.

Your room?

Sami moaned. She had to be all kinds of a fool not to have realized this was his home. But the grandeur of it astounded her. How many men born in such circumstances would consider doing away with their title? Seeing where he lived gave her new insight into Eliana's pain.

She looked down at the baby asleep in his carrycot. When she'd told Ric their little boy reminded him of a prince in a fairy tale, she hadn't realized she was only speaking the truth.

"If you've caught up with your thoughts, we'll go in." His low voice curled beneath her skin to resonate through her nervous system.

The men took their things so he could cup her elbow. Bemused, she walked through the doors of the side entrance with him. He introduced her to an older-looking staff member named Mario who spoke in rapid Italian to Ric calling him Excellency. Uh-oh.

Ric guided her to an ornate staircase, not giving her a chance to ask questions. They started up the white marble steps to the next floor lined with paintings and tapestries. Halfway down the hall Mario opened the double doors to a sumptuous suite.

"This is your room, Sami," Ric explained, "and next door is the nursery."

She was so staggered by the opulence, she forgot to walk, and then had to hurry to catch up with him as he strode to another set of open doors. A female staff member he introduced as Sofia was waiting for them.

A cry escaped her throat when she saw the lavish nursery. Her eyes went to the exquisite crib that must have been in their family for years. "This just couldn't be real!"

One of the only grins she'd seen come from him unexpectedly appeared, making her heart leap. "I assure you it's as real as we are. It was made for the firstborn son of the fifth Count Degenoli. Shall we see how our son likes his new room?"

Before she could respond, a disturbance on the other side of the door had her turning around to see a man who was questioning Sofia in Italian. Sami might not understand the language, but she knew an interrogation when she heard one.

"Vito?" Ric called out. "Speak English, *per favore,* and come in."

Another drop-dead-handsome Italian with black hair entered the room. He was the same height as Ric with certain Degenoli traits that were unmistakable. Sami winced when she noticed a scar on the side of his neck. It came up a little above his jawline, no doubt a burn injury from his military experience.

"Vito? I'd like you to meet Sami, born Christine Argyle from Reno, Nevada. Sami, as you know, Vito's my only brother. He and Donata live in the other wing of the palace."

His brother nodded to her, scrutinizing her from head to toe.

"Sami's the mother of my son, Ric, who so far hasn't awakened since we got off the plane."

She could tell the other man was in shock. He stared at the baby, then at Ric. "So it's true what Claudia told me on the phone last night?"

"Every last word." Ric kissed his son's little cheeks again, then picked him up from the cot and put him on his shoulder. "Come take a good look at him and there'll be no doubt."

Vito walked over to inspect the baby. Pretty soon a smile lit up his dark brown eyes. "With that shape of his hairline, he's yours all right. Donata will have a heart attack when she sees him. She's not feeling well this morning, but she'll be up later."

"Would you like to hold him?" Sami asked.

"It's permitted?" He could be a tease like Ric.

"With my blessing. You and Claudia's husband are his only Italian uncles. His American uncle is married to my only sibling, Pat."

He stared at her a moment longer, digesting her words. Then he took the baby and put him against his shoulder the way Ric had done. "What's his name?"

"Ric Argyle Degenoli."

Vito shook his head. "Who would have thought? Monsignor Tibaldi would say when God took one away in the avalanche, he provided another."

"I believe he *would* say that." Ric responded to the dark humor before his gaze slid to Sami's. "I have to say *we* were the most surprised parents on the planet."

His brother's features sobered. "There's only one person more surprised."

"You're talking about Eliana, of course."

"Who else but your fiancée?"

"I'm going over there at noon to talk to her."

His brother handed the baby back to Sami before he looked at Ric. "Answer me one more question. Is it true you got rid of the title?"

"Yes. We're all on the same playing field now. No more firstborns. After centuries, the Degenoli line is free of its nemesis." Sami heard the fierceness in his voice.

Vito must have heard it, too. He looked stunned. "When did you start proceedings?"

"Soon after Father's funeral, but I had to go through a lot of red tape to make it official."

A nerve throbbed at Vito's temple. "Does Eliana know about it?"

"Yes."

He whistled. "*Mamma* always said you played with fire."

Sami's eyes went to the scar at the side of Vito's neck. Both men had them, though Ric's had been hidden.

"She played with it herself by marrying Papa, wouldn't you agree?"

Silence filled the nursery while the two men communicated in silence. Whatever was going on between them was private. Sami and Pat had shared similar moments throughout their lives. Neither of them had to say a word to get what the other was thinking.

There was still a whole part of Ric she knew nothing about. Though it was none of her business, she wanted to know all his secrets and felt deprived.

Vito broke the silence. "I'll be seeing you later, Signorina Argyle." He touched the baby's cheek with the back of his hand before leaving the room.She went over to the crib and laid Ric down. His lids had closed again. "He looks so cute in there. I do believe he's even made your brother baby-hungry."

"For several reasons, the Degenoli family will never be the same again."

Sami heaved a sigh, dreading what was coming. "Are you going to leave now?"

"Not until you're properly settled."

"Consider it done."

"I've never known a woman so easy to please. In case you do need anything later, just use the house phone and press zero. One of the staff will help you."

"Thank you. Now please stop worrying about me. You go on and meet with your fiancée. I have a feeling it will mean everything that you decided to surprise her," Sami's voice shook.

"Not until you and I have another talk first."

She frowned. "Another talk?"

"I saw your face before Vito left. It's time you knew certain facts about my life I hadn't chosen to reveal yet, but the event facing me today has dictated the moment." She had a sudden foreboding she wasn't going to like it. "Let's go in your room so we won't disturb the baby. What I have to tell you will take a while."

Alarmed by his words, she walked out of the nursery first. Ric followed, but he left the door ajar so they could hear the baby if he cried. Whatever he had to say had made her nervous and she sought refuge in the first available upholstered chair.

He remained standing while he leveled his gaze on her. "Eliana's father is from Milan and one of the wealthiest industrialists in our country. He married a Genovan princess, which makes Eliana one, too. For years I've known of her and many other eligible prospects my parents had in mind for me one day. When I turned twenty-one I told them I wasn't the marrying type so they could stop hoping for something that wasn't going to happen.

"They despaired of me, but didn't take me seriously.

Before my mother died, she begged me to stop being foolish and marry Eliana Fortulezza who would make me a wonderful wife and a beautiful one. It surprised me she had a preference. Because she was so ill, I told her I'd think seriously about it in order to bring her peace of mind. But I had no intention of following through. After Mother's funeral, I put it out of my mind.

"Less than half a year after her death, Father and I traveled to Imst for the wedding of my cousin to an Austrian of nobility. I didn't want to go because I knew Father would harp on me about my bachelor status, but he'd had a bad case of the flu and needed help, so I accompanied him. We stayed at the hotel that brought you and me together. The wedding was held in the Maria Himmelfahrt Church."

"I remember seeing it as I was coming in on the train. You couldn't miss it."

He nodded. "Before we went back to Innsbruck for the flight home, Papa wanted to relax in town for a few more days to get back his strength. On the night before the avalanche hit, he broke down and told me he was in financial trouble. That didn't surprise me. Years earlier Vito and I had learned through our uncle in Paphos that our father was an inveterate gambler."

Sami moaned. "That must have come as a terrible shock."

"At the time, you could have no idea. Considering how much money our father had the ability to lay his hands on, it raised terror in our hearts. The family wealth earned over hundreds of years could be like a gift that kept on giving. But squandered long enough if no one stopped him, one day it would come to an end and be the downfall of the family.

"Vito and I confronted him. He laughed and told us to mind our own business. He told me I had no right to question him because I didn't hold the title yet. In the same breath he told Vito he would never have the right to question what he did because he wasn't the firstborn. I'm convinced that rebuke was the reason my brother signed up for the military.

"He was fed up with Father. Already disillusioned by Father's womanizing, Vito didn't want any part of watching our father gamble away his legacy. Unfortunately Donata thought he'd lost interest in her. Vito was so ashamed of our revered father, who had to be the laughingstock of Genoa, he couldn't talk to her about it. The silence on his end did serious damage to their marriage, yet Donata has held on. Vito's luckier than he knows."

"I'm so sorry, Ric."

He threw his head back. "This gets worse. When I asked Father just how deep his problems were, he told me Eliana's father had covered some big debts for him. The mere mention of her father hit me like a bomb blast because it meant he'd needed help from someone like her father who had the kind of money necessary.

"Father had been living in denial for years and now his problems were horrific. He didn't need to spell it out.

The implication was painfully clear. If I married Eliana, those debts would be forgotten."

Sami shot to her feet. "But that's monstrous!"

"Perhaps now you understand my aversion to the title and all it represented. Evidently my mother had known about my father's gambling problem. It suddenly made sense why on her deathbed she'd pushed me in Eliana's direction as hard as she could. She was always loyal to my father, so she wouldn't have come right out to tell me the truth."

"Oh, Ric..."

"I was sickened by his confession, disgusted. Wounded. And still he wouldn't discuss amounts of money with me. He was too cowardly. For him to force me to marry Eliana meant the stakes were astronomical. Nothing less than her father obtaining the title and possession of the existing Degenoli family assets through his daughter Eliana would satisfy the debt.

"Father must have seen the distaste in my eyes because he actually broke down and cried like a baby. I'd never seen him do that before and I realized he was a broken man cursed by two vices that got a stranglehold on him early in life. When he begged me to marry Eliana to save him, I had to get out of the room."

Sami put a hand to her mouth, too horrified to speak.

"As I opened the door to go downstairs, he screamed at me to make that promise to him. He was on his hands and knees and looked so frail he could have been a hundred years old. I finally told him that in time there would be a marriage in the future, but I would do it for the family's sake, not his. That was the last time I ever saw him alive."

What he'd told her was too awful. She loved him so much and felt so helpless in the face of what she knew. "Does Eliana know all this?"

"No. Her father never worries about stooping to criminal behavior to get his own way. He rules her life in what I consider a criminal way and has shielded her because he's been so sure of the final outcome. For a truly greedy man, money isn't enough. He wanted the title to legitimize him once and for all. I'm the target he's been after all this time, which is why he enabled Father to get in deeper and deeper till he had him completely sewn up with no squirming room."

Sami couldn't stop her shivering. "What will he do when he finds out the title's gone?"

"I have a good idea. Rest assured I'm ready for him."

Ric's life was in danger. Sami could feel it.

"But what about Eliana?" she cried.

He sucked in his breath. "Sadly she's a victim of the same system as her father, whose god is money. She's ruled by him. Since June I've done my best to be good to her in order to save my own sanity and make our forthcoming marriage work. But my father's unexpected death put certain dynamics into motion that forced me to act sooner on my promise to him. In the process I hadn't counted on seeing you again in this life."

Another tremor passed through her body. If anything happened to Ric...

"Our emotional connection created a complication that's had a ripple effect. Instead of immediately getting to know Eliana with the goal of marrying her, I spent time looking for you first. Even though Father had died, I knew at one point I had to honor my commitment. But there's another truth to all this. If it weren't for the promise I made to him, I'd still be looking for you."

Ric...

When Sami had been defending him in the hotel room before learning his identity, she'd said he was the most honorable man she'd ever known. She'd believed it at the time and believed it now to the depth of her soul.

"After you and I were buried under the snow, I was positive my father was already dead. While we waited for the end to come, I realized that promise would never be fulfilled. I prayed for Claudia and Vito who'd be at the mercy of Eliana's father once the funeral services were over. He would swoop in and take everything out from under them. It would read like a novel and make headlines felt throughout the country."

She trembled. "But you *did* live through that avalanche." Since then he'd been carrying this nightmare on his shoulders and standing on the edge of a financial precipice.

History had taught her that kingdoms had been lost or won on the promises sealed with lands and dowries. In this case his father's scandalous behavior had cost their family the Degenoli empire. It wasn't fair. It was an archaic, evil system, just as he'd said.

Her thoughts flew back to the day she'd asked him if he were rich. He'd responded with what she now knew was a riddle. The second Eliana called off the wedding, Ric's family would be ruined. Sami couldn't stand it. If she hadn't come to Italy, none of this would be happening. Ric was in real danger now.

He'd told her he had his own reasons for asking Eliana to marry him. Now that Sami understood what they were, she needed to leave the country. If Eliana's father were pushed too far, he might come after the one thing Ric valued above all else. *Their baby...*

At this point there was only one thing to do, but she needed to get rid of Ric first. "After what you've told me, I can't bear for you to be here any longer. Please don't let me keep you. You need to go to her father and work this out."

He gave an elegant shrug of his shoulders. "There might be nothing to work out now he knows there's no title involved in the transaction. We'll see."

"Ric—there has to be some way to make this right."

"That could be asking too much, Sami. You've heard of the sins of the father, and I'm my father's son with a baby and no title."

There might even be bloodshed. Was that why Ric never took a step without his bodyguards?

Tears coursed down her cheeks. "I'd give anything to help you. What are you going to do?"

He looked so grim, she thought he must be ill. "Whatever I have to." His pain-filled eyes devastated her. "What will you do while I'm gone?"

No matter his pain, he was still worried about her.

Put on a face, Sami. Don't let him know.

"None of us got much sleep last night. I'm going to catch up on mine while the baby has a long nap. Later on I plan to phone my sister and let her know I'm installed in a real palace with the man who refused to be king."

Ric's sharp intake of breath reverberated against the walls. "I don't know when I'll be back. It'll probably be late."

"Take care," she called after him.

CHAPTER NINE

THE second he strode from her room, Sami moved over to the table and pulled out her cell phone to call her sister. Pat wouldn't appreciate being awakened at two in the morning, but this was an emergency. After three rings she picked up.

"Sami?"

"I'm sorry to do this to you, Pat, but I need a favor and don't have time to talk. It's 11:00 a.m. my time. Will you book me on a flight out of Genoa anytime this afternoon or evening my time, leaving for the States? Phone me back when you've got the reservation booked. Love you."

After hanging up, she moved over to the table to use the house phone. When a male staff member answered she said, "Could you connect me with Claudia Rossi, please."

"One moment."

In another thirty seconds Ric's sister came on the line. "Sami?"

"Hello, Claudia. I'm so glad you answered. I'd like to talk to you in person. Do you think we could get together for lunch today? Maybe we could meet at a favorite restaurant of yours?"

"Of course. I'll come by for you at the side entrance. Shall we say in a half hour?" Claudia knew something was wrong and was playing right along. Sami could hug her for it.

"That would be perfect. Thank you."

She put the phone back on the hook.

Since she was already dressed in her suit and white blouse, all she had to do was pack the diaper bag with some formula and diapers she'd need for the flight. She couldn't take her luggage. That would be a dead giveaway. She needed to look like a mother going out for an afternoon with a friend.

When it was time, she put Ric in his carrycot. Just as she was about to walk out, her phone rang. She picked up. "Pat?"

"It's done. Five o'clock on TransItalia to New York. You'll connect with a Continental flight to Reno."

"Bless you. Now I've got to go."

She left the suite and walked down the magnificent hallway with the baby. Several staff people nodded to her. Claudia's limousine was waiting at the side entrance as planned. Little Ric was still asleep.

As Sami climbed inside she whispered, "Can your driver hear us?"

"Not unless I turn on the switch."

"That's good, because I need your help. We need to devise a plan to get me to the airport without Ric's bodyguards catching on."

"You're *leaving?*"

"I have to. Do you know about your father's gambling debts?"

"A little."

"Then I need to tell you everything so you'll understand." On the drive to the villa, Sami poured it all out. It was time Ric's family knew the terrible burdens he'd been carrying and the danger he could be in. "After hearing what a ruthless man Eliana's father is, I wouldn't put it past him to target our baby as a way to make Ric conform."

"I wouldn't either," Claudia said with conviction. "You're doing the right thing and I'm going to help you. Even if Ric never speaks to me again, it will be worth it when he finds out why you left."

Sami squeezed Claudia's hand. "Ric can't stand for me to take the baby away. After the avalanche, he has this fear he might never see him again. But the situation is too volatile for me to stay in Italy any longer."

"Do you know Vito phoned me before you did? Knowing about the rescinding of the title, he's put two and two together and wants you away from the palace. We both agree you need to be gone until this thing with Eliana is resolved one way or another."

Sami heaved a relieved sigh. "Do you have any ideas how to accomplish this? My flight leaves at five o'clock."

"I've eluded my bodyguards from time to time. Leave this to me." For a moment she sounded like her brother in one of his teasing moods.

Claudia pressed the switch and said something in

Italian to the driver. Then she turned it off. "I told him to take us back to the villa where we'll have lunch and stay until five o'clock when you're due back at the palace. He'll pass that information on.

"When we get to the villa, we'll go inside and have lunch. Then we'll hide you in the back of my secretary's car. Signora Bertelli comes every weekday morning at eight and leaves by three. Her car is parked in the rear near my study. The guards won't have any idea. You can give her your instructions on the way to the airport."

Though Sami was in deep pain, she smiled at Claudia. "You're brilliant."

Ric left the Fortulezza estate for the last time. His business was finished and his agony over. Every asset including money and properties of the Degenoli fortune were now in the hands of Eliana's father.

Thanks to Ric's father, neither he nor Vito had a job, and neither he nor his siblings had a roof over their heads.

At least not in Genoa.

But he'd managed to salvage his mother's assets, enough for all of them to start a new life on Cyprus and be a real family.

He was free. Free in every sense of the word.

His heart pounded like steel striking an anvil. All he could think of was Sami and his son. He climbed in the limousine and told the driver to take him back to the palazzo. Once they arrived at the side entrance, he raced inside and took the steps two at a time to reach the second floor.

"Sami?" He knocked on her suite door. When she didn't answer, he opened it and called her name again. No answer. Her things were still around. He hurried through to the nursery. Ric wasn't in there. Maybe she'd put him in the stroller and had taken him for a walk.

He phoned Mario. "Have you seen our guests?"

"No. She and the baby left with your sister for lunch at her villa around eleven-thirty. As far as I know, they're still there."

"Thank you."

He hung up and called Claudia. All he got was her voice messaging. Frustrated, he phoned Carlo. "I understand Signorina Argyle and my son are still with my sister."

"That's right. Your sister told the driver the signorina would be leaving at five to return to the palazzo." Ric glanced at his watch. It was four-thirty. "She's not answering her phone. Do me a favor and go to the door. I need to speak to her. Tell her to call me."

"Bene."

A minute later his phone rang. "Claudia? I understand Sami's still there. Will you put her on?"

"I'm afraid she's no longer here."

"Then where is she? I'm at the palazzo and there's no sign of her or Ric."

"Listen, Ric—"

He heard her hesitation. A band tightened around his lungs. Whenever Claudia started out a sentence like that, she was afraid of something. "Where is she?"

"A-at the airport," she stammered.

He knew it. "When does her plane leave?"

"Five."

"What airline?"

"TransItalia to New York. Don't be angry. She was afraid Eliana's father might come after your baby and—"

"I know exactly how Sami's mind works." He cut her off. "But I know something she doesn't and everything's going to be fine, so don't worry. I'll tell you all the details later."

He hung up and phoned Carlo. "Get out to the airport and stop the TransItalia flight that's supposed to leave at five for New York. Signorina Argyle and my son are on it."

"But how could they be?" he asked in bewilderment.

"You're dealing with my sister, who knows every trick in the book. I'm taking the helicopter and will meet you there."

On his way to the pad at the rear of the palace he phoned Mario. "Instruct the staff to gather up everything Signorina Argyle left in the suite and have it delivered to my private jet ASAP."

"This way, Signora." One of the flight attendants helped Sami to the window seat in the coach section at the rear of the plane. With so much commotion, Ric was awake. On the flight over, nothing had seemed to faze him, but he was a different child right now and growing fussier by the minute.

As soon as she was settled, she picked him up out of his carrycot and held him close while she patted his back.

"We're going home, sweetheart." She'd cried so many tears, she thought she'd be dry by now. But the baby's tears started hers up all over again.

The plane filled fast. Every seat looked taken. Pat must have pulled a few strings to get Sami on this flight. She couldn't credit that they were really leaving. She felt as if her heart was being torn out of her body.

Knowing Ric, she knew she'd see him again, of course, but he'd probably be a married man when he could find the time to fly to Reno. She had no doubts he'd work out all the complications with Eliana and her father to preserve his family's honor, but nothing between Sami and Ric would ever be the same again.

Visions of their week together played through her mind like a movie, torturing her to death. The final blow came when the Fasten Seatbelts light went on. This was it.

She had to put the baby back in his cot and fasten the straps. He didn't like it at all. She pulled a bottle out of the diaper bag. Once she was strapped in, she held it to his mouth so he'd drink, but he wasn't interested and fought her.

She gave up. Once in the air, she'd be able to hold him and get him to settle down. She let his fingers curl around hers, hoping the contact would keep him preoccupied. The male passenger in army fatigues seated next to the baby smiled at her. "Hi. I'm Gary."

A real live hero from the military. He looked so totally American with his butch cut, she couldn't help but smile back. "I'm Sami. This is my son, Ric."

"He's awfully cute."

"Thanks, but he'd be a lot cuter if he weren't so upset."

Whatever the soldier said back was lost to her because she noticed a couple of Italian men in nondescript suits who didn't look like passengers walking down the aisle toward her. They were scanning the packed plane.

As they drew closer, Sami recognized one of them and gave a little gasp of shock. *Ric's bodyguards.* Her heartbeat took off at a breathtaking pace.

The men reached her row in a hurry. "Signorina Argyle? There was an irregularity with your passport before you boarded the plane. You will have to come with us please on orders of the Chief of Police." Chief Coretti was involved?

The soldier's eyes widened before he got to his feet and stepped out in the aisle to make room. One of the bodyguards took the diaper bag while the other picked up the carrycot holding her baby.

"Good luck," the soldier said as she stepped past him.

She was in too much shock to answer him, because by now another man stood behind the security men. The glint of glittering eyes black as jet was unmistakable.

"Ric!"

He must have noticed her legs start to buckle. The next thing she knew he crushed her in his strong arms. "Hold on to me, darling. Keep holding on and never let go."

"Tell me what this means," she half moaned.

Ric buried his face in her hair. "It means I'm free to ask you to marry me. If you don't say yes this instant, you're in a lifetime and beyond of trouble."

Sami didn't even take an instant before she found his

mouth to give him her answer. After having to hold back for so long, her hunger for him had taken over.

The passengers began clapping. She heard a few wolf whistles. In the background above the din she could hear their son wailing loudly enough to wake the dead, but for once she had to attend to her own needs first.

"I love you, Enrico Alberto Degenoli the thirteenth, but you've always known that."

"Sami, Sami. *Tesora mia.* I adore you."

She heard throats being cleared.

"Excellency," one of his bodyguards whispered. "We need to exit the plane so it can take off."

Sami giggled for happiness. "I'm afraid it's harder for you to get rid of your title than you thought."

"As long as it haunts everyone else, that's all that matters. Give me your mouth one more time."

Three days later she walked down the aisle of the church in Paphos with her new husband, beaming at the small crowd of beloved faces of friends and family members on both sides who'd come to see them married. Their baby rested against Pat's shoulder. When Sami looked at her sister, they had one of those communication moments.

They were both remembering Pat's warning over the phone. *You might be walking into something you wish you could have avoided. Not all people are as nice and good as you are, Sami. I don't want to see you hurt.* Was it only ten days ago?

Pat blew her a kiss. It said, *You were right to look for*

Ric's grandfather. You were on the path to your destiny.
Sami flashed her a brilliant smile.

The doors at the back of the church opened to the sun-
light. What a glorious wedding day! She looked at the
handsome man she'd just pledged her life to. Sami was
so in love with him she couldn't contain it. "Oh, Ric—"

"I know," he said, reading her mind. "We've got to get
each other to ourselves quick."

"Just a few more pictures, then we'll kiss the baby
and go."

Everyone followed them outside. So many hugs and
kisses, but it was clear Ric had trouble letting go of their
son. Sami could be jealous, but she wasn't.

Finally they climbed in the back of the car and Vito
drove them to the harbor where the cabin cruiser was
waiting. As he helped them get on board, he hugged her,
then his brother. Sami heard him say, "I've talked it over
with Donata. She's excited to move here with everyone."

Ric gave him a bear hug back.

When they moved below to the galley, she caught his
face in her hands. "What was that all about?"

"I'll tell you later. First, I need to get you out of your
wedding dress. You looked like a golden-and-white angel
in there today, Sami." He kissed her pliant mouth. "But
will you forgive me if I confess I've been waiting to take
this off you since the second I saw you in it?"

She gave him a playful smile. "I have a confession of
my own to make. For eleven endless months I've longed
to lie in the arms of the man who held me in the avalanche. All we had was each other and very little air

to breathe. I want to re-create that time over and over again, forever."

His eyes burned like black fire, filling her with longing as he carried her to the bed. She embraced him with a love she no longer had to hide.

They lost track of time in their desire to give each other pleasure. Her unseen lover was now her husband, a man whose lovemaking brought her the most ineffable joy. Hours later they surfaced to discover it was night.

She half lay on top of him. Sami rubbed the side of his jaw with her cheek. "Hmm. I feel a little stubble. Do you know I love every single thing about you whether we're in the dark or the light?"

His deep chuckle thrilled her. "It's still not as dark in here as it was that day. I can see enough of you to want you all over again. My appetite for you is indecent."

"Then we were made for each other," she cried.

"Tell me something," he whispered, kissing a favorite spot. "Was that soldier coming on to you?"

She lifted her head. "What soldier? Oh—the one on the plane?"

"Do you know another?"

"No," She laughed because he sounded so possessive. "He thought Ric was adorable and said so."

"Then I guess I forgive him."

"Darling." She kissed him hungrily. "Now tell me about Vito's plans."

He rolled her over to look into her eyes. "With all the money assets including the palazzo and Claudia's villa turned over to Eliana's father, the debt my father accrued is paid up in full."

"I can't believe it took all that!"

"My father's vice was his own undoing, but I don't want to talk about him. The best news is, Vito has agreed to go into business with me and run a new shipping line with the assets from Mother's legacy."

She covered his face with kisses. "I know how much it means for you to be close to him."

"I believe you do. It'll be fun to see if we can build a new Degenoli empire with our own hard work, shoulder to shoulder. Both my siblings are going to buy villas here on Paphos so we can all live together."

"It's perfect, except for one thing. You haven't told me how things went with Eliana."

"That's because her father wouldn't allow me to go near her. After our business meeting concluded, he told me she was spending time at Prince Rudolfo's winter palace in Torino while she recovered."

"That's awful."

"I don't think so. She couldn't handle my having a son, and I don't blame her. Rudolfo's her type and eligible. I think they could even have a good marriage because she'll be marrying a prince. That's much better than a count."

"Ric—" She buried her face in his neck.

"But I don't want to think about any of that again. The only thing that matters is you. You came to Italy as I'd hoped you would, bringing me a Christmas gift that's brought me joy beyond measure. I think I willed you here."

Her breath caught. "I'm positive you did. I felt a force stronger than my own will. Ric and I need you desperately."

"Then prove it to me again, Sami. I couldn't live without you now."

Neither could she without him.

Neither could she.

* * * * *

THE ITALIAN'S
CHRISTMAS
PROPOSITION

CATHY WILLIAMS

CHAPTER ONE

'ROSIE! ARE YOU going to focus on what I'm telling you?'

The cut-glass accent was a mix of despair, impatience and long-suffering love and Rosie guiltily dragged her eyes away from the far more stimulating sight below of people coming and going, skis on shoulders, imbued with the unique excitement of being on holiday in the run-up to Christmas.

The luxury five-star resort—a jewel nestled in the heart of the Dolomitic Alps in the Veneto region of northern Italy—was the last word in the very best that money could buy and as good as a second home to Rosie, who had been coming here with her family for as long as she could remember. She could close her eyes and accurately visualise every beam of deep burnished wood, every swirl and curve of marble, the timeless cool greys of the exquisite indoor swimming pool area and the oversized chandeliers dominating the Michelin-starred restaurants.

Right now, sitting in the galleried landing with a *latte* in front of her, Rosie was in prime position to admire the dramatic twenty-foot Christmas tree sweeping upwards by the reception desk, a vision of tasteful pink and ivory and tiny little electric candles. She could almost *smell* the pine needles.

'Of course I am,' she said with a suitable level of sincerity and enthusiasm. Across from her, her sister was on the verge of another of her laborious, long-suffering sighs. 'You were asking me what I intend to do once the ski season is over. I don't *know*, Diss. Right now, I'm just enjoying the ski instructing. It's *fun*. I'm meeting some really lovely people and plus, let's not forget, I'm looking after Mum and Dad's chalet while I'm here. Making sure it…er…doesn't get burgled…or anything…'

'Because burglars are a dime a dozen here in Cortina?'

'Who knows?'

'You can't keep flitting from place to place and from job to job for ever, Rosie. You're going to be twenty-four on your next birthday and Mum and Dad…well, *all* of us—me, Emily, Mum, Dad…we're *all* concerned that it's getting to a point where you can't even be bothered to try and…you know what I mean…'

'Become an accountant? Get a mortgage? Find a decent man to look after me?' Rosie flushed and looked away. She was particularly sensitive on the subject of men and, in her heart, she knew that this was what her parents were worried about—that she was never going to find Mr Right, as both her sisters had. That she was going to spend her life drifting from Mr Wrong to Mr Really Bad Idea to Mr Will Take Advantage. She had, as it happened, been down several of those roads in the past and, whilst she had put a cheerful face on each and every disappointment, each and every one had hurt.

At this point in time, if she never had another relationship in her life again, she wouldn't lose sleep over it. The last guy she had gone out with had been a fellow traveller in India. He had been out there buying cheap

Asian artefacts to sell for a profit in a market somewhere near Aldershot. They had had fun before he had taken a shine to a tall brunette and disappeared with her, leaving only an apologetic note in his wake.

The only saving grace in all these disappointing relationships, as far as Rosie was concerned, was that she hadn't made the mistake of bed-hopping. One guy. That was it. The one guy all those years ago who had broken her heart. She'd been nineteen and finding her feet all over again, having dropped out of university, and he had been there to catch her as she was falling. A biker with a refreshing disdain for convention and the first guy who had been a world away from the upper-class posh boys she had spent a lifetime meeting. She had loved everything about him, from his tattoos to the ring in his ear.

He, in the end, had loved the financial package she came with more than he had loved her for who she was, and had thrown a fit when she had promised to dump all her worldly goods for him. She still shuddered when she thought about what could have been the biggest mistake of her life. Since then, she'd enjoyed life without getting in too deep.

'Whoever said anything about becoming an accountant?' Candice rolled her eyes and grinned, and Rosie grinned back, because Emily's husband, wonderful as he was, could be a little tedious when he began pontificating about exchange rates and investment opportunities.

Still, he earned a small fortune, so he had obviously played the game right.

Whilst she, Rosie, hadn't started playing it at all.

'With Christmas just three weeks away...' Candice shifted and Rosie looked at her sister with narrowed eyes, smelling a conversation ahead that she would not want to have.

'Don't worry, I'll make sure the chalet is in tip-top shape for the family invasion. You know how much I love the whole decorating thing. Plus, I'll make sure there are lots of chocolates hanging on the branches of the tree for Toby and Jess.'

'There has been a slight change of plan. The snow is so magnificent at the moment that everyone's coming over a little earlier than originally planned.'

'Earlier than planned?'

'Tomorrow, as it happens. I'm the advanced warning party, so to speak. I know you and I had planned a couple of girly days together but you know Mum and Dad…they can't resist the slopes and the atmosphere here at Christmas. And there's something else,' Candice said in a rush. 'They're thinking of asking the Ashley-Talbots over for a long weekend. Bertie too. He's something or other in the City and doing quite well, I hear. They think it might be nice for you two to…er…get to know one another…'

'No.'

'It's just a thought, Rosie. Nothing's confirmed. He's always had that crush on you, you know. It might be nice!'

'Absolutely not, Candice.'

'Mum and Dad just thought that there's no harm in actually meeting someone a little less…*unorthodox.*'

'When you say that you're the advance warning party—' Rosie narrowed suspicious eyes '—does that actually mean that you've been sent to start preparing me for lots of lectures on getting my house in order, starting with dating Robert Ashley-Talbot? Well, no way will I be getting involved with him! He's…he's the most *boring* guy I've ever met!'

'You can't say that! You might find that you actually enjoy the company of someone who has a *steady job*, Rosie! Emily and I both happen to agree with Mum and Dad! Give me *one* good reason, Rosie-Boo, why you won't at least give it a go. If you find that you really don't like Bertie, then that's fair enough, but you haven't seen him in *years*.'

'A year and a half, and he can't have changed that much.' Nerdy, prominent Adam's apple, thick-rimmed glasses and a way of getting onto a really dull topic of conversation and then bedding down for the duration.

Rosie looked down. Down to the lively buzz of excited guests, down to the glittering Christmas tree, down to the clutch of leather chairs in the foyer, where a group of three people was gathering some papers, shaking hands, clearly about to leave.

'And—' she turned her clear blue-eyed gaze back to her sister '—I wasn't going to say anything but…but… I'm just not in a good place for meeting Bertie, Diss. Or *anyone,* for that matter.'

On her lap, she crossed her fingers and told herself that this was a perfectly sensible way out of a situation that would turn Christmas into a nightmare. She didn't want Bertie coming over. She didn't want to have to face the full force of her family gently trying to propel her to a destination she didn't want to go because they were concerned about her.

She leaned forward. 'I've had my heart broken while I've been out here.'

'What on earth are you talking about, Rosie?'

'You say that I never go for the right kind of guy?

Well, I did. I fell for one of the guests here. A business-man. As reliable and as stable as…as…the day is long. He was everything you and Ems and Mum and Dad would have wanted for me, which just goes to show that those types just aren't for girls like me. I bore them in the end. It was just a holiday fling but I guess I got more wrapped up in him than I thought I would.'

'I'm not sure I believe you,' Candice said, eyebrows raised. 'It's very odd that this is the first I'm hearing of this and we've been sitting here for what…an hour? What a coincidence.'

'I wasn't going to mention it but I felt I had to when you told me that Mum and Dad were thinking of asking Robert and his parents over for the weekend. I'm just a little shaken up, that's all. I know I've dated the wrong sorts but I really felt that this guy might be the one. I went into it with my eyes wide open and I was hurt. So… I just need a bit of time out to lick my wounds.'

'And where is this mysterious disappearing man right now?' But her voice was hesitant, on the cusp of be-lieving.

'As a matter of fact…'

And there was that group of three again. She recog-nised the elderly couple—Bob and Margaret something-or-other. She had given them both a lesson, filling in for their usual instructor who had called in sick when Rosie knew for a fact he had been suffering from a hangover. They had said were there to try and learn to ski because, although they were in their late sixties, they believed that old dogs could be taught new tricks and, since their daughter loved her skiing, they were up for giving it a try. They were going to be retiring. Selling up. A nice young man, Matteo, would be coming in for a flying visit to do the deal. Exciting times.

With his back to her as he shook hands with the older man, Matteo—or the man she assumed was Matteo, because who else could it possibly be?—was just the candidate for the role of businessman heartbreaker. There was no way she intended to spend her Christmas dodging Bertie, and a broken heart was the only excuse she could find that might save her from that dreadful possibility.

'There he is. Matteo. With that couple about to leave. He's here on business with them. He doesn't know that I'm up here looking down at him. Thinks I'm out on the slopes giving a lesson. He's probably completely forgotten about my existence already.'

She looked at her sister who stared down to the group of three, eyes narrowed.

'*That* creep was the guy who hurt you?'

Rosie mumbled something inarticulate, meant to convey an affirmative reply without going into further detail. Not a liar by nature, she was guiltily aware that she was blackening a perfect stranger's character with her little white lie.

Distracted, what happened next took her by surprise. It was so out of keeping with her cool, collected, elegant blonde sister. Candice was *always* so controlled! But here she was now, angrily rising to her feet, hands slapping down on the table, and then she was hurtling between tables, feet flying at a pace while… Rosie watched, mouth open, horror slowly dawning because she knew that this was not going to end well for her…

She would have to stop her sister before things went any further. She didn't waste time thinking about it. She leapt up and followed in hot pursuit.

* * *

For once, Matteo Moretti wasn't looking at his watch. He usually did. The end of a deal always awakened a restlessness inside him, an impatience to move on to the next thing. True, the signatures on the dotted line were technically not there yet, but that was a formality. Hands had been shaken and, as soon as the horror of the Christmas season was over and done with, the lawyers would be summoned and the finishing touches put to a purchase that meant a great deal to him.

Bob and Margaret Taylor, the most unlikely of clients, were beaming up at him. Bob, yet again, was congratulating him in his bluff, Yorkshire accent for getting past the post.

'Land's worth a bob or two.' He slapped Matteo's arm and winked. 'Can't tell you how many wanted to get their greedy paws on it but you're the first person the missus and I feel we can trust to do the right thing.'

'Honoured that you think that,' Matteo responded with sincerity.

He'd been here at this eye-wateringly pricey resort for the past three days, wooing Bob and his wife. A different type of approach for a very different type of deal.

Around him, Yuletide merriment had been a constant backdrop, getting on his nerves, reminding him that it was high time he did what he always did every single Christmas—escape. Escape to his villa on the outskirts of Venice, which was a mere couple of hours from here.

He worked in London and had a penthouse apartment there, indeed lived most of his life there, but his elegant, yellow-stone villa here in Italy was his bolt-hole and the only place where he felt perfectly at peace. Every year he removed himself from the canned carols, the ridiculous Santa lookalikes ringing bells outside supermarkets and the pounding of crowds on pavements, frantically hunting down presents, wrapping paper, Christmas decorations and all the paraphernalia that seemed to arrive earlier and earlier in the shops with every passing year.

Two weeks away from it all, isolated in his sprawling manor with two trusted employees to cook and clean for him while he worked. God bless broadband and the Internet. It enabled him to avoid the chaos of the festive season while still keeping on top of each and every detail of what was happening in his various offices across the globe. He might live in England but he was Italian and this bolt-hole in Italy reminded him of his heritage and everything that went with it. He threw money at his PA, told her to do as she wished when it came to entertaining the troops at various office Christmas parties and he disappeared.

'Just a couple more "i"s to dot and a couple more "t"s to cross and it's yours, lad, and we couldn't be happier.'

Intensely private and remote, Matteo felt the twist of something highly emotional swell inside him because this was the one and only deal he had ever done that had real personal significance. His background, his childhood—in a way the very reason he was where he was now—all lay in that land he was on the verge of buying and the halfway house within it. It was a place of retreat for foster kids, an escape where they could feel what it was like to be in the open countryside, with nature all around them. Horses to ride, quiet, secret places to go and just *be,* chickens to feed and eggs to collect. An idyll.

So many years ago, but a fortnight spent there, when he had been just ten and about to go off the rails in a big way, had done something to him, had given him something to hold onto. He had found an anchor in a restless, rudderless existence and had somehow held onto that. Bob and Margaret hadn't been in charge at the time. They had come later, and of course he'd kept that connection to the place to himself, as he kept everything of a personal nature to himself. But with ownership of that special place within his grasp... Yes, he felt strangely emotional.

Shaking Bob's hand as they made plans for their final meeting, Matteo was ill prepared for what happened next.

A scene.

A blonde woman bearing down on them from nowhere. The high pitch of her voice was as piercing as the scrape of fingernails on a blackboard. Heads spun round, mouths opened and closed and there was a flurry of activity as stunned hotel employees and guests alike gasped and wondered what was going on.

For a split second, Matteo was utterly lost for words. Next to him, Bob and Margaret were also stunned into immobility.

'Who do you think you are... Matteo whoever you are...? How *dare* you mess with Rosie? People like you should be strung up! And I guess you're going to run away and leave her all broken-hearted. And I bet you won't even look back. You have no morals at *all*! She's been hurt too many times!'

'Are you talking *to me*?'

'Who else could I be talking to? Is your name Matteo?'

'Yes, but there seems to have been some kind of misunderstanding...'

Matteo, already on the back foot, peered around the tall blonde to see a shorter, plump girl, wearing an expression of dismay, borderline panic and acute embarrassment.

For a few seconds, he was utterly nonplussed. She was staring directly at him and she had the bluest eyes he had ever seen. Her hair was vanilla-blonde, a tangle of unruly curls framing a heart-shaped face that was, just at the moment, suffused with colour. Her mouth was a perfect bow shape and her skin was satiny smooth.

Words failed him. He stared. He registered that she was calling his name and then, somehow taking advantage of that moment of weird disorientation he had experienced at seeing her, he realised she was leading him away from the others with a sharp tug on his arm.

'Please, please, *please...*' Rosie was whispering, simultaneously tiptoeing and tugging him down so that she could whisper into his ear, 'Could you just play along with this for the moment? I'll explain in a bit. I'm really, *really* sorry, but all you have to do is…'

Is what? Matteo thought. Through the confusion of his thoughts, he felt her small, delicate hands clutch at his arm. She was so much smaller than Matteo, his tall form and muscular body towering over her.

'Who the hell are *you*?' Matteo kept his voice low, a whispered conversation that he knew looked a lot more intimate than it was. He was thinking fast but was disconcerted by the softness of her body and the sweet, floral scent of her hair. She was much shorter than him and her reaching up to him somehow emphasised the fullness of her breasts, pushing against her jumper, just brushing against him.

'Rosie. Sorry. Sorry, sorry, sorry. I had no idea my sister would rush down here like a tornado...'

'This isn't what I expected from you, son. You know how traditional I am when it comes to treating other people the way you would want to be treated yourself.' This from behind him—Bob's voice, thick with disappointment.

How the hell did the woman know his name? And who was she anyway? His head was clearing and one thing was certain—the ramifications of what was going on were becoming patently obvious.

No deal.

Lengthy unravelling of this mess was going to take time and time was not on his side. Bob was making noises under his breath, wondering whether he hadn't made a dreadful mistake, while his wife was trying to be the voice of reason. The deal was disappearing into the ether. He had no idea who was the woman imploring his help. His assumption was it was some kind of set-up somehow to extract money from him. He was made of money. Public accusations of some kind? Blackmail? Press somewhere waiting in the wings, cameras at the ready?

His levels of anger bordered on volcanic. Of key importance was to take this scene away from Bob and his wife and sort out the consequences later. Damage limitation was essential. He wanted this deal and he was going to do whatever it took to seal it.

And the only thing he could think of doing right now was to follow the lead of the pink-faced girl still looking at him and play along, much as he didn't want to.

He smiled and Rosie went a shade pinker.

'Rosie,' he murmured, spinning her round and edging

them both back to the group, who had fallen silent during their whispered *tête-à-tête*, including the screeching sister. 'You know we talked about this...'

He looked at Bob and Margaret with a self-deprecating smile and anchored the fiery little blonde closer to him so that she was nestled against his side. 'She's gone off the rails because she thinks I'm going to be one of those fly-by-night guys...' He shook his head, leant down and brushed his mouth against her cheek. 'How can I convince you, my darling, that this isn't just a fling for me?'

Rosie looked at him. Her skin burned where he had brushed it with his mouth. His arm, hooked around her waist, was doing all sorts of things to her body, making her squirm.

In the heat of the moment, she hadn't quite appreciated just how stunning the guy was. Raven-black hair, bronzed skin and eyes as dark as midnight. She knew that she was breathing quickly, just as she knew that she wasn't thinking straight. She was conscious of her femininity in ways she hadn't thought possible.

'Um...'

'This feels like the start of something big, Bob,' Matteo said in a darkly persuasive voice. 'I would have mentioned it to you but I didn't want to jinx it.'

'So romantic,' Margaret was saying with approval.

'Isn't it?' Matteo commented neutrally. He tightened his hand on Rosie's waist and gave her the tiniest of squeezes, nudging her ever closer, thigh against thigh, his arm resting just below her breast now.

Rosie felt the tightening of her nipples. She had no intention of catching her sister's eye but she could feel Candice looking at the pair of them and heaven only knew what was going through her head. Candice was astute but it had to be said that this dark stranger, dragged into a charade not of his making, was doing a fine job of pulling it off and her only question was *why*?

'You should head back to your hotel.' Matteo's primary objective at this point was to put distance between Bob, Margaret and the combustible situation unfolding in front of them. 'Long day tomorrow finalising our deal.'

'You're getting a good man in this one,' Bob said warmly, moving in to shake Rosie's hand. 'Glad everything's sorted, lad. Misunderstandings can get out of control! Nice to see you've got the makings of a family man within you. A good woman is always the making of any man.' He chuckled and gave his wife a hug.

Matteo thought it best to speed things along. He had no idea what was going on but the threat of it all blowing up was a distinct possibility and one he intended to divert with everything at his disposal. He mentally bid a temporary farewell to his Venetian villa that was waiting for him the following evening. It wasn't going to happen.

'So they say,' he murmured as he thought ahead to how he intended to squash whatever machinations were afoot. 'Comprehensively' was the word that sprang to mind.

'Hope we get to spend some time with the two of you before we head back to Yorkshire. Family is everything, like I say, and I wouldn't mind raising a glass or two to celebrate young love.'

Matteo murmured, nodded, half-smiled, brushed his lips against Rosie's hair... He exerted every ounce of charm to smooth over the sudden, alarming pot holes that had surfaced on the very smooth road. He walked them to the glass door, where they were waiting to be met, the little blonde still by his side because question time was about to begin.

Rosie watched with mounting dread as Matteo disposed of her sister with ruthless speed. He was the essence of charm, even though his hand on her waist carried the hint of a threat that sent shivers racing up and down her spine. She could hardly blame him. She listened in mutely as he smoothed over Candice's doubts, laying it on thick until Candice was smiling and telling him how relieved she was that things were back on track, apologising for the fuss and then, somehow, laughingly blaming *Rosie* for having given her the wrong impression.

Rosie couldn't believe the way events had transpired. Who knew that her five-foot-ten, ice-queen sister could let rip with such uncharacteristic drama? Candice was the one who flinched if someone raised their voice slightly too loudly in a restaurant. She moaned about people shouting into their mobile phones in public! She'd once told Emily off, when they had just been kids, for laughing too much.

Candice out of the way, Matteo dropped his hand, stood back and surveyed the blonde coldly.

'So,' he said flatly, 'Let's find somewhere nice and cosy and private and have a little chat, shall we?'

Rosie quailed. The man was sexy, dangerous…and from the expression on his face in the presence of his quarry.

'I'm really sorry, I—I know how this must look…' she stammered, only dimly aware that he was leading her out of the crowded foyer. She found she couldn't quite meet those wintry eyes.

'Do you, now?' Matteo purred.

Where was he taking her? She cast a desperate backward glance behind her, back down to the marbled foyer with the tall Christmas tree. The low buzz of curious voices that had greeted the little scene earlier had died down but there would still be curious eyes looking to see whether it might kick off again.

'Where are we going?'

'Somewhere private,' Matteo murmured, voice as smooth as silk and as razor-sharp as a knife, 'Where we can have our cosy little chat.'

'I've already apologised…' Her legs, however, were obeying his command. She stood up and began walking alongside him, hyper-aware of his presence. There was a leashed power to the guy that made her quiver with a combination of apprehension, downright fear and a weird sort of breathless excitement that stemmed from a place she couldn't quite put her finger on.

He wasn't saying a word and seemed unaware of the cluster of well-heeled people around him that parted to allow him passage as if in the presence of royalty.

It was extraordinary.

She had no idea where they were going but eventually they reached a door which he slid open, standing back to allow her to brush past him.

She'd never been into this particular inner sanctum, even though she had been coming to this very resort with her parents for as long as she could remember, before they'd bought their own chalet just a bit further up the slopes.

It was a large, square room, richly panelled, with a gleaming wooden floor that was largely covered by an expanse of expensive, silk Persian rug. A cluster of deep, comfortable sofas was positioned here and there and a long bar extended along the back of one panelled wall. Rosie assumed this was the chill-out area for the senior management who ran the resort, somewhere where they could relax and unwind, away from the clamour of what might be going on outside.

She stared around her and, when she settled her eyes back on Matteo, it was to find that he had made himself at home and poured a whisky for himself. Needless to say, there was no offer of any form of refreshment for her.

'Okay,' Rosie began. 'I know what you're going to say and I'm sorry.'

'First, you have no idea what I'm going to say, and secondly, if you're sorry now, then you're going to be a whole lot sorrier when I'm through with you and your accomplice.'

'Accomplice?' She gazed at him, bewildered, and then wished she hadn't because he seemed to have the most peculiar effect on her. He made her feel as though the room was beginning to spin and if she didn't sit down fast she would topple to the ground in an undignified heap.

'The blonde with a voice that could shatter glass. Sit.'

A voice that could shatter glass? That was a first when it came to a description of her sister. Of either of her sisters, for that matter. Both were tall, sophisticated and impossibly beautiful in an ice-queen kind of way. Whereas she was... Rosie: short, way too plump because of the siren call of chocolate and all things sweet, with shoulder-length blonde hair that refused to be tamed, breasts far too abundant to be fashionable...

She recalled the heat of his hand so close to her breast and shivered.

Conscious of each and every one of those downsides, and aware of those cool, cool eyes on her, she haltingly headed for the closest chair and dropped into it, little knowing what was coming but all too ready to take the blame.

'If that little scene was some half-baked attempt to screw money out of me then you messed with the wrong guy,' he said flatly. He didn't raise his voice or move a muscle but for all that the single sentence was imbued with threat and Rosie shivered and licked her lips.

'I came here to do a deal that means a great deal to me,' he continued, in the same deathly subdued, almost conversational tone. 'Which is why I played along with whatever game you fancied you'd set in motion. I'm going to play along just until my deal is done, and then, let's just say you'll understand the meaning of regret.'

'You can't threaten me,' Rosie objected weakly. 'And that woman was my sister, not an accomplice!'

'Can't threaten you? No, you've got that wrong, I'm afraid. Here's the thing, whoever the hell you are—whatever scheme you and your sister or whoever she was have concocted, you can bury it, because there's no money at the end of this particular rainbow.'

'Money?'

'Did you really think that you would create a public scene to grab my attention, hurl baseless accusations against me to grab the *public's* attention and then somehow manoeuvre me into a place where I would part with hard cash to shut the pair of you up?'

'I have no idea what you're talking about.'

'Don't play games with me, miss!'

'I'm *not* playing games! I honestly have no idea what you're getting at! Are you saying that you think my sister and I are out to get money from you? Why would we want to do that?'

Matteo clicked his tongue with blatant incredulity, reached into his pocket and extracted a card from his wallet, which he tossed onto her lap. Then he sat back and crossed his legs.

'How *rude*!' Rosie exploded, her face bright red. 'Is this how you treat women? How dare you just…just fling something at me?'

'Spare me the self-righteous outrage,' he returned smoothly. 'Why don't you have a look at the card?'

Still fuming, Rosie looked at the card, which had just a name on it and three telephone numbers. She politely reached forward to return it.

'I'm sorry but this doesn't mean anything to me. Well, I guess it's your name. Matteo Moretti.' She sighed. He'd taken the card back and was obviously waiting for her to expand. His expression was unreadable and she got the impression that this was a man who knew how to conceal what was in his head and that it was something he was accustomed to doing. He emanated a certain amount of menace but she wondered whether that hint of menace wasn't amplified by the fact that she was just so *conscious* of him in a way she had never been conscious of any man in her life before.

Suddenly very much aware of her physical shortcomings, she fidgeted in the chair and tried to get herself into a suitably more elevated, commanding position.

'I suppose you're someone important, which is why you think I should recognise your name, but I don't know who's who in the world of business. You must be rich, because you think that I'm some kind of master criminal who wants your money, but you're wrong.'

'Your sister knew my name,' Matteo said bluntly. 'Care to explain?'

'Her name is Candice.'

'Irrelevant. Just answer my question. Time is money.'

Sinfully good-looking he might be but Rosie was beginning to think that he was the most odious guy she had ever encountered. Rude didn't begin to cover it.

'I teach skiing here,' she said stiffly. 'For the season. I happened to meet your…your friends on the slopes. Pierre was supposed to be giving them a lesson but he went out last night with his girlfriend and he didn't show up for—'

'Get to the point!'

'I'm getting there! Bob and Margaret told me that they were here mixing business with pleasure. They told me your name—Matteo. They said you never left the hotel, then they laughed and said that if they didn't get to grips with skiing then you were to blame because they were too busy feeling guilty about you being cooped up inside to concentrate on getting their feet in the right place. Obviously I didn't know it was *you* at the time, but that's how I happened to know your name. It was just coincidence that you happened to be where you were when…'

When all hell broke loose.

Matteo gritted his teeth. 'How much more tortured can this explanation get? I feel as though I'm being made to sample a vision of hell. Are you ever going to get to the point or do I have to bring the police in to question you?'

'Police? How *dare* you?' She glared at him and he stared back at her without batting an eyelid.

'Just. Get. To. The. Point.'

'Okay, here's the point!' Rosie snapped, leaning forward and gripping the sides of her chair tightly. 'I had to pretend that I had broken up with someone, because I didn't want to be condemned to seeing Bertie over Christmas, and I spotted you down there in the foyer with Bob and Margaret and I... I...figured that you were the businessman called Matteo so I lied and told my sister that I'd been seeing you! Is that enough of an explanation for you? I'm really sorry but you were the fall guy!'

CHAPTER TWO

THEIR EYES MET. Matteo was beginning to feel a little unsteady. He had never before heard such a garbled non-explanation from anyone in response to any question he had ever posed in his life. Her mouth was parted and she was leaning forward, her body language speaking of an urgency for him to believe what she was saying.

The woman was distracting.

It wasn't just the breathless, convoluted workings of her brain which he was finding extraordinarily difficult to deal with. It was *her,* the entire package. The second he had laid eyes on her, something inside him had kick-started and now…staring back into her impossibly turquoise eyes…

He shifted, frowning. There was enough on his plate without losing focus over this nonsense. His eyes roved over her flushed face, subliminally appreciating the satin smoothness of her skin and the juicy fullness of her lips. As he watched, her tongue flicked out, nervously licking her upper lip, and his whole body jack-knifed in sudden, heated response.

A libido which had been dormant for the past six months surged into life with shocking force. He gritted his teeth together but he had to shift position because his erection was rock-hard, pulsing against the zipper of his trousers.

Was she leaning forward like that on purpose? Making sure that those lush, heavy breasts were on tempting show, begging to be fondled?

Matteo had a very particular type of woman. Very tall, very slim and very brunette. He went for the career woman, the woman who challenged him intellectually. He liked the back and forth of informed conversation about politics and the economy. He liked them cool, confident and as driven as he was. He'd fought hard for his place in the world and he appreciated a woman who had battled against the odds as well. An ambitious woman with a career of her own was also not a needy woman, and he disliked needy women. He didn't want anyone needing him. He operated solo and that was the way he liked it.

So why was he staring at this woman in front of him with the rapt attention of a horny teenager? She was breathy and ultra-feminine and didn't strike him as the sort who would be winning awards for her thoughts on world finance. She was the antithesis of what he sought in any woman.

Furious with his lack of self-control, he leapt to his feet to prowl through the room, at the same time finishing the glass of whisky he had poured, tempted to help himself to another but resisting the urge.

He had to remove his eyes from the sexy woman on the chair but, when he finally glanced at her again, it was to find that he was still in the grip of whatever ludicrous spell she had temporarily cast on him.

He positioned himself in front of her and then leant

down, gripping either side of the chair, caging her in so that she instinctively drew back.

Her breathing was fast and shallow, her breasts heaving.

'Not going to work,' he growled.

'What are you talking about?' Rosie whispered. 'I've tried to explain what happened.'

'You expect me to believe that I was just some random target? That you really have no idea as to the reach of my power? And, if that's the case, why are you coming on to me?'

Rosie's mouth fell open and she stared.

'I beg your pardon?'

'Don't think that you're going to get me into any sort of compromising situation! I wasn't born yesterday. That garbled nonsense about dragging me into this situation to avoid a guy—unbelievable.'

'Compromising situation?'

'You're a sexy woman but I'm not a fool.' Matteo gritted his teeth, controlling his hands with extreme difficulty, because what he desperately wanted to do was take what was obviously on offer, starting with those luscious lips and moving on to the even more luscious breasts.

'You're telling me that *I'm sexy*?'

'And advertising it isn't going to work. Where's your sister? Lurking behind the door? Ready to take an incriminating photo, perhaps?' He pushed himself away from the chair but his body was still on fire as he strolled through the room, purposefully maintaining distance between them.

Eventually, he sat down. He was still hard, still turned on.

'I can't believe you'd imagine that I was coming onto

you,' Rosie said faintly. The thought alone was enough to suffuse her with colour.

Her? She was the one who had drawn the short straw when it came to looks. Her sisters had always been the ones to turn heads. She, Rosie, had been the girl the boys enjoyed hanging out with. She self-consciously folded her arms over her breasts and then realised that, in doing so, she had simply drawn attention to them.

She wondered whether that would lead to another crazy accusation that she was trying to come on to him. Her skin prickled. He had called her *sexy* and she didn't think that he'd been kidding.

'And it wasn't garbled nonsense,' she belatedly continued. 'If you'd just listen! My family…' Her voice was staccato with suppressed nerves. 'Well, you've met Candice, my sister. They've been a bit concerned about me…they think I need to settle down, find a job, a life partner…'

'A *life partner*?'

'Yes.' She flushed. Why had she launched into this brutally honest explanation? Why hadn't she skimmed over the details? The way he was looking at her, frowning in silence with his head tilted to one side, was bringing her out in goose bumps. She should have left him puzzled about the nonsensical reason for her behaviour because now she would have to confess that the last thing she was was *sexy*. *Sexy* women didn't have their entire protective family twitching with concern about their life choices.

'How old are you?'

'Twenty-three.'

'Let's suspend disbelief for the moment and go along with your story: why are you supposed to have a *life partner* at the age of twenty-three?'

Matteo realised, with frustration, that the woman was doing it again. Distracting him. He raked his fingers through his hair and reminded himself that this was the woman who had probably scuppered his deal, the one deal that mattered even though he had nothing to gain financially from it.

She looked as pure as the driven snow but he knew better than to trust the way people looked. Scratch the surface and there was usual a healthy store of avarice and general unpleasantness to be found.

She was gazing at him with those incredible aquamarine eyes.

Matteo was beginning to think that she wasn't the Machiavellian character he had first assumed, working in cahoots with a partner in crime. For once, his cynicism might be misplaced. He wasn't going to give up the notion willingly, but…he was getting there.

Nor was he convinced that she had been trying to come on to him, he grudgingly conceded. She was either an actress of Oscar winning standard or her shock at the accusation had been genuine.

He was so accustomed to women making a play for him, that the idea of one actively horrified at the thought of it was as novel as discovering a fish riding a bike in the centre of Hyde Park.

No ulterior motive, which just left her explanation that she had started an ill-thought-out act of impulse to escape some guy's advances.

This time, when he looked at her, it was with lazy interest. He was thirty-two years old but his palate was lamentably jaded. This slice of novelty was strangely compelling.

'Aren't you a little young to be told that you need to

start thinking about settling down?' He shifted, making a concerted effort not to give in to the urge to stare at her fabulous body. 'And, conversely, a little old for your family to be the ones giving the lectures?'

Rosie bristled. 'They care about me. Not that that's any of your business.'

'Everything is my business when, thanks to you, the deal I've been nurturing for the past eight months will probably come to nothing. Whether what you and your sister did was a deliberate ruse or not, the upshot remains the same.'

'Bob and Margaret seem very reasonable people, not the sort to jeopardise whatever agreement you reached with them because of a scene in a hotel lobby.' Rosie flushed as her guilty conscience ate away at her. She couldn't understand why he needed any deal so badly when it was obvious that he was made of money. Her parents were rich but she suspected that this guy was in a different league altogether.

'Bob and Margaret are deeply traditional people,' Matteo informed her coolly. 'Church goers with an extremely healthy respect for the family unit, as you may have gathered. My integrity has been paramount to winning their trust.'

'I'm really and truly sorry. I had no idea that my sister would fly down there and let rip. It's not like her at all. She *never* makes a fuss. She's probably at the chalet right now broadcasting our relationship to the entire family.'

'The chalet?'

'My parents own a chalet about fifteen minutes from here.' She stared off into the distance and wondered what the next step was going to be.

Her gaze slid over to where Matteo was still staring at her, his loose-limbed body relaxed and her heart picked up speed. He was so perfect...so stupendously good-looking.

'You still haven't properly explained what went on down there,' Matteo prompted, his voice clipped. 'Now Cupid has supposedly targeted us, you might as well fill me in on this guy you don't want to meet and why you're having to in the first place. I didn't ask for this but it's landed on my lap and I'm going to have to make the best of it. I'll need some personal details about you.'

Rosie looked at him and then found that she couldn't stop looking and, when she looked, her brain went into overdrive and she started thinking about the way his mouth had felt against her cheek.

'I...well...as I mentioned, my family think it's time for me to start settling down—and please don't tell me that I'm too old to have my sisters and my parents fussing around me. I know that. Fact is, Candice came over to warn me that they were thinking of inviting some family friends to the chalet over Christmas.' She grimaced. 'Bertie is their son.'

'And?' Matteo tilted his head and looked at her with raised eyebrows. 'You don't like him? Ex-lover? Bad break-up? Where are we going with this one?'

'You're very rude, aren't you?' She scowled and then, without warning, he smiled at her and all that sexiness was thrown into such stark focus that she was temporarily shocked into silence.

The harsh beauty of his face was no longer forbidding. All of a sudden, Rosie glimpsed at what true sexiness in a guy was all about and in an instant every boyfriend she had ever had faded into insignificance. She had gone out with silly little boys. The glorious specimen sprawled in front of her was just the opposite. He was all man, an alpha male in the prime of his life. She felt faint.

'No one has ever said that to me before,' Matteo drawled. 'Should I be irritated, bemused or intrigued?'

Rosie squirmed. She wasn't sure how to answer that question or whether he even expected an answer. She felt hot and bothered, as if she was coming down with something.

'My parents think that Bertie and I might be a good match and I guess...' She hesitated. 'I acted without thinking. Candice was sitting across from me, ruining my entire Christmas. I just looked down and spotted Bob and Margaret and the guy they said they'd been doing business with, and I knew that you were all leaving, so I...told my sister that I couldn't possibly face Bertie because I'd been having a fling with you, which hadn't worked out and I was all broken up. It seemed safe. You were going and there was no way I thought she was ever going to...do what she ended up doing.'

Hearing it spoken out loud, Rosie couldn't imagine why she had done what she had. Why hadn't she just stood her ground and refused?

She knew why. Because it had always been her nature to follow the path of least resistance and that had evolved into her just going with the flow.

'I should have just told Candice that if Bertie was going to be on the scene then I would make sure not to be there. I should have had a bit more will power. Instead, I acted on impulse, and I'm sorry.'

'I'm getting the picture of someone who lets her family run her life for her. Am I right?'

'Is there anything I can do to make it up to you?'

'You shouldn't make offers like that,' Matteo murmured. 'A guy could get all the wrong ideas.'

Heat coursed through her body, a slow burn from the inside out. Her breasts ached and her nipples, straining against her bra, felt ultra-sensitive, tingling. She imagined the pads of his fingers rubbing them and her breathing became shallow and laboured. She had no experience when it came to this kind of sophisticated, lazy flirting. If that was even what it was. All she could do was stare at him while her mind continued to play with all sorts of graphic, contraband images.

What on earth was wrong with her?

This guy reeked of danger and yet the pull she felt was overpowering.

'So, now that we're an item, what happens next?'

'I...well...'

'In the thick of this relationship, our hot, two-week clandestine fling, where were we supposed to be meeting? My room at the hotel? Your parents' chalet? Neither of the above? It's a mystery that Bob and Margaret didn't jump in with a string of questions about our so-called affair, bearing in mind most of my time over the past few days has been spent with them working on finishing touches to my deal.'

'How am I supposed to know?' Rosie retorted truthfully. 'I didn't stop to think things through.'

Impulse on that scale was unheard of in Matteo's world and it was strangely refreshing to glimpse a life where variables were given a chance to survive. Not for him, and yet... 'Well, we're going to have to come up with some sort of plausible story or else the whole thing falls apart, and I'm not about to let that happen.'

'Because of this deal you're working on?'

'I just need to get past the finishing line.'

'Why?'

'Come again?'

'Why would a deal mean so much to you that you would go along with this charade instead of just calling me out? I mean, you seem to have enough money…'

'You've lived a life of comfort,' Matteo said coolly. 'From that vantage point, it's easy to come out with platitudes about not needing money or having enough of it. Tell me, have you ever told anyone that the best things in life are free? Take it from me, they seldom are. Now, back to my question—what happens next? Your sister is staying with you. Having witnessed our show of love, presumably she expects nothing less than a formal meeting with the man who's head over heels in love with you?'

Rosie's brain was only just beginning to move on from what he had said about her attitude towards money. She was mortified to realise that he was right. She'd led a charmed life and it was easy to take all that for granted when you knew that it would always be there. For all her free-spirited travelling, she would never have fallen very far, because there would always have been a cushion waiting for her.

'She's probably curious,' Rosie admitted.

'And the over-protective family? Will the grape vine be buzzing with news of our whirlwind romance?'

Rosie shot him a sheepish smile and pushed some tangled blonde curls off her face.

'"Buzzing" might be an understatement,' she confessed.

'But at least the ex-lover won't be on the scene now you're spoken for.' He'd felt it again. A charge of electricity, powerful and disorientating. Primal. She represented everything he steered clear of when it came to women, and yet she was uniquely appealing and he had no idea from where the appeal stemmed.

'Bertie was never an ex,' Rosie was obliged to point out. 'Never even came close! Our families have known each other for ages and, somewhere along the line, he got it into his head that he wanted to ask me out on a date. I was seventeen at the time. I've never fancied him but now he's a big shot in the City somewhere and everyone thinks he could be a suitable match.' She rolled her eyes.

Matteo didn't say anything. His dark eyes were lazy and thoughtful. 'So I'll be meeting the family,' he murmured.

'You don't have to. I could tell them that you've been called away on business. Candice has met you. She'll understand.'

'Why will she understand?'

'Because...' Rosie thought that, for someone as forbidding as he was, it was oddly easy to talk to him. 'Because she has two children now, but before that she was a successful lawyer, so she understands the demands of work. She'll get it if you pay a flying visit and then disappear.'

Rosie frowned and sat forward. 'That would work,' she said slowly. 'If you disappear, then there won't be the complication of your meeting my parents and the rest of the family. That way, I can gradually warn them that the big romance isn't actually going as planned. These things happen,' she thought aloud. 'People meet and think that they've fallen in love but it turns out to be a mistake.'

'And naturally,' Matteo said soothingly, 'That's exactly what will happen but, for the moment, that solution is off the cards.'

'Why?'

'Because my deal hasn't been finalised. Bob and Margaret are here for another week. Skiing, having fun and making sure the last details of my purchase are drawn up and inspected via email by their lawyers in London. Until signatures are on the dotted line, we're in love and thinking of building a future together. Once everything's signed, sealed and delivered, then the hasty unravelling of our relationship can begin.' He gave an elegant shrug which implied that that was the way forward and there was nothing she could do about it, whether she wanted to or not.

'It'll be harder on my parents if they actually meet you face to face.'

'Tough.' Matteo didn't bother beating about the bush. 'I didn't ask for this.'

His dark eyes scoured her face. He could read the tension and anxiety there, and of course she had a point. She clearly came from a tight-knit family unit. The less they were hurt by her behaviour, the better, but as far as he was concerned that was not his problem. Matteo didn't allow sentiment to rule his life. It simply wasn't in his nature. He had managed to remain focused, to stay on course with his life—unlike many of the kids he had grown up with, who had ended up either in jail or six feet under. That said, a life spent in foster care had toughened him. He had known what it meant to have nothing, to be a face and a name in a system and not much more. He had climbed out of that place and forged his way in the world.

That brief spell of respite at the place he was in the process of buying had shown him that there were alternatives in life. He had held onto that vision and it had seen him through.

He had realised that the only way to escape the predictability of becoming one of the victims of the Social Services system was to educate himself and he had applied himself to the task with monumental dedication. By the time he had hit Cambridge University, he had been an intellectual force to contend with.

He'd known more than his tutors. His aptitude for mathematics was prodigious. He'd been head-hunted by a newly formed investment bank and had swiftly risen to the top before breaking free to become something of a shooting star in the financial firmament. Money had given him the opportunity to diversify. It had allowed him to get whatever he wanted at the snap of a finger. Money had been his passport to freedom and freedom had been his only goal for his entire adult life.

Money had also jaded his palate, made life predictable. Being able to have whatever and whomever you wanted, he had reflected time and again, did not necessarily guarantee excitement.

He hadn't had a woman in months and he hadn't been tempted.

Now here he was and, in that instant, Matteo decided that he was going to go with the flow and make the best of the situation into which he had been catapulted. Moreover, he was going to enjoy the experience.

'I have a suite here, at this hotel,' he mused. 'Bob and Margaret are at another location, further down the slopes. If I'm the new man in your life, then I'll be expected to be at your parents' chalet with you, I presume?'

'Wait. What? Now, hang on just a minute...'

'It's hardly likely that we're in the thick of a stormy, passionate affair and I'm bedding down on my own in a hotel room while you're miles away in a chalet somewhere with nothing but the telly and a good book for company. Is it?'

'Well, no. but...'

'But?'

'But this isn't a normal situation, is it? I mean, we're not actually involved with one another, are we?'

'You need to follow the plot line here,' Matteo imparted kindly. 'There will be people we will need to convince and no one, not even traditional and church-going Bob and Margaret, will be persuaded that this is the affair of a lifetime if we're crossing paths off and on.'

'Stop being patronising,' Rosie said absently. What did he mean by being at the chalet with her? Sharing a bedroom? She paled at the thought because suddenly her little white lie had taken on a life of its own and was galloping away at speed.

Matteo burst out laughing and she focused on his handsome face and glared.

'I hadn't banked on this,' she said tightly. 'You may find the whole thing hilarious but I don't.'

'I don't find anything hilarious about this situation,' Matteo shot back and, she thought for the millionth time, there was no need for him to remind her that she had brought this mess on herself. 'But here we are. I'm going to move into your parents' chalet today.'

'Candice will know that you haven't been living with me,' Rosie pointed out.

'How?'

'There would be signs of us sharing a bedroom. You would have left stuff behind. Clothes on the backs of chairs. Shaving foam. Bedroom slippers. Aftershave...'

His eyebrows shot up, his expression halting her in mid-flow.

'I have never spent a night in any woman's house and, if I had, I certainly wouldn't have left anything behind.'

Rosie's mouth fell open and she gaped at him. 'You've *never* stayed at a woman's overnight?' He was so arrogant, so beautiful, so sophisticated—she found it impossible to credit that he had never spent the night with a woman.

What woman, she guiltily thought, would let him out of her bed? It was an inappropriate thought but it lodged in her head, pounding with the steady force of a drum beat.

Matteo made a dismissive gesture with his hand that was both elegant and strangely exotic and she watched him from under lowered lashes, fascinated and mesmerised by the strong, proud lines of his handsome face.

'I'm a normal, red-blooded man with a healthy libido,' Matteo told her wryly. 'I work hard and I play hard, but I don't do love, and I never encourage a woman to think, even for a second, that I might.'

'And if you spent a night with a woman...it would mean that you're interested in more than just *sex*?'

'Forget about me,' Matteo drawled. 'The danger would lie in *her* believing that there might be more to it than sex.'

'And yet you're okay with spending time in the chalet with me?'

'Oh, but you're not my woman,' Matteo purred silkily. 'And this isn't about sex. This is a little pretend game that'll be over just as soon as I get what I'm after...'

CHAPTER THREE

ROSIE THOUGHT THAT it was one thing to produce Matteo as a boyfriend, like a magician pulling a rabbit from a hat then yanking him off stage before anyone had time to suss that it was all sleight of hand. It was something else to hold him up to scrutiny, which was what she would be doing by having him in the chalet with her. He would be spun around for inspection, asked questions, quizzed about his intentions. How was she going to deal with all that without cracking? How was *he*?

Her sisters, in particular, had all made it their mission to make Rosie keep them posted on her love life and she had always obliged. They had met a couple of her fleeting boyfriends and had not held back from making their opinions known, politely but firmly. She was so much younger than them and they had never really stopped treating her like the baby of the family.

Hence, Rosie thought with uncharacteristic bitterness, the reason why she was where she was now.

She had bolted from the prospect of having their idea of a suitable partner presented to her instead of standing her ground—but why on earth had it occurred to them that they could actually match her up with someone of their choosing in the first place?

This time, she was going to deal with the situation calmly. If there were too many questions, she would just stop answering. If the quizzing from Candice and Emily went too far, she would tell them to back off.

Matteo was a perfect stranger, but some of his remarks had been a little too perceptive for comfort. They had made her see herself in a different and more critical light than she had ever done before.

She wasn't silly and she didn't feel entitled but she *was* a trust-fund baby in the truest sense of the word and she had felt embarrassed to acknowledge the fact.

'You're going to be held up to the spotlight,' she warned. 'Five minutes with Candice is quite different to several days with my entire family.'

'I can take the heat,' Matteo drawled. 'Can you?'

Rosie looked at him steadily. 'I know what you think of me,' she said, matching him for self-composure and liking the way she felt empowered by it. 'That I live off my parents, and float from one thing to the next and allow my entire family to have a say in my life, but this time round I am definitely going to take the heat.' She grinned suddenly. 'They'll be shocked.'

'Good,' Matteo murmured approvingly. 'Sometimes it's worthwhile to shock.'

'I just have one condition.'

'I'm all ears,' Matteo said wryly.

'I'm the one to do the breaking up.'

Matteo looked at her, at a loss for a suitable response.

'I can tell from your stunned expression that no one's ever broken up with you before, am I right? None of those women you refuse to spend the night with, just in case they get ideas, has ever broken up with you...?'

'Fate has smiled on me in that respect.'

'Well,' Rosie countered drily, 'Either smiled on you or else made you incredibly arrogant.'

Matteo grinned and then he burst out laughing. 'You're the most unexpected woman I've ever met,' he murmured. His eyes were lazy and shuttered and feathered over her like a caress. 'I've never met anyone as honest and outspoken. You contradict your background. So…you want to break up with me. I don't see why not. Maybe it's high time I suffered from a broken heart, and it works for you, doesn't it?'

Rosie nodded slowly. 'I'm tired of my family feeling ever so slightly sorry for me.'

'So you dump the eligible guy and you instantly gain their respect. Well, we'll have to make sure that I'm the very besotted boyfriend, won't we? Now, why don't I check out of my suite here and we can both go to your chalet and begin this game…?'

His suite was breath-taking. Huge, with several rooms, including an open-plan kitchen, fully equipped but, she imagined, seldom used.

'You want this to be a convincing act?' he had put to her as they had emerged from the private room where they had been ensconced for ages. 'You come with me to my suite while I pack my things. Then we check out together. I was here on business when we met. Now that your family are coming over, it's only natural I shift base so that we can be together and meet them as a couple.'

Rosie looked at him as he efficiently gathered his belongings. While he packed, he conducted a series of calls in Italian, phone to his ear as he wandered from bedroom to living area, from bathroom to office, picking things up and tossing them in a case he had dumped on the glass table in the living area.

She got the feeling that he had forgotten about her completely.

'I don't know anything about you,' was the first thing she said when he was finally off the phone and the last of his things had been flung into the suitcase.

Here, in his suite, nerves assailed her. There was something so sleek and so innately *dangerous* about him that she found it impossible to think that they could convince her very perceptive and inquisitive family that they were really an item. Up close and personal, the force of his personality was more powerful, not less. She'd told herself that she wasn't going to be browbeaten by their curiosity and their questions, but how on earth were they going to believe that she, Rosie, bubbly, extrovert and carefree, had lost her heart to someone like Matteo?

Add to that the fact that he really was a stranger and the uphill task of convincing *anyone* seemed insurmountable.

In the act of zipping his suitcase, Matteo paused and looked at her for a few seconds.

She hadn't moved from her position by the door. She looked nervous and he marvelled that a lifetime of privilege—which had clearly been her background, judging from what she had told him—had managed to leave her unscathed. He hadn't been kidding when he had told her that she was unexpected. He met a lot of privileged people. Young and old, and even the most charming—they all had a very similar veneer of confidence borne from the assumption that the world was theirs for the asking. They all spoke loudly and with booming confidence.

Most drew distinct lines between the people who served them and the people on their own level.

Rosie was as skittish as a kitten, open, guileless and honest to a fault, and that surprised and charmed him.

Now, looking at her, Matteo wondered whether he hadn't agreed to this charade because a part of him found her intriguing.

Rosie took a few hesitant steps forward and peered at the half-shut suitcase.

'You haven't brought any ski wear? Or have you stored it somewhere else?'

Matteo strolled to the small kitchen and withdrew a bottle of water from the fridge, which he held out to her. When she declined, he unscrewed the cap and drank.

'I don't ski,' he admitted. He dumped the empty bottle on the counter and hesitated momentarily, then he moved to the sofa and sat down, watching as she followed suit to sit facing him. 'And stop looking so nervous. I'm not going to pounce on you.'

'I know you're not.' She stifled a wave of nerves brought on by him telling her to stop looking nervous. 'We're not in public now. You know a lot about me, but I don't know anything about you, and I'm going to have to if our story is going to be credible. I'm surprised you don't ski,' she admitted.

'There's a time for learning to ski,' Matteo said wryly. 'It's fair to say I missed the slot.'

'Those obligatory school trips to the slopes can be a bore,' Rosie reminisced. 'I guess I'm lucky my parents were crazy about skiing. I can remember staring down fields of snow with little skis on when I was about three.' She laughed, throwing her head back, catching some of her hair in her hand and twisting it into a pony tail before releasing it.

Matteo smiled. 'Tell me more about your family. Your sister is married with two children and was a lawyer before she settled on motherhood…'

Rosie was transfixed by that smile. It was so genuinely curious that she felt her nerves begin to abate. She told him about Emily, sister number two and a chartered surveyor. Also married. Pregnant with her first. She chatted about her parents. Her mother had been a lecturer and her father a high-ranking diplomat before they'd retired three years ago.

'And they didn't approve of past boyfriends,' he encouraged. 'Hence Bertie…'

Rosie grimaced. 'Hence Bertie. Not at all my type.'

'No? And what is your type, Rosie?'

Rosie opened her mouth to recite what she had always taken for granted—that she, free-spirited unlike her sisters, was attracted to other free spirited souls, unlike her brothers-in-law. Except, was she really?

He saved her from having to stumble through an answer by saying gently, 'You're very lucky. Riding lessons…skiing holidays from the age of three…house in the country and *pied à terre* in London. I'm guessing you dated guys your family didn't approve of as a form of quiet rebellion.'

'That's not true,' she countered but she could feel his observations too close to the bone. 'I've always been adventurous,' she concluded unconvincingly.

Matteo shrugged, ready to let it go and surprised that he had been lured into psychoanalysing her when he rarely felt inclined to plumb the depths of any woman.

'You wanted to know about me,' he said indifferently. 'Think of an upbringing as far from yours as it is possible to be.'

Rosie frowned. When she looked around her, all she could see was the trappings of wealth. He was clearly far, far richer than her parents or indeed anyone that she had ever known. He was in a league of his own and she didn't understand where he was going with that enigmatic remark.

He was sophisticated, polished and, if there was something of the street fighter about him, then she presumed that the richer you were the more ruthless you had to be.

'Did you grow up here? In Italy? I heard you on the phone, speaking in Italian...'

'I was born here but my parents went to England in search of a better life when I was a baby.' Matteo paused, uncomfortable with sharing details of his past but knowing that she was entitled to information up to a point. 'There was nothing for them here in Italy and they were young and hopeful. Unfortunately, life did not quite work out the way they planned. My mother contracted a virus shortly after they arrived in England, and was taken into hospital, but by the time they diagnosed meningitis it was too late.'

Rosie covered her mouth with her hand and stared at him. There was a remoteness about his features that mirrored the cool briskness of his voice. He was stating facts with all emotion removed from the recital. More than anything, she felt her heart twist at that. It was a defence mechanism to protect himself from the pain of losing a parent at such a young age. That was something she felt instinctively, just as she also knew instinctively that this proud, arrogant man would not appreciate her sharing her thoughts with him.

In that moment, he was so very human that she wanted to reach out and touch him. She sat on her hands just in case they decided to disobey the warning bells in her head telling her to avoid any such spontaneous show of affection.

'I'm so sorry, Matteo,' she contented herself by saying and he lowered his eyes, thick lashes brushing his aristocratic cheekbones, before he looked at her once again, fully composed.

'Don't be. It's history.'

'And where is your father now?' she asked. 'Does he live over here? He must have been devastated at the time. Did he return to Italy?'

'My father died when I was four and I was taken into foster care. No, he did not return to Italy. I have maintained my links, however. I have a villa on the outskirts of Venice and at the moment I'm in the process of expanding my operations to Naples. Hence my conference call earlier.'

'Foster care?'

'It's of no importance.' He stood up and glanced around, making sure that he was leaving nothing behind.

Rosie thought differently. It was of monumental importance and it gave her valuable insight into this forbidding stranger now phoning down for a porter to come and collect his belongings.

He was so cold, she thought, so contained, and there was a very good reason for that.

He was walking towards the door and she shot to her feet and hurried behind him. Instead of opening the door, however, he stared down at her, his dark eyes shuttered.

'The only reason I've told you what I have,' he stated, 'Is because you have a point. Relationships aren't built on two people knowing absolutely nothing about one another, and this has to be a credible relationship until all the paperwork is done on the deal I'm working on with Bob and Margaret.'

'You haven't told me why it's so important.'

'Nor will I. And I should tell you that you should save the questions if any of them involve further delving into my past. I've given you sufficient information for us to pull this charade off. The confidences end there. The fact is we are not in a relationship. This is a temporary and fictitious arrangement and all we need to establish is a sufficiently credible basis from which we can answer the most straightforward questions.' He opened the door and they walked in silence to the lift, then rode down to the busy foyer.

All the while, thoughts were buzzing around in her head like wasps. He had opened a door and, having peered in, she wanted to have another look.

As soon as they were back in the public domain, he slung his arm over her shoulders, only breaking apart to sign himself out.

There was a background hum of Christmas carols being played which followed them out of the hotel onto the snow-covered slopes.

Rosie had been to many ski resorts with her family over the years but they had fallen in love with this one and had made it their annual destination. The ski resort was situated in the heart of the Southern Alps in the Veneto region of Northern Italy. From here, Venice was a couple of hours away, and she figured that Matteo had probably arranged for his clients to come to this particular resort because it had suited him. He couldn't have picked a more beautiful spot for the uninitiated.

The mountainous, pink and orange backdrop of the Dolomites was picture-postcard perfect, soaring up, commanding the valley and everything nestled inside it. The vista never failed to impress and Rosie stopped and stared at the sight.

'You don't know what you're missing.' She turned to him impulsively.

'Meaning?'

'You should learn to ski. I could teach you.' She laughed at the horror etched on Matteo's lean face and slowly he grinned.

'You don't give up, do you?' he murmured, staring out at the panoramic view with her. Out here, everything was shrouded in silence, and the hue from the rising mountains was quite special. He had always used his Venetian villa as a bolthole. It had never occurred to him that this glorious place existed. But then again, he didn't ski, so why would it have?

He gazed back down to her upturned face. She had dimples when she smiled. She had stuffed a woolly hat on her head and her tangled white-blonde curls trailed in disarray from under it. Wrapped up in countless layers, her small, curvaceous body was tempting beyond endurance and Matteo spun around on his heels, indicating that they should make for her car now.

'What do you mean?' Rosie tripped alongside him, keeping some distance but feeling the impact of his presence slamming into her at every step.

'I mean, others would have tactfully retreated once I warned them off trying to get to know me.'

'That's very egotistical of you.' She swerved into the hotel car park, heading towards the four-wheel-drive car that was kept on permanent standby, as the villa was used by the family out of season as well.

'Egotistical?'

'I don't want to get to know you,' Rosie lied, beeping open the doors and hoisting herself into the driver's seat. She waited until he was sitting in the passenger seat before turning to him. In the late-evening light he was all shadows and angles, and he sent a shiver of fierce excitement racing down her spine. 'I just thought that, if we're going to be stuck with one another for days on end, it might give us something to do aside from arguing, and anyway, it's a shame to be here and not try your hand at it.'

She started the engine and the car shuddered into life.

'I've never had any woman tell me that she has to think of things to do if she's going to be stuck with me,' Matteo said, amused in spite of himself. 'Sure you know how to handle this thing in snowy terrain?'

'The road to the chalet is clear and gritted, Matteo, so there's no need to be nervous—and of course I know how to handle it.' She glanced across at him. 'Don't tell me that you think women can't drive as good as men?'

'Can they, though?'

Rosie heard the lazy teasing in his voice and she burst out laughing.

Her heart skipped a beat. A thread of something beyond excitement suddenly sparked and sizzled in her veins.

'Probably better.' She was focused one hundred percent on the road ahead of her, taking it very slowly, but she didn't want to lose the moment. She liked this. 'Are you scared of giving it a go? The skiing, I mean?'

'Terrified,' Matteo drawled.

'I'll make sure you're all right.'

'Will you, now? That's an offer that's almost too good to pass up.'

They were nearing the chalet—a left-hand turn off the main road and then just a short drive to the warmth of the ski lodge. The drive was short but hazardous, but the car was equipped for all conditions and handled the steep climb to the chalet with aplomb. Ahead, the bright lights were welcoming.

Candice was waiting for them, dressed to go out but making sure she stayed put to ask questions. Having shaken off the snow, hung various jackets and coats and dumped shoes and boots and all the other paraphernalia, Rosie faced her elegant, glamorous sister with a strength of purpose she had never really experienced before.

From behind, she was aware of Matteo approaching, but the touch of his hand on her waist, curving to rest just under her breasts, still made her flush. She hesitantly slipped her arm around him to complete the picture she knew he was striving to convey. The pressure of his palm on her rib cage and the crazy tingling of her nipples in heated response fogged up her brain and she knew that she was beetroot-red.

She wanted to moan and chewed down on her lip in horror, especially when he lazily circled his fingers on the woolly jumper, applying just the right amount of pressure.

She had whipped off the woolly hat and in a matter of a few heart-stopping seconds he sifted his fingers into her hair and tilted her chin so that she was gazing up at him. Then he lowered his mouth to graze over hers... and all those things she had read about in magazines suddenly made complete sense. Lust…desire…whatever you wanted to call it…

She had had one serious relationship that had, in retrospect, been nothing more than the optimism of youth to be loved and a need to be rescued from her abortive university career. It had lasted a matter of months and had certainly not prepared her for the high-voltage charge of craving that shot through her body when his lips met hers. Nothing she had ever experienced had. Confusion tore into her, darkening her eyes, sending a slight tremble through her body.

Her vocal cords seemed to have dried up, but it didn't matter, because Candice was smiling and Matteo had eased into charismatic gear and was saying all the right things, asking all the right questions, giving her cool, contained sister little chance of asking questions back.

'I'd really love to hear about the two of you and how you met.' She glanced at her watch, while from the sidelines Rosie breathed a sigh of relief. 'But I'm going to catch up with some friends I haven't seen for ages. Before the family descend tomorrow evening. By the way, they can't wait to meet you. Hope you don't mind but I couldn't help but share the news with everyone—and get them to hold off on trying to set you up with Bertie.'

'Actually,' Rosie heard herself say, 'I do mind, Diss. It was my place to tell them that Matteo and I are…er… going out.'

'Yes, I suppose so but…' Bright colour poured into Candice's cheeks. For the first time in living memory, she was discomfited by her much younger sister, and Rosie realised that this was what she should have been doing all along. Taking control of her life and owning her decisions.

'It's done now,' she said quietly. 'It doesn't matter.' Oddly, Matteo's hand cupping the nape of her neck gave her a certain amount of strength.

'I do apologise, Rosie. I was just so excited that you'd actually met someone...'

Candice shifted, aware that she was treading in un-chartered waters, accustomed as she was to compliance from her younger sister.

'Socially acceptable?' Matteo interjected coolly. He tightened his hold on Rosie and she leant against him, loving the strength he imparted. He was as solid as a rock.

'That's not quite what I meant.' Candice reddened.

'My track record hasn't been great,' Rosie said ap-peasingly.

Candice gave her a bright, relieved smile and moved towards her for a quick hug before standing back and looking at them both with her head to one side.

'You two make a fantastic couple,' she said. 'I was quite prepared to thump you when Rosie told me that you'd let her down. I can't tell you how happy I am for the both of you that whatever misunderstanding you had has been sorted. I can just tell that you're meant for one another.' She winked at her sister.

'Hang on, Candice,' Rosie interjected, horrified and embarrassed that 'holiday fling' was morphing into 'marriage on the cards'. 'We've really only just met! We're still getting to know one another.'

Candice was laughing, heading for the door. 'That's how all relationships begin, Rosie! Anyway, don't wait up for me, guys. That car could pull a sled in an avalanche, but if I feel too tired to head back then I'll just stay over with Mick and Carol. They've already invited me and they've got oodles of room. I'll text and let you know.'

With which she left in a flurry of air kisses, slamming the door behind her, leaving Rosie alone with Matteo.

'So…' He looked around him. 'Nice place, Rosie.' It was open-plan, big but not huge, and with all the clutter of hectic family life left behind from one holiday to the other—well-thumbed books, games, toys and all sorts of bits and pieces collected over the years. The floors were deep, rich wood and there was a clutter of artwork on the walls, pictures done by Rosie and her sisters. In the sitting area, colourful throws were tossed onto the deep, comfortable sofas, and in the corner the television was rumbling on, volume low, because Candice had forgotten to switch it off.

Looking around her, Rosie saw the place through his eyes. It was the essence of upper-middle-class comfort.

'Can I ask you something?' She waited until he had turned full circle to look at her.

'Ask away.'

'I know you said you didn't want me prying into your private life…'

Matteo realised that her prying was a lot less objectionable than expected. He wondered whether that was because, for the first time in his life, he had opened up about his past with another human being. Of course, he had had very little choice, given the situation, and none of it mattered anyway, because they would be parting company before Santa dropped down the chimney with his sack of goodies, but it was still a little unnerving.

He wasn't the confiding sort and he grimly told himself that he wasn't going to change any time soon. A leopard never changed its spots and his reticence was solidly ingrained. He had always lived his life with the assumption that, when it came to other people and his private life, information was purely on a need-to-know basis.

Like now, was what sprang to mind.

'Then don't,' he informed her silkily.

'I was just curious to find out how you…ended up where you did.'

'Rich and powerful?' He sat on one of the squashy sofas, which was a lot more comfortable than the pale leather ones in his place in London. He thought of that halfway house and the boisterous fun he had had there all those years ago. He'd never thought he would ever laugh again after he'd been put into foster care, but he had. The place had been designed to broaden the horizons of the underprivileged kids who went there and it had worked, at least for him.

'There's that modesty of yours again,' Rosie teased lightly, but her curiosity was getting the better of her fast and she joined him on the sofa, opposite end, but close enough to hear every word he was saying.

'When you're a kid in care, you have to make an effort not to slide down to the lowest common denominator,' Matteo told her conversationally. 'No one has any dreams for you. You have to make sure you have dreams for yourself or you sink to the bottom fast. I was lucky. I was bright. I learned the value of education.' He shrugged. 'I studied. I never skipped class. I set my sights on the only thing that mattered.'

'What was that?'

'Freedom. When you grow up without any advantages, money is the only thing that buys freedom, and by the age of eighteen I'd come to the conclusion that I would just have to make money and a lot of it. I was gifted at maths and got into Cambridge University. Got a first-class degree and was lucky enough to get taken on by a burgeoning investment bank. By twenty-five I'd made my first million. The bonuses were insane, but that life didn't suit me. I don't like taking orders or working for other people. So I jacked it in and began scouting around for companies to buy. Small IT companies, mainly. That's the long and short of it. Rags to riches.'

'Your opinion of me must be very low.' She thought of her cosseted background, the trust fund that kept her going, the university career she had jettisoned because she had been bored stiff.

Matteo looked at her. She had such a transparent face. Yes, he really should have a low opinion of her, but there was something about her...

'You're not the sort of woman I would normally be drawn to,' he was forced to concede.

She raised aquamarine eyes to his, and his jaw tightened, because she was hurt.

'That's not meant to be an insult, Rosie,' he said roughly.

'I know that. It's the truth. What sort of women *are* you drawn to, just out of interest?'

'Career women,' he admitted.

'Of course.'

'We're poles apart,' he reminded her. 'I'm sure you wouldn't, under normal circumstances, go for someone like me.'

'Definitely not.' Rosie tilted her chin at a mutinous angle, pride coming to her rescue, because it cut to the quick that, whether he found her sexy or not—and she hated herself for dwelling on that stupid, throwaway compliment—he would never have given her the time of day if he hadn't been dumped into playing out this charade. 'I'm just shocked at how easily Candice fell for the charade,' she mused truthfully.

'People believe what they want to believe,' Matteo said with a shrug. 'Human nature. Your family want what they think is best for you and someone rich, powerful and wearing a suit fits the narrative.' He looked at her. 'And here's another reason why no one will question this too deeply…'

Matteo looked at her flushed, pretty face ,but then his eyes drifted down to the tightness of her jumper straining over full breasts and the curve of her hips.

The atmosphere shifted. He could feel it and he knew that she would as well. He was just looking, he thought, because he wasn't going to encourage any further complication to an already complicated and annoying situation. He was going to be sticking around for a handful of days and then he would be off, leaving her to assert her independence and damn him for the bastard he really wasn't at all.

'What's that?' Rosie asked breathlessly.

'The most obvious reason of all. Opposites attract…'

CHAPTER FOUR

ROSIE COULD ONLY concede the truth behind that statement. Matteo was sinfully good-looking but he wasn't her type. Take away the dark good looks and the perfectly honed, intensely masculine physique, and what you had was your basic businessman, the sort of guy to appeal to her entire family but not to her.

It was true that she had never met any businessman quite in this one's league but he was still nothing like the free-spirited adventurers towards whom she always gravitated. She shouldn't be attracted to him at all but she was.

But then, he wasn't exactly Mr Typical Business Tycoon, was he?

That background in foster care...

Not exactly your run-of-the mill CEO...

And those cool, cool eyes...seeing everything and revealing nothing...also not typical.

And that thread-like scar...where had that come from? Surely not filling out profit and loss columns with his fountain pen?

'She took it for granted, your sister,' Matteo said conversationally. 'That it was okay to break the news about us in a group family chat without asking whether you might have preferred to do the news-breaking yourself. That par for the course? Because, if it is, then you did well to put her in her place.' He settled his gaze on her.

'I know,' Rosie said simply. She didn't add that his presence had given her backbone. 'The problem is that Candice wouldn't have relayed the information the way I would have.'

'Explain.'

'You heard her. She thinks this is some great romance and that's what she would have told everyone. I would have been a little more realistic. I would have prepared them for the fact that there was a chance this wasn't going to work out. It feels as though things are getting more and more difficult to control.'

'That's the problem when a lie begins to spiral out of control.'

She was hovering.

Things had taken an unexpected turn and he could see that she was uncomfortable with the situation. Her edginess was apparent in the way her gaze was flicking towards him, then flicking away...in the way her whole body seemed alive with restlessness even though she wasn't actually moving around. Underneath the feisty, open exterior, real apprehension was creeping in. The consequences of that little white lie were dawning on her.

'It's also the problem with acting on impulse but, if you think you've been inconvenienced, then I should tell you that the last thing I'd banked on doing was remaining here for longer than strictly necessary.'

'I'm sure you have commitments. It's Christmas.'

'I don't do Christmas. The only reason I'm here at this time of year was because of the timing on this deal.

My only commitment was to retreat to my villa outside Venice and escape the madness.'

'Escape? *Escape?*' Distracted, she angled her bright, blue-eyed gaze in his direction.

'Don't look so bewildered.' Matteo's eyebrows winged up. 'Not everyone is in love with the festive season.'

'You have no family…' Rosie said slowly.

'Don't go there,' Matteo told her, voice dropping by several degrees.

Rosie frowned. 'It must be a lonely time of year for you,' she said simply and Matteo vaulted to his feet and frustratedly raked hands through his hair.

'What is it about *stay out of my private life* that you don't get?'

Rosie didn't apologise. Her mind was busy with images of him in foster care. He had given her a sketchy description of what it had been like but she knew that it probably would have been far more soul-destroying. He had expressly set up No Trespass signs and he had made it clear that the only reason he had said anything at all was because he'd felt it necessary.

Except…her heart went out to him. She knew that she was going where no doubt angels feared to tread, but there was a generosity of spirit inside her that found it difficult to leave the subject alone.

'Everyone needs to talk to somebody about the distressing things that happen in their lives.'

'I don't believe I'm hearing this! I don't think you quite understood…'

'You don't want to talk about it.' She shrugged but her clear blue eyes were stubbornly fixed on his face as he towered over her, looking down, expression forbidding.

'No,' Matteo said with angry force. 'I don't.'

'Which says a lot.'

Matteo leant over her, hands on either side of her, depressing the soft sofa cushions and caging her in. His face was dark with enraged incredulity that someone had dared cross the boundary lines he had laid down. Did the woman have *no* limits when it came to saying what was on her mind? Matteo was accustomed to people editing their behaviour around him. Her lack of interest in following those rules left him practically speechless. From the second she had appeared in his life, normal rules of behaviour had been suspended.

'Don't make me regret having told you what I did.'

'Why would you regret it?'

'Are you hearing a word I'm saying?'

She held his outraged stare. 'You're accustomed to everyone doing what you tell them to do, aren't you?'

Matteo stood up but remained standing in front of her.

'Yes, I am!'

'Okay. You win! I won't ask and you don't have to tell me anything. Would you like something to eat? Drink?' She stood up and swerved around him, heading to the kitchen and straight to the fridge to peer inside.

As always it was crammed with food. A lot of optimistically healthy options that were probably past their sell-by date. She had been staying at the chalet since the season had begun and she was an impulse shopper. Things in attractive jars always held so much promise but often it was the easiest way she ended up taking.

He was still scowling when she looked at him quizzically. 'Well?' she snapped. 'You don't want to talk to me about anything of any importance, so we can talk about food options instead. I know you'll think it's safer. What do you want? I can make you something.'

Matteo wasn't into women cooking for him. In fact, he actively discouraged it, just as he always made sure that a night of pleasure never turned into breakfast together the following morning.

'I usually just eat stuff that comes out of boxes or cans but I don't suppose you do.'

'I don't,' Matteo said flatly. He paused. 'You ask a lot of questions.'

'So do you.' Her azure eyes were innocent and her voice was sincere because she meant it.

'Show me the rest of your house.'

Rosie shook herself back to earth, hesitating and on the cusp of barrelling past his Keep Out sign but reluctantly accepting that, if he wasn't into sharing, then he wasn't into sharing. They meant nothing to one another and she would have to put her curiosity to bed because it wasn't going to get her anywhere.

She gave a perfunctory tour: open-plan living area with a huge, modern fireplace and lots of comfy chairs, perfect for settling in for the long haul—just her, a book and the fall of silent snow outside. The kitchen, which was the hub of the house, and a study in which her father occasionally worked, although now that he had retired those instances were few and far between. He had forgone offers of consultancy jobs and opted for quality time with his family instead.

Wooden stairs led to the floor above: six bedrooms all leading onto a broad landing that overlooked the space below. Next to her, Matteo's silence was oppressive, and she wondered what was going through his head.

She found out soon enough.

'So where is our bedroom?'

About to head back downstairs, head still buzzing with unanswered questions, Rosie spun around on her heels and stared at him with consternation.

'You can choose which bedroom you'd like,' she told him politely. 'Mine...' she nodded in the direction of the bedroom at the end of the long, broad landing '...is down there.'

'Well, I suppose that's where I'll be dumping my bags.'

He headed down at pace towards her bedroom and, as he flung open the door, she was right behind him.

She'd waved an arm to indicate the bedroom floor, only opening the first door and standing back while he'd looked inside like a prospective buyer doing a tour of a house. Now, with him standing in her bedroom, her personal space, she felt invaded. She was on show here, with all the little pieces of her childhood for him to see. A framed photo of her on her first horse, with her dad proudly standing next to her. The ridiculous chair in the shape of a big, pink heart which had been her favourite when she'd been about eight, and which her parents had stashed away in their attic, shipping it over when they'd bought the chalet years before. Pictures of her family over the years.

'You're not staying in *my* bedroom,' She folded her arms and watched, tight-lipped, as he strolled through the bedroom, peering at this and that and ignoring her. He had dumped his bag on the ground like a declaration of intent that sent a chill of forbidden excitement racing up and down her spine.

He commanded the space around him. He was so tall...so muscular...so *there*.

'Oh.' He spun round and stared right back at her. 'This is exactly where I'll be staying.' As if to confirm what he'd said, he picked up the designer bag and flung it on the mattress of her four-poster bed.

It landed with a soft *thud* and then sat there, challenging her to remove it.

'But…'

'No *buts*. You got me into this mess and, now I'm in it, for better or for worse you're just going to have to suffer the consequences. We're supposed to be an item. Hot off the press, so to speak. Your sister is going to be extremely suspicious if she thinks that we're not sharing a bedroom. Particularly given the fact that she probably assumes that you've been sharing my suite at the hotel while we've been conducting our torrid affair.' He glanced at his watch then back to her, where she had remained hovering at the doorway to her own bedroom, almost as though, having asserted his authority, *she* was now the guest in her own space.

'I can tell her that we're in separate rooms here out of respect for Mum and Dad.'

'That's ridiculous.'

'You don't know my parents!'

'Are you telling me that you would be exiled to the Arctic wastes if they discovered that we were sleeping together?' He pinned his eyes to her reddening face. 'Right. Enough said on the subject.'

Rosie's face was a picture of dawning dismay. Their love-at-first-sight scenario invited enough questions without those questions reaching fever pitch because they were in separate bedrooms, like a Victorian couple.

'Now,' Matteo declared, jettisoning the subject as if suddenly bored with the whole thing, 'I would come down and have something out of a box or a can with you, but right now I want a shower, and I have a stack of emails to get through, so I'll have to forfeit the feast.'

He reached for the button on his trousers and Rosie stared open-mouthed for a few seconds before gathering her wits.

'I hadn't banked on this,' she said tightly and he stared at her with disbelieving eyes.

'And I hadn't banked on it either,' he informed her coolly. 'Right about now, I should have been getting in touch with my housekeeper and readying her for my arrival. Instead…'

Instead, she mentally filled in, *here you are, sharing a room with a woman you don't know, who keeps getting on your nerves with her constant questions, caught up in a crazy game of make-believe.*

'If you're sure you're not hungry…' she muttered, inching a couple of steps back, eyes still fixed on him. She didn't want to, but she couldn't help feverishly wondering what he looked like underneath the expensive clothes. Bronzed and sinewy, she imagined, every cord and muscle defined. She felt faint thinking about it and, when she contemplated the prospect of sharing her bedroom with him, she went into a positive mental tailspin. She eyed the *chaise longue* by the window.

'You can make that up.' She nodded in the direction of the *chaise longue*. 'It's very comfortable.'

Matteo didn't say anything. He glanced at it, his hooded silver eyes revealing nothing. 'Like I said,' he drawled, 'I'll do without the food. Now, unless you have no objection to seeing me strip off in front of you…?'

Colour high in her cheeks, Rosie fled, shutting the door behind her.

In the quiet of the kitchen, she hastily prepared some pasta for herself, making good use of a number of tins. Comfort eating. Her head was full of the ramifications of her very small, practically invisible little white lie. Everything had snowballed and now here she was, with the sexiest man on the planet upstairs in her bedroom. Her nerves were shredded. When she thought of Matteo, everything inside her went into meltdown. Physically, she felt faint when she closed her eyes and pictured him in all his over-the-top sexiness. He was just so breathtakingly *beautiful*.

But it wasn't just confined to the way he looked. If that had been the sum total of it, then she could have steeled herself against the impact, because a good-looking guy without personality was just a cardboard cut-out to be admired without any threat of him getting under your skin.

No. Matteo's extraordinary effect on her was all wrapped up in the power of his personality, his air of command, and now that she had eked out a couple of personal details the fallibility she could sense underneath the cloak of arrogant self-assurance.

He posed questions, he ignited her imagination, he stirred depths of curiosity she'd never known she possessed.

Absorbed in hectic speculation, she ate without thinking—the pasta, some salad that looked dangerously close to needing last rites performed then a slab of chocolate dessert that was just the thing to settle her mind.

She was startled when she heard the sound of the door opening and then there was Candice, shedding outer layers of snow-covered gear as she breezed into the kitchen, pink-faced and smiling.

'I really miss the little monsters.' She headed straight to the fridge to pull out a bottle of mineral water. 'But—' she looked at Rosie with a grin '—some time out is a wonderful thing. Had a ball. So nice to catch up with that crew. Where's Matteo?'

'He…um…working.'

'Working?' She kept her eyes fixed on Rosie's flushed face as she drank from the bottle before lowering it. 'Where? In Dad's office? Surely he can pack in the work for a few days…if he's head over heels in love with you?'

'Well, you know how it goes when it comes to men and…er…work.' Rosie offered vaguely. Her sisters had always had the ability to pin her to the spot with their penetrating blue eyes and she was pinned to the spot now, unable to move forward and incapable of shuffling back.

'Tell me.'

'Lucien works all the hours under the sun, or have you forgotten?'

'He's a surgeon,' Candice responded drily. 'Lives depend on him. It's early days for you both, Rosie. I would have expected him to have made a little time for you, especially considering the time of year, when most businesses are operating at a much slower pace.'

Rosie remained steadfastly silent. A fierce defensiveness for her so-called boyfriend suddenly kicked into gear allied to the stubborn need to stand her ground. Where had that come from?

'He isn't where he is because he's a slacker, Candice,' she said without the usual note of apology in her voice. 'Sometimes work can take over, and not necessarily because lives are at stake. Lucien might save lives on an operating table, but Matteo and how he runs his businesses can affect the livelihoods of lots of people who work for him.'

Candice stared.

'I consider myself duly told off. Second time for the evening. The only reason I sound nosy…' She sighed. 'Okay, I've researched the guy,' she confessed, 'And he's big stuff, Rosie. Somewhere at the back of my mind, I recognised the name, but I honestly thought I was mistaken because I couldn't believe that someone who doesn't even breathe the same air as we do could… well…'

'Find me attractive? Thanks very much.'

'It's not that at all!' Candice said quickly. 'I can't help being protective of you—he's out of your league, Rosebud. For a start, the sort of women he dates…'

'I know. He likes high-powered career women.'

'So he told you? I'm impressed with his honesty on that front, at least. Of course, Emily's heard of him, and so has Robert. But, from everything I've read and heard, he's so far up the pecking order that you literally have to be a billionaire to have much personal contact with him at all on the business level.'

Frankly, Rosie couldn't help thinking, the more Candice elaborated, the less likely it seemed that someone like Matteo would even glance in the direction of someone like her. Not unless they had temporarily taken leave of their senses. Christmas madness. Except, he didn't do Christmas.

'But of course,' Candice continued, flipping open the bin and dumping the plastic bottle into the recycling section, 'Opposites *do* attract, I'll give you that.'

'They do…' Rosie smiled to herself, remembering what Matteo had said earlier.

'There's no accounting for people when they fall in love.'

Fall in love? Was that the story doing the rounds? And was it spreading like a forest fire beyond the family unit?

'Well...' She laughed lightly and managed to galvanise her body into action, walking across to sit opposite her sister, wishing she had opted for a restorative glass of wine, for some Dutch courage would have done wonders right now. 'I don't know about *falling in love...*'

'What do you mean?'

'Relationships aren't all about *falling in love*,' she asserted, glancing away.

'That's not what you've always maintained,' Candice told her drily. She paused and delivered a searching look to her sister. 'I don't want you to get hurt,' she said quietly. 'And I'm very much afraid that you will. I just don't think you're tough enough to handle a guy like Matteo.'

Into the brief silence came the last voice either of them expected to hear.

'Maybe that's what I find so charming about your sister.'

They both looked up to see that Matteo had silently pushed open the kitchen door and was now lounging in the doorframe.

How long had he been there?

Rosie tried to remember if she had said anything incriminating and was certain that she hadn't.

He'd showered and changed into a pair of faded jeans and an old tee shirt and he looked drop-dead gorgeous— easy, relaxed, wildly sophisticated and with that edge of danger about him that made her whole body go on full alert.

'Maybe,' Matteo continued, 'It's a breath of fresh air to be with a woman who isn't as tough as nails and doesn't want to spend every minute of her time discussing the state of the world and how it should be fixed.' He strolled towards Rosie and then remained standing behind her, his hands on her shoulders, lightly caressing her neck and feathering shivers of pleasure through her body.

He leant to brush his lips on the nape of her neck and she nearly passed out.

She had never seen Candice out of her depth but Matteo unsettled her, Rosie thought. It was his self-assurance, his bone-deep confidence that his opinions carried weight. He didn't *allow* anyone to take advantage of him and, before they thought that they could try, he made sure to establish the lines of command.

'And what makes you think that your sister will be the one to be hurt?' he enquired coolly.

'Exactly.' Rosie finally entered the conversation but her usual spirited response was seriously compromised by the continuing, caressing motion of his fingers on her neck. 'Candice, please don't worry about me.'

'I intend to take very good care of your sister.' Matteo's voice was still cool.

'Really?' Candice's eyebrows shot up. 'I mean, I hope so. We all do.'

'Why would I say it if I didn't mean it?'

'But,' Rosie interjected, 'It's only been a couple of weeks so…we're taking each day as it comes.'

'And you were always the impulsive one, Rosie,' Candice teased. 'Is love changing you already?'

'Don't be ridiculous!' Rosie spluttered. How much deeper could the hole she had dug for herself go?

'I know it's not wedding bells yet!' Candice laughed and stood up, her movements graceful as she strode towards the door. 'But please don't forget to give me ample warning so that I can start planning my outfit!'

Rosie managed to stammer out something, grateful that Matteo seemed to be taking it all in his stride, and it was only when the kitchen door was shut and her sister well and truly gone that Rosie looked at him with alarm.

'You should never have encouraged my sister to think that there was more to this than there is!' was the first thing she said, leaping to her feet, irritated at Matteo's composure as he helped himself to a bottle of water from the fridge.

'We should head up,' was all he said.

'Why on earth did you come down here, anyway? I thought you said that you had a mountain of emails to get through!'

'The prospect of working suddenly didn't seem quite so enticing.' He circled her and stared down at her for a few seconds until she reluctantly lifted her eyes to his.

'I was trying to ease the way to us breaking up,' she confessed. 'Until you came along and demolished all my efforts. Why couldn't you have just taken the lead from me and backed me up when I started insinuating that this was probably just a fling?'

Matteo shrugged. 'Maybe I'm so arrogant that the thought of being written off as a fling dented my ego.'

'I don't believe you,' Rosie muttered.

'Maybe…' he murmured.

Rosie didn't know what was going through his head, but his expression wasn't the expression of an arrogant alpha male with a sore ego.

'Just maybe it got on my nerves hearing your sister

assume that a man like me could never look twice at someone like you.'

'I'm not asking for your pity.'

'If you don't assert yourself, you'll be walked over.'

'Thank you very much for the words of advice.'

'You've stood up to your sister once. You can do it again. Try it a few times and you might find that it becomes a way of life.'

'You don't like me prying into your private life, Matteo, and I don't like you thinking that you can analyse me.'

'But you've set a precedent. Don't get me wrong,' he grated. 'Your life is none of my business but it affronts something in me when I hear you being treated like a kid who needs other people to look after her. You're not a kid.'

'I know that,' Rosie muttered grudgingly. She sneaked a glance at him from under her lashes. 'I did actually stick up for you when she told me that it was strange for you to be working when you should be desperate to spend time in my company.'

'Did you, now?'

Rosie could see the speculation in his eyes at that admission. 'I thought it might be a good idea to let her know that work came first with you.'

Matteo burst out laughing, his grey eyes darkening with appreciation. 'More of those foundations being laid down.'

'It might have been if you had got on board with me instead of branching out and doing your own thing.'

Matteo shrugged, the smile lingering on his lips, and began heading towards the door. 'I'm hitting the sack. Coming?'

'I'll… I think I'll stay down here and finish tidying the kitchen,' Rosie told him. For a while she'd forgotten the prospect ahead of sharing her bedroom with him but it was all coming back to her now at great speed. On the spot she decided that she would stay out of harm's way in the kitchen, at least long enough for him to fall asleep so that when she finally joined him he would be dead to the world.

She couldn't picture him being dead to the world, though. In fact, she couldn't imagine him sleeping. More lying still with his eyes closed but primed to leap into action at the sound of a pin dropping.

'Don't wait up. There's linen in the cupboard on the landing for the *chaise longue*.'

'Sure.' He didn't bother turning around to look at her but left the kitchen, shutting the door behind him, leaving her to take as long as she possibly could filling the dishwasher, wiping the counters and in the end going through the contents of the fridge and binning everything that no longer had any lifespan left whatsoever.

It was after midnight by the time she finally headed up to the bedroom and she was dead on her feet.

So he was going to be in her bedroom. That meant nothing. She was going to be cool and composed because he was right—she wasn't a kid and she was going to stop behaving like one. She was the only one who could determine the direction of her life and her choices and she was going to remember that.

This felt like a crucial moment for her. She was at a crossroads. She either carried on in no particular direction, escaping her family's well-intentioned guidance by drifting from one job to another, or else she buckled down and asserted herself. It was odd that a perfect stranger had been the one to bring her to this point.

He told her things that she didn't want to hear but it was thanks to him that she had actually stood up to Candice instead of backing away. She had always been treated like the baby of the family and she had followed through, fulfilling their expectations, becoming the family member happy to drift through life while other people got on with responsible living and grown-up decision making.

When she stood back and looked at it through objective eyes, she was mortified.

From now on, things were going to change. They already had.

Filled with the rosy glow of assertiveness, Rosie pushed open the bedroom door and there he was on the *chaise longue*, semi-reclining, and it looked painful. His laptop was open and his legs looked as though they weren't quite sure where they should go. Over the end of the sofa? Uncomfortable. On the ground? Likewise. He was way too tall and too big for the piece of furniture to which he had been consigned but the fact that he had obeyed orders touched her.

He shifted his big, muscular bulk as she walked in, drawing attention… Forget about the inadequacies of his makeshift bed, the guy was semi-naked.

Low-slung, loose-fitting jogging bottoms. That was it. He was half-naked and she stood by the door, shamelessly gaping for a few seconds, before walking in and shutting the door behind her.

Thank God he hadn't switched on the overhead light. Instead, he had swivelled the angle-poise lamp by the bed in the direction of the *chaise longue*. Rosie hoped that in a half-dark room the beetroot red of her cheeks wouldn't immediately be visible.

'You took your time,' Matteo said, now standing up and stretching before dumping the laptop on her dressing table.

Rosie's vocal cords had dried up. She cleared her throat and stared straight past his spectacular, burnished bronze body to the window just behind him. Seemed a safer option. That said, he still managed to intrude into the entire periphery of her vision. He was so tall, muscles densely packed, the flat lines of his stomach tapering to a narrow waist and spirals of dark hair arrowing down...

'There was a lot of tidying to do in the kitchen,' she croaked. 'You... I see you've made yourself comfortable on the *chaise longue*.'

Matteo glanced over his shoulder and grimaced. 'I'm not sure that *comfortable* would be the appropriate word.'

Rosie had expected complaints. Maybe a show of resentful acceptance of the boundaries she had laid down, possibly even fully fledged refusal to accommodate her wishes. But his voice was remarkably even and she felt something...quite different from those waves of taboo attraction. She felt the stirrings of affection.

She glanced at her lovely king-sized bed and Matteo followed the direction of her gaze.

'I'm in your house,' he said, walking to the window and back to the sofa, exercising his long limbs. 'The bed is yours.'

'I'm half your size.'

'Rules of the house apply here,' Matteo drawled drily, flexing his muscles again and then sinking back down onto the *chaise longue*, his dark eyes pinned to her face as she remained hovering like a visitor in her own bedroom. He grinned. 'Relax. There's no need to start thinking about playing the self-sacrificing martyr by giving up your bed for me, Rosie. If the shoe was on the other foot and you were in my house, I'd be sprawled out on the bed and you'd be trying to squeeze into the clothes hamper in the bathroom. It's late. Forget I'm here and go to sleep.'

CHAPTER FIVE

THE BEDROOM WAS empty the following morning when Rosie woke up. In that moment between sleeping and waking, she had a brief respite when she actually forgot about Matteo being in her room at all, then she shot up into a sitting position and squinted at the *chaise longue* which was as tidy as though it had never been slept on. No rumpled linen. No pillow tossed onto the floor and no six-foot-two, drop-dead gorgeous Italian scrunched up asleep.

No Candice either.

There were messages waiting for her the second she checked her phone, including a lengthy voicemail informing her that one of the kids had come down with hand, foot and mouth disease.

'Absolute nightmare!' Candice had sounded rushed and a little frantic on the voicemail. 'It's only a passing virus, and Toby will be over it in a couple of days, but of course Lucien is freaking out, so I've caught the first flight out, darling. Don't despair, though! I'll be back at the end of the week with the gang—and don't let that hunk of yours go anywhere! Lock him away if you have to! Everyone's dying to meet him!'

A long text message from her mother warned her that

they, too, would be delaying their arrival so that they could lend a hand with two-year-old Jess while Candice was playing Florence Nightingale to her elder brother.

Probably a good idea to give you a little more private time with your young man! her mother had messaged, with a winking face next to it. So you can breathe a sigh of relief, darling.

With several skiing lessons booked for the day and behind time, Rosie raced through the room, flinging on the appropriate gear, and headed down, taking the short flight of stairs two at a time and screeching to a halt by the kitchen door. Matteo was in the kitchen. It was a little after eight, but he looked bright-eyed and bushy tailed, as though he had had a splendid night's sleep.

'Coffee?' He greeted her equably, shutting the laptop which was in front of him on the kitchen table.

He was in a black polo-neck jumper and faded black jeans and he took her breath away.

Rosie blinked.

'How long have you been up?'

'A couple of hours. Hard to say.' He stood up and strolled towards the kettle to switch it on.

'Because you didn't manage to sleep well on the sofa?' Rosie inched into the kitchen, then told herself that it was ridiculous to feel uncomfortable in her own space. She needed to eat something before she shot out or she'd faint on the slopes. Her tummy was rumbling.

'It was a challenge,' he threw over his shoulder, 'But I've never been one to shy away from a challenge.'

Rosie had a vision of him on the *chaise longue*, half-naked, dwarfing it and yet accepting without complaint that that was his designated sleeping spot, and she felt it again—a stirring of tenderness that was disconcerting.

'Well, you're in luck,' she offered brightly. She headed for the bread bin and extracted a sandwich loaf that was, thankfully, fresh enough to pop into the toaster. 'Candice has had to rush off back to England because Toby has a virus.'

'Hand, foot and mouth,' Matteo murmured and Rosie looked at him with surprise.

'How do you know?'

'I was in the kitchen when she was heading out of here.'

'You were?'

'Like I said, sleeping was a challenge. I threw in the towel just in time to catch her before she left. She explained the situation.'

'Right.' Rosie hesitated as it dawned on her that there was no need for Matteo to stay at the chalet at all because there would be no one around to observe the lovers in action. He could return to the hotel and check himself in for however many nights before the family descended.

The chalet would feel very empty without him there, she thought, and just as quickly she banished that thought from her head. She had been in it on her own for weeks and it had been absolutely fine.

She had been ensnared by his personality and by the way he looked, and she had probably been a bit lonely without realising it. The instructors and all the young people working in the hotel were very friendly, and there was a brilliant social life on tap for anyone who wanted to dip in and out of it. There were always things happening in various groups in the evenings, depending on who happened to be working what shift. But many of her friends had paired up and she could only think that

Matteo had lulled her into enjoying time with a guy on her own.

She had to remember that this was an artificial situation, though, and it annoyed her to feel that nudge of disappointment at the thought of him not being around.

'So I guess you've worked out what this means,' she said casually, offering him some toast, which he politely refused, even though he didn't appear to have eaten anything. There were no dirty plates to be seen and she had a feeling that he wouldn't have been meticulous about washing, drying and putting away anything he'd used.

'What?' Matteo strolled back to the chair and swivelled it so that he could watch her as she buttered her toast and then stood pressed against the counter, looking at him.

'You can return to the hotel and stay there until the family show up. I mean, Candice won't be here, and Mum and Dad are hanging back with her so that they can help with the kids while Toby is poorly. Emily and Rob will come later as well. It'll be a sudden onslaught but in the meantime there's no need for us to pretend because there will be no one around to see us.'

'No can do.'

'Sorry?' Rosie had bitten into her toast and she chewed it slowly. One slice. She'd be starving in an hour but thinking about all those career women Matteo was attracted to had got her thinking that she could do with shedding a few pounds and redirecting her love of chocolate into something else. Celery, perhaps.

'Bob and Margaret are still around,' Matteo elaborated. 'They're not staying at that hotel but they're there on a regular basis, enjoying one of the restaurants, drinking in one of the bars. There are only so many watering

holes in this resort. Since the whole purpose of this arrangement was to convince them that we're the happy
couple, it's hardly going to do if they spot me back at
the hotel without you.'

'I hadn't thought of that,' Rosie admitted.

Which brought her to another realisation and that
was that they would now be here, in this lodge together,
without Candice and her entire family around to dilute
the situation.

She dropped the toast into the bin and looked at him
in consternation.

'Don't worry,' Matteo drawled, 'I'll make myself
scarce.'

'That's not what I meant.'

'You have a face that's as transparent as a pane of
glass. I have a mountain of work to get through, as it
happens. This deal isn't the only thing on my plate at
the moment. I'd planned on having time out at my villa
in Venice to work solidly over the Christmas period, but
now that that's been shot out of the water I'll have to get
as much done as possible before your family get here.'

'At least you won't have to sleep on the sofa now.'

Matteo didn't say anything. The night had been a hid-
eous lesson in physical discomfort and not because he
was averse to sleeping on anything that wasn't a feather
mattress. Growing up in a foster home, there had been
no luxuries. He had become accustomed to a single bed
with a mattress that seemed about as thick as a pound
coin.

No, his discomfort had stemmed from the fact that he
was way too big for such a delicate item of furniture.

And, as if that wasn't bad enough, he had been aware
of her tossing and turning and then, at some point in the

early hours of the morning, she had stumbled past him to go to the bathroom, mostly asleep, and after that getting back to sleep had been impossible.

Her body…

Even under the baggy tee shirt and the shapeless shorts he had glimpsed luscious curves that had sent an ache of desire straight to his groin. There was something about the light in this part of the world… The luminosity had penetrated through a crack in the curtain and as she had yawned her way past him, oblivious to his presence because she'd been dead to the world, the shadowy outline of her heavy breasts had been clearly visible.

His erection had been hard and immediate and he had had to suffer in silence, gritting his teeth while his imagination had taken flight.

Never had he felt such an intense craving to have any woman. It had shocked him and had been intensely unsettling because he hadn't been able to control his response.

If he'd managed half an hour's sleep for the entire night, he would have been surprised.

'You can have one of the guest bedrooms,' Rosie elaborated, breaking eye contact and then hovering. 'They're all made up and I can just replace the linen before the family arrive later in the week.'

She couldn't read his expression. If he always seemed to know what she was thinking because her face was 'as transparent as a pane of glass', then reading his thoughts was about as easy as groping a way forward in dense fog wearing a blindfold.

Right now, he was staring at her with hooded eyes, pinning her to the spot, even though she knew she had to run because her first client was in forty-five minutes.

'Good idea.' Matteo dropped his eyes and glanced at the laptop.

Her cue to go, Rosie thought. Enough small talk.

'I'll be on the slopes until this afternoon,' she said, edging past him to the door. 'And then I might go out with some of the gang this evening. So I won't be in your way.' They were talking to one another as though they were strangers and, although she knew that this was to be expected, given the fact that there were no witnesses in the vicinity to make judgement calls on their relationship, she couldn't help but miss the easy, teasing banter he was so good at whenever they were in public view.

'That's not going to work.' He caught her wrist, stopping her in her tracks.

A sizzle of electricity zapped through her and she froze. She wanted to shut her eyes because he was so clever at reading what was in her head and, right now, what was in her head was *I want this man.* She licked her lips but her mouth was dry and she couldn't seem to get any words out.

'Want to know why?' Matteo was gazing at her flushed face.

He rubbed the pad of his thumb absently over the softness of her inner wrist.

He could feel it. He could sense a physical response rippling through her, mirroring his.

This was playing with fire. He wasn't on the lookout for a relationship with anyone and certainly not with a woman who was as soft as meringue, no sharp edges, no defence barriers. Despite her wealthy background, she was so sweetly disingenuous that he would be crazy to go there.

He banked down the tide of images flooding his

mind—pictures of her in bed naked, her plump, ripe body opening up for him.

He dropped her hand and sat back. 'You keep forgetting that we're supposed to be an item.'

'I don't think that Bob and Margaret will be partying at a club.'

'That's not the point. I expect glad tidings of our hot and heavy relationship have already reached the ears of most of your fellow clubbers. How's it going to look if you show up without me?'

'You could always come.'

'I'm not big into the club scene.'

Rosie distractedly rubbed her wrist where he had been touching it. 'Well, if everyone has heard all about us, and I honestly don't think that's the case, wouldn't it be a good idea if we were to do something outdoorsy?'

'Like gyrating on a dance floor at two in the morning?' He raised his eyebrows and Rosie shot him a reluctant grin.

'Everyone's too tired after being on the slopes all day to stay out until two in the morning. Gyrating.' Her smile widened. 'You sound like an old man.'

'I'm old compared to you,' Matteo told her irritably. 'I'm thirty-two. You're twenty-three. I've lived a life of responsibility. You've had the pleasure of doing just as you've always pleased without fear of consequences.' He paused, hating himself for wiping the easy smile off her face. 'It's what makes you who you are,' he said roughly. 'And that's no bad thing.'

'What do you mean?'

'I happen to like the way you approach life, as though each day is filled with the promise of something new and enjoyable.'

'It often is.'

'Is it?' He shrugged. 'You could be right but it's an optimism that usually gets ground into dust by the time reality takes over.'

'What do you mean by reality?'

'Work. Responsibility. Life in general.'

Rosie was so tempted to reach out and touch him. There was a vulnerability there and she was sure he wasn't even aware of it. He'd had a tough life and Lord only knew what sacrifices he had had to make along the way to get where he had.

'How did you get that scar?' she asked suddenly, expecting him not to offer a reply. She had done what he seemed constantly to be telling her not to do, namely push past his boundaries to invade his inner sanctum.

'Fight.' He smiled at her. 'I was a teenager at the time. Fights happened all the time. Someone had a knife and I got in the way of it.'

Her heart twisted and she backed towards the door. 'I should be going.'

'And I need to carry on with this work. What time are you wrapping it up with your lessons?'

'Last one at three.' Rosie knew she had to go and yet she didn't want to leave. Every small entry into his life felt magical. 'I need to go and buy some food,' she said, fidgeting. 'I've been lazy when it comes to buying stuff. It's easy to live off junk food because we get discounted prices at most of the cafés around here. One of the perks of being a ski instructor.'

'I noticed a lot of greenery,' Matteo remarked, enjoying the way she blushed, which was something that never failed to surprise him.

Rosie grimaced. 'I know. I always think that if I buy

lots of lettuce and vegetables then I'm going to actually eat them. I should. I should never go anywhere near chips or burgers.'

'Why?'

'Can't you look at me and tell?' She laughed and then sobered up when her eyes collided with his and she saw that he wasn't laughing along with her.

His expression was...darkly hungry.

She shivered, a core of excitement reaching fever pitch as he continued to stare at her. By the time he lowered his gaze, her nerves were in crazy freefall and there was a heat between her thighs that made her want to rub them together.

'No, I can't, as a matter of fact,' Matteo intoned in a driven undertone that was quite unlike his usual lazy drawl.

'I'll see you later.' Rosie fled. Any longer in his presence and she would start having heart palpitations. Could he see the effect he had on her? For a minute, just then, she had seen something in his eyes that had sent her pulses racing out of control. It was an attraction that had gone to her head like incense. He'd wanted her. She was sure of that.

Her mind was all over the place for the rest of the day. She waved at Bob and Margaret, who were trying out the slopes on their own. She discovered that Matteo had been right to think that news of their whirlwind romance had done the rounds. She had to think fast on her feet when questions were asked, building a picture of a relationship that had been clandestine. He'd been busy wrapping up a deal and she'd been busy with her ski lessons so they had enjoyed snatched time together and things had gone on from there.

Fortunately, due to the nature of the business, there were a lot of arrivals and departures and the few friends she had made who had been there as long as she had, doing the season, seemed to have such frenetic social lives after their duties were done, that they accepted her stammering explanations without delving too deep. Indeed, the thought of 'snatched time together' had struck her girlfriends as wonderfully exciting.

She was pleasantly tired by the time she saw off her last client. She was preparing to head back to the hotel to dump her stuff and change when she happened to glance to her left and there he was. Her heart skipped a beat, then it skipped a couple more as he made his way towards her, dressed in ski gear.

'I didn't think you skied,' she said breathlessly when he was standing in front of her.

She didn't think it was possible for anyone to look as good as he did in ski clothes. Aside from a thin orange strip along the top, he was dressed completely in black. His sunglasses were propped up and he hadn't shaved. She could make out the shadow of stubble on his chin.

At this hour, the slopes were emptying out, and from the resort below she could hear the distant strains of Christmas carols being played. Something about the stillness in the air seemed to trap the sound and hold it within the confines of the mountains rearing upwards, red, gold and white in the fading light.

'I don't.' He flashed her a smile. 'But you had a point when you said that some outdoor time together might be a good idea. Bought the gear, so here I am.'

'It's a little late...' Her skin was burning. 'But... I guess I could take you through the ropes. I mean, it's not as though you actually *want* to learn to ski.'

'Who knows?' Matteo murmured. 'With the right teacher, I might find I have untapped talent.'

Nervous as a kitten, and aware of her roundness thanks to the layers of ski gear, Rosie went through the paces with him.

'Feet together…take it slowly…keep the skis parallel… No, not quite like that. Here, let me show you. Don't forget to keep your eyes ahead! Are you scared of heights, by the way? Will you be spooked in the cable car?'

Rosie had never had so much fun. She was in her comfort zone and, as she laughed and tried to give him some handy tips, she caught herself telling him about when she had first taken to the slopes. It was the one thing she was better at than her sisters.

'They were clever,' she said, eyeing the distance between his skis, 'But I was always the sporty one.'

'I'm surprised you didn't think about making a career in it,' Matteo murmured.

'I'm a good skier,' Rosie laughed, 'But I'm not great enough to compete on an international level!'

'There's more to making a living in sport than practising it at an international level.'

This as they were making their way to the car, Matteo having managed to get hold of a personal driver to bring him down from the chalet.

Rosie paused for a fraction of a second and looked sideways at him.

'You mean like a sports teacher or something?'

'I mean…'

Matteo stopped and turned to look at her so that she was obliged to stop as well and stare up at him.

'The key thing is to find what you enjoy, because chances are you'll probably be good at it, and then with a favourable following wind you can make a career out of it.'

'You enjoyed making money and you were good at it so you made a career out of it?'

'I enjoyed the thought of being free. Money was just my passport to getting there. I've bought food.'

'Sorry?' Rosie's brain was lagging behind, dwelling on what he had said.

'Food. You said you needed. I've bought.'

Rosie felt a tingle of pleasure and for a few moments, a real sense of *contentment*. So this was what her sisters had, she thought with a pang. Someone to laugh with. Someone who bought food. Someone to open the car door for them.

She'd never had that.

This was just an illusion, and she didn't want to get sucked in, but it was hard when he was chatting to her as they slowly bumped their way back up to the chalet, which was in darkness by the time they got there.

Around them, the snow blanketed everything in white. The air was dry and cold. The house, however, was toasty warm as they entered, shaking off the snow and dumping coats, gloves, scarves and boots in the spacious cupboard by the front door.

The intimacy of their surroundings, just the two of them in the house, hit her with the force of a sledgehammer as they headed towards the kitchen, Matteo with two carrier bags in his hands.

He switched on lights as they went. He'd dumped the outer layers and was down to a thermal tee shirt that clung lovingly to his muscular torso.

'I'll just go and get changed…showered.' She was trailing behind him and she didn't give him time to look around, carolling gaily as she veered off to the staircase. 'And I'll pop a towel in the guest bedroom for you!'

Not that there's anything to worry about, she told herself. *He might have glanced at you with a show of interest but you're not his type. And he was the perfect gentleman last night. So making a point of telling him about the towel in the guest room is at best not very subtle and at worst a hint that you are downright terrified of sharing a bedroom with him when there's no sister conveniently lodged two rooms along.*

He had unpacked the carrier bags and the contents were laid out on the kitchen table in ceremonial fashion.

Rosie relaxed and grinned. She looked at what was there: tomatoes, some vegetables, duck eggs, an assortment of expensive pâtés, smoked salmon, various cheeses, an enormous box of the finest Swiss chocolates and a gateau that instantly made her mouth water.

'You don't need to watch what you eat.' Matteo followed her gaze to the gateau.

Rosie ignored him. She was so conscious of his presence that the hairs on her arms were standing on end.

'Duck eggs?' She held the blue box up to him.

'That was a mistake,' Matteo admitted.

'It's a very interesting assortment of food and thank you very much for going to the trouble of buying it. I'm not sure what I do with some of these ingredients. Maybe we should just have a salad for our supper.'

'There's bread,' Matteo informed her.

'I guess you don't cook at all?'

'I try and avoid it.' He found himself telling her that cooking had been *de rigueur* at the children's home when he'd been growing up and the very fact of that had instilled a healthy dislike for anything to do with pots, pans and food preparation.

What he didn't add was that he'd suffered from the realisation over the years that pots, pans and food preparation was what at least some women enjoyed doing in an attempt to whet his appetite for more than just the dishes they had lovingly prepared.

He watched as she fetched plates and busied herself opening the packets he had bought.

Did that count as food preparation? Nothing went into preparing a cold meal. It was ready in under half an hour and, looking at the spread, Matteo found himself wishing that he was about to eat something hot.

'Do you…enjoy cooking at all?' he queried, opening a bottle of wine.

It was a little after six. Early for supper, but it was dark outside, with flurries of snow reminding them of the time of year.

'I wouldn't say it's the love of my life.' Rosie had tactfully stuck the gateau out of sight and she eyed the array of pâtés, cheeses and smoked salmon with a distinct lack of enthusiasm.

He'd obviously bought the sort of food he personally enjoyed.

'This wouldn't be your choice of food?' he quizzed and she looked at him sheepishly.

'I've always liked food that's a bit more…more…'

'Tasty?'

'This is all very good.'

'Wine will improve the flavours. Hang on for five secs.'

He disappeared and returned a few minutes later with two bottles of champagne.

'Forgot I bought these at the wine merchant.' He opened a bottle, found glasses, poured them a glass each and then returned to his seat.

Rosie was ashamed at just how good this felt, sitting here with this guy, eating a meal together, almost as though they weren't caught up in a charade, a game of make believe.

She was uneasily aware of how slender the line could be between reality and fantasy.

This felt real.

This felt more real than any of the passing connections she had ever made over the years with guys and she knew that it was because, very quickly and purely because of the situation, they had shared things with one another. He had shared his background—reluctantly, she knew—but still…

She had opened up to him, he had listened and somehow he had seen right into the very heart of her. That had promoted a feeling of…*closeness*.

The champagne was excellent. The best money could buy.

'I thought you had planned on working all day,' she said a little drowsily after champagne had been drunk and a dent made in the food.

'Bob and Margaret weren't available for comment.'

'I saw them on the slopes.'

'Did they approach you? Ask any questions?'

'They were too far away, but you were right about my friends seeming to know that we're involved. When this started, I had no idea that it would grow legs and start running away from me.' She sighed.

'Like I've said before…' Matteo fetched the gateau from where she had earlier hidden it behind the canisters of sugar and tea '…once you start lying, it's impossible to know where it's going to end up.'

'You must hate all of this.' She looked at the slab of cake in front of her and was indecently keen to tuck in. He produced two forks and gently pulled the plate between them.

'Care to share?'

Rosie's eyes widened. This felt truly intimate. They weren't touching one another—not even their forks touched!— yet as they at the slab of cake it felt weirdly *intimate.*

'You asked me whether I was hating all of this,' Matteo mused.

Her eyes were even more amazing up close, he distractedly found himself thinking. She couldn't quite meet his gaze and he knew, with the instinct of a man well versed in the way women reacted, that her response was a physical one. The champagne had relaxed her but she was still wary. He could sense it. He could almost smell it.

What would she do if he touched her? He found the thought of that so erotic that he had to grit his teeth together to ease the ache in his groin.

'You must be.'

'I should be,' he admitted, 'But I suppose that a change is as good as a rest.'

Rosie wanted to feel relieved at that, but all she could think was, *You're enjoying the novelty of the situation. The novelty of being with someone like me. You've practically said so yourself.*

She didn't want to be a novelty but she wasn't going to give that away.

'I've put you in the room to the left of the staircase,' she said, changing the subject.

'There's a towel on the bed,' he added politely and she blushed.

'I'll tidy in the morning.' She staged a yawn which turned into the real thing. 'I'm exhausted. I always am in the evenings.'

'And yet you wanted to go clubbing tonight.'

'It was optimistic.'

'You don't have to try and run away from me,' he said kindly, which made her blush even more. 'As this evening has shown, we're two adults perfectly capable of passing the time of day together without any major disagreements. I'm going to stay up for a couple of hours, finish some emails. I think, if we can agree to stick to this routine until your family show up, life shouldn't be too overwhelming for us. Wouldn't you agree? And, as soon as my deal is signed, we can begin the process of… disentanglement.'

CHAPTER SIX

ROSIE STARED UP at the ceiling. She hadn't drawn the curtains and the silver light, the reflection of the moon shining down on endless white outside, illuminated everything in the bedroom.

This had always been her favourite time of the year—the run up to Christmas. The entire resort was a winter wonderland of tiny lights, Christmas trees and carols booming through the village, ratcheting up the excitement. Every year, the entire family would meet for a week at the chalet and it would mark the beginning to the countdown for them. They would put up a tree and the board games would come out. Family time.

She should have been alive with anticipation. Instead, she eyed the empty *chaise longue* and realised that her thoughts had been entirely occupied with Matteo.

At a little after one in the morning, he would be sound asleep in a proper bed instead of lying awake, cramped and uncomfortable, on a sofa that she, inches shorter, would have found a challenge.

She thought about him bedding down without complaint and then waking up and busying himself on his computer at some ridiculously early hour in the morning, also without complaint. She knew that he would have spent his entire time at the chalet falling off a sofa in the middle of the night, perfectly accepting that, if that was his designated sleeping area, then so be it.

He had a childhood without any luxuries. As a small boy growing into a young man learning how to be tough and ambitious enough to ignore the siren call of violence—all that had prepared him to accept discomfort should it come his way. He might be worth billions now but she got the feeling that the past he seldom discussed was never forgotten.

Caught up in the fruitless exercise of thinking about him and trying to work him out, she finally decided to get out of bed and head down to the kitchen for something to eat.

She'd barely touched a thing all day and the gateau was beckoning.

The chalet was in darkness as she made her way downstairs to the kitchen. Through the vast glass doors, she paused to take in the expanse of snowy white outside.

She shivered, feeling the chill, because the central heating had switched off at midnight. She should have slung on a bathrobe but satisfying her rumbling tummy had been far too pressing. Plus, she was sick of thinking about Matteo and then mentally asking herself why she couldn't put him out of her mind.

She'd managed to find every excuse under the sun for her relentless absorption with him, starting with *It's perfectly understandable, considering the way we were thrown together* then going on to *It would be unnatural for me not to think about him* and *There wouldn't be a woman alive who wouldn't be thinking of him if she was sharing a house with him...who could ignore someone who looks the way he does?*

She didn't bother turning on the kitchen light due to the unfounded suspicion that it might filter all the way upstairs to where Matteo was sleeping and alert him to the fact that there was someone downstairs.

As a consequence, she banged her foot against the edge of one of the chairs and hopped in agony for a few seconds until the pain subsided, then she opened the fridge and knelt down to inspect the contents.

She wanted to resist the cake but the alternative of eating whatever remained of the options Matteo had generously bought didn't tempt.

She reached out to cut a sliver of the gateau which Matteo had shoved in the fridge, not bothering to remove the knife he had earlier used to cut it, when the sound of his voice coming from behind her almost shocked her into having a heart attack.

With a yelp, she scuttled back and shot to her feet, heart pounding and mouth dry, and she spun round to look at him. The kitchen was still in darkness but to her horror that didn't last long because he banged on the switch and the room was flooded with light.

Never had Rosie felt more conscious of her state of undress. The tee shirt might be baggy but she was excruciatingly aware of the heavy weight of her bra-less breasts pushing against it, and her shorts were tiny. Way too small.

For a few seconds, she couldn't speak at all. She studied him, her thoughts in frantic disarray. She'd glimpsed him without a shirt on but this time... The man was *awesome*, she thought weakly, so very tall, so very well built. So very, very under-dressed. Not only was he half-naked, but the safe option of tracksuit bottoms had been jettisoned in favour of boxers that revealed long, muscular legs and a stomach as flat as a wash board.

'What are you doing here?' she managed accusingly. In timely fashion, she reminded herself that this was, actually, *her* house and he was the guest so why should she feel as though she'd been caught red-handed stealing the family heirlooms? How was it that he somehow found it so effortless to exert control and thereby give the impression that he owned everything around him even if he didn't?

'I heard a noise.'

His voice was terse and, reading into that abrupt response, Rosie could only imagine his annoyance at finding his sleep disrupted yet again.

'I made sure to be quiet!'

'Noise travels around here.'

They stood and stared at one another and, suddenly conscious of herself, she crossed her arms over her breasts and was disconcerted when he followed that gesture. Was he trying to embarrass her on purpose? She swung away but the heavy silence was getting to her.

'I just came down to get something to drink.' She thought of the gateau and silently bid farewell to the chunk of lovely, comforting calories. 'Are you just going to stand there? I'm sorry if I woke you up. I had no idea I made any noise. I banged my toe but I didn't think I yelped loud enough for you to hear.'

'I might as well get myself something to drink as well now that I'm down here,' Matteo muttered, moving forward with the quiet grace of a panther to open the fridge and extract two bottles of water, one of which he handed to her.

Instead of walking towards the door, he remained standing next to her, unsettling in his masculine beauty, holding her transfixed gaze until her legs began to feel wobbly.

Water in hand, she began backing away towards the door, eyes on him the whole time.

'I thought someone had broken in.' He moved towards her, his voice lacking its usual cool self-control. He sounded as though he needed to clear his throat.

'That's rare over here.' Rosie breathed, watching wide-eyed as he stopped in front of her. There was nowhere else to go so she remained where she was, staring up at him and trying hard to play it cool when her pulse was racing and her heart was slamming against her rib cage. 'You could sleep with the doors open and no one would break in.'

'You have the most amazing eyes,' Matteo murmured.

'Matteo…'

'I like it when you say my name in that breathy little voice.'

'Matteo, don't.'

'I'm not doing anything.'

But he was. Right now, he was. He was lifting one hand to sift it through her wildly tousled fair curls. Her mouth ran dry. She badly wanted to touch him but she had no idea how this kind of game went. He traced the outline of her mouth with his finger, then cupped the side of her face and stared at her for a long moment until her head was swimming.

'What's going on?' she whispered.

'As if you don't know.' He laughed softly. 'Haven't I told you how sexy I find you? I'm attracted to you, *mia bellissima*. And it's mutual, or are you going to deny it?'

'You're a good-looking man,' Rosie prevaricated.

'Would you like this good-looking man to kiss you?'

Rosie nodded, an unfamiliar, but powerful heat running through her body.

He lowered his head and the kiss…took her to heaven and left her there. His mouth was cool and when he inserted his tongue she reached up on tiptoe and wrapped her hands around his neck to pull him down closer to her.

A little groan escaped her. Her breasts felt heavy, her nipples sensitised to the point of painful. She ached for him and curved her body in a wriggling movement that invited him to slip his hand underneath the tee shirt.

For a second, Rosie stilled, but only for a second. He brushed her waist with his hand while he continued to ravish her with a never-ending kiss. Of its own volition, her body seemed to have closed what little gap there had been between them.

Lost in a world of sensation, and feeling as though her body was alive for the very first time, Rosie only realised that he had gently propelled her towards the kitchen table when she bumped against the edge of it.

He eased her apart from him and kept his eyes locked to hers when he began to slip the tee shirt up.

Mesmerising eyes, Rosie thought. Bottomless and fringed with indecently long lashes. Inch by inch the tee shirt was lifted until she was standing in front of him, her breasts exposed.

She felt a surge of feminine power when his nostrils flared as he looked down at her body.

She reached behind to prop herself against the table, clutching the edge with her hands and leaning ever so slightly back so that her body was inclined towards his, towards his heated, appreciative gaze.

He cupped her breasts in his hands and massaged them, simultaneously rolling his thumbs over the stiffened peaks. The groans became restless whimpers.

She wanted much more than this.

She wanted everything.

And suddenly, she realised that she was never going to get what she wanted. She was never going to get anything deep or significant with this guy.

Was this her?

Everything that was rooted in principle and tradition flared into life and she caught his hands in hers and looked at him with troubled eyes.

'I'm not sure I can do this,' she said on a miserable sigh, and just like that he dropped his hands and she lowered the tee shirt. 'I know we're adults, and this is what adults do when they fancy one another, but I'm not sure this is...*me*.'

'You're not...sure?'

'I've only had one serious relationship, Matteo, and that was a long time ago and it didn't end well. I thought we were going somewhere, heading somewhere, but it turned out that he was using me. Maybe not to start with, maybe there was something genuine there at the beginning, but in the end the family money, the trust fund... it all meant more to him.'

'What does a relationship you had years ago have to do with this?'

There was genuine bewilderment in his voice, and that threw her, because in her head the two seemed to be tied together, but why? Did he have a point? Did one bad relationship have to influence every relationship thereafter?

Confusion seeped in. She wondered what, exactly,

she was looking for. Permanence? Of course, she came from a secure and loving background. Her parents had been with one another for a lifetime and beyond. But did that mean that the only route open to her was with a guy she would end up marrying and settling down with?

What about the benefits of just having fun? Despite all the adventures she had had on her travels, hadn't she been at pains to avoid the greatest adventure of all—getting involved with someone? Opening up to them, whatever the outcome? Relationships had lasted five minutes because split decisions had been made that he wasn't the one.

'If you have to turn this into a drama in five acts, then maybe I misjudged things.' Matteo's voice had cooled and he stepped away from her, leaving behind an icy-cold void. 'I'm sorry.' His eyes were as dark and as deep as a glacier.

'Matteo…'

'I'm going to head up, Rosie. I'll see you in the morning.'

He spun round on his heels and soundlessly left the kitchen. In his wake, she subsided onto one of the kitchen chairs and thought, but she couldn't make sense of any of her thoughts. Matteo came from a different world from hers and not just in the material sense. He was hard, tough, had dragged himself up by the bootstraps and had battled whatever adversities he had faced to do it. He had money now but he had learnt from his experiences and now lived his life accordingly.

Something inside her shifted, adjusted and settled into another place and she began heading up the stairs, straight to the bedroom where he had been put.

He was up, lounging on the bed with his hands clasped behind his head, staring at the ceiling.

She could see him in the silver light filtering through the windows because, like her, he hadn't drawn the thick curtains, preferring the distant view of craggy, soaring, snowy mountains.

'I know I'm soft,' Rosie began, walking into the room, fired up.

'What the…?'

'Just let me say what I have to say!'

'Go to bed, Rosie. I'm not in the mood for a raging sermon from you. You don't have to justify your decisions to me.'

'I know I'm soft. I've been spoilt. I don't take anything for granted, believe me I don't, but that doesn't mean that I'm not aware of all the privileges I've grown up with. Maybe you think that that has something to do with me wanting the fairy-tale ending when it comes to romance and you could be right. My big relationship ended with a whimper but don't you dare tell me that you don't see what that has to do with anything.'

Matteo had sat up and she was propelled towards the bed—towards *him*.

Against the white bed linen, his burnished gold body, the deep, rich colour of someone in whom exotic genes ran like a thread of gold, was a powerful, lithe reminder of his intense masculinity.

'We're *all* affected by our pasts.' She perched on the edge of the bed and stared at him. His face was in shadow but she knew that he was watching her. She just didn't know what he was thinking, but when did she ever? 'You are. You haven't had *my* past, but you're as affected by yours as I am by mine. Our pasts are what shape us, and I'm not going to have you tell me that you have no idea what one broken relationship has to do with anything. You don't let anyone into your life because of what you went through. You don't like Christmas, and there would be a reason for that somewhere, buried in your past. So, I was hurt once and I never want to be hurt again.'

'You've said your piece and I've listened, Rosie. You should go to sleep now.'

'I'm attracted to you.'

'Don't go there,' Matteo warned in a dangerously low voice. 'I don't like game playing.'

'Isn't that what we've been doing ever since we met one another?'

'Wrong phrasing. I don't want any woman thinking she has to play games with me.'

'I'm not,' Rosie told him abruptly. She felt a surge of empowerment from her decision taken with eyes wide open. 'We're attracted to one another, and it's not about whether this will lead anywhere or not. I *know* it's not going anywhere. I *know* I'm not your type and you're not mine. So I'm not going to be hurt. I'm going to have fun.'

'What are you saying?'

Reckless daring swept through her in a *now or never* moment as she pulled the tee shirt over her head and stood in front of him, fighting hard not to succumb to crippling self-consciousness.

He wasn't saying anything but his silence wasn't the silence of someone politely about to channel her out of the bedroom and that was encouraging. The silence was still and thick with electricity.

She stepped out of the rest of her clothes and for a few seconds squeezed her eyes shut.

'Come.'

One word and it was enough.

This was a situation far removed from both their comfort zones and, if she only subliminally recognised the danger that particular novelty carried, then Matteo was all too aware of it.

Novelty, in his rarefied world, was a scarce commodity. He'd suffered the indignities of being the poor kid at a rich school, where he'd earned a scholarship to board at the age of thirteen. He'd learned the hard way to ignore every single thing that wasn't worth taking on board and that had included all manner of insults and verbal abuse. Ambition, an intellect that was in the stratosphere, an ability to take risks…all of those things had propelled him onwards and upwards, and he had had no time to relax…until now.

He'd made it. He had more money than most people could dream of. Enough to turn his back on work and live on a beach, drinking cocktails, for the rest of his life. But, in the cold light of day, there was a part of him that acknowledged that he was *bored.* What else was there to get? He could have anything he wanted. Any *woman* he wanted. All those top-notch career women, brainy, beautiful and independent, would still do anything he asked. He could read it in the way they looked at him, the way they listened to what he said, even in the way they sometimes played hard to get.

But she was right. His past had made him the person he was today, locked in a controlled world where he called the shots and there were no unpleasant surprises on any front—material or emotional.

Then into his safe, predictable and obscenely wealthy life this woman had parachuted and she was nothing like any woman he'd met before.

On paper, she made no sense. Life had taught him

to walk away from poor little rich girls with their ag-grieved air of entitlement and their healthy trust funds. He had no time for anyone for whom life was easy. His admiration was reserved for those who had faced at least some of the tough mountains he had had to conquer. Most of the women he had dated had worked hard to climb the ladder of success. They had gone beyond the call of duty and battled in a world that was largely, and stupidly, male dominated. Some had made marks that would live on after them.

There was no way that Rosie Carter could possibly qualify for any of those categories. She came from a privileged, private-school background but she surprised him at every turn. It had taken guts to do what she had just done. She was a breath of fresh air and he wanted her more than he had ever wanted any woman in his entire life.

Temptation had never looked so irresistible.

Rosie pushed her fair, curly hair behind her ears and stared at him. Her heart was pounding like a sledgeham-mer in her chest. It was chilly in the room, but her body was on fire, as if someone had taken a match and lit a bonfire under her feet.

He flung back the duvet, inviting her in, and she could see that he was completely naked. Her mouth went dry and the fire burning up inside her went from sizzling to molten.

She stifled a groan as their bodies met and she felt the push of his erection against her.

'I don't get it,' she whispered. 'I can't seem to help myself.'

'What's going on here,' he said, 'Is something that neither of us had banked on. There's a chemistry here that defies logic. Like you said, I'm not the sort of guy you're accustomed to dating and the same goes for me with you. Sexual attraction has a way of defying logic.'

Rosie's breath hitched in her throat at the feel of his hand gently smoothing her thigh, circling just by her crotch. She moaned softly and lay back, eyelids fluttering shut, parting her legs just a bit more so that he could nudge the dampness between her thighs with his knuckles. It was gentle, seductively rhythmic, and her breathing quickened in response.

'You have no idea how much you turn me on,' Matteo rasped shakily, tugging her so that he could plant a series of kisses on the side of her neck. 'You're breathtakingly sexy.'

'So are you.' Rosie's eyes were hot and drowsy as she caressed the side of his face before cradling the back of his head with her hand and pulling him into a kiss that melted everything in her body. His mouth was cool and firm and the feel of their tongues meshing was indescribable.

It was a kiss she never wanted to end. She curved into him, her body pale and smooth in the dim light.

He didn't talk but he didn't have to. His appreciation of her body was in the way he touched her and the hot fire in his amazing eyes.

He bent to suckle one throbbing nipple, drawing it deep into his mouth, tasting and feasting while sensations spiralled in her, making her wriggle and writhe underneath him.

She'd never wanted anyone so badly. Had never come close.

Her body was flushed and tingling all over when he eventually straightened. The contrast in their colouring was dramatic—she so pale, he burnished gold. He stepped off the bed and she could see that he was rummaging in his wallet for a condom. He dropped it on the wooden table by the side of the bed and looked at her with brooding intensity for a few silent seconds.

'What are you doing?'

'I'm looking.' He held himself in his hand and absently pleasured himself for a few seconds.

.Without thinking, she reached up. On cue, he stepped towards her, and she traced the sinewy ridges of his erection with a trembling finger, starting at the base and working slowly to the tip, which she circled until his fists were clenched at his sides in an attempt to maintain some semblance of self-control.

He finally caught her wrist and breathed deeply.

'Any more,' he said roughly, 'And I'll come—and when I come I want to be deep inside you.'

He slowly joined her back on the bed but, instead of kissing her, he lowered himself to her belly and kissed her there, along her rib cage, while she trembled under the caress.

He circled her belly button with his tongue and then darted it into the sensitive hollow there before moving down lower to her panties, in an intimacy she had never experienced before.

She fought against snapping her legs shut and, as if sensing the impulse, he placed both flattened palms on the inside of her thighs, holding her open for him.

That very first sensation as he began to nuzzle the dampness between her legs was electrifying.

She wanted to thrash around, arch up against his questing mouth. The breath caught in her throat and then what emerged was a guttural groan of utter pleasure as he began working his tongue along the slippery groove that shielded her clitoris.

When he delicately began tracing the delicate, throbbing bud of her clitoris, she fisted her hands and moaned against her knuckles. It was exquisite. Transporting. She began to move against his mouth, finding his rhythm and matching it to her own.

She couldn't stop the shattering force of her orgasm. It ripped into her and she spasmed against his mouth, stifling her cries of pleasure, reaching to curl her fingers into his hair so that she could press his face harder between her quivering thighs.

The strength of her orgasm left her weak, flushed and drowsy and it took her a few moments before she surfaced.

'I'm sorry,' she uttered, dismayed, but he was smiling.

'For what? Enjoying yourself?'

'This wasn't what was supposed to happen.'

She wrapped her arms around him and buried her face against the side of his neck because there was something shockingly intimate in what had just taken place, at how her body had reacted.

The freedom she had felt at that moment of coming made her feel as though her soul had opened up.

Suddenly, she wanted *more*, but she wasn't too sure what.

She tentatively rested her hand on his lean, firm buttocks, then stroked him. He flipped her over and positioned her so that she was lying on top of him. Like this, his pulsing manhood against her was a powerful reminder of the chemistry uniting them against all odds. She had just had an explosive orgasm, and her body wanted a repeat performance, but this time she wanted him inside her, moving deep and hard.

X-rated thoughts made her feel faint. She arched up so that her heavy breasts dangled invitingly close to his mouth and their eyes tangled in the subdued darkness.

'Very sexy,' Matteo murmured shakily and, when he contained her breasts between his hands, squashing them gently together, he couldn't contain a groan of utter pleasure.

That did something to her. A strain of wanton recklessness that she had never known she possessed sizzled through her with lightning speed.

She angled her body lower and levered her nipple into his mouth, propping herself up so that he could suckle on it while she watched. It was erotic, giddily so. Very slowly, she began to move against him, sinuously and seductively, inching left to right, and then in small, circular motions that heightened his responses and brought a flare of scorching lust to his eyes.

In the end, he couldn't stand it any longer. He groaned, pulled her down to him and then kept completely still for a few seconds, breathing himself back into a place of some self-control.

'I need to be inside you,' he said hoarsely. 'You're driving me crazy.'

That was music to Rosie's ears. She felt as though she was waking up, stepping into the real world, for the very first time in her life. She watched him heave himself off the bed, every movement clumsy and uncoordinated, testimony to the fact that, whatever he was feeling, it had complete control over him. He donned protection, easing the condom over his erection, taking time because of his size.

She was aching for him…couldn't stay still. She whimpered as he levered himself over her and then the whimper turned into a cry of intense satisfaction when he finally pushed into her.

He moved slowly at first, driving deeper into her, and then faster, holding them both at bay until, on one final thrust, he groaned and she felt him swell inside her. Indescribably turned on, she wrapped her legs around him and let wave after wave of pleasure surge over her. Their bodies were as one. She could never have imagined feeling so close, so united, with anyone.

Spent, her breathing took its time returning to normal, but then she sighed happily and wriggled against him.

Her head was against his chest and Matteo trailed his fingers through her hair, sifting free the tangles. Her warm breath puffed against him. She had one thigh across his and he felt her dampness. She was so soft… sexy curves and bountiful breasts…with an eagerness that was as sweet as the summer sun.

For the first time in his life, Matteo felt exposed. Had sex ever been that good? He had only just come down from a high and he wanted to go there again. He had no inclination to head straight for the shower. His mind wasn't moving on to other things. There was no creeping urge to free himself from the presence of another body sharing his bed.

Disquieted, he eased himself back with a frown and lay flat to stare up at the ceiling and, immediately sensing the shift in atmosphere, she pulled back as well.

The urge to get her back close to him, pressed against him, was strong but Matteo resisted, asserting control over a situation that seemed to have pulled against the reins and galloped off in directions unknown.

'I know you're going to say that this was a mistake,' Rosie began and he turned to look at her.

Matteo thought that she would do well to steer clear from mind reading because she couldn't have been further from the truth. If what had just happened between them was a mistake, then he had been well and truly caught in the grip of it, and furthermore wanted a repeat performance. What was going on? He had encouraged the situation. He would be the first to admit that. He had wanted her and he had finally succumbed, had laid his cards on the table, made a pass, did what came so naturally to him. He just hadn't predicted that their love-making would be so explosive. Disturbingly so.

'You have no idea what I'm going to say,' he managed.

'I can tell from your silence...'

'I wouldn't call it a mistake.'

'Then what would you call it?'

'A complication. I'd call it a complication, and now we need to think about what we're going to do about it...'

CHAPTER SEVEN

'WE DON'T HAVE to do anything about it,' Rosie said, mouth down-turned as she stared at her pale hands clasping her knees. 'You're right. It shouldn't have happened. These things do.'

But never, Rosie thought with a rapidly beating heart, *to her.* In *her* world she'd become friends with some guy, there would be a little bit of flirting, but nothing, in the end, would lead anywhere—because sooner or later she would lose interest and there had never been the driving physical need she had felt with Matteo.

Nothing like it.

In her world, nothing had ever happened. No lights had been ignited. No breathless excitement. No *wanting* so big that it drowned out all the little voices urging caution.

In *her* world, she thought, life had never really been lived.

And, now that she had tasted what living to the full felt like, it was going to be snatched out of her grasp, because what had been momentous for her had been routine for him.

'Not to me,' Matteo said seriously. He reached to clasp her hands and held them in his, and Rosie relaxed a little.

The last thing she wanted was for him to see how vulnerable she felt.

'What do you mean?' she asked cautiously.

'I mean…' Matteo raked his fingers through his hair and frowned, as though trying to get his thoughts in order. 'Life doesn't spring surprises on me.'

'What, never?'

'Never.' He paused and looked at her. 'We don't come from the same world,' he said flatly. 'I may have as much money as I could ever want now, but life is more than just the sum total of the present. Life is a series of small sums, adding up to the person we eventually become, to the way we deal with what life throws at us. You have always lived your life in the exclusive conclave of the wealthy. You, I am sure, have always been open to surprises because there was always a comfort blanket waiting to break your fall if the surprise didn't turn out to be a good one.'

Matteo felt safe saying that. Black and white he could deal with. Grey occupied unknown territory and something inside resisted the threat of dealing with it.

Rosie blushed. 'That's not fair.'

'No, I don't suppose it is, but you can see what I'm getting at.'

'Yes. You're going to tell me that I'm not the sort you're attracted to because I don't have a hot-shot career in the City. Not everyone does and hot-shot careers aren't what they're cracked up to be. Have you any idea how stressed out some of those women are?'

'Stress can be an issue,' he murmured.

'I would rather be outside teaching sport than cooped up in a building popping anti-depressants because I'm finding it hard to deal with the anxiety.' Rosie wasn't going to roll over and play dead.

Matteo grinned, eyebrows raised, expression so unconsciously sexy that it was making the blood in her veins hot with a resurgence of desire.

How was it possible to be so fiercely turned on by someone who was in the process of giving her her walking papers because she wasn't suitable? But she was and she shifted uncomfortably.

'You don't have to bang the drum for people who don't wear power suits.' He shrugged. 'My point is that neither of us anticipated this but it doesn't mean that…'

'That?'

'That I didn't want it to happen and don't want it to happen again.'

'What are you saying?' She licked her lips and registered the way his eyes followed that tiny movement. With hunger. The same hunger she was feeling inside her. Like a match set to tinder, it ignited a series of popping explosions inside her.

Matteo Moretti, self-made billionaire, had come to this five-star Italian ski resort for one reason and one reason only—to close a deal that meant a lot to him.

He hadn't banked on suddenly having his life go off the rails because of her. One minute he had been politely shaking hands with his prospective clients, the next minute he had been on the back foot trying to justify bad behaviour of which he wasn't guilty. He'd been forced into a situation not of his making because of circumstances he could never have predicted. He wanted to do what it took to make his deal happen, and what that took involved a pretend romance with the least likely woman on the planet, as far as he was concerned.

So far, so bad, but on top of that here they were. Unlikely lovers. Had she expected that? She'd certainly acknowledged his massive sex appeal but no way had she projected that thought further into the realms of actually making love.

Now he was being honest and telling her like it was. He'd enjoyed what had happened between them. He wanted more, but there were a lot of conditions attached to that and a lot of sub-clauses he wanted her to understand.

She wasn't his type. She led the sort of privileged lifestyle he had commandeered for himself and made his own but his respect was reserved for people who had fought their way up, as he had. He dated bankers and lawyers and she was an intellectual lightweight—she would be the first to admit it. She'd never been in the league of either of her sisters and she'd packed in trying to be years ago, roughly around the time when her form teacher had kindly suggested to her parents that she focus on sport and arts and crafts.

Rosie was at a crossroads. Back away and put that one night down to a fantastic experience, never to be repeated, or else do what he wanted to do and prolong that one night for just a tiny bit longer, until the charade was over and they went their separate ways. An amicable break-up, initiated by her, between two people who had fallen for each other in haste but had thankfully come to their senses before any permanent damage could be done.

In a flash, she trawled back through the years and could see that her rebellious behaviour, her travelling and changing jobs and all those brief, barely notable liaisons with unsuitable boys had been as predictable as the rising and setting of the sun. He'd been right when he'd said that a comfort blanket of financial and emotional security had made all her choices safe. None of his choices had ever been safe. He would always have had a lot to lose and that dangerous edge to him was so appealing.

For the first time in her life, she knew in her heart that to follow him to where he was now pointing would be the most challenging and exciting choice she would ever make. It was so far out of her comfort zone that she had no idea where it might lead.

Not together in some happy-ever-after scenario, was the thought that flashed through her head. *But would she still be in one piece...?*

'I know what you're saying,' she said in a rush. 'You don't want this to be a one-night stand but you want me to remember that it isn't going to be anything more than a brief fling.'

Matteo was looking at her carefully, his silver eyes hooded and watchful.

He was waiting for her to accept his proposal on his terms. No involvement.

'I'm not looking for any kind of relationship,' he told her flatly. 'Here we are and the sex was fantastic.'

'Have you *ever* been interested in having a relationship with someone?' Rosie asked with genuine curiosity.

'That's not on my radar.'

'Why?'

'Why? Because everything I've ever seen has taught me that romance and all the fairy-tale nonsense that accompanies it comes with a lamentably short lifespan. I prefer to hedge my bets where the odds are better for a successful outcome.'

'Making money.'

'Works for me.' His voice hardened and she was reminded of the gaping chasm between them.

Common sense was making her question how she could be attracted to a guy who was so brutally honest when it came to his intentions.

'We *are* going to be stuck together for a few days more…' she began, yielding to the riptide of physical attraction.

Matteo's slow smile was the smile of the victor and he angled her so that their bodies were pressed together, stomach to stomach, her generous breasts squashed against his muscled chest.

She rested the palm of her hand firmly on his chest, just in case he thought that she was a rag doll, helpless and obedient. He was so staggeringly sexy, so stupidly good-looking, that she knew without a shadow of a doubt that women would trip over themselves to get an invite into his bed. 'And I get it. You don't have to warn me that you're not interested in a relationship with me. I'm not interested in any kind of relationship with you either.'

'So you're not into flowers, chocolates and romance?'

'I never said that. I'm just not interested in flowers, chocolates and romance *with you.*'

'I like that we're on the same page.'

'I can keep things separate,' she assured him, ignoring the shadow of doubt that whispered over her skin. 'Business is the fact that we have to present a certain front for a short while, and pleasure is…'

'What happens when the lights go off?' He traced the side of her cheek with his finger and she shivered, eyelids fluttering, body responding instantly to that gently, teasing caress. 'Or on…' he murmured seductively. 'Either way works for me.'

'What works for me,' Rosie told him, 'Is some sleep. I

have to teach tomorrow and then in the afternoon there's a little Christmas thing for the kids at the resort.'

'A Christmas thing?' He frowned.

She remembered what he'd said about Christmas not being his thing, but it was *her* thing, and if he was to convince her sister that they were an item, and by extension her family who would be trooping over only days from now, he would at least have to pretend to enjoy the festive season.

'It's no big deal.' She shrugged. 'You don't have to come but it'll only be for an hour or so. My sister will be there and some of her friends.'

'I'm getting the picture. If I'm a no-show, doubts might start being cast on our love-struck, whirlwind relationship.' He shrugged. 'I think it's fair to say that the rewards when we get back to this bed will more than compensate for sitting through some festive carols...'

Matteo was unprepared for what awaited him later that evening. Rosie had disappeared to work promptly at ten, and he had closed the door and settled down to make full use of the seldom used office, but having set up camp he instantly realised that his focus wasn't totally what it should have been.

Responding to emails had taken longer than usual because he caught himself sitting back, chair pushed away from the desk, contemplating what the night held in store for him. He'd spent a lifetime winning at everything he undertook but this victory felt so much sweeter.

The woman had cast a spell. He'd told her things he'd never divulged to anyone else. He'd opened up in ways that were hardly earth-shattering in the great scheme of things, and pretty routine by most people's standards, but which were earth shattering *for him*. He was a man who never confided. There had never been any pillow talk. People had no right of entry to his private life, he had long concluded, and if along the way some might have been offended by the rigidity of his Keep Out signs, then he really didn't care.

But there was something about this woman...

He told himself that there had been a perfectly good reason to confide in her. They were supposedly in a serious relationship and he had found himself on the back foot, having to explain his intentions to her sister, to his clients and to her family when they rolled up. It made sense to fill her in on some of his background, if only for the sake of verisimilitude, and it wasn't as though he was ashamed of his past. It had made him the pillar of strength and single-minded purpose that he was, hadn't it?

That said, Matteo was uneasily aware that something had shifted inside him, although he couldn't quite put a finger on what exactly, or how seismic the shift was.

So it was a relief when, at a little after four, the time arranged to meet Rosie at the resort for festive fun, he abandoned his work and headed down to the five-star hotel.

He smiled when he remembered her earnest attempt to teach him how to ski. He figured there was no harm in having another lesson.

He took a taxi to the resort and was deposited at a scene of outlandish Christmas extravagance.

At least, as far as he was concerned.

For a few seconds, he stood and stared. The hotel was lit up with hundreds of thousands of lights. He thought that up in the heavens, a million light years away, some alien life forms would be wondering what the hell was going on down here on planet Earth because the light display would surely be visible from outer space. The glittering, twinkling lights were weirdly hypnotic against the soft fall of snow and the whiteness of the landscape.

There were flurries of people everywhere, entering, leaving, skis on shoulders, holding hands with their kids. Evidently, this was something of a popular tradition. He steeled himself to sit through whatever lay ahead, now that he was here, and dialled Rosie's mobile, which remained unanswered.

Someone jostled him from behind, laughing and wishing him season's greetings in Italian, and that galvanised him into joining the throng of people heading into the hotel.

His irritation levels were rising fast when he heard her from behind, and he swung round.

He had already concluded that coming here had been an error of judgement. He was uncomfortable with the chaos and the over-the-top Christmas decorations everywhere. He had somehow expected the festivities to be of a more sombre nature: a choir singing carols in a dining area cleared of tables, perhaps. Instead…

He was scowling as he swung round, already formulating how he could politely make his excuses and clear off back to the chalet and wait for Rosie there.

And there she was. Santa's Christmas helper—red-and-white-striped tights, knee-high black boots with red *faux* fur at the top, small mistletoe-green dress with matching red fur swishing round the hem and at the cuffs of the sleeves, and a jaunty red-and-green hat set at an angle under which her flyaway, curly blonde hair peeped out with unruly abandon.

His breath caught in his throat and he stared.

'You're…' he managed to say hoarsely, raking his fingers through his hair.

'An elf. I know.' Rosie laughed but she was blushing madly because he was making no attempt to conceal the hot appreciation in his eyes. She'd seen him standing there, so perfectly still and watchful while the crowds swarmed around him. His tension was evident in his rigid posture and, from behind, she had pictured him frowning, irritable, about to glance at his watch. All of those things.

The guy didn't do Christmas, and why would he when he had spent his childhood in a children's home? Yes, maybe there had been the usual celebrations there, but without family it would still have been a lonely time. She hadn't thought but, hot and bothered as she was by the way he was looking at her, she still managed to reach out to circle his arm with her hand and draw him away from the centre of the vast lobby where pandemonium reigned.

'I'm sorry,' was the first thing she said when they were in a corner which was relatively quiet and she could hear herself think. There was still too much hubbub around. She pulled him into one of the smaller rooms where Tim, one of the managers, held his briefings with the ski instructors every morning. She shut the door and turned to face him, back to the door.

'I'm sorry,' she repeated quietly, and Matteo frowned, then strolled towards the large rectangular desk and perched against it, long legs extended and linked at the ankles.

He was such a specimen of pure physical perfection, she thought helplessly. Black jeans, black ribbed jumper, black coat—inappropriately non-waterproof and so stupidly elegant. He removed the coat and dumped it on the desk behind him.

'What are you sorry about?'

'I shouldn't have asked you to come here.'

'I don't recall you asking and, just for the record, I'm not in the habit of doing what other people tell me to do unless I want to. I'm here because I chose to come.'

'But you don't do Christmas.' She didn't back away from saying what was on her mind, doggedly bypassing the uninviting expression on his face. 'And this is the most Christmassy a place could get. You must hate it. I don't suppose,' she continued, tenderness sprouting shoots as she thought of him young and alone in a home without the jolly family chaos she had had growing up, 'That Christmas was great in…er…when you were growing up.'

'Is that the sound of you feeling sorry for me?'

'Yes. Is that a crime?' Rosie tilted her chin at a stubborn angle and folded her arms.

'You always say what's on your mind, don't you? I'm here, and I'll bet Bob and Margaret are somewhere in the throng of people. No need to pull out the sympathy card.' He thawed and appreciatively ran his eyes over her. 'I like the outfit, by the way.'

Rosie reddened. 'I don't think elf outfits were designed for my particular shape, but I promised. Barry, the guy in charge of the entertainment over Christmas, has always been good to me.'

'Good? In what way *good*?'

He looked at her with sudden, brooding intensity. He had no idea from where it had come, but out of the blue a spark of white-hot jealousy had suddenly ripped into him. He thought of her warmth and her voluptuous sexiness curling against his body and all thoughts of her sharing herself with someone else, anyone else, sent his brain into instant meltdown.

It was disconcerting, bewildering. He had never considered himself to be a jealous person. A man who was jealous was a man who lacked the sort of iron-clad self-assurance which he possessed in bucket-loads.

Never had he gone out with any woman and paid the slightest bit of attention to lovers she might have had in the past or, for that matter, to any men who might have come on to her in his presence. He had always had the supreme confidence of a man who knew in his gut that he had everything it took to keep a woman glued to his side for just as long as he wanted her there.

Why would he ever have been jealous of any other man? Emotions, like every other aspect of his life, were there to be controlled. A childhood in which control had always lain in the hands of other people, with rules and regulations there to be obeyed, had resulted in an adulthood where he made his own rules and regulations and was controlled by no one.

And a childhood devoid of the love of a parent, where efficiency had come a poor second to love and affection, had nurtured in him a healthy wariness when it came to his heart and handing it over to anyone. Frankly, that was something he would never do.

So, with those two factors firmly in place, why the attack of irrational jealousy?

'You're not *jealous,* are you?'

Matteo lowered his fabulous eyes for a split second and, when he next met her headlong stare, his expression was as controlled as always.

'I don't do jealousy.'

'There's an awful lot of things you don't do.'

'I do sexy, little red-and-green elf outfits.'

'If you don't *do* jealousy, then why does it matter how Barry is good to me?'

Rosie folded her arms and gazed at him, mouth set. She had never been one to let anything go. Yes, she was non-confrontational when it came to her family, because the path of least resistance had always been the most convenient one to take, but in all other respects she could be as stubborn as a mule when it came to getting answers to questions she asked. And Matteo Moretti seemed to have an amazing knack when it came to arousing her curiosity. Five minutes in his company and she could feel a thousand questions piling up in her head.

She imagined him jealous of her—possessive, guarding her with caveman-like, finger-crooking ownership—and, much as her logical brain instantly revolted against the sexist image, a very feminine part of her twisted with simmering excitement.

'You're doing it again,' Matteo said with exasperation. He shook his head. 'Has it occurred to you that, if we're supposed to be the loved-up couple, the last thing I need is an intrusive old flame entering into the picture and trying to pick up where he may have left off a couple of months ago?'

Simmering excitement was replaced by full-blown anger and Rosie took a step closer to him.

'First of all,' she hissed, glaring, 'How dare you imply that I'm the sort of person who lets a guy *pick up where he left off* as though I have no mind of my own? Do you honestly think that I'm that sort of woman? For your information, Matteo Moretti, I'm extremely selective when it comes to men! I've been on my own, even though I've had boyfriends, for *years*!'

'And then I come along?' Matteo asked speculatively. 'My mind is beginning to work overtime.'

What could she say to that?

'I didn't foresee…what happened between us.' Rosie suddenly found herself on the back foot.

'Even though you're extremely selective.'

'We were thrown together in a highly charged situation…'

'I was very happy to be the perfect gentleman and sleep on the *chaise longue*, although the ground would have been more comfortable.'

'Yes, well…'

'Let's drop this conversation. It's not going anywhere.'

He reached out, curled his fingers into her unruly, vanilla-blonde hair and tugged her gently towards him.

With helpless fascination, she watched as his mouth descended, and she closed her eyes and whimpered as his cool lips met hers. She curled her fingers onto the waistband of his trousers and felt herself slowly being propelled backwards, ever so slightly, until she bumped against the table behind her.

They were in a public place. A room that was only vacant temporarily because everyone happened to be outside, where the Christmas choir would be starting shortly. What on earth was she doing?

But right now, right here, he *owned* her body and what he was doing with it was turning her on so much she was melting from the inside out. He was kissing her, his tongue lashing against hers…cupping her bottom, massaging it with his big hands…pressing against her so that she could feel the rock-hardness of his erection bulging against his zipper.

Neither heard the door opening behind them. Rosie was certainly oblivious to everything until she heard her mother's shocked voice and then Candice laughing with genuine delight. At which point, she shoved Matteo away. When she looked at her parents—at her entire assembled family, because Emily was there as well—she just wanted the ground to open and swallow her up.

'What are you doing here?' She gasped. 'You're not supposed to be here for another couple of days.'

'Surprise, surprise!' Candice trilled. 'We couldn't wait to come over as soon as we could, and thank goodness that beastly virus was over sooner than expected! We just had time to dump our stuff at the chalet and here we are! Harry spotted the pair of you vanishing into this room so we thought we'd give you a happy surprise!'

Happy surprise? Rosie thought in horror. Of all the adjectives she could come up with, *happy* wasn't one of them. And whatever happened to that old-fashioned courtesy of knocking?

She cleared her throat but her father was already striding towards Matteo, and Rosie could tell from the expression on his face that he wasn't going to oh-so-politely pretend that he hadn't seen them a hair's breadth away from doing more than just a bit of kissing and groping.

She was hot with mortification. She'd always been a daddy's girl and she hated the thought of him being shocked at what he would consider inappropriate behaviour, given the surroundings. They were in a resort in which they'd all been well known as regulars for many years.

'Dad…'

'So you're the young man Candice has told us about!'

'We were just about to go back outside,' Rosie said weakly. 'Great that you're all over! Hi, Em. Is everyone here? The kids and Lucien and Robert as well?' Her voice was letting her down badly, but that was only to be expected, given the nightmarish turn of events.

'Rosie, I'd like to have a word with your young man on his own.'

'Dad…' She cast a panicked sideways glance at Matteo who, after looking momentarily disconcerted, had somehow managed to gather his composure while hers was still all over the place.

Her tall, beautiful mother, so much alike to her two eldest daughters, had opened her arms for a hug and Rosie walked towards her even though her heart had plummeted. Her dad could be ferocious when the mood took him, and especially so when it came to his daughters.

'Ken…' Debbie Carter said in a warning voice, halting him in his tracks. 'I'm sure Rosie's young man would like to relax before the cross examination begins.'

'Besides.' Emily was joining the family circle. 'Lucien and the kids are waiting outside with Robert.'

Rosie stifled a groan of utter despair.

But, Matteo, she noted with grudging admiration and relief, seemed to have everything under control, making suitably polite noises, clearly unfazed that they had been caught in the middle of a groping session worthy of a couple of horny teenagers.

'Just one question, young man,' her father eventually boomed. Whatever Matteo had been saying, she hadn't clocked all of it, because her mother had been chattering away a mile a minute about this and that.

'I've looked you up on the Internet, although I've heard your name before.'

'Of course.' Matteo accepted the recognition with a sweeping lack of false modesty.

'You're rich,' Ken tabulated on his fingers, 'You have a history of going out with beautiful, high-flying women and yet here you are with my baby.'

'Dad!' Rosie couldn't have got any redder but her father paid absolutely no notice to her horrified interruption.

'I don't take kindly to anyone dabbling with any of my daughters.'

'Don't blame you,' Matteo returned equably, giving Ken Carter as good as he got without any show of disrespect. He certainly wasn't in the least intimidated by the older man. 'If I had a daughter, I would certainly not want anyone fooling around with her feelings.'

'I *am* here!' Rosie interjected in a high voice, breaking free from her mother and moving to stand between the two men.

They couldn't have been more different physically. Matteo, tall and so dramatically good-looking. Her father, short and rotund, but with the sort of fiercely determined face that advertised why he had managed to get as far as he had.

'My intentions towards your daughter are entirely honourable.'

'Are they?' Ken growled.

'Honourable enough to ensure an engagement ring will soon be on her finger.'

The silence that greeted this statement was so complete that they could have heard a pin drop.

Then screeches of delight came from her sisters, who

rushed towards her, warm pleasure from her mother, who was trying to get a word in edgeways, and a grunt of approval from her dad, now shaking Matteo's hand vigorously, warmly, clapping him on the back and announcing that a weight had been lifted from his shoulders.

'She's my little baby,' Rosie was aware of him saying, while sick perspiration began rising from her toes upwards. 'Needs someone to look after her. Glad she's found that person.'

In a daze, Rosie was vaguely aware of her family all leaving the room *en masse*. Lucien and Robert had apparently chosen to stay outside with the kids, who were in seventh heaven, because Santa was due to make an appearance.

In her elf outfit, and shorn of all festive spirit, all Rosie could think was, *what the heck has just happened...?*

CHAPTER EIGHT

THE REMAINDER OF the evening passed in a blur. Rosie mingled with all the guests, entertaining the kids as Santa's jolly helper while frantically trying to keep her eye on a roaming Matteo. Roaming where and doing what? She wished she had eyes on the back of her head and consoled herself with the thought that he couldn't do any more damage than he had already done.

Engaged? Diamonds on fingers? What on earth had he been thinking?

She fumed internally, because a complicated situation had suddenly got a whole lot more complicated, and yet…

Something inside her burned with treacherous heat at the thought of being engaged to Matteo, wearing his ring on her finger, looking forward to a lifetime of making love with him and finding out more and more what made him tick.

From the very moment he'd entered her life, a curiosity had been awakened inside her that she knew, realistically, would never be sated. Whatever mess he had landed them both in, whatever *further* mess—she had started the ball rolling with her little white lie—this was and never would be a real relationship, one in which sharing and confiding played a part, in which discovery was part of the package.

She was one of the last to leave, because the staff were asked to volunteer for tidying up duties, and it was after eight by the time everything was more or less in order and normality had been restored.

She was standing uncertainly by the Christmas tree in the foyer, fiddling with her hat and wondering how her overwhelming family could be swamping her one minute and nowhere to be seen the next, when a dark, amused and familiar voice said from behind, 'The elf looks somewhat worse for wear.'

Rosie spun round, heart picking up pace and body racing into fifth gear at the sight of him. *He* certainly didn't look the worse for wear. If anything, an evening spent immersed in the Christmas spirit appeared to have relaxed him, although he was so clever at projecting a public face that she wasn't sure whether this was accurate or not.

He'd shoved up the sleeves of his shirt and her eyes were helplessly drawn to his powerful forearms, liberally sprinkled with dark hair. Her mouth went dry and for a few seconds she forgot that she was fuming and angry with him, and had been all evening for the extravagant lie he had told.

'Where's…everyone?' she asked.

'Gone to a French restaurant for dinner. *En masse.*'

'They didn't tell me that that was the plan.'

'That's because I assured them that we would be far keener to break bread together, just the two of us.'

'You're right.' Rosie was proud of her composure as she began walking towards the cloakroom so that she could retrieve her coat, bag and everything else. 'We need to talk.' She felt a lot less jumpy saying this with her back to him. The second he was staring at her with those amazing eyes, her thoughts began going haywire and she couldn't seem to string a coherent sentence together.

She disappeared into the cloakroom and emerged back in sensible clothing but feeling just as dishevelled.

'Let's get something to eat,' Matteo drawled, lounging against the wall with one finger hooked into the waistband of his trousers. 'Long, meaningful conversations are always more productive over food. Where do you want to go?'

Rosie couldn't think of doing anything as relaxing as eating when her mind was buzzing with all sorts of angry, confused thoughts, but she was ravenous. There had been a lot on offer in terms of canapés, but those had been out of bounds to the staff, and she had been too wired to eat any of the leftovers once the tidying had been done. Her stomach growled.

'I'm not actually hungry,' she returned coolly.

'Let's go to the restaurant here. The food is decent enough, from what I recall. And, before you start trying to convince me that you couldn't eat a thing, your stomach has just given you away. You're right, we have to talk, and I won't be doing that standing here outside the cloakroom.'

He pushed himself away from the wall and looked down at her and while she was dithering, loath to give in to his calmly spoken statement of fact, he spun round on his heels and began heading towards the flight of stairs that swept up to the restaurant on the mezzanine floor.

Gritting her teeth with frustration, Rosie pelted behind him, caught up with him. She had a moment of feeling utterly awkward when they were shown to a corner table in the restaurant because, although the coat, scarf and long, black cardigan were all in place, underneath was the elf outfit which wasn't exactly appropriate wear for a serious conversation.

However, there was nothing to be done about that, and she reluctantly surrendered the coat and long, winding scarf to the *maître d'*, making sure to keep the cardigan tightly pulled around her as she took her seat.

Her breasts felt huge, pushing against the stretchy outfit. She had removed the jaunty hat but her fair hair was all over the place and she ran her fingers through it now, trying to get it into some kind of order, her blue eyes very firmly fastened to Matteo's dark, lean face.

'I can see that you can't wait to tell me what's on your mind.' He lounged back in the chair, summoning the waiter over with the smallest of nods and ordering a bottle of Chablis without bothering to look at either the waiter or the wine list, instead keeping his gaze very firmly pinned to her flushed face.

'Can you blame me? How could you?'

'Why don't you take the cardigan off? You must be hot.'

'Thanks for the concern, Matteo, but I'm just fine. And you haven't answered my question—how could you tell my parents, *my whole family,* that we're going to get engaged? How could you pretend that this is actually a serious relationship!' Tears of frustration sprang to her eyes and she rapidly blinked them away.

The waiter came and poured the wine and she muttered what she wanted to eat—the first thing she spotted on the menu that she liked, knowing that she wouldn't do justice to the food that would be placed in front of her.

Matteo leaned towards her, his voice low and cool. 'When I met your sister, I got an idea of how your family operated. She flew down to attack me out of nowhere because she mistakenly thought that I had led you on and broken up with you. She was as ferocious as a tiger looking out for her cub. When you told me that you had lied about being involved with me in order to get out of an uncomfortable Christmas spent with your family trying to match-make you with some guy you weren't interested in, well, needless to say I had never come across a situation like that in my life before.'

Rosie reddened, knowing just how that made her sound—feeble, childish and not in control of her own life.

'We've been over all of this before,' she muttered with simmering resentment. 'It still doesn't explain why you said what you said.'

'Rosie.' He raked his fingers through his hair and sat back, sipping some of the wine and looking at her carefully, as though doing his best to marshal his thoughts. 'Your sister was just the tip of the iceberg. You are surrounded by family who clearly feel it's their duty to protect you.'

'It's not that unusual.' She squirmed and when she met his eyes his expression was remote.

'In my world, it's very unusual.'

With a tug of compassion, Rosie reached out, but he didn't take her hand and she withdrew it and returned it to her lap.

Of course, he wouldn't understand her family dynamics, she thought, ashamed because she had thoughtlessly put her foot in it. Again.

'I'm sorry, Matteo…'

Matteo held up his hand impatiently to cut short her stammered, sympathetic interruption. 'No need to be. I'm getting accustomed to your outbursts of sympathy. It's irrelevant. The fact is that your father, in particular, is extremely protective of you. I'm guessing that's because you're the baby of the family.'

Rosie shrugged and lowered her eyes. 'We have a lot of shared interests,' she admitted. 'My sisters have never been interested in sport and I was always the one he took to football matches. He used to tell me that it was the best relaxation he could think of after slaving away in an office five days a week.'

He, more than her mother, had been the one to indulge her nomadic lifestyle, she was now forced to concede. Her mother had made lots of noises over the years about her settling down, but her dad had always been the one to overrule those small protests.

Now, she wondered whether it hadn't been partly because her father, born into privilege, had had his life conditioned from an early age. He had been sent to the right schools and gone to the right university and maybe there had been a part of him that had always longed to rebel. Just a little. And that part had led life vicariously through his youngest daughter who had always been a free spirit.

Perhaps that was why, when Bertie had been presented as a possible suitor—her dad had climbed on board that wagon with the rest of the family—it had panicked her because everything had suddenly seemed very serious. A serious, suitable candidate to rescue her from her enjoyable but essentially irresponsible life.

If she hadn't been so panicked, she would never have

done what she had done—told that little white lie, never realising what the consequences might be.

'He was never really worried by all those dalliances you had in the past, was he, *cara*? Your father?'

'What makes you say that?' She lifted startled eyes to his and frowned.

'It was a conclusion I reached off my own bat,' Matteo admitted. 'And he said as much to me when I had a conversation earlier on with him.'

'What?' She stared at him furiously and he stared right back at her without blinking an eye. 'What were you doing talking to my dad?'

'Don't be disingenuous, Rosie.'

'What did he say?'

'Exactly that. You deserved to have some fun. You were never academic like your sisters, and if you wanted to stretch your wings a little then he could more than afford to indulge you. But he finally reached the conclusion that it was time for you to discover the joys of leading a more grounded existence, so to speak.'

'You had no right to discuss me behind my back!' she snapped, her voice steeped with dismay. 'And I'm not just a carefree twenty-something!'

'Aren't you?' Matteo questioned and that hurt. For a short while, she couldn't speak at all, and it was a relief that their starters were being positioned in front of them, small, tasty dishes, because it relieved her of the need to say anything.

'You think I don't find that an attractive trait?' he asked gruffly, and her eyes shot to his face.

'What are you talking about?'

'You're like a breath of fresh air and I think I may have mentioned that to you before,' Matteo admitted with rough sincerity. 'I've never met anyone like you in my life before.'

'What does that have to do with…anything? Matteo, it would have been so much easier if you hadn't said what you had. Relationships come and go, and if this one crashed and burned, then…'

'Then it would have joined all the rest of your relationships that had crashed and burned in the past?'

Rosie gazed at him with down-turned mouth.

'Why should you care?' Her voice was so low that Matteo had to strain forward to hear what she had said.

Good point, he thought uncomfortably. There was no reason why he *should* care. He just knew that what he had seen in her during the short time he had known her had fired up in him something strangely protective. Her entire family had descended and when her father had cornered him he had reacted utterly on impulse. For once in his life, Matteo had been galvanised into behaviour that was alien to him.

The only thought that had run through his head was, *they know who I am and they're already predicting the outcome. Another failed relationship, and this time one deserving of even more tea and sympathy because of who I am.*

Underneath the sunny, plucky exterior was someone both sensitive and oddly brave. She needed to find her place in the family dynamics and suddenly he had been driven by the urge to help her along.

Matteo wasn't going to delve further into his motivations. Introspection never got anyone anywhere because, when it came to the crunch, action and not thought was what mattered.

But tugging away at the back of his mind was the notion that perhaps not everyone fought the same battles he had. It wasn't always about carving out a place for yourself in the world of money. Sometimes, there were other forces at work. It didn't mean that the fight was any the less significant.

He shrugged. 'Maybe I didn't care for either the idea that I would be just the sort to take advantage of an innocent like you, because of the person I'm reported as being in the media, or the idea that you would be disingenuous enough to walk straight into a trap from which you could only end up hurt, requiring your over-protective family to go into rallying mode.'

'So you decided to become the knight in shining armour?'

'That wasn't the intention but I'm happy to go along with the description.'

'Except,' she said ruefully, 'That still leaves us the problem of breaking up from a so-called serious relationship where we're about to get engaged.'

'No,' Matteo corrected, 'That leaves *you* walking away from a serious relationship where we're about to get engaged. That puts *you* firmly in the role of heartbreaker.' He grinned. 'I have a feeling that if you play your cards right your family will have a lot of respect for your decision.'

'Why would you do that for me?'

'Maybe I think you're worth it.'

Rosie nodded with a thoughtful frown but inside her nerves were all over the place.

What did it mean?

They had been thrown together because of her rash outburst and she had assumed, from day one, that they were so dissimilar that, even having slept together, there was no way he could ever find her interesting. Not really.

And vice versa, naturally.

But a tiny voice now asked…did they actually have what it took to have a relationship? A proper relationship?

A curious thrill rippled through her, the thrill of the great, big unknown, of an adventure waiting to happen.

'Yes.' She unconsciously glanced at her finger and wondered what a diamond ring would look like on it, then she closed her hand into a fist and banished the thought, because this wasn't real. There would be no genuine 'for ever after' relationship. He'd felt sorry for her. Underneath the tough exterior, she couldn't have found a nicer guy even though she didn't think he'd thank her if she pointed that out.

'You have no idea what kind of Pandora's box you've opened,' was what she said instead. 'My parents aren't going to be casual about this. My mum will already be planning what outfit she'll be wearing, and whether it would be too premature to have a chat with the local vicar, and they'll both be debating whether they should have a marquee on the lawn like they did for both my sisters.'

She closed her eyes and contemplated the dreadful scenario unfolding in front of her. 'But you're right. You're such a catch, they'll respect me for turning down your proposal.' She smiled, a wide, sunny smile. 'A passing fling, well, they would have been sympathetic, but a full-blown marriage proposal—I'm not sure if they'll know quite how to react.'

'You're fortunate,' he said in a husky undertone and

Rosie glanced up at him in bewilderment. 'You have people who care deeply about you.'

'They care so much that they don't understand that there were times when I felt stifled,' Rosie said bluntly. She felt as though something inside her had toughened up. The girl who had rushed into a little white lie to spare herself the annoyance of Bertie, his nerdy persistence and irritating habits was gone for ever. In its place was someone slowly realising that she needed to be in charge of her future, stronger, more assured, more focused.

'There were times when *I* didn't realise just how stifled I felt.'

'So you took to the hills and ran as fast as you could?'

Rosie laughed, marvelling that he could be so perceptive. 'They were always terribly understanding about my academic failures.'

'Maybe they shouldn't have been,' Matteo said mildly. He reached forward absently to graze her knuckles with his thumb.

'We're having a deep and meaningful conversation,' Rosie remarked and then wished she hadn't because he immediately withdrew his hand with a frown.

'We're discussing a way forward with this,' he responded quickly. 'I took this charade past the bedroom door and into the bed.'

'You slept on the sofa,' Rosie was quick to remind him. She wanted him to reach out and take her hand again. She missed the warmth, the feel of his finger casually stroking her bare skin. 'And you would have carried on sleeping there until your deal got signed and you were free to leave.'

'I opened the Pandora's box,' Matteo said drily. 'But let's forget about who did what. We weren't having a deep and meaningful conversation. We were discussing what happens next and how best to deal with the fallout.'

He shifted, uneasy and suddenly restless.

The logic of his argument was reassuring. 'Let's face it, Rosie—when I walk away from this, I won't have any further contact with you or your family. You will be the one left to handle the inevitable post mortem. It's to your advantage if you're given a helping hand in tackling the aftermath.'

'Of course.' She linked her fingers together and stared at them. That told her, she thought, just in case she started getting any ideas. She doubted he even realised the subliminal warning. 'What if word gets out?'

'What do you mean?'

'Social media is everywhere. People with mobile phones taking pictures. What if someone you work with finds out that you somehow got yourself engaged while you were over here on business? And then got cruelly dumped?'

Matteo grinned. 'I like the way you're going to cruelly dump me. I'd bet that there might be a few women out there who would enjoy hearing that.' He became more sober. 'Go ahead and be as heartless as you like. I don't care what other people think of me.'

Somewhere along the line, food had been eaten and wine had been drunk. Matteo hadn't really noticed. He had been way too absorbed in the woman sitting opposite him, absorbed to the exclusion of everything else, and that in itself was a source of wonder because he couldn't recall the last time any woman had commanded that sort of attention from him.

Work absorbed him. Women relaxed him. Not this

one. His life had been a rollercoaster ride since meeting her and it surprised him to acknowledge that, as hair-raising experiences went, this one was pretty exhilarating.

He watched her with brooding intent, his keen eyes noting everything about her softly appealing face, from the delicate tinge of colour staining her cheeks to the glittering blue of her eyes and the fullness of her parted mouth. Then he thought of her in bed, naked and eager, her full roundness, her heavy breasts, such a sexy contrast to the angular women who constituted his usual diet. He felt himself harden at the thought of her.

'I envy you not caring what other people think of you,' she was saying as their eyes tangled. 'If I had half of your indifference, we wouldn't be sitting here right now.'

'But you wouldn't be you if you had half of my indifference and who says that I'm not enjoying myself sitting here right now?'

Her tongue darted out, moistening her upper lip, and Matteo had to stop himself from groaning.

'Stop doing that,' she whispered, lowering her gaze, but almost immediately returning greedy eyes to his lean, handsome face.

'Doing what?'

'Staring at me...like that.'

'Like what?'

'You know.'

'Oh, I know.' He laughed under his breath. 'I just want to hear you say it.'

'You're looking at me as though you could...'

'Eat you?' He raised his eyebrows expressively. 'It's exactly what I want to do, *mia cara*. I want to feast on your body, suckle your breasts until you're squirming underneath me, and then I want to take you until you cry out and beg for me to never stop.'

'Matteo!' She squirmed and looked around her, red-faced.

'Let's get out of here.'

A thought suddenly struck her. 'We should. We can't have the whole troop return to the lodge to find that your things are in the spare room!'

'Don't panic. I removed myself for the night, not for the long haul, and if the bed isn't made quite as it should be then who's to say that we haven't spread ourselves around the house in our uncontrollable need to pleasure one another, irrespective of whether it's your bedroom or not?' He burst out laughing as crimson colour stole into her face. 'Don't look so shocked. It happens.'

He beckoned across a waiter with a crook of his finger and tossed his credit card down without bothering to check the bill. 'I'll enjoy showing you the ropes.'

Rosie had no need to ask what he meant and she blushed furiously, her whole body going up in flames with anticipation and excitement.

'Come on.'

'Where are we going?' she asked, breathless, cardigan still pulled tightly around her as she followed him out of the restaurant. Instead of heading towards the cloakroom so that she could fetch her coat, they headed towards the reception desk where she was greeted like an old friend.

'I think we can spend the night here, don't you?' He slid her a sideways glance.

If he wanted their pretend relationship to hit the gossip grapevine fast, then he couldn't have chosen a more efficient method. They all knew her here at the hotel, and sharing a room with him…?

A flare of adrenaline-charged excitement coursed through her. She felt faint and she had to look away as he sorted out the most expensive suite for them.

'This is crazy. Mum and Dad…everyone…will be expecting us to show up at the chalet after dinner.'

'Mum and Dad and everyone else will be raising their glasses to the wildly enamoured couple. If you're planning on forging a way forward as someone with a voice, then you could start using it right now. Besides, I can't wait, and I don't want to get back to the chalet to find myself bogged down making small talk until midnight.'

'I can't wait, either,' she confessed, as they made their way to the lift, on a heated sigh. Her hand was trembling as she extracted her mobile phone and punched in Candice's number. She sent a text because she didn't know if she would be able to sound controlled should a conversation ensue.

The lift doors opened and as soon as they had whirred shut behind them he pulled her to him. His head descended and his mouth crushed hers hungrily, his tongue plundering her mouth until her legs felt as weak as jelly and she had to cling to him for support, like a rag doll. She pushed her hands underneath his clothes, finding bare, warm skin, and she shoved them up to rub his flat nipples. His body was hard and sinewy. She wanted to explore every inch of it, to feel every corded muscle, sinew and tendon.

In a minute, she thought weakly, the lift doors were going to open and they would be faced with some shocked faces, but they made it to their floor in privacy, and by the time he was unlocking the door to the suite with the gold-and-black card she was desperate to get rid of her clothes.

They stumbled into the huge sitting area, bodies urgently pressed together. He was stripping along the way, blindly leading her in the general direction of the bedroom until he abandoned their stumbling progress and swept her off her feet, kicking open the door.

The bedroom was bathed in the peculiar glow only falling snow outside could cause and he left the curtains open. She was on the mattress of the super-king-sized bed without even realising how she had got there, and she hastily propped herself up on her elbows, watching as he stripped off.

He was so glorious he took her breath away. So glorious that nothing else mattered. Not her family, not what other people might start thinking, not the aftermath of this madness waiting to catch her out.

The only thought in her head was, *I want this guy more than anything.*

The wretched elf outfit had to come off but he stilled her frantic hands as she began to scrabble with buttons, the zip and various bits of Velcro, all of which seemed to be oddly positioned in ridiculously unreachable places.

'I want to see you do a striptease,' he murmured, his voice as dark and as seductive as chocolate. 'I want to enjoy watching you. You have an amazing body.'

He held out his hand, their fingers linked and then she was on her feet and he was on the bed, places reversed. He, utterly naked, and she…

Bit by bit the clothing was removed and bit by languorous bit she began to enjoy herself. Initial nerves were replaced by brazen relish. His eyes on her were such a turn on and she was wet and on fire by the time the last strip of elf costume had been flung to the ground.

She sashayed her way towards him and stood by the side of the bed, and he sat up to slip his hand between her thighs, parting them, feeling the wetness there against his hand. Then he gently parted the delicate folds of her womanhood and flicked his tongue along the groove, finding the stiffened bud of her clitoris with ease.

Rosie moaned and arched back, automatically opening her legs wider to receive his exploring tongue. She moved against him, hands reaching down to press his head harder against her so that he could taste her even more thoroughly.

As he licked, he caressed the soft flesh of her inner thighs, stroking lightly until she was going crazy with desire. She wanted to come against his mouth and yet she never wanted the rolling waves of sensation to end.

He took her so far and then pulled her down to the bed to join him. This time, their love-making was fast, hard and furious and her orgasm was explosive, coming even as she felt him arch back and groan loudly, succumbing to his own release.

She was utterly spent when he eventually positioned her onto her side so that they were facing one another. She looked at him drowsily, smiled and stroked the side of his face.

'We're not in a trap.' Matteo kissed the side of her mouth, the angles of his lean face thrown into shadow because his back was to the window. 'So the charade went a little further than originally intended but is that such a bad thing?'

'What do you mean?'

'I mean this…us.' He swept his hand along her thigh

and she shivered. 'This ridiculous chemistry… So, we're chalk and cheese and what we have isn't going to last. You know that and I know that but for now… God, I want you, *tesoro mio*. When I think of you, I want you, and I want you immediately. I touch you and I don't want the touching to end. This charade…why don't we enjoy it for what it is and forget about tomorrow?'

CHAPTER NINE

ROSIE DIDN'T WANT to think it but she did anyway: *this is perfect.*

She and Matteo were standing on an incline, looking down at a Christmas extravaganza. It was a little after seven and the slopes were ablaze with lights. The sound of laughter and kids screeching with excitement were only just drowned out by the harmonious singing of the Christmas choir, who were perched on a makeshift stage just outside one of the five star resorts in radiant reds, whites, *faux* furs and boots.

For the first time in days, the snow had stopped falling, conspiring to provide a picture-postcard image of what the perfect December evening should look like.

Of course, she guiltily acknowledged to herself, the reason it was perfect was because Matteo was standing next to her with one arm carelessly slung round her waist. They were both drinking mulled wine and Rosie was heady with happiness.

She'd never thought that it was possible for her to be quite so happy. Her family adored Matteo. After her father's initial misgivings, they had all succumbed to his charm. He could hold court without seeming to and what she might once have considered the hugely annoying trait, being just so self-assured, she now found deliciously mesmerising.

It was really no wonder her entire family had been sucked into his magic circle. She could only imagine their giddy relief at the fact that she was supposedly engaged to a guy like him, settled with someone of whom they heartily approved.

She didn't want to think about how they would react when it ended. She didn't want to think of all those scary tomorrows and what they might herald. Three days ago, he had dangled that carrot in front of her: enjoy the chemistry they shared and forget about tomorrow. She had grabbed that carrot with both hands. She was going to live for today. She was going to savour the excitement, the wonder of being with an unsuitable guy who still, somehow, managed to make her blood boil hot in her veins. She was going to enjoy losing herself in the glory of his love-making. Beyond that, anything could happen. In theory.

'Miss your family not being here?' Matteo inclined his head to murmur into her ear and Rosie shivered and looked up at him. In the reflected glow from all those thousands of lights that illuminated the snow-covered slopes, his face was all shadows and angles.

She thought about it. 'Normally I would,' she confessed. 'But I'll be seeing them on Christmas Eve when we…er…when I go back to England. It's unusual for me to be here at this time of year. It's because I'm instructing.'

She gulped down some of the mulled wine. Would Matteo be returning to England with her? And would he be spending Christmas with her entire family at her parents' country house in the Cotswolds? Or would he be going his own way, doing his own thing? She didn't want to ask the question because she was afraid that the answer might not be to her liking. The deal with Bob and Margaret had been signed and now there was nothing binding him to her, aside from the chemistry.

In his *let's enjoy this and forget about tomorrow* suggestion he had failed to clarify what counted as 'tomorrow' and she didn't want to press him for an answer.

'Are *you* going to miss them?' she asked teasingly. 'I expect you've found it all a little…chaotic. It always is when we all get together, especially with the kids, and especially at this time of year.'

'It's been an experience.' Matteo shrugged. 'This would not be how I would usually spend the run up to Christmas Day but, as experiences go, I am certainly glad I've had it.'

'That's good,' Rosie said uncertainly. She laughed. 'I think.'

'I'll certainly be glad to have the place to ourselves once again.' Matteo lowered his voice and brushed his lips against her cheek. 'There's something unnerving about making love when outside there's the danger of two little people banging on the bedroom door and demanding interaction in whatever game they've decided to play.'

'They liked you,' Rosie said.

'Don't sound so shocked,' Matteo commented wryly, leading her down towards the lit slopes where the carollers were finishing the last of their repertoire. He still had his arm around her waist and she was leaning into him.

'I bet you never come into contact with anyone under the age of…let me think about this…maybe twenty-one?

The average age for new recruits to join a company after university?'

'You forget,' Matteo surprised himself by pointing out, drawing her closer against him, 'That I grew up surrounded by a lot of kids. When I hit twelve, I was given the task of looking after a number of the younger ones.' He laughed at the surprise on her face. 'And don't tell me that you're sorry because you've suddenly remembered my very different childhood.'

'You took care of the other kids?'

'It was company policy, so to speak. You would be surprised at how many of them were off the rails by the time they hit six.'

'You don't like talking about your past.'

'I've never seen the point of dwelling on things that cannot be changed.'

'Have you ever confided in anyone?'

'By anyone, you mean a therapist?' Matteo burst out laughing. 'That touchy-feely stuff isn't for me.'

'There's a lot to be said for that touchy-feely stuff,' Rosie said pensively. She shivered as his hand crept under her thick, padded, heavily insulated jacket to caress a sliver of skin under the waistband of her ski trousers. 'I'm a great believer in sharing…what's on your mind.'

'I know.' Matteo grinned down at her. 'You're excellent at letting me know all the highways and byways of what you're thinking.'

'Do you find it boring?' She stiffened and pulled away from the light caress.

'You'd know about it if I did.'

'How? Would you tell me?' She looked up at him seriously, wishing she could read his face, wishing she had as much insight into the workings of his mind as he obviously thought he had into hers. Wishing that the playing field was a little more level.

'I wouldn't have to.'

The carollers disbanded and normality returned, although skiing was now being replaced by *après ski* and the crowds were dissipating, with clusters of warmly wrapped people hiving off in whatever direction their various resorts, chalets and hotels lay.

The loss of that background carolling suddenly made the cold, wintry slopes feel very quiet, very still. 'I meant have you ever confided in any of your girlfriends in the past?'

'No,' Matteo said abruptly.

Rosie ventured boldly into the unknown. 'You've never felt close enough to anyone to talk to them about your past?'

'I'm trying and failing to see where this conversation is heading.'

'It isn't heading anywhere.' She sighed.

'Good,' he said silkily. 'Now, where do you want to eat? Are you hungry? We could always skip an elaborate meal and head back to the chalet. I'm looking forward to having the place to ourselves.'

'So you've said.' She kept her voice as bright as she could but this time it felt like an effort.

He was looking forward to an empty chalet because without anyone around he could, taking his time and without fear of interruption, do what he did best. Make love. Wonderful, stupendous, fabulous sex. But that was where it ended. He wasn't interested in being alone with her so that they could share anything more significant than their bodies.

Rosie hated herself for letting her thoughts stray into that dangerous territory. She was determined to think and live in the moment but her heart clenched in disappointment and frustration.

'Eat, I think.' She needed a bit of time to get back into the right frame of mind, away from the barrage of muddled thoughts assailing her. 'The café in that resort halfway down the hill is very good. Although it might be packed.'

He *had* confided in her, Rosie thought as they slowly made their way past busy, brightly lit restaurants, cafés and boutiques, past the laughing, chattering crowds. He had told her stuff about his past, but did she occupy a unique position because of that? Or had he said as little as he possibly could simply because, in this game of theirs, he'd decided that she needed, at the very least, to have some sketchy background information about him?

And the information had been delivered without the benefit of emotion. He had simply told her facts about himself without telling her how those facts had impacted on him, made him the person that he had become.

It wasn't his fault that his omissions had left her more curious rather than less.

The café was crowded but a table was miraculously produced for them from thin air. She had noticed that he had that impact on people and it wasn't simply because he oozed wealth. It was a combination of his striking good looks and his cool assumption that the duty of everyone around him was to jump through hoops to give him what he demanded.

That curious blend of urbane sophistication and dangerous, wrong-side-of-the-tracks toughness inspired awe, fascination and a healthy respect in everyone he met.

She couldn't imagine what it might be like to work for him. He had offered her a job in one of his companies as a way to becoming independent once they returned to London but she had immediately turned him down. It had felt like a salve to his conscience for any discomfort he might subconsciously feel when their time was up. But, when she thought about him no longer being in her life at all, she felt sick. He had made her question her life and her choices and that had been a good thing, long overdue, but had his offer been genuine? It would certainly be useful, at least to start, if she were to enter the work force as opposed to returning to full-time education, which was also an option.

And she might get to see him. He wouldn't vanish completely out of her life. He would still be *there*. Maybe, subconsciously, by offering her a job, he had been thinking the same thing…?

All those questions were finding air time in her head as she sat down so it was hardly surprising that the woman's voice from behind her took a while to penetrate.

She wasn't expecting it. She wasn't expecting anyone to recognise Matteo and she spun around as he stood up, his silver-grey eyes revealing nothing, although he was smiling at the tall, striking brunette weaving her way towards them.

Rosie watched.

An old flame. That was the thought that raced through her head. The woman was in her thirties, with a sharp, dark bob. She was very tall, very slender and very pale.

'Bethany.' Matteo made the introductions, his voice formal and polite. 'This is… Rosie.'

'Rosie…' Bethany's curious brown eyes looked at Rosie, gauging, intelligent, speculative. 'Have we met anywhere? I don't believe I recognise you. Are you and Matteo…?'

'Tell me what you're doing here, Bethany. Didn't think you found much time to take to the slopes. Join us for a drink?'

'Quick Chablis? Rob's going to be joining me in twenty minutes. You remember Rob, don't you? Melstorm? Head of Asset Management at Frazier and Co? We're an item now.' She flashed an enormous engagement ring in their general direction and sat at the chair Matteo had pulled out for her.

At which point, Rosie was relegated to spectator.

It wasn't so much an intimate catch-up as a conversation about finance and what was going on in their relative worlds of law, asset management, mergers and acquisitions and big business. Names were bandied about and small in-jokes made that elicited the sort of secret smiles from the brunette that made Rosie's teeth snap together.

Chablis finished and about to leave, Bethany finally turned her attention to Rosie and asked pleasantly what she did for a living.

'Don't tell me,' she drawled lightly, head tilted to one side as though trying to work out a conundrum, convinced that the right answer would be found. 'Maybe company lawyer for one of those start-up companies? Dylan Sync, maybe? If this rogue's dating you—and I gather he must be, because it's not exactly his thing to be in the company of any woman he isn't dating unless he's in an office wearing a suit—then you surely must be big in the corporate world.'

Rosie stiffened, sensing an attack under the glossy smile.

'I must be the exception to the rule because I... I'm currently employed as a ski instructor at the resort a little further up the slopes.'

'You're a *ski instructor*?' Bethany stared at her as though she had suddenly grown two heads and then she burst out laughing. 'I don't believe it!' She waggled her fingers in a little wave at the fiancé who was obviously behind them 'Matteo Moretti and a ski instructor! That's a first. You must have something special, my dear!'

'I suppose I must have.' Rosie realised in that instant that Matteo wasn't going to intervene, he wasn't going to stand up for her, and that hurt because it put everything in perspective. 'What do you think, Matteo?'

'I think it's getting late and it's probably time we headed back to the lodge.'

'How did you two meet? I'm curious.' Bethany's eyes darted slyly between the two of them.

'How we met is irrelevant,' Matteo drawled. 'Good luck with the wedding, Bethany. Should I expect an invite to land on my doormat in due course?'

'Oh, I shouldn't think so, Matteo.' Her brown eyes cooled. 'I don't think Rob would like that very much. Ex-heartbreakers always pose a threat.'

Then she laughed again and said to Rosie, 'Have fun with Matteo, Little Miss Ski Instructor, but be warned— he's not a guy who likes sticking around for any length of time!'

'Don't worry about me.' Rosie bared her teeth in a stiff smile. 'I won't be leaving this with a broken heart.' She saw, from Bethany's face, that her jibe had hit home. It wasn't in her nature to be uncharitable, but this time it felt pretty good.

Little Miss Ski Instructor? No way was she going to get away with that dismissive insult.

But this was the sort of woman Matteo enjoyed and not just for her novelty value. This was the sort of woman who appealed to him on an intellectual front. Rosie had watched the way they had talked to one another, their conversation on a level she could barely keep up with. They had friends in common, work in common—an interest in the business of making money in common.

'Apologies,' Matteo said, turning to her.

'Why?'

'You were uncomfortable. I had no idea Bethany would be here.'

'If you thought that I was uncomfortable, then why didn't you say something?'

'Say something?'

'I get it that she was an ex-flame, and you had lots of exciting catching up to do about the stock market and which dull company was doing what, but it got personal, Matteo.' Rosie's heart was thudding so hard, it was making her giddy. 'She was just plain nasty to me and the least you could have done was to say something. When did you two break up anyway?'

Matteo looked at her narrowly and in silence. 'Where are you going with all this?'

'I'm not *going* anywhere. I'm reacting just the way any other woman you were sleeping with would react!'

Pinned to the wall, Matteo experienced a surge of searing discomfort. She never backed down. He should know that trait of hers by now. She was persistent with him in a way no one else was. She didn't wince or back away in the face of his obvious, unflinching disapproval. He didn't want to discuss Bethany, or any of his ex-girlfriends, for that matter. She should be able to suss that out. He knew that she did, but she just kept crashing through his boundary lines as though they didn't exist.

What was it with the woman? Did he need this?

'How would *you* feel if some ex-flame of mine showed up and was rude to you? How would *you* feel if I just stood there and didn't say anything?'

'I wouldn't have a hysterical outburst,' Matteo returned grimly. 'I also wouldn't expect you to rush to my defence.'

'Well, you might have rushed to mine!'

They stared at one another in silence and Rosie was the first to look away. She was feeling so many things. Hurt, disappointment and most of all the sinking knowledge that he felt nowhere near for her what she felt for him. She'd let herself get carried away, had let her imagination play tricks on her, and she was paying the price now. He wasn't going to defend her because he didn't see the point.

'You did a pretty good job of taking Bethany down a peg or two.' Matteo shifted, deeply uncomfortable with the raw emotion of this conversation, yet seemingly unable to shut it down the way he knew he had to.

What was she looking for? He was no one's knight in shining armour. He'd never applied for that job and he never would, and he knew that she deserved better than someone whose entire life had geared him towards turning away from rescuing damsels. But something twisted inside him at the expression on her face.

'You're right. I did.' She paused and looked him in the eye. 'Would you have told her that I was your girlfriend, Matteo? If she hadn't jumped to the conclusion off her own bat? Or would you have passed me off as the ski instructor you were having a drink with because you'd just had a good lesson and wanted to say thank you?'

'Don't be ridiculous,' he said, flushing darkly. 'Why is that women can fixate on one small thing and magnify it to ridiculous proportions?'

'It's patronising to stereotype women and to try and diminish what I'm trying to say. I'm not fixating on *one small thing.* I'm being perfectly reasonable.'

'I can't believe I'm having this conversation.'

'You mean you don't *want* to believe that you are, because the only talking you're interested in doing is between the sheets.'

'It works, doesn't it?' he grated, crashing into the barrier of her arctic coldness and not knowing how to deal with it, because he had become so accustomed to her soft, sweet accommodating nature. She was so ultra-feminine. He angrily wanted to backtrack and rush to her defence, as she'd wanted, just so that he could have her back.

But maybe this was for the best. In fact, it *was* for the best. This was supposed to be fun. He wasn't interested in having to justify his behaviour to anyone. He'd never done that in his life before and he wasn't going to start now.

'You might think it's terrific being repressed,' Rosie said through gritted teeth, getting angrier and angrier by the second, 'But it's not. It's just sad and I feel sorry for you. And, if you don't want to be having this conversation, then that's fine. I'll head back to the chalet and you can do whatever you want. Stay here at the hotel. You've signed your precious deal so there's really no reason for us to carry on with this any more.'

She didn't rush or run off, and anyone might have thought that she was simply getting up to go to the bathroom, but she wasn't looking at him as she weaved her way towards the door, heading straight for the cloakroom so that she could collect her padded jacket.

Would he follow her? Rosie didn't know and she didn't care. She knew that he didn't *do* so many things, of which emotion was obviously one, but his indifference to her feelings hurt her beyond belief.

She thought of Bethany and she felt a rush of pure misery. It was one thing knowing that he went for women like that but it was another thing actually to be confronted by one of them.

That unexpected meeting had really brought home to her that to Matteo this really was just a game and she was no more than a passing indulgence.

Whilst for her...

She couldn't be casual about him the way he was about her because she had made a crucial mistake in her dealings with him. She had somehow managed to pretend that she could be as tough as he was. She had forgotten that she had a heart, and that hearts got broken, and hers was breaking now because she knew, without a shadow of a doubt, that she had stupidly gone and fallen in love with the man.

From pointing at a random stranger in the foyer of the resort, a stranger clearly removed from the festive chaos all around him, she had galloped towards heartbreak. He had seduced her with his wit, his charm, his intelligence and with those glimpses of someone he was at pains to conceal. He had thrown her tantalising titbits about himself and about his childhood and she had gobbled them up and wanted more. What had started as a charade because he wanted to complete a deal, and he needed to go along with the pretence of a relationship with her in order to get there, for her had become an obsession.

And now they were lovers and everything was...*a mess.*

She knew that he was behind her before he said, in a low, gritty voice, 'You don't get to make outrageous statements like the one you just made and then run away.'

'Go away. I don't want to talk to you.'

'Tough. You opened a box and now you don't get to shut the lid until we've gone through all the contents.'

Rosie felt the chill of an imminent break-up whisper over her. Pride came to her defence.

'You're right.' Somehow, they were outside the hotel and heading towards the car. Her feet had propelled her in the right direction and she hadn't even noticed. She wasn't looking at him as she headed to the car and she was revving the engine before she deigned to glance in his direction, and then only briefly. ' I thought that I could do this. I thought I could have a fun fling with you, but you're a stranger, and having a fun fling with a stranger doesn't make me feel good about myself.'

'Where is this coming from? One crazy encounter with an ex?' He frustratedly raked his fingers through his hair.

'It's not about your ex, Matteo. It's about the fact that I don't know you. You keep everything to yourself.'

'You know more about me than any other woman I've ever gone out with.'

And that was why she had deluded herself into thinking that what they had was somehow special. He'd opened up about his past and she had read all sorts of things into that. She'd been wrong to do so.

'Because, as you pointed out,' she said coldly, 'You

had no option because of the situation. You were desperate to get your deal done. You had to pretend to be my boyfriend and so you ended up having to share a few details about your past to keep the fiction believable.'

She laughed shortly. 'You couldn't take any chances that Bob and Margaret or someone from my family might ask a question, only to find out that I didn't know a thing about you aside from your name. You shared what you did because you didn't think you had a choice. I don't even know what your deal was all about or why it was so important to you! You never shared *that,* did you?'

'Want to know about the deal, Rosie?'

'Nope. You can carry on being as secretive as you like, Matteo.'

She wasn't going to beg. She'd made the biggest mistake of her life falling in love with him and she only had herself to blame because he had been honest from the start about his intentions: sex, fun and nothing else. She'd chosen to ignore the hand in front of her because trying to rearrange the cards into a different, more exciting hand had been too tempting to resist. In the end, it was always going to come back to the same place, though. They were never going to have a relationship, not the sort of relationship she craved.

It was going to end but she wasn't going to cry, plead or declare her undying love.

They were back at the lodge. She'd barely noticed the short drive. Now, she flipped open the door and jumped out, landing squarely on pristine white, then she trudged to the front door and opened it to let herself in without bothering to look back at him.

'Jesus, Rosie...' He pulled her towards him as she was

striding off towards the kitchen. 'The deal…' He shook his head and scowled. 'They own a farm.'

'You don't have to share, Matteo. I told you that.'

'It's no state secret.'

'Then why act like it was?'

'It's who I am.'

Rosie didn't think much of that answer and her expression said as much.

'They're very particular about…the plot of land that this farm sits on. The land is valuable. It wouldn't be impossible for a developer to get planning permission to stick up a load of executive houses with manicured lawns and double garages. It's in a prime location in the north of England.'

Rosie opened her mouth to repeat that he could keep his story to himself, because it was too late, but curiosity got the better of her.

'Why would making more money by developing land matter so much to you, Matteo? Haven't you got enough?' She wished that she could pigeon-hole him as a greedy capitalist but it didn't work. He had got under her skin by being complicated.

'There's a…for want of a better word…facility there that provides…' He shook his head and stared at her in silence for a few seconds.

'A facility?' Rosie prompted coldly. Was this his idea of a concession? He didn't want to explain his past to her. He had brushed their relationship aside, when put to the test, because for him it didn't actually qualify as a relationship. She had asked him about the deal but did she really care about it? She had cited it because it had been the first example to come to mind of something else he felt compelled to keep silent about. It would be just something else to do with making lots of money. As if he didn't already have enough. He wasn't interested in talking about what she wanted to talk about, which was his emotional past. *That* was very firmly off-limits!

'Maybe *facility* is the wrong word,' Matteo said brusquely, heading for the kitchen. She followed him, marvelling at how he somehow managed to convey the impression that he was master of all he surveyed, even though he was a visitor in her parents' chalet.

He was firing up the coffee machine, his back to her, and there was tension in his posture. When he finally looked at her, his lean, beautiful face was closed.

'Bob and Margaret,' he said quietly, 'have a place on the grounds that provides a working holiday for…the kind of kid I used to be.'

Rosie's heart skipped a beat and she stared at him.

'It's partly educational, with facilities for learning various crafts, but there's also a football field, tennis courts and horse riding on tap. The quality of the buyer is very important to them because they don't want those facilities to be scrapped. There is an enormous amount of acreage and, whilst they concede that some might be developed, they insist as part of the deal that the main place for foster kids remain intact. Naturally, it wouldn't be a legally binding situation. More of a gentleman's agreement.'

'And gentlemen don't lead young girls up the garden path, play with their feelings and then dump them without further ado. You could have told them the truth, which was that you had no idea who I was.'

Matteo shrugged. 'Why waste time on laborious explanations that would still have probably left a sour aftertaste in their mouths when another, far less onerous solution presented itself?'

'You intend to…develop some of the land?' She was enthralled by what he was saying, sliding deeper into love with him, as helpless against her own emotions as a piece of driftwood blown across stormy seas.

'I intend to develop quite a bit of the land,' Matteo told her. 'I intend to expand on the facilities there so that more underprivileged kids can come and stay there and see that there's life beyond the bleak walls of whatever foster care situation they're struggling with. I will ensure that the best of professionals are at hand for educational purposes. I will make it the sort of place… I would have benefited even more from as a youngster. So there you have it, Rosie. Has it lived up to the hype?'

'Why did you tell me?' she asked quietly.

Because I love you, was what she hoped he would say.

'Because you deserve to know,' Matteo told her roughly. And that was as far as he was prepared to go.

His wintry-grey eyes collided with hers and just for a moment…just for a second…something stirred inside him, one of those confusing, inexplicable, seismic shifts that only seemed to happen in her company, a strange feeling of disorientation that defied common sense.

He gritted his teeth together, despising himself for that fleeting loss of self-control.

The truth was that this crazy charade had not panned out the way he had foreseen.

It should have been easy, controllable. He never allowed himself to enter into situations he couldn't control. It was too much like opening the door to a room without knowing what was happening behind it, and there had been way too many of those doors in his childhood.

A sheen of prickly perspiration broke out over his body and he scowled.

Memories. Who needed them? He'd done a great job of banking down on them over the years, locking them away, always moving onwards and upwards, refusing to be dragged back to a past that was no longer relevant.

Had they begun to wriggle free when he had started dealings with Bob and Margaret?

The land with the care facilities on it—had that kick-started a trip back in time which seemed to have picked up pace just recently?

Or had the woman in front of him somehow opened that door, letting them flood out?

And, if that was the case, how the heck had it happened? Matteo wasn't going to stick around analysing the situation.

'I deserved to know?' Rosie questioned.

'We were where we were because I wanted that land. It's only fair, in the end, that you know the reason why it meant so much to me.'

And no one could accuse Matteo of not being fair, she thought bitterly. He'd been the perfect gentleman who'd kept his distance, and slept on a bed of nails in her bedroom because she'd asked him to, and thereby had opened the first crack in her heart. And he'd been as fair as anyone could be when he'd warned her that he 'didn't do love'. Or sharing. Or jealousy. Or confiding. Or Christmas. He certainly hadn't led her up the garden path with phoney promises about a future that was never going to happen!

And he was being fair now. Giving her the explanation she'd asked for, digging a deeper hole into her heart and showing her just how complex a man he was.

He'd been a gentleman, and he'd been fair and honest, and now it was over because she wanted much more than a fair and honest gentleman. She wanted the whole package, but she was never going to get it, and she couldn't pretend that sleeping with him for a bit longer, until he got bored of her, was better than nothing, because it wasn't.

'Thank you for that,' she said with a stiff smile and keeping her distance. 'I'm glad you told me. I would always have been curious. I've enjoyed being with you Matteo. It was all so unexpected…the turn of events… but I've grown up. I partly have you to thank for that but I can't carry on making love to you until we both get bored. I feel like I'm facing a new chapter in my life and I want to get on with it.'

This was exactly as it should be, Matteo thought. So why wasn't he feeling good about it?

It had to end and, the longer it carried on, the higher the chances of her getting hurt. She wanted more than he was ever going to be able to give her.

He wanted a stiff drink. He wanted to punch something. That lack of control was as powerful as a depth charge and he detested the weakness it represented.

'You need to. We had fun but it's time for us to go our separate ways. What will you tell your family? What are your plans moving forward?'

Rosie shrugged and met his dark, shuttered eyes without flinching. Fear of the future gripped her like a vice.

'I'll think of something. It's not your concern and, don't worry, I wouldn't dump you in it. Now, if you don't mind, I think I'll head up.'

'Take care, Rosie. I'll be gone by the time you wake up tomorrow morning.'

CHAPTER TEN

FOR THE FIRST time in her life, the frenzied excitement of a fast-approaching Christmas day left Rosie feeling flat and miserable.

True to his word, Matteo was gone by the time she awoke the following morning. She'd barely slept but she must have dozed off at some point because surely she would have heard him leaving the house? Naturally, he hadn't slept with her, and the bed had felt as vast as an icy ocean. How had she managed to become so accustomed to the warmth of his body next to her in such a short space of time? Didn't she have *any* inbuilt defence mechanisms that could have come to the rescue? How had she been so ill-equipped to deal with this situation?

She stayed at the ski lodge just long enough to pack her things. Her parents had a housekeeper who came to clean when the place was not in use, and usually Rosie would have made sure to do some rudimentary tidying before she arrived, but this time she hadn't the heart to do anything but plaster a phoney smile on her face and do the rounds with all her friends at the hotel and on the ski slopes.

Then she headed back to London, to her parents' apartment, which she had always used as a base whenever she was in the country.

She looked around her through new, wide open eyes. She was a woman in her twenties who had always thought that travelling the world was a courageous and daring way of life. Her sisters, in her view, had been solid, grounded, unadventurous souls who had buried themselves in having careers when there was so much world out there waiting to be explored.

Thanks to Matteo, all those notions had been turned on their head.

Since when had it ever been courageous to live at home with Mum and Dad when you didn't have to? Since when was it a daring decision to live off a trust fund and sneer at the tedium of responsibility?

It was an ordeal to face her entire family when she returned.

She spent two days in London, catching up with friends, seeing everything in a whole new light. Then she headed up to the Cotswolds, where her mother was in the thick of Christmas preparations, bulk-making mince pies and Christmas treats for the entire family while her dad sheepishly read the newspapers and watched from the side-lines.

Emily, Candice and entourage were all going to be spending Christmas Eve at the Cotswold mansion where her parents lived.

'Darling, it's such a shame that that gorgeous young man of yours can't join us for at least some of the Christmas celebrations,' her mother sighed when on the first night they all sat down for a family dinner at the kitchen table. 'Surely he could have spared a day or so even if he had to disappear for Christmas day?'

'Work commitments,' Rosie had muttered vaguely. 'You know how it goes...'

She needed some breathing space before she told her parents that the whirlwind romance had crashed and burned. She planned to tell them the truth. She would reassure them that she didn't need protecting, that she wasn't a kid any more. She had decided that she would return to university to study sports science. The ski season and teaching at the resort had pointed her in the direction which she now intended to go. Lots of mature decisions had been made and that chapter she had talked about had been opened. She just wished she felt better about it because right now, right here, staring at her reflection in the mirror a mere couple of hours before her sisters descended in a flurry of excitement, presents and stockings that would sneakily be hung for the kids once they were asleep, the world felt like a very lonely place.

Downstairs, her mother would be getting everything ready for the meal of the year, the crowning glory that was the turkey for Christmas Day. It would be put in brine and, at the crack of dawn in the morning, it would be all systems go and Rosie would be expected to be her usual self—excitable, up early before everyone else, fussing over the Christmas tree, the food and everything that would need doing before her sisters, the kids and the other halves woke up and trooped downstairs.

Bubbly, sparkling Aunty Rosie was her designated role and she would have to live up to it or else invite curiosity and anxious questioning. All that was going to happen soon enough, post-Christmas Day and Boxing Day, once she had had time to get over some of the raw pain. Once she had got her thoughts in order. Once she could manage to go for five minutes without thinking about him, which she did constantly.

As soon as she started thinking about him, her body did what it was accustomed to doing—it tensed up, all her muscles contracting and her nerves going into over-drive. And her brain did what it had also grown accustomed to doing—it began wandering down all sorts of pointless dead ends marked *what if?* and *if only.*

She was bracing herself for an evening of pretend-ing to be jolly when there was a bang on her bedroom door and her mother pushed it open, giving Rosie just enough time to get her face in happy mode.

'Darling, there's a surprise downstairs for you.' Her mother smiled. She was wearing a red-and-white apron which was dusted with flour. Underneath it, in a pair of jeans and a long-sleeved tee shirt, she looked twenty years younger than she was.

'Father Christmas come early? Drawn by the smell of your mince pies?' Rosie forced a smile and stood up. She was dressed and ready to start the evening in a pair of culottes and a fitted stretchy top with lots of sparkle and glitter, as befitting a Christmas Eve gathering. She was counting on the clothes to give the right impression just in case her expression ended up letting the side down. 'Have the girls and kids arrived already?' She glanced at her watch with a frown. 'It's not yet six. I thought they were going to pile up around seven. Sorry, Mum, I should be downstairs helping you!'

'Don't be silly, Rosie. Too many cooks spoil the broth. And no, your sisters aren't here just yet. No, guess again.'

'I can't guess.'

'Your young man has shown up out of the blue. Isn't that wonderful? He's come bearing gifts, which is sure to go down well with the little ones.'

'What young man?' It took some seconds to register

who her mother was talking about but, even when she had, she still couldn't quite believe her ears.

'How many have you got, Rosie?' Her mother chuckled. 'I can't possibly be seen like this. I'm going to have a quick shower—give you two love birds time to catch up. Your father has disappeared down to the pub for a drink so you won't be disturbed!'

Debbie Carter looked at her daughter seriously. 'I'm so thrilled for you, Rosie. You deserve a decent, lovely chap and I think you've struck jackpot with this one. I told him that I thought he was too busy with work to pop up here but he said that work would just have to take a back seat. Not many business moguls adopt that sort of attitude! I despaired of your father back in the day, when he was sometimes far too busy to remember that there was such a thing as *family* waiting for him to appear! Which makes Matteo such a rare find.'

Rosie contorted her face into something she hoped might pass for a smile and not a grimace of despair. Truth to tell, her heart was beating so wildly in her chest that she didn't have time to think about anything much at all.

'Maybe,' she muttered inaudibly. It was too late to climb out of her glittery, sparkly outfit but she felt like a fool as she went downstairs to the sitting room, to where, she had been told, he had been directed with a glass of wine.

And there he was. Behind him, the Christmas tree which she had helped decorate was awash with tiny white lights and heavy with ornaments that went way back to when she and her sisters had all been kids. Rosie could recognise each and every one of them. The curtains of the big bay windows were pulled back and the outside lights illuminated a panorama of stretching gardens and the light fall of snow, nothing like the sweeping fall that had covered the ski slopes, but still somehow graceful and strangely romantic.

Rosie walked over to the window on trembling legs and briskly yanked the curtains shut.

She had to sidestep a ridiculous mound of presents, all professionally wrapped and covering most of the ground by the tree and spreading in front of the sofas.

She had closed the door behind her, because there was never any telling in her parents' house just who could come bombing into any room without warning, and now she turned to him and folded her arms.

'What are you doing here?'

God, he looked so spectacular, so gorgeous, that she could feel her heart going into freefall.

He hadn't shaved and the roughness of dark stubble covered his chin. Looking closer, his eyes were ringed with slight tiredness. She wondered whether all those important deals had been keeping him up at night.

Conscious that she was hardly looking her most sophisticated in her sparkling attire, Rosie remained standing by the window, as tense as a piece of elastic stretched to breaking point. She'd barely had time to get her hair in order when her mother had barged into the bedroom and it fell in feathery, unruly waves around her heart-shaped face.

'I've come…to talk.'

'Talk about what?' She glanced at all the presents strewn on the ground. 'And why have you brought all this stuff?'

'Because it's Christmas.' He smiled crookedly and

took a step towards her, but then stopped, as though uncertain.

'You don't do Christmas,' Rosie said scornfully.

'There were a lot of things I never did until I met you,' he said in a low undertone that she had to strain to hear.

'I can't deal with this, Matteo,' Rosie whispered. 'I don't want you here…spoiling Christmas for me. I just can't handle pretending that everything's fine between us in front of my family. We broke up, for good reasons, and I've begun coming to terms with what I'm going to tell everyone—because, as you've seen, they're still in the dark.'

'I…understand.'

'You've ruined everything coming here with all these presents. My family are going to be doubly upset when I break it to them that it's over between us. They're going to be horribly confused because one minute you…you're showing up pretending to be Father Christmas and, the next minute, you're just a part of my history and you've moved on with your life.'

'Not if I can help it.'

'Don't!'

'Come and sit on the sofa with me. I can't have this conversation standing a hundred miles away from you. I need you…to be closer to me.'

'It's not going to work.'

'I'm not here to try and revive what we had. I haven't come to try and persuade you into carrying on with any charade because I still…want to sleep with you. Because you still haunt my dreams.'

He sat on the sofa and waited, his fabulous eyes focused on her with such unwavering intensity that she could feel her body burning up as she stumbled towards the sofa and sat down, pressed up at one end, because any closer would have made her already fast-dissolving nerves dissolve even faster.

'Rosie.' There was urgent sincerity in his voice and, more than anything else, more even than the brutal impact of his physical presence, that made her still, made her focus her wide blue eyes on his. 'I let you go and I should never have done that.' He raised his hand to halt any interruption, even though she had no intention of interrupting because she had been thoroughly silenced by the tone of his voice. 'I…was afraid.'

'Afraid? *Afraid?* Matteo, there's no way I… I can believe that. Isn't being afraid just one of the hundreds of things you don't *do*?' Bewilderment nudged a way past her defences. She felt as though she was suddenly standing on quicksand.

'Used to be.' He pressed his thumbs briefly over his eyes and then looked at her with none of his usual self-assurance.

Rosie had no intention of melting but she knew that she was straining towards him, closing the gap without really realising it. She had pressed her hands on the squidgy sofa and was leaning forward.

'Don't say anything you don't mean, Matteo.'

'I'm not. This comes from the heart, and if I'm not as fluent as I usually am it's because I'm not accustomed to this sort of speech. Rosie, my life, before I met you, was so well-ordered,' Matteo confessed in a roughened undertone. 'No surprises. Relationships, women… I knew how to deal with both. I never wanted any sort of long-term, committed involvement with anyone and I always made that clear at the start of a relationship. I wasn't raised to see the up sides of forming any emotional attachments.'

Rosie was holding her breath. She reached out to cover his hand with hers, her heart softening even as her head tried to be stern and unforgiving.

He didn't remove his hand. In fact, he curled his fingers into hers and tugged her ever so slightly closer to him so that their knees were touching and she could feel the warmth flowing from his body towards her.

'I wasn't abandoned as a baby,' he said roughly. 'My mother—shockingly, in this day and age—died in childbirth. I know this because I was told when I was old enough by one of the carers at the home. I was raised single-handedly by my father until I was four. I remember him. A kind man—this is simply what I have managed to put together over the years using all the resources at my disposal, including hunting down some of the staff who worked there when I was a child, and people who briefly knew him where he worked. My father died at Christmas. He'd left me with a neighbour so that he could go buy some presents. It was an accident. Poor weather conditions.'

'Matteo!'

'It was a long time ago.' Matteo smiled. 'But I suppose you could say that the experience toughened me up. I learned very young that no one was going to rescue me. I had to make my own way in the world and I couldn't depend on anyone. I had lost both my parents. My faith in loving anyone had taken a fatal beating.'

'That's why Christmas is the one time of year you avoid,' she said slowly.

'I have pictures. Not many. Memories.' He sighed.

'When I met you, you couldn't have been more different from the women I was accustomed to going for.'

'As you made crystal-clear,' Rosie murmured. Her mind was taken up with images of a young Matteo, lost, confused and bewildered by the abrupt death of his father, abandoned to fate. Her heart constricted and she had to swallow back tears. He did this to her. Showed her sides to him that made him irresistible. Beneath the harsh, controlled front there was so much humanity.

'I got sucked in without really understanding how. A first for me. And then I met your family, all of them, and what I experienced was also a first. I experienced what it felt like to be surrounded by the closeness of people who cared about you. I experienced what it felt like to be a part of something bigger. It was…disorienting.'

'We can overwhelm.'

'In a positive way.' He angled a smile. 'You're very lucky, Rosie, but not as lucky as I am to have met you. What started out as a charade turned into something else very quickly. We became lovers and it was nothing like I'd ever felt before.'

Keep talking, Rosie thought, *please don't stop.*

'It was…unsettling. When you confronted me after meeting Bethany and laid into me because I hadn't defended you, well, it made me take stock of just how far I'd been drawn into a situation that had somehow spiralled out of control. All my old habits kicked back into gear big time.' He grimaced. 'I was programmed not to care, to focus on what was tangible, namely work. You wanted what was not in the brochure and I told myself that it was for the best that things ended, not just for me, but for you as well. I told myself that you deserved better. Maybe, Rosie, you do.'

'Never,' Rosie breathed shakily. 'I met you and you turned my life upside down in five seconds flat. I didn't want to fall in love with you, Matteo, but I just couldn't help myself, even though my head was telling me all the time that I was being an idiot.'

'You fell in love with me.' He flung his head back for a few seconds, eyes closed, and then when he looked at her there was no doubt in her mind that her feelings for him were returned. The love and tenderness in his eyes brought a lump to her throat. 'I wasn't sure. I'd hoped. Then you left and it felt as though my world had come to an abrupt stop. I was greedy, Rosie. Greedy for you and hungry for the chaos and joy of having an extended family. I thought I'd locked up my heart and thrown away the key, but I was wrong.

'I came here, bearing gifts...lots of them.' He squeezed her slender fingers. 'In a gesture of shameless blackmail. I intended to ingratiate myself until I won you over. Anything, my darling. I realised that I would have done anything.'

He'd brought something else aside from sack-loads of presents but Rosie didn't find that out until later, when the carols were blaring in the background and her entire family was scattered between the living room and the kitchen, with Candice's children weaving between them in a state of high excitement.

He gathered them all in one place and he took out from his pocket that last thing he had brought with him. A little black box.

Rosie watched in stunned silence as he showed her that her beautiful, arrogant, guy...the guy who claimed to have lost the key to his heart...could be breathtakingly romantic after all.

He knelt in front of her, in front of her entire congregated family—including the kids, who had fallen silent for ten seconds—and he proposed.

And what else could she do but say yes? *Yes, yes, yes!*

EPILOGUE

MATTEO LOOKED DOWN at Rosie from the towering heights of a precariously balanced ladder. In his hand he held a star. In his head he was trying to figure out how he was going to get the damn thing to sit perfectly atop the massive Christmas tree that adorned the living room of the townhouse into which they had moved three months previously.

It wasn't quite the countryside, but neither was it the heart of the city. It was perfectly located in the leafy borough of Richmond.

'Please be careful up there,' Rosie said anxiously. 'You look way too big for that ladder.'

'Finishing touches.' Matteo smiled. 'You want everything to be perfect for when the troops arrive in a week for turkey with all the trimmings, don't you?'

He angled the star, waited until approval from his beloved wife was given, and then slowly dismounted. Then he stood back to look at their creation.

Arm around her, he pulled her gently against him. Outside, the darkness was blocked out by thick curtains. Inside, the glittering lights on the tree and the presents waiting to be handed out to family was a Christmas scene worthy of a postcard. Or a fairy tale. Matteo thought that it was certainly *his* fairy tale.

He'd found his princess, even if he hadn't immediately known it, and he had married her. In record time, a mere few weeks after he had proposed in front of a delighted audience of people who were now as close to him as he could ever have hoped.

He smelled the floral sweetness of Rosie's hair and murmured softly, 'Do you wish we could have returned to the slopes and celebrated our first proper Christmas together there?'

Rosie twisted and looked up at him, smiling.

'You know you put your foot down when I suggested popping over for a few days.' She smiled, reaching up to stroke his face.

'Can you blame me?'

'My darling, I'm six months' pregnant. I think travelling is still allowed.'

Matteo rested his hand on her swollen stomach and felt it again, that surge of pride, love, tenderness and a fierce need to protect the beautiful woman who had become his wife.

He'd gone from tough, hard-as-nails tycoon to a guy who was happy to admit that he was vulnerable.

'You can't be too careful,' Matteo growled, swivelling her gently so that they were facing one another. He gazed down at her with love. 'But we'll get there. Maybe next year. Maybe next Christmas. Return to the place where all this began.'

'And maybe bump into Bob and Margaret.' Rosie smiled, thinking of the couple who had been almost as thrilled at their wedding as she and Matteo had been themselves. 'I gather from her email that they're getting quite proficient.' She reached up on tiptoe to kiss him and, as always, the touch of his cool lips made her squirm with sudden desire. 'Who knows? You might get there one day.'

'I intend to.' Matteo grinned and deepened his kiss, his hand curving over her breast, caressing it and knowing that she would be wet for him. 'I can't have you teaching our kids how to ski so that they can taunt their old man that they're better than him on the slopes.'

'In that case, we can get cracking as soon as this baby arrives.'

'And until then...' he ushered her over to the sofa and settled her into it as delicately as if she was a piece of priceless china '...feet up, young lady. I can do more than just stick a star on a tree. Your wish is my command.'

'You're here, Matteo.' Rosie looked at him lovingly. 'I have no more wishes.'

* * * * *

LET'S TALK
Romance

For exclusive extracts, competitions
and special offers, find us online:

[f] facebook.com/millsandboon

[🐦] @MillsandBoon

[📷] @MillsandBoonUK

Get in touch on 01413 063232

For all the latest titles coming soon, visit
millsandboon.co.uk/nextmonth

MILLS & BOON
A ROMANCE FOR EVERY READER

FREE delivery direct to your door

EXCLUSIVE offers every month

SAVE up to 25% on pre-paid subscriptions

SUBSCRIBE AND SAVE

millsandboon.co.uk/Subscribe

WANT EVEN MORE

ROMANCE?

SUBSCRIBE AND SAVE TODAY!

'Mills & Boon books, the perfect way to escape for an hour or so.'

MISS W. DYER

'Excellent service, promptly delivered and very good subscription choices.'

MISS A. PEARSON

'You get fantastic special offers and the chance to get books before they hit the shops.'

MRS V. HALL

Visit millsandboon.co.uk/Subscribe and save on brand new books.

JOIN THE
MILLS & BOON
BOOKCLUB

* **FREE** delivery direct to your door

* **EXCLUSIVE** offers every month

* **EXCITING** rewards programme

50% OFF
YOUR FIRST
PARCEL

Join today at
Millsandboon.co.uk/Bookclub

MILLS & BOON

THE HEART OF ROMANCE

A ROMANCE FOR EVERY READER

MODERN

Prepare to be swept off your feet by sophisticated, sexy and seductive heroes, in some of the world's most glamourous and romanti locations, where power and passion collide.

HISTORICAL

Escape with historical heroes from time gone by. Whether your passion for wicked Regency Rakes, muscled Vikings or rugged Highlanders, aw the romance of the past.

MEDICAL

Set your pulse racing with dedicated, delectable doctors in the high-pre sure world of medicine, where emotions run high and passion, comfort love are the best medicine.

True Love

Celebrate true love with tender stories of heartfelt romance, from the rush of falling in love to the joy a new baby can bring, and a focus on emotional heart of a relationship.

Desire

Indulge in secrets and scandal, intense drama and plenty of sizzling ho action with powerful and passionate heroes who have it all: wealth, stat good looks…everything but the right woman.

HEROES

Experience all the excitement of a gripping thriller, with an intense ro mance at its heart. Resourceful, true-to-life women and strong, fearless face danger and desire - a killer combination!

To see which titles are coming soon, please visit

millsandboon.co.uk/nextmonth

JOIN US ON SOCIAL MEDIA!

Stay up to date with our latest releases, author news and gossip, special offers and discounts, and all the behind-the-scenes action from Mills & Boon...

 @millsandboon

 @millsandboonuk

 facebook.com/millsandboon

 @millsandboonuk

It might just be true love...

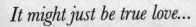

GET YOUR ROMANCE FIX!

Get the latest romance news,
exclusive author interviews, story
extracts and much more!

blog.millsandboon.co.uk